SOPHOMORE

SURGE

Sophie Fournier, Book Two

K.R. Collins

A NineStar Press Publication

Published by NineStar Press
P.O. Box 91792,
Albuquerque, New Mexico, 87199 USA.
www.ninestarpress.com

Sophomore Surge

Printed in the USA
First Edition
November, 2019

Print ISBN: 978-1-951057-88-6

Also available in eBook, ISBN: 978-1-951057-86-2

Warning: This book contains depictions of emotional abuse by a parent.

Thank you to my family, my parents, my sisters, and my brother. And thank you to my writing group, Lis and Ray.

Chapter One

SOPHIE BRAVES THE Manchester airport, her ball cap pulled down low over her eyes so she won't be recognized. On a different day, she wouldn't mind being noticed by kids or even their parents. It would be a sign of how quickly hockey has caught on since she made her debut with the Concord Condors last season. Today, though, she's on a mission.

Theodore Augereau, one of her teammates, is flying in, and she promised him a place to crash during the convention. Fan Fest is Concord's first event of its kind, a weekend-long celebration of Condors hockey. They've planned autograph signings, player panels to answer questions, photo-ops, everything their PR team could think of to drum up support and excitement for the 2012-2013 season.

Sophie's been in town for a few days helping to prepare, and her teammates are finally trickling in to join her. She spots a familiar figure in the crowd. Teddy has his hat tipped to hide his eyes, same as her, but she'd recognize those scrawny chicken legs anywhere. His goalie pads make him appear twice as large as he is, but in shorts and a T-shirt he looks small.

"You're too skinny," she tells him once they're together. "Don't you know the off-season is for bulking up?"

Teddy taps her shoulder where her shirt stretches thin to accommodate the breadth of her muscles. "You hit the weight room enough for both of us."

She grins, pleased he noticed. She spent the summer training, determined to drag Concord into the playoffs this year. The last time she saw Teddy, his shoulders were hunched, the same misery in his eyes reflected in hers because it was locker room cleanout day, and their season ended too early. It'll be different this year. They'll have a postseason for the first time in franchise history.

"The guest room is made up for you," she says as the baggage claim belt begins to move. "I even stocked the fridge."

"You'll spoil me."

"You're my goalie." Goalies are meant to be protected—and spoiled—at all costs. Happy goalies make for happy teams. Jakub Lindholm—Lindy—is their starter, but he was Matty's long before Sophie came to Concord. She knows better than to think she'll separate their number one goalie from their captain. But she claimed Teddy last year, fair and square.

Teddy finds the black suitcase with a white 30 embroidered on it and hefts it off the belt. "Will you carry my bag?"

He grins as if he's teasing. Sophie matches his smile. "Sure. I mean, it looks like I'm the only one who worked out this summer."

"I tried!" Teddy slaps her hands away as she makes a grab for his bag. He lifts it up even though it has perfectly functioning wheels. His muscles flex, but where Sophie is thick and solid, he's wiry like one of those Gumby figures she played with at her grandparents' house.

"Men and their egos," Sophie sighs.

"The summer didn't make you any nicer."

"I picked you up from the airport, I'm feeding you, and I'm giving you a place to stay." She ticks each reason off on her fingers. "But you're right. I'm not nice at all."

"I'm not going to win this one."

She laughs as she playfully bumps his shoulder. "I rarely lose."

"WELCOME TO MY apartment." Sophie opens the door and ushers Teddy in. Last year, given her status as the first woman in the League, the Condors organization felt it was best for her to live with her general manager and his family rather than with one of her teammates. The Wilcoxes had been kind, but she's ready for something different.

Sharing an apartment with Elsa will be new, but, more importantly, it'll make her feel normal. Most players don't eat dinner with their GM after practice or babysit his kids on their off days. They play video games with their teammates and eat too many tacos. She's spent so much of her career set apart from what typical hockey players do. She's excited to finally be like them.

She and Elsa haven't talked much this summer which means Sophie's done most of the decorating for their apartment on her own. The living room, the first thing anyone sees when they walk through the door, is all Sophie. The floors are hardwood, which is how the apartment came, but she picked out a slate-gray suede couch. It's extra wide to accommodate hockey players, and she bought the matching love seat. The smaller couch won't work for napping, but it's somewhere for people to sit if they ever have company.

The coffee table is the same one displayed when she went furniture shopping. It's square, with a glass inlay in the wood. The woman at the store said it's ideal for displaying magazines without cluttering the top of the table. In deference to the saleswoman, she placed a few copies of *After the Whistle* inside. Carol Rogers, the reporter for the segment, also publishes weekly articles on the state of the League. At the end of each season, they compile her articles and interview transcripts into one large publication. It's a look-back on the season, and Sophie can trace the history of the sport she loves by paging through the issues.

"Do you want a snack before your shower or after?" Sophie asks Teddy as she moves into the kitchen. It's smaller than her parents' kitchen, but it's functional. There's an oven with four cooktops and a fridge with a freezer big enough to store all the ice packs she and Elsa will need.

"The shower isn't optional?" Teddy grins as he slides his shoes off near the door. "What're you trying to say about me?"

"You smell like airport. You can't take forever, we have places to be today." Matty—Daniel Mathers—offered Lindy's house for a team get-together before the convention. It'll be a good opportunity to see everyone before they have to be on their best behavior for the fans. "The guest room is the one at the end of the hall. The bathroom's the one with the toilet."

Teddy laughs as he wheels his suitcase down the hall. Sophie pulls two bags of tortilla chips out of her pantry and takes out the salsa dip she made after a frantic Google search last night. It's a layered dip with shredded buffalo chicken, and she hopes it tastes good. Cooking's still new to her. At Chilton Academy, all their meals were provided to them and not much has changed since she made the jump to the North American Hockey League. Last year, Amber Wilcox and the team accounted for the majority of her meals.

When she asked Elsa if she has any hidden talents in the kitchen, Elsa sent back a picture of an open-face sandwich with either pickles or cucumbers on top. Sophie reapplied herself to finding easy, but trainer-approved recipes. At least if things become dire, she and Elsa can always order takeout.

"What are these?" Teddy pops back into the kitchen, holding a powder-blue hand towel with a seashell border.

"They came as a set; shower curtain, rug, towels. It means everything matches."

Teddy stares at the towel. "Seriously?"

"It's the guest bathroom. There are no seashells in mine."

"Do they make towels with embroidered hockey pucks or do you have to custom order them?"

"Fuck off and shower."

THERE ARE ALREADY cars lining the curb when Sophie and Teddy pull up. Music reaches the street from the backyard, and Sophie and Teddy exchange looks before they race each other around the side of the house. Teddy's legs are longer, but Sophie's more motivated. As soon as they round the corner, Sophie skids to a halt to avoid knocking into Theo and Kevlar.

Theodore Smith and Kevin Faulkner are a defensive pair, but their similarities end there. Theo's over six and a half feet tall and pushing two hundred fifty pounds. When he smiles, there's a gap where he's missing two teeth. He lost them in a fight years ago and figured he'd wait to replace them until the end of his career. Kevlar's a few inches shorter and almost fifty pounds lighter. He has a full set of teeth, and he shows them off as he smiles.

"Woah there," Theo says. "Where's the fire?"

Teddy crashes into Theo and they pop the bags of chips between them.

"I win," Sophie says.

"You fucking did not!"

Kevlar laughs as he steps back, careful of the casserole dish Sophie's holding. He pats her shoulders and then her biceps, and his eyebrows climb upwards. "Did you live in the gym this summer?"

"I wanted to make sure I was ready for the season. I've been watching some fighting videos." Kevlar is the one who worked with her on the punching bags last season. He taught her to throw a punch, a skill she won't ever use, because the NAHL has unofficially forbidden her from fighting.

"We can progress to sparring."

"Don't break our Sophie," Theo says. He reaches an arm out and reels Sophie into a three-way hug.

She wriggles out of Theo's hug so she can safely set her dip on one of the long tables in the backyard. Garfield, his shoulder length black hair tucked behind his ears, leans over to inspect her dip. Where Garfield is, Nelson isn't far behind, and she's unsurprised to see the other winger wander over, holding a plate of cookies.

Garfield plucks one off the plate and mumbles a thank-you through a mouthful of chocolate chip cookie.

"Once Zinger's gotten his ass kicked by J-Rod, you're up."

Hockey players like their nicknames. Some, like José Rodriguez, have their names smushed together. Jeffrey McArthur told everyone he has magic hands and became Merlin. Nelson is called Odie because he's always with Garfield. It's from a comic she's never read. Faulkner's called Kevlar because of all the shots he blocks. Petrov was dubbed Marinara Man after face-planting in his spaghetti and meatballs last year. For brevity's sake they mostly call him Peets unless they're recounting the story or giving him a hard time.

"Mario Kart tourney," Garfield tells Sophie as he scoops her dip into a paper bowl. "Do you want in?"

"I'm good but thank you."

They take their food and head back inside, arguing over which one of them gets to be Princess Peach. Sophie shakes her head and inspects the table to see if anything catches her eye.

"Look who finally made it."

She turns to spot Merlin opening one of the drink coolers. Merlin was her right winger last season, and they played good hockey together. This season, they'll be even better. His copper beard is trimmed short, but as soon as he starts a point-streak, he'll grow it out until his streak is snapped. For the sake of the team she's almost grown to like the scraggly mess he calls a beard.

He snags a second beer from the cooler he stands guard over. "Want one?"

She holds up her car keys. "I'm in charge of driving home." It's an easy excuse not to drink. Plenty of her teammates do, even when they're underage, but she refuses to give the League an excuse to drop her. Besides, years of playing hockey have taught her she can't always trust her team. Being the only sober one means she's often accused of being boring but it's better than the alternatives.

"Are you sticking around until the start of the season?" Sophie asks.

Merlin tosses her a purple Gatorade and she catches it and twists the cap off. He shakes his head as he sips his beer. "Marissa and I are visiting her parents before the season begins. What about you?"

"I'm making sure the apartment's ready for Elsa."

"Am I being replaced as your favorite winger?"

"I don't have favorites."

"Liar!" Teddy calls from the snack table. He has a bowl full of her buffalo chicken dip. "I'm your favorite."

And, well, he's not wrong. But goalies are different.

"He's your favorite goalie," Merlin says, stubborn. "I can still be your favorite winger."

"*I'm* her favorite winger." Witzer—Eli Aronowitz— her left winger from last season, comes over to argue his case. His brown hair floofs today without the usual product slicking it down.

Sophie holds her hands up. "I am not stepping in the middle of this."

"You're my favorite center," Merlin says.

"One might even say, you're the center of our universe," Witzer adds.

They glance at each other before they squish her between them in a hug. She laughs, happy to be back and surrounded by her team.

TEDDY STUMBLES INTO her kitchen the next morning, bleary-eyed and adorably miserable. His Condors T-shirt is loose, baring a bony collarbone. "Coffee?" he asks, hopeful and longing.

Sophie takes the scrambled eggs off the burner and pushes half of them onto Teddy's plate and half of them onto her own. "Elsa's picking out the coffeemaker, because I don't drink it."

"No coffee?" He sinks onto one of the island chairs, looking lost.

"I have tea?"

"We're stopping at Dunkin."

WHEN THEY ARRIVE at the hotel for Fan Fest, Teddy's still clutching his large coffee in both hands. He breathes in the scent of it as if he can get caffeinated this way until it's cool enough to drink.

"Go find a chair to curl up in," she tells him. She has a cup of coffee too but it's for Mary Beth Doyle, their PR manager. She's in the middle of the room, giving instructions to the six eager men and women crowded around her. She's wearing a smart business suit, her hair pulled up in a tight, professional bun. Her ever-present phone is in her hand, and she glances at it a few times as she speaks.

Once she sends her underlings on their way, she spots Sophie and smiles, or maybe it's the coffee which brings out her smile. "For me?"

Sophie hands the coffee over. "Your day is longer than mine."

"Easier too." Mary Beth takes a cautious sip followed by a longer one. "You're starting with the media. It isn't the fun part of the weekend, but it's how we grow the game."

As the first woman in the League, Sophie stood in front of more cameras last season than some guys will over their entire careers. She knows why media exposure is important, but she still wishes she had a panel to kick-start her day. The fans are who she cares about, and she'll answer what her favorite color is fifteen times if fifteen kids come up to a microphone and ask.

She wants to know how many young girls have shown up to see her. She doesn't play only for them—first and foremost she plays for herself—but inspiring girls was a big factor in why she's playing here in the NAHL and not overseas. She has vivid memories of lying on her grandparents' rug and watching Bobby Brindle lift the Maple Cup for Montreal. She knew the first time she saw him do it *she* wanted to lift the Cup one day. Now, she hopes, when she does, there will be a girl on her grandparents' living room floor who sees her and thinks *I can do it too*.

But Sophie doesn't start with a panel and kids who ask her who on the team has the best pranks and whose gear stinks the worst. Instead, Carol Rogers from *After the Whistle* says, "You were focused on making a place for yourself last season. Will we see a better balance of hockey and a social life this one?"

Sophie's brain screeches to a halt. *This* is her first question of Fan Fest? As a rookie she broke a hundred points to notch 101 and earn herself the Maddow Trophy. She lost out on the Clayton, the trophy awarded to the best rookie, but she'd rather talk about her disappointment than—

"You must be on the radar of a lot of young men," Rogers continues.

A boyfriend question. She wants to seek out Mary Beth and share an eye roll, but she's too well-trained. She fixes her media smile firmly in place. "I'm as committed to hockey this season as I was last season."

"Have you been encouraged by the front office to remain single?" asks Marty Owen, a sports writer for *The Concord Courier*. He's wearing a rumpled suit, seemingly the only kind he owns. His eyes, too close together, are especially piercing this season. He's always hunting for the angle which makes the team look the worst. She doesn't understand why he covers a team he appears to hate.

"The front office doesn't interfere with my personal life." Though maybe they will now. "The NAHL isn't an easy League to play in, and I don't want any distractions."

"You think a boyfriend would be distracting, then?"

"A hypothetical boyfriend has already created a distraction. We're here for Concord's first Fan Fest and instead of asking me about the upcoming season, you want to talk about someone who doesn't exist." She scans the crowd until she finds Ed Rickers, her favorite reporter of the bunch.

He works for *The Granite State Sports Network*, and his tie today has Concord's condor on it. "You bulked up this summer."

"I always strive to be better."

It's the perfect opening to ask about her summer training or her expectations for the season, but Marty Owen says, "Concord drafted Elsa Nyberg at this year's draft. Was it wise to take a chance on another woman?"

One day, she'll strike the phrase *take a chance* out of everyone's vocabulary. It's all she heard last year even though Concord picked her last which was the opposite of taking a chance. Drafting Elsa wasn't a gamble. She's an elite goal scorer, able to come up big at the vital moment. In addition, she plays on the left wing, and her goal scoring combined with Sophie's playmaking...a line with the two of them could be exactly what Concord needs to propel them into a winning season, then the playoffs.

"If you've seen Elsa's game tape, you'd know Concord isn't taking a chance," Sophie answers, as bland as she can manage. She locks her indignation down deep. "She'll be an asset to our team."

"She has an edge to her game you don't," someone in the crowd says. She doesn't recognize him which means he's probably a blogger. If he thinks he can pit Sophie and Elsa against each other, he must be new.

"One of the reasons I'm looking forward to playing with Elsa is because her skill set complements mine. Not all women in the NAHL are the same."

Rickers is smiling as he asks, "What about Gabrielle Gagnon? Would you say the two of you are different players?"

Gabrielle is the third woman to be drafted into the League. She and Elsa both went first round at the last draft. Elsa, tall with sharp blue eyes and a bright smile, will be Sophie's teammate and roommate this upcoming season. Gabrielle, who is striking in her own way, is the first female goalie in the League. They're both proof Sophie did something right last season. The "Sophie Fournier Experiment" as her critics, and even some of her supporters called it, must have been a success since two more women have been added to the League.

Sophie allows the reporters to see a flash of her smile before she answers. "I'd say I'm more offensively minded than Gabrielle, but she has me beat as a defensive player."

Rickers grows serious. "Do you think she'll be a good fit for Quebec? They're notoriously hard on their goalies."

Most teams put statues of players they're proud of outside their stadiums. They erect monuments to franchise players, the ones who have led the team on a great playoff run or scored an iconic goal or blown team records out of the water.

Not Quebec.

Quebec's stadium is guarded, or maybe haunted is the better word, by a statue of William Loiseau. He was the Bobcats' goalie when they won five straight Maple Cups, and he was the one who lost them their sixth. With a win, Quebec would take the record for consecutive Maple Cup victories from Montreal, their longtime—and bitter—rival. But in triple OT of Game Seven of the Finals, the puck trickled through Loiseau's legs and Quebec lost.

They ran the man out of town. From the rumors Sophie's heard, he was run out of the country too. They put up a statue of Five-Hole Billy to warn future goalies against repeating his mistakes. It was the birth of the Quebec Curse. They haven't held on to a goaltender for more than five years since.

"Quebec does have a reputation," Sophie agrees. "Gabrielle is a steady goalie, and she's always performed well for Team Canada, another tough hockey critic. There are a lot of aspects of her game for Quebec to like."

It's uncommon for a goalie to make their team right out of being drafted, but maybe Gabrielle will be an exception. Sophie's most excited for Elsa, to have another woman on her team, but it'll be good to compete against Gabrielle.

AFTER SHE'S RELEASED from the media, she sits for a signing session with Matty, Lindy, and Delacroix. Benoit Delacroix—X—is their veteran defenseman and as much as this weekend means to Sophie, it means more to him.

The last expansion took place during the League's seventy-fifth year. Concord was one of the teams added. X was recruited out of college, the first player signed to the team.

X, and Concord, have been in the League for eighteen years now. He's dedicated his entire career to this team, and Sophie will see him lift the Cup before he's done. No one has given this franchise more than he has, and she wants him rewarded for it. There are lines in his face she doesn't remember from last year, and his beard, while trimmed short, has more gray than brown in it this year.

She sits between X and Matty with Lindy on Matty's other side. They're the pillars of the franchise, the Condors building up around X then Matty and X then Matty, X, and Lindy, but a solid structure needs *four* pillars. Maybe it's cocky for her to elect herself Concord's fourth support, but she does it anyway. The four of them, they'll bring Concord to the playoffs for the first time in franchise history, then they'll win the Cup.

"You're my favorite player."

Sophie's pulled out of her thoughts by a girl in a Condors T-shirt. Her curls are pinned to keep them out of her face, and she hands a second T-shirt to Sophie to sign.

"It used to be Justin Rust, because he's American and my brother says I'm not allowed to like Canadian players best, but it's a stupid rule so I like you anyway."

Matty's doing his best not to laugh, and Sophie has to turn away from him so she can control her smile. "Thank you. Do you play?"

The girl nods and it shakes some of her curls free. "I want to play with the boys like you. I have your poster on my wall and my brother told me it was stupid because girls can't play as good as boys but you scored the most points in the League."

"If you're good enough to play, you can play, whether you're a boy or a girl. What's your name?"

"Eliza Bennett. My mom named me after some girl in a really old book. I'm going to name *my* daughter Sophie like you."

All three of her teammates are openly laughing at her now. Fighting a blush, Sophie writes *To Eliza* above her signature. "You seem too young to have kids."

Eliza rolls her eyes. "Duh, I'm only in sixth grade. Mom says I have to wait until *college* to have a boyfriend." She squints at Sophie. "If you didn't go to college then when are you allowed to date?"

Thankfully, one of the convention attendants moves Eliza along before Sophie has to answer.

AFTER THE CONVENTION, the team piles into one of their favorite bars. They take up two sets of booths near the back, and Sophie sits between Witzer and Merlin with a bottle of water rather than a beer. She fiddles with the plastic label. "It has been *one* day, and I've fielded more questions about dating than I did all of last year."

The table falls silent. Nelson looks away as if the word *date* is something to be afraid of even though she listened to him regale the locker room with stories of his various hookups last year, in more detail than anyone needed. Next to her, Witzer has gone still as if she'll forget he's here if he doesn't move or speak.

"Sorry." Sophie twists and untwists the cap on her water bottle. She forgot there are some topics off-limits to her.

"You don't need to apologize." Merlin glares at his phone.

She leans over his shoulder. *The Sin Bin*, which is more an online tabloid than a hockey news site, is running the headline *Sophie Fournier–Hockeysexual?* She's heard variations of the same ever since her male teammates realized they wanted to be near girls instead of running away from them. There were several awful months in the locker room where the boys strutted around with their shirts off and their chests puffed up.

She was eleven and completely uninterested.

Over the years, with different teams and in different locker rooms, Sophie has remained uninterested. Sometimes, she wonders if there's something wrong with her. She's never felt a spark when she sees someone or experienced the stirrings of a crush. She's seen plenty of abs and asses and dicks in the locker room and never thought anything besides *put some clothes on before a camera catches you.*

"This article says instead of watching porn you get off on hockey highlights." Merlin keeps his voice light, trying to make a joke out of it because if they can joke, then everything will be okay.

She doesn't need him to guard her feelings, but she appreciates the effort. She's tempted to say she gets off the way she imagines most women without a partner do—with her hands and her favorite vibrator—but this isn't the right time or the right audience.

Instead, she grins and bumps his shoulder with hers. "I guess you don't have to worry about me having a crush on you. You're certainly not on my hockey highlight reel."

The table, if possible, grows even quieter.

Then Matty slaps the table as he bursts into laughter.

"Hey," Merlin grumbles, but he looks too relieved to mean it.

Chapter Two

MOST OF HER teammates leave town after the convention. Garfield returns to Montana to spend as much time as possible with his grandmother before the season begins. Matty takes his wife and kids on one last vacation before his schedule becomes so packed they don't see much of each other.

Sophie opens her apartment to Derek Napoli and CondorsTV so they can film a special episode of *In the Nest*. It's a web series which also airs on *The Granite State Sports Network*, and it provides a behind-the-scenes experience for the fans of the Condors. She understands why it's important, but she resents her home being invaded.

Her entire life has been open to anyone who wants to poke at it. All her schoolteachers have been interviewed over the years as well as coaches and teammates from every team she's played on. Already, there are a dozen of specials on *The Making of Sophie Fournier*. She has *biographies* about her life, and she isn't even twenty. Sometimes, she's afraid people will scoop every story and memory from her until there's nothing left belonging to her.

She dips her fingers into the waistband of her pants so she can touch the tattoo she knows is there. This, at least, is a secret she's managed to keep. Her tattoo is two crossed hockey sticks, with the number 93 inked to the left of them. She intended the right side to hold an equally important number, her draft selection maybe. But after she was chosen dead last, she didn't want a 224 on her body, a permanent reminder of how her team undervalued her. Instead, she has a blank space, waiting for the right thing to fill it with.

There's a knock at her door and she stops touching her tattoo. She shakes her Condors T-shirt out to cover the waistband of her jeans so there's no chance Napoli will see something she doesn't want him to see. Then she opens the door, covering a yawn as if she woke up only moments ago.

She's been awake for two hours.

"Coffee?" she asks Napoli and the camera crew who follow him in.

Teddy dragged her to the store and made her buy a Keurig after the first day of the convention. He claimed her lack of a coffee machine was "a crime against humanity" and assured her Elsa wouldn't abandon Sophie and get her own apartment because there was already a coffeemaker.

"We're good," Napoli tells her. Behind him, the red light on the camera blinks. "Can you tell me about your apartment? Did you pick it out yourself or did one of the guys help you?"

Last season, Sophie asked Matty for help buying her first car. She doesn't think Napoli or Ed Rickers have forgiven her for not taking a camera crew along with them. The apartment hunting had been done on her own. She felt it was an important step and, more importantly, she didn't want anyone teasing her for how long it took her to decide. She needed the perfect apartment so Elsa will be happy and want to stay.

"I found it on my own. Um, you guys came up so you know there's a doorman. I never thought I'd live in a place with a doorman, but here I am." She smiles even knowing it's as awkward as she feels. Over the years, she's learned to be as bland and boring as possible, the best defense against the intrusive media, but CondorsTV is all about being warm and inviting.

It's difficult to be inviting when she doesn't want them here.

"Why don't you tell us about your couch," Napoli suggests.

She glances at the piece of furniture. She ordered it online and it serves as a visual block between the kitchen and the living room. She did some reading on apartment staging to make sure she did it right. She doubts Napoli will care. "It's extra wide because sometimes I fall asleep on the couch, and there's nothing worse than waking up because I've fallen off."

"Your TV is smaller than I'd expect."

Sophie hadn't wanted a TV at all, but the wall looked too empty, and the TV takes up space. "I don't plan on watching much."

Napoli, who is out of the video frame, looks pained. "There aren't any shows you follow?"

"I watch hockey, but on my computer or my iPad if the coaches have loaded my shifts for me to review."

"Do you have any game consoles?" Napoli asks, desperate.

"No. I texted Elsa to see if she wanted me to buy any, but I haven't heard back yet."

Even accounting for the time difference, she should've answered Sophie already. They exchanged numbers at the draft, and Elsa has had no problem bombarding Sophie's phone with vacation photos; Elsa at the beach, Elsa climbing mountains, Elsa at a petting zoo. She loves animals and she loves being outside, and almost every picture has been a selfie, Elsa's bright smile taking up most of the frame.

"You have a roommate next year." Napoli latches onto this new topic. "Are you looking forward to it?"

"I am." Her first genuine smile spreads across her face. "I'm grateful to the Wilcoxes for giving me a place to stay last year, but I'm excited for an apartment and a roommate to share it with. Do you want a tour?"

Napoli grimaces even as he nods. They've already seen the couch and the TV so she moves into the kitchen which is modern and functional. Napoli waves the cameras over to zoom in on the pictures on her refrigerator. They were housewarming gifts from the Wilcox girls. Kaylee drew Sophie a pretty good picture of Sophie on the ice with her teammates. Jessi drew her Biscuit, the Wilcox family hamster.

"They're from the Wilcox girls," Sophie says. Kaylee is in fourth grade now, and Jessi is in second. Jessi's still campaigning for Sophie to serve as show-and-tell in her class. It's brought up every time Sophie visits the family, and Kaylee tries to appear aloof and disinterested, but she never leaves the room as if she's invested in the answer. Sophie makes another mental note to ask Mary Beth about setting something up.

Sophie leads the cameras into her bedroom next. It's large enough to comfortably fit a queen-size bed and a dresser. The closet has the space for all of her suits. Her walls are bare, because she feels weird hanging up hockey posters the way she did in her childhood bedroom.

"Still getting settled, I see."

Sophie looks at the neatly made bed and the quilt folded at the end of it, a present from her mom. A framed family photo rests on one nightstand. A picture of the team is on the other. Napoli clearly thinks something is lacking so Sophie says, "Early days," and hopes he doesn't come back to see if she makes any changes.

She brings him to Elsa's room next, and it's even barer than her own with only a bed, a dresser, and two nightstands. She's learned, though, and jumps on the offensive right away. "I didn't want Elsa to feel as if her room isn't hers. I want it to be a blank slate for her. The guest room is more decorated."

She leads them into the last bedroom in the apartment. There's another queen bed, and this one has a bed skirt and everything. Everything in the room matches from the dark blue comforter to the sailboat pictures on the walls. She saw this room in a magazine she was flipping through and ordered the whole thing. The furniture is white, the bedding is navy blue, and the walls are a light blue to bring out the color of the ocean in the pictures. According to the catalogue, at least.

"This is...nice," Napoli says.

"It's for family."

WHEN THE PREVIEW for the special goes up, Sophie's mom sends her six different links for throw pillows, because her couch doesn't have any and apparently they're essential.

Merlin sends her a plastic plant.

ELSA SIGNS A one-year extension with Gothenburg and Sophie finds out from *the media*. Her alert on Elsa's name pings and sends her to an article in Swedish. At first, Sophie hopes it's a Google Translate issue even though, deep down, she knows it isn't. Still, she sticks a link into her chat with Elsa to confirm.

It barely takes any time for Elsa to respond.

Mamma says Concord is far away.

It's like a blindside hit, knocking the breath out of her. Elsa isn't coming.

Disappointment pierces the fog in her brain. The sharp twist of it makes her want to cry. She was supposed to have another woman on the team. She was supposed to have a *roommate*. She looks at the matching sectional she ordered for the couch so there would be space for both of them. Then she sweeps all the stupid throw pillows onto the floor.

She takes a deep breath. Her Google alert warned her of the article, but it won't be long before it's translated and the news trickles down to the American media.

Elsa has added a bunch of sad face emojis to their chat. Sophie takes another deep breath and closes their conversation.

She calls Mary Beth.

"What happened?" Mary Beth asks.

"Elsa's staying in Sweden. My schedule is open. Whatever interviews you need, I'll do them."

"Thank you." Mary Beth sounds distant as if she's already compiling a list of reporters and outlets. "You know for sure?"

"The news broke in Sweden. Elsa confirmed it when I asked. It won't be long before North America catches up."

"Are you still in Concord?"

"I am and I'm staying until the season."

"We'll do a mix of in-person and phone interviews then. We'll get you on the ice for some of them to remind everyone Concord's future is already here and it looks bright." There's a pause. "I'm sorry. I didn't ask how you're doing with the news."

"Concord's future is bright," Sophie parrots. "Fan Fest was only a preview of what this season will be."

"CONCORD TOOK A chance on Elsa Nyberg," Marty Owen from *The Concord Courier* says.

Sophie did phone interviews with *Representation Matters* and *After the Whistle*. *The National Sports Network* flew someone in to talk with her and she sat down with Ed Rickers from *The Granite State Sports Network*. She wishes her interview with Marty Owen had been over the phone.

Of course, if her wishes were being granted, she wouldn't have to talk to him at all.

Today, Owen's suit is too big in the shoulders and too short in the sleeves. He has ink stains on his fingers and he brandishes his phone like a weapon. She's never had a comfortable relationship with the media. They're always demanding *more* and trying to trick her into headlines to sell articles. She isn't dynamic like Dima or funny like Merlin. She can't even quite capture the serious but personable vibe Matty goes with.

Bland and boring is her fallback, and she relies on all her years of practice to keep her expression neutral as Owen stares her down, challenging. "Elsa isn't the first player not to come over in her first year, and she certainly won't be the last."

"You don't think this is a sign Concord made a mistake?"

"Elsa's committed to playing another year for Gothenburg. It means she'll be another year stronger and better when she joins Concord." *If* she comes. Sophie keeps the thought off her face. Elsa *will* come. Next year. All Sophie has to do is prove Concord is a team worth being a part of.

"The *In the Nest* special on your apartment has already come out. What will you do without a roommate? Do you think it was premature to rent an apartment before Nyberg signed with the team?"

"I moved into an apartment for me. It was the next logical step. Obviously, I would've enjoyed having Elsa for a roommate, but I'll manage on my own."

She's gotten used to it over the years.

AFTER THE LAST of her interviews, Sophie plops down on her couch with a pint of vanilla frozen yogurt. She pops the lid as she calls Dima and puts the phone on speaker.

Dmitri Ivanov was the first overall pick at the 2010 draft, selected by the Boston Barons. When Sophie was selected last by the Concord Condors in the next year, the NAHL tried to create a rivalry. A lockout led to them debuting in the same season, and the League hoped to use them to draw attention after an entire year without hockey.

She and Dima chose not to follow the NAHL's narrative. They're competitors on the ice, but off it they're friends. She trusts him enough to ask, "What if Elsa never comes?" voicing doubts she refuses to even share with Mary Beth.

"Then you play good hockey, same as if she is here."

She scowls at her phone even though Dima can't see her. She wants to *wallow*, not be practical. "I wanted to play good hockey with Elsa. She switched to left wing after we played against each other in Zurich so we could play on a line together one day. I thought it meant something."

She's whining and she'd be embarrassed by it except Dima's already seen her at her worst. Last year, after he won the Clayton, the trophy for the best rookie, he had a front row seat to the tantrum she threw in her hotel room. *She* was supposed to be the best. Her dad always told her growing up, *if you're not the best then you don't get to play*. She was afraid being the runner-up meant everyone was right, she deserved to be the last pick of the draft. She was afraid it meant the League wouldn't invite her back and it would close its doors to all women.

A few days later, she selected Elsa fifth overall.

Dima tsks at her. "For you, go to States is easy. Short flight, parents can visit and call. Is hard for me. Is hard for Nyberg."

"Oh." Guilty, she stares at her frozen yogurt. Elsa even told her she was staying because Concord is too far away, but Sophie didn't understand. It *is* easy for her family to fly out for her games. Last year, her parents came to her first three games. This year they'll be at the home opener. She's never asked Dima what it's like for his family to be so far away. Yaroslavl and Boston aren't exactly close.

Not for the first time, she thinks he got the short end of the friendship stick.

"I should let you be with your family, then."

"Can talk for little bit. Hiding from Mama."

"What did you do?"

Dima squawks, offended she thinks he's done something wrong, but launches into a story about trying to smuggle a dog into his house without his mom noticing.

TRAINING CAMP IS around the corner when Sophie's mom calls.

"Are you sure it's not too late for you cancel your lease?" she asks.

It's the same thing she's asked, in different ways, through four phone calls and six text messages. Sophie bites back her sigh. "I'm sure."

"Ronnie and Amber would open their house up to you again. And you liked spending time with their kids."

"The Wilcoxes were very nice." Living with them her first year had been important, a safety net to fall back on when the season seemed like too much for her to handle. But she's in her second year in the NAHL, and she's an adult. It's time for her to have her own apartment even if she doesn't have a roommate.

"I worry about you."

And here they go again. Sophie's almost relieved when her dad takes the phone. Then he opens his mouth. "Nyberg was a waste of a high draft pick."

Should they have picked her in the last round like me? There's no risk there. "She deserved to be picked high. She's hardly the first player to take an extra year. Guys do it all the time to play another year in college or even finish out their degree. And European players rarely come over in their first year."

"She should've been more grateful for the opportunity Concord gave her."

Now her dad sounds like Lenny Dernier. His show *Rinkside* is on *The National Sports Network*. Growing up, she watched it religiously, soaking up everything he said like his words held the path to the NAHL for her. Of course, if Dernier had his way, Sophie never would've stepped foot on NAHL ice. He's what people like to call an old school hockey personality as if age is an excuse to constantly deride anyone who isn't *a good Canadian boy*.

"You mother says you're moping."

"I'm not."

"You can't link your happiness to other people. They'll always let you down."

"Pierre!" Her mom's voice is loud enough to be heard through the phone. A moment later, she's snatched the phone back. "Don't listen to your father, sweetie. People are important."

"Hockey is important," her dad says.

"Maybe having your own apartment will be a blessing in disguise," her mom continues, talking louder as if she can drown out her husband. "Maybe you'll meet a nice boy. There are nice boys in Concord, aren't there?"

"Ugh," Sophie says.

THE DAY BEFORE training camp starts, Merlin invites her over for dinner with him and his girlfriend. Marissa answers the door in teal scrubs with an oversized Condors sweatshirt thrown over the top. She smiles as she ushers Sophie inside.

"You brought me flowers?" she asks as she takes the bouquet. "You didn't need to."

"I'm not old enough for wine." Sophie takes her shoes off by the door and sets them against the wall. There aren't any other shoes there. Maybe Marissa has a shoe closet? She looks up for help, but Marissa's already halfway to the kitchen, waving her flowers.

"Jeffrey, your teammate brought me flowers. How come you never get me flowers?"

"I told you, as soon as we have a house, I will buy you a garden so the flowers won't die."

"Mmm, sweet." Marissa bops him on the nose with the bouquet. "But bullshit."

Merlin shrugs. "Worth a try." He waves a wooden spoon at Sophie in greeting. "How's the plant I sent you? Is it still alive?"

"It's a fake plant."

"Which would make it doubly sad if it was dead." Merlin flashes her a smile as he opens the cabinet to the left of the stove. "Do you want coffee? Tea? Wine?" He goes up on his tiptoes to reach the top shelf. It's full of silly coffee mugs. One of them is red with Elmo's face on it. Another has a toucan handle.

Is this what her apartment is missing? Weird mugs?

Merlin waves his hand. "Drink?"

"Water's good. Sorry." She stares for another moment before she gives in. "Is that a *toucan*?"

Merlin raises his eyes to the ceiling as Marissa laughs. She links her arm through Merlin's. "Jeff bought it for me on our first vacation."

"You were staring at it! I thought you liked it."

"It's a phallic bird thing." Marissa laughs as she plucks the mug from its hiding place. "But it's ours. I think I'll have tea with dinner."

"Seriously?" Merlin groans and tries to snatch the mug.

Marissa grins as she dances away from him and to the pantry. "Sophie, has Jeffrey told you how we met?"

"We mostly talk about hockey."

"This relates to hockey. I was doing an internship at UMass Memorial when this dumbass kid limps into the ER. He and his teammates were doing flips on a trampoline and he fell off and sprained his ankle. He thought his coach wouldn't find out if he went to the hospital instead of his team trainer."

"Coach found out," Merlin says, picking up the story. "He was pissed but I met Marissa so it was worth it."

"Aw." Marissa flashes her boyfriend a smile.

Sophie feels a pang of jealousy as she watches the easy way they move around each other in the kitchen as they finish dinner. They tell stories, started by one of them and finished by the other. This is what Sophie could've had this season. Well, not exactly, because she and Elsa would be roommates, but she'd have someone to come home to and talk to, someone to share inside jokes with.

The third time Merlin catches Marissa stroking the toucan, he groans. "Okay, you win."

She smirks as she hands the mug to him. He wraps his hands around the mug part, careful not to touch the handle as he takes a drink of her tea.

"You're welcome to come over whenever," Marissa says as she takes the chicken out of the oven.

"You have to be more specific in your invitation," Merlin says. "Sophie's Canadian. She doesn't like to impose."

Sophie, who was about to politely decline, scowls at him.

"At least once a week then," Marissa declares. "The shine of having an apartment to yourself wears off pretty quickly. And if you ever want girl time, we can kick Jeff out and binge watch *The Bachelor* and eat cupcakes."

It sounds...nice. Well, she doesn't care much for *The Bachelor* and kicking Merlin out of his own apartment seems rude, but she wouldn't mind having people to hang out with. Hockey hasn't given her many opportunities to spend time with other women.

"We can do dinner at my place too," Sophie offers.

"I dunno, your TV is pretty small."

Merlin's smirk turns into a yelp when she kicks him under the table. She smiles sweetly at him. Marissa holds her hand up for a high five.

Chapter Three

DESPITE HAVING AN entire year in the League under her belt, Sophie's as nervous for the start of training camp this season as she was last. Coach Butler's personal philosophy is no one walks into camp on the team. Not Matty who has worn the C for them the past few seasons or X who has been with the team since its inception.

And if they don't have a guarantee, Sophie certainly doesn't.

Even letters are stripped away for training camp. Everyone knows Matty will wear the C once preseason begins, and they'll still treat him as the leader he is, but Coach Butler doesn't want anyone feeling safe. He thinks it leads to complacency.

It's why no one wears their numbers during training camp either. She steps into the locker room for the first day, and all the stalls have a piece of tape at the top with their last name and then their first name in alphabetical order. Like last year, she's between Faulkner, Kevin and Garfield, Luke.

Unlike last year, her clothes already hang in her stall. She changes into her T-shirt and mesh shorts and hits the weight room. She's the only one here so she hops on her favorite bike, puts her headphones on, and warms up. After the bike, she stretches and rolls out on the foam roller. By the time she grabs one of the elastic bands, someone else has joined her.

Zinger waves and pushes his sweatband higher on his forehead. It makes his bangs stick up, and she can't help her laugh as she steps into the band. Then she squats and steps sideways, the band providing resistance as she moves.

"Gotta look good to do good, he tells her. Jiāháo Zhang was one of her teammates last year. Unlike most hockey players who have a first name, last name, and nickname, he has his Taiwanese names, his English name, and his hockey name. To his family he's Jiāháo, to the media, he's Justin, and to the team, he's Zinger. She asked him once why he picked Justin as what he wanted to be called when he moved to the States from Taipei. He deflected, badly, but one night when they were at a bar during karaoke, he did a full set of NSYNC's greatest hits and drunkenly confessed to her his love of Justin Timberlake. It's a secret she's kept for him. His love of Timberlake, not his love of karaoke. Merlin filmed the whole thing and periodically busts it out on plane flights when he's bored.

"This is looking good?" Sophie gives him an obvious once-over and shakes her head.

He flashes her a double thumbs-up and claims an elliptical. They work out in silence until Zinger joins her near the free weights. He lies down on his back and stretches his leg across his body. "Will you help? I'll do you after."

She places one hand on his right hip and her other hand on his right knee and pushes down. He groans before he takes a deep breath and releases it slowly. When he relaxes, she pushes more and holds to a count of thirty. He switches sides and they repeat the process. Then it's her turn to lie down.

Some more of their teammates join them. X goes straight for the stretch-bands. Kevlar and Theo each hop on an elliptical and immediately race each other.

"Save some of it for camp, eh?" Sophie calls out.

"Eh." Theo cracks up as if he's never heard a Canadian speak before.

Sophie and Kevlar flip him off at the same time.

MATTY'S IN CHARGE of the first day of training camp, and he takes them on their customary historic run through downtown Concord. Afterward, they lay out exercise mats in the parking lot and Matty puts them through a series of core and general strength exercises.

This year, Sophie sets her mat up next to her captain's. It means they're side by side when they begin the plank challenge. It's easier to focus without Kevlar and Theo making a fuss next to her. It helps too to have Matty in her sights.

He was her direct competition last year, and they're shaping up for a repeat. Sophie's stomach quivers, and her shoulders ache as they tick upwards of five minutes. Sweat pools in the small of her back and drips off her face onto her mat. Matty adjusts his position and almost slips on his own puddle of sweat.

Sophie keeps her gaze locked on Matty and breathes as deeply as she's able. Matty trembles, from his shoulders to his toes, and she knows she won't have to hold out much longer.

"You're looking tired there, Cap," Merlin says.

"Oooh," several of the guys chorus.

Sophie and Matty exchange an eye roll.

Matty breaks first. He drops to his mat with a grunt, and Sophie holds out for another five-count before she drops down too.

"I'm never moving again," Sophie decides.

"Do you practice this during the summer?" Merlin pokes her shoulder.

"I only let myself watch TV if I'm planking."

"This explains so much." Merlin pokes her again. "Come on, shower time."

She pushes herself to her knees and then to her feet. She adds her mat to the pile near the doors to their practice facility. They troop inside for the first shower of the day. Sophie pulls her soaked shirt over her head and tosses it in her laundry. She tosses her shorts in next.

"Woah!" Kuzy exclaims. "What are you doing?"

"Undressing for my shower."

The locker room falls quiet, everyone looking to Matty for help. Sophie, in her spandex and a sports bra now, wraps her towel around herself. Last year, she showered in her closet-turned-locker room. This year, Ben Granlund, their equipment manager, curtained off a shower in the main locker room for her.

This is the locker room she belongs in, not banished down the hall. She doesn't intend to ever strip down completely in front of her teammates, but if they can't handle seeing a bit of skin, they're the ones who have to leave, not her. She arches her eyebrows at Matty, challenging.

"You should take a shower too," Matty tells Kuzy. "You smell like shit."

There's a beat of silence before Merlin shouts, "Captain's a shit-sniffer!" and the locker room dissolves into uproarious laughter.

She slips into the main shower room and grins at the shower curtain. It's red with the team's condor on it, exactly what she would expect from Ben. She hangs her towel on a hook, out of the reach of the shower spray, and strips the rest of her clothes off.

She can still hear her teammates laughing at each other when she steps under the stream of water.

THE SECOND DAY of training camp is even better than the first, because they're allowed on the ice. They're geared up by the time Coach Butler barges into the locker room. The first time she saw him, she thought he had a severe face. It hasn't relaxed in the year she's known him. The closest she's seen him to happy is when they battle with another team, blood and teeth on the ice by the end of it.

"Welcome to training camp," Coach Butler tells them. "Yesterday, Mathers was in charge of you. Today, it's my turn. Get ready to work."

Despite the serious tone he struck, everyone is all smiles as they troop up to the ice. They're all here because they love hockey, and none of them would be here if they were afraid of work. She's the second one on the ice after Matty, and she beams as she skates a full loop of the rink.

"What a smile," Theo says as she reaches the bench again. "Long dry spell?"

She rolls her eyes and pulls him onto the ice. Kevlar trips him so he falls on his face. "Long dry spell for you maybe. You've forgotten how to skate."

Theo hauls her into a headlock and she twists out of his grasp. They play-fight until Matty skates over. He grabs Theo in a bear hug from behind which turns into *them* wrestling. She drifts over to where X is watching the scene unfold.

"We have the best captain in the League," she says.

X takes one of his gloves off so he can put a hand to her forehead. "Did you forget everything this summer? Our captain is a loser."

"Yeah, but he's *our* loser."

AT THE END of training camp, there's the first round of cuts. Guys are sent back to Juniors or college or home, depending on where they are in their development. Sophie's cooling down in the weight room when her phone buzzes. She checks the notification. Gabrielle Gagnon has been assigned to the Trois-Rivières Bobcats, Quebec's minor league team. It isn't surprising; goalies rarely start right away, but it means Sophie's still the only woman in the North American Hockey League.

Her shoulders slump and she slows down her biking until she comes to a complete stop. Then she moves to the far side of the weight room where the punching bags are set up. She tapes her hands the way Kevlar taught her and squares up against the bag.

She isn't allowed to fight, the League has made it very clear to her they want her gloves to stay on, but this is good stress relief. Besides, if she ever does have to fight, she wants to be prepared. Today, she locks her core and twists as she extends her arm the way Kevlar showed her. Her fist thuds against the bag. She hits it again. Then again.

Sweat beads along her hairline. This is the opposite of cooling down, but she isn't ready to go back to her empty apartment. The last thing she needs is a reminder of how alone she is. No Elsa, now no Gabrielle.

"Why am I not surprised to find you here?"

She turns to see Kevlar leaning against the lat pull-down machine. His own hands are bare which means he isn't planning on joining her. She pulls her shirt up to wipe the sweat off her face. "I have some things to work out."

"We already have double and triple sessions. There's no need to make more work for yourself."

"Gabrielle was assigned to Trois-Rivières."

"Uh huh."

Sophie shrugs. "It was a longshot, but I was hoping she'd make the team. I really thought I'd have another woman in the League this year."

Kevlar crosses his arms over his chest, making himself comfortable. "You're the only one like you? Gee, what's it feel like?"

She stares at Kevlar's hands again. They're dark brown, a sharp contrast to her own pale ones. She flushes as she realizes how self-centered she's been. She's the only woman in the League, but it isn't like it's easy for Kevlar either. "Do you want to talk about it?"

He laughs. It's a stupid question. He's a hockey player. Of course he doesn't want to talk about it. But then he unfolds his arms. "Selfishly, I wish I wasn't alone, but part of me is glad I am. No one else needs to hear the shit I do."

She knows about taking shit from fans and other players and even coaches and commentators. It's different for her than it is for him. She's accused of being soft, of being weak, of never living up to expectations. Kevlar's a brute when he plays too aggressively and a waste of a roster spot when he backs off. Neither of them can ever win.

"If there were more people like you..."

He laughs and shakes his head. "It wouldn't stop. They would feel threatened and get louder. Reporters scoff when you say you want more women in the League. Could you imagine if I said I wanted an army of black men?"

"No. You have too much media training. You'd put it more diplomatically."

"But it's what I would mean. Right now, if someone says 'hey, do you know that black guy who plays hockey' then there's a one in ten chance you'll answer right. I want us to quit being an anomaly in this sport. I want two black players on the team to stop being headline material. It isn't news when 75 percent of a roster is white."

"It should be."

"But we *are* diverse. Swedes and Danes and Norwegians, even some Finns for good measure. Northern Europe is very well represented."

Sophie laughs as she unwraps the tape from her hands.

THIS YEAR, COACH Butler takes them to Mount Washington for their post-training camp team-building activity. They pile onto the team bus, storing their Condors backpacks above them and fighting over who sits where.

Most hockey players have militant superstitions which dictate where they sit on the bus or plane, what food they eat the day before and of a game, and even what clothes they wear. Sophie's never had the luxury of being superstitious. Her play isn't determined by a lucky sports bra or whether she eats chicken and pasta for breakfast on game day.

She sits next to Teddy, because he doesn't spread his thighs into her personal space. She taps his shoulder and points to where Merlin is shifting restlessly in his seat, because he's in Row Ten and has the window seat. The guy next to him, George Cullen, keeps looking over, amused. He played for the Regina Rapids last season, and he's here on a professional tryout contract. His hands are good, but he's too close to forty, and his speed isn't great.

He seems like he'd be a good guy to have in the locker room—anyone who gives Merlin shit is okay in her book—but she's not sure he'd be an asset on the ice.

"We're climbing a mountain?" Peets asks as the bus finally begins to move.

"Not just any mountain," Matty answers. "Mount Washington. Did you know the Summit House was one of the first tourist attractions in the United States, in 1832?"

Merlin groans. "You and your fucking history boner."

"Once we reach the base of the mountain, you'll be assigned hiking groups. We're not losing anyone on the mountain."

Teddy leans in to whisper. "We're definitely losing someone on the mountain. I'm thinking one of the new guys, but I could be persuaded to make it Theo."

"Still jealous about the nickname, *Teddy*? Don't say it too loudly or you'll end up at the bottom of a cuddle pile again." Last year, Theodore Augereau was traded to their team and when he met Theodore Smith, there wasn't even a question of who'd get to keep Theo as their nickname. Teddy made one valiant attempt, claiming Theo looked far more like a teddy bear. He didn't win the argument, he'll be Teddy for his entire career in Concord, and ended up in the middle of a group hug as Theo and Kevlar proved he was cuddly enough to be a Teddy.

Sophie photographed and videoed the moment to preserve it for future mockery. Teddy, no doubt remembering, pokes her, a vicious jab to her stomach, and she has to bite back her laugh because Matty's still talking. She pokes him back and it turns into an all-out poke war. Hopefully, Matty didn't have anything else important to say because they stop paying attention.

Sophie's hiking group is Teddy, Kevlar, George Cullen, and Christian Spitzweg. Spitzweg played for Manchester last season, and he's supposedly twenty, but he has enough baby fat lingering on his face to make him look closer to twelve. His eyes are bright blue and his hair is so blond and fair, it reminders her of a dandelion. She's afraid if the wind picks up, all his hair will blow away.

"I'm Sophie." She introduces herself as she adjusts the straps on her backpack. She has two water bottles and some food, but most of her backpack is taken up by clothes. They were warned the temperature at the base of the mountain varies drastically from the temperature at the top, and she wanted to be prepared.

The kid laughs. "Uh, yeah. Peets talked about you a lot last year. Before he was called up."

"We call him Marinara Man," Kevlar says. "He face-planted in his spaghetti during preseason. Did he tell you the story?"

"For some reason, he forgot." Spitzweg grins, lighting up in a way which means he'll cheerfully give Peets shit about it next time they see each other.

"It happens every year," Cullen says. "One year, the rookie fell asleep in his sushi and got wasabi up his nose."

Teddy flinches in sympathy, but Cullen only shrugs with the air of someone who has seen everything.

THERE ISN'T ANYTHING to do on the hike except walk up a mountain and talk to each other. Sophie has the lead, which means she has to strain to hear what the guys are talking about.

"Oh man, we did it one time in Juniors," Kevlar says, responding to Cullen's story. "We were stuck on the bus for eight hours and we were bored so we broke into the med kit. We slapped some Icy Hot on our junk. Coach was pissed when we woke him up with all our yelling."

"We did it too," Teddy says. "Well, because I'm not an idiot, I put it on my thigh. Duke put it on his balls. I've never heard a guy's voice hit a note so high after puberty."

Sophie twists to look back at the line of guys. Spitzweg looks to her, horrified, as if he's waiting for her to share her own version of this story.

"You're still an idiot," she tells Teddy. "But apparently every boy who's ever played hockey is an idiot."

"It's a natural curiosity."

"You see something and wonder what it would feel like on your dick?"

Kevlar shrugs but nods.

"This is why we need more women in hockey."

"In Germany, we don't have sex with Icy Hot," Spitzweg says.

"It's not a sex thing!" Teddy objects.

"Maybe for Canadians it is," Cullen says.

"Hey!"

The two of them squabble over whether it's America or Canada with the Icy Hot fetish. Sophie laughs to herself as they wind their way up the mountain. Kevlar speeds up so they're side by side. "Look what you've done. I hope you're proud of yourself."

"I'm doing my part to disrupt border relations."

WHEN THEY STOP for a snack break, Teddy takes his right sneaker off and frowns as he rubs his heel.

"Blistering?" Kevlar asks. He's in sturdy boots, the laces done up tight. Sophie thought about boots, but she doesn't have any broken in and didn't want to risk ruining her feet with preseason around the corner.

"I have Band-Aids in my bag if you want one." Sophie tosses her backpack to her goalie.

He catches it and opens the front pocket. A tampon falls out. The rest of the guys stop eating and stare as the little white cylinder rolls until it's stopped by a rock. Teddy picks it up and puts it back in her bag and grabs a Band-Aid.

"I'm not a nature guy," Teddy grumbles as he opens the Band-Aid. "Can we go down instead?" He looks longingly back at where they've been.

"Sounds like a question for Alyssa, not us." Kevlar laughs as Teddy flips him off.

"Snack time's over," Sophie decides. She stands up and brushes the granola bar crumbs off her clothes. "If the next group catches up to us, Merlin will never let us live it down."

Chapter Four

THEY RETURN FROM their team-building trip. The next day, Sophie's called into Coach Butler's office. Mr. Wilcox and Mr. Pauling are both there. Mary Beth is too, her phone out because she's always working. Sophie glances around the room and wonders what's gone wrong.

She was brought to Concord to give the team a spark, but more often than not, she finds herself polishing Concord's image. When Michael Hayes couldn't give a half-decent interview to save his life, she was trotted out in a nice blouse with her hair curled to talk about what a great organization Concord is. When they missed the playoffs for the seventeenth straight year, the spotlight was on the final stretch of her rookie season and whether she'd break a hundred points or not. And, when Elsa Nyberg chose to stay in Sweden for another year, it was up to Sophie to smooth everything over.

She's shiny, she's distracting, and as much as she hates being paraded around, it's what she has to do in order to play hockey.

The team had their retreat this weekend which means they were supervised. If something bad happened, she should already know about it.

"We're giving you an A this season," Mr. Pauling says.

She stops imagining worst-case scenarios, but it's a sharp turn to make. *Alternate captain?* A year and a half ago, she didn't know if there was a place for women in the

North American Hockey League. Only a few months ago, she didn't know if Concord would invite her back to camp. And now they want to give her a letter?

She looks to Coach Butler for confirmation.

He's frowning, but since Mr. Pauling and Mr. Wilcox stand behind him, they can't see. "You'll wear it during the preseason. *If* you prove yourself worthy of it, we'll talk about you wearing it during the regular season."

Coach Butler has never been as openly supportive of her as Mr. Pauling, but it's because he knows how well she responds to challenges. If the preseason is her opportunity to prove she deserves the A, she'll damn well prove it.

She straightens her shoulders. "I won't let you down."

"You haven't so far." Mr. Pauling's eyes are warm as he smiles at her.

"We're not making a fuss about it," Coach Butler says. Mary Beth's gaze cuts to him, but he doesn't notice. "It'll be on your jersey for your first game. We don't need a circus to start the season."

"Of course not." She's never asked to be singled out the way she is. All she's ever wanted was to play hockey. It's everyone else who makes a big deal out of it.

Mary Beth slides her phone into her pocket. "Once we're done here, you and I will prep on how to handle your postgame. As soon as people notice, there will be questions."

WITH NO ANNOUNCEMENT, the first time her teammates see the A on her jersey is in the locker room before their game against Seattle. She's nervous for their reactions. She learned to ignore the media out of self-preservation. She cares what the people in this room think. She's only in her second year in the NAHL, and, because of the cuts, she's still the youngest.

Last year, after they were eliminated from playoff contention, the team rallied around her. With no postseason to look forward to, they focused on helping her win the Maddow Trophy. This team supports her, and she's grown more comfortable around them, but the letter is a big step. In her experience, her teammates like her best when she's in the background, giving them assists, the spotlight trained elsewhere.

"Holy shit!" Merlin exclaims when he spots the A ironed onto her jersey. "About fucking time!"

Sophie's shocked enough to actually look surprised.

"You bossed me all over the ice last season. It's not like we didn't know it was coming."

She smiles, pleased with his acceptance. To cover it up, she says, "I wouldn't have to tell you what to do if you weren't so clueless."

"Matty, Sophie's being mean to me," he whines.

Matty is sitting in his stall, in his game day suit because he isn't playing in this game. It's normal for players to sit out preseason games. There are too many in the squad for them all to play in every one, but she finds it strange their captain isn't playing in their first home appearance of the season.

"Take it up with your alternate captains, I have today off."

Merlin turns back to Sophie. "Sophie, Sophie's being mean to me."

She laughs and throws a balled-up piece of tape at his head. "Focus, we have a game to play."

"It's *Seattle*," he huffs but he changes into his gear.

The Seattle Seafarers were added to the League in the same year as Concord in order to keep the Eastern and Western Conferences balanced. Somehow, they've struggled even more than Concord, selecting in the top three of the draft for year after year. Despite all the high draft picks, they've never managed to put together a winning team. They draft high then, a couple of years later, trade those top picks for more picks which they eventually trade.

Concord's been trapped in a similar cycle, but Sophie is determined to be the draft pick who will make the difference in Concord. And tonight, with an A on her chest and facing off against last year's first overall pick, she's going to prove it.

WITH MATTY OUT, Sophie is the first line center tonight. Her name is announced as part of the starting lineup, and she raises a hand to acknowledge the fans as the entire stadium rises to their feet for her. The crowd is a sea of red, everyone in the vibrant home jerseys. She drops her hand back down as Zinger's announced. The crowd cheers for him too but they aren't as loud as they were for her.

Next, they bring out the anthem singer. Because it's a Concord-Seattle matchup, Carolyne only sings the American anthem. Sophie hums *O, Canada* to herself as she skates to the bench for one last word from Coach Butler.

"I want you hard on the puck and even harder on the body," he says. "This is your first statement of the year. Make it a good one."

The crowd swells with noise. A glance at the Jumbotron shows the camera's zoomed in on Sophie's A.

Coach Butler taps the letter with his pointer finger, and the fans grow even louder. She knows what he's telling her. *Earn it.*

She leads her line onto the ice for the opening faceoff.

She takes her place at center ice across from Carruthers. He has dark circles under his eyes even though the season has barely begun. The puck is dropped, and she springs into action, knocking the puck to Zinger before Carruthers has a chance at it. She trails Zinger into the offensive zone so they stay onside and picks up his pass before she skates the puck around the back of the net.

Carruthers skates in after her. He stays with her as she rounds the net. She stops sharply and changes direction, and he falls on his ass. It gives her the space to make a clean pass up to J-Rod at the point.

J-Rod rifles a shot on net. It deflects off one of Seattle's defenseman and slips past the goalie.

First shift, first goal.

The crowd leaps to their feet again.

Sophie glances at Carruthers. *All night long*, she thinks as he slowly pulls himself off the ice. She blows past him to join J-Rod's celly.

MIDWAY THROUGH THE first period, she steals the puck off Carruthers's stick and goes the length of the ice for a goal of her own.

Later in the period, she crushes Carruthers into the boards and pins him there as Zinger nets the third goal of the game.

Merlin makes space for her next to him on the bench and holds his water bottle out to her. "The kid has it bad enough in Seattle without you trying to break him in the first preseason game."

"I thought a first overall pick would be tougher." She snatches the water bottle from Merlin and takes a drink. "If Seattle crumbles, they crumble. We won't play down to their level. We play *our* game, even if it means running up the score."

"Aye, aye." Merlin tosses her a lazy salute.

THEY WIN 7-2 with two goals and three assists on the night for Sophie. Matty's there in the tunnel to offer fist bumps and back slaps as they head down to the locker room. She's the last one on the ice, and Coach Butler puts a heavy hand on her shoulder as she tucks her helmet under her arm.

"It's a start, but it's only one game," he tells her.

Settling means stagnating. Another one of her dad's catchphrases, second only to *If you're not the best then you don't get to play.* She wouldn't be where she is without people to challenge her, and she's glad to have Coach Butler here, pushing her to be her best.

"My defense can use work," she agrees. She was on the ice for Carruthers's even strength goal. It was late in the third period and the game was basically over by then but there's no excuse for the turnover which led to Carruthers's opportunity.

Coach Butler ushers her down the tunnel. Matty's still there, and he slings an arm over Sophie's shoulders even though she's sweaty and gross and he's wearing a nice suit.

"Not bad out there, rookie."

"I'm not a rookie anymore."

He shrugs. "You'll always be my rookie. Nice goal you scored on the power play."

It had been but, "I followed it up by letting Carruthers score on my next shift."

"It's important for players to be well-rounded," Coach Butler says, trailing behind them.

Matty's arm tightens around her shoulders for a moment before he drops it back to his side. "Of course. My trainer introduced me to some new backchecking drills this summer. I can come in before practice tomorrow and show them to you."

They make plans, and Sophie slips into the locker room so she can shed some of her gear before the media pours in.

SHE PLAYS IN all three home games, and she stamps her impact on every shift. She battles in the corners, she threads passes through sticks and skates, and she pays special attention to her backcheck.

It doesn't stop her from having Decision Day jitters. Last season, when Coach Butler thought she was too complacent, he scratched her to teach her a lesson. He has no qualms about benching her or even scratching her if she doesn't live up to his expectations.

She wouldn't put it past him to start her in Manchester if he wanted. *I wore an A during the preseason. I led the team in points.* But was she good enough? Sophie corrals a loose puck and passes to Zinger. He has to settle it before he passes it back. After the second shaky pass she sends him, he holds onto the puck. "You're not nervous, are you?"

She scoffs, aiming for unbothered and missing by about a kilometer. Zinger raises his eyebrows as he flips her the puck. "Why are you nervous? You and Matty are the two guarantees."

"There are no guarantees in hockey," she says in her best Lenny Dernier voice. She juggles the puck a few times before she flips it back to him.

Zinger drops his voice an octave and adopts a horrific Canadian accent. "Hockey is about tough work and tough players." The way he says player sounds more like "pl'r," as if he swallowed a handful of marbles.

Her shoulders shake as she laughs. "That's not what Dernier sounds like."

"He sounds more like this—foreigners? In *my* league?" Zinger slaps a hand to his chest as if he's some offended '50s housewife.

She laughs even harder. By the time X taps her on her shoulder, she's almost lost her nerves. Of course, as soon as he says, "You're up," they return full force. His expression softens and he squeezes her shoulder.

She skates off the ice and heads up to Coach Butler's office. Their whole coaching staff is there, along with Mr. Pauling and Mr. Wilcox. She sits in the empty chair in front of Coach's desk.

"Congratulations," Mr. Wilcox says.

She breathes easier.

"A double congratulations is in order." Mr. Pauling smiles as if he's amused himself. "The A is yours."

Coach Butler slides a piece of paper across his desk to her. It lists the numbers 1 to 99, save for those retired by the League. There are only three names on the list so far; Matty, Lindy, and X. She adds her own name, next to the number 93.

"You'll have to come over for dinner," Mr. Wilcox tells her. "Kaylee and Jessi miss having you around."

Coach Butler clears his throat. "Send Nelson up."

"We'll talk later," Mr. Wilcox tells her.

She nods and troops back down to the ice. Nelson's by the bench with Garfield, and she taps his shoulder. "Your turn."

Last year, Nelson wore the second A after Thurman was traded at the deadline. Since no one starts the season with a letter she didn't take it from him, but it still feels like she did. There's always been an undercurrent of tension in their relationship. If he thinks she's taken his letter, things could get rocky again.

"What's the verdict?" Garfield asks.

"Still with you."

"And the letter?"

"Coach Butler says I've earned it."

Garfield rubs his smelly glove in her face. Nelson pats the top of her head and heads up for his own meeting. A bunch of the other guys skate over.

"Are we celebrating?" Kevlar asks.

Theo wraps her up in a bear hug and lifts her off the ice.

ONCE ALL THE meetings have happened, the remaining players have a short practice. Afterward, they all pile into the locker room. Matty stands up, stripped down to his spandex. "This is our team. I know you've fallen into the familiar during preseason; the Americans or the Canadians, the vets and the new guys—"

"Cliques," Lindy volunteers.

"We're not *girls*," Wilchinski mutters.

Everyone's gaze swings toward Sophie. There are always moments when she can't escape the feeling of being the only woman. She was acutely aware of it when her tampon fell out of her bag on the hike. She's acutely aware of it now too.

"I'm not a girl, I'm a woman," Sophie says.

Merlin sniffles and wipes away a fake tear. "They grow up so fast."

There's scattered laughter and the tension in the room breaks. Everyone turns their attention back to Matty. "We're a team now. Get to know each other."

"Do you know what would bring the team together?" Lindy asks.

"A party at Matty's?" X grabs a marker and flips their whiteboard over to the blank side. "Time to draw up a game plan." He writes *dessert, appetizers,* and *healthy shit* across the top and the locker room dissolves into its usual shouting as everyone tries to claim the category they want.

SOPHIE STOPS BY the grocery store on her way home from practice. Last year, she resorted to online grocery orders after too many people offered her advice on how to play better. The guy ringing her up recommended she get into more fights and the well-meaning father of two who cornered her by the eggs wanted to go over zone entries as if she didn't already have three coaches, a captain, and a dad of her own telling her what to do.

She suspended the online orders for the start of this season, because she actually enjoys going to the store. Wandering through the aisles with a neatly bulleted list makes her feel normal. It reminds her of trailing after her mom when she was a kid. Her mom would send her down the rice aisle to pick up a box of brown rice or a box of couscous or ask Sophie to pick out the granola bars she wanted for the week.

Every time her mom put something in the cart, Sophie would peer at it and ask what it was for. She listened as her mom explained what she intended to do with the chicken or how she was going to prepare the fish or which vegetables paired well with each meat. Sophie was never around for the actual cooking part. She was always at school or practice or stuck at the table doing homework.

Today, though, Sophie's here on a simple mission. She's doing dessert for the party, and she stands in the baking aisle, staring at the wall of boxed and packaged mixes. There are too many options. Brownies? Cookies? Cake? There are regular brownies, fudge brownies, triple chocolate brownies, and more.

"Cupcakes are the best dessert." Next to Sophie, a young girl in jeans and a Condors jersey joins her in staring at the wall. "The serving size says I'm allowed to eat two, but my mom never lets me."

Sophie obediently shuffles toward the cake side of the wall. "If a serving size is two, how many cupcakes will I need for a team of hockey players?"

"A lot. Theodore Smith is *huge*." The girl grins and pulls three boxes of Funfetti off the shelf. She drops them in Sophie's basket. Then she takes three tubs of pink frosting and adds them too. "You shouldn't let anyone forget you're a girl."

"Uh, thank you." Sophie looks at her basket, amused. "Does your mom know where you are?"

The girl huffs. "I'm getting cake mix and meeting her by the deli. My brother's getting a slice of cheese, but only *babies* get snacks at the grocery store." She grabs a box of Funfetti for herself and holds it out. "Will you sign this for me?"

Every coat, windbreaker, and purse she owns has at least two Sharpies stashed in it. This coat has a black one and a red one. She lets the girl pick the red one before she writes *Thank you for the cake advice. Sophie Fournier 93.*

"Thanks!" the girl says before she sprints off, hopefully to find her mother.

MERLIN MAKES A face at the pink frosted cupcakes when Sophie shows up to the party. She sets them down between a plate of brownies and a plate of chocolate chip-walnut cookies. "I was told not to let anyone forget I'm a woman."

"I don't think it'll happen any time soon."

Sophie shrugs and looks out at the backyard. A bunch of the guys are kicking a soccer ball around, and she grins as Theo throws a second ball into the mix to confuse everyone. To the left, there's a badminton net set up, and Peets and Spitzweg look as though they're trying to play volleyball with a rubber kickball.

"There's no way this ends well," Sophie says.

"Already being responsible?" Merlin herds her over to the coolers. There's three of them, all different colors and all with a different label. Beer in the red cooler, soda in the blue one, and "other stuff" in the green one.

"Other stuff?" Sophie laughs as she opens the lid. It turns out to be water and Gatorade. She plucks a purple Gatorade out of the ice.

"First pink, now purple? We all know you're a woman."

"I like purple Gatorade. Don't make it weird."

She twists the lid open and takes a long drink. Merlin is looking past her at the grill so she leaves him to play assistant to Matty and wanders over to where Theo and Kevlar are huddled around Kevlar's phone. Hanging out with them doesn't follow Matty's suggestion to branch out, but she'll sit with some of the new guys while she eats.

"Who're we pranking?" She has to go up on her tiptoes to see over Kevlar's shoulder. He jumps at the sound of her voice and tucks his phone into his pocket.

"Pranking? Us? Never."

She laughs and takes another drink. It's still hot and humid, her thin tank top sticking to her skin with sweat. She's waiting for the first crisp, fall day, the one which means hockey is right around the corner. "You want a cupcake?"

"You made cupcakes?"

"They're only for my friends." She pretends to think. "I guess you can't have one then."

Kevlar gasps and claps a hand to his chest as if she's mortally wounded him. "I need to fix this."

He lunges at her, and she jumps out of the way, avoiding what she thinks is an attempt to hug her. Then she has to run, because Kevlar chases her all over the yard. She loses her Gatorade somewhere between dodging a kickball and almost being tripped by the guys playing soccer. She weaves in and out of teammates until she can hide behind Lindy.

"You're a goalie," she says as she keeps Lindy between her and Kevlar. "Protect me."

"I only protect my net."

"This is why you aren't my favorite."

"I'm not protecting you either," Teddy tells her as he picks his way through the snack table. "What'd you do to him, anyway?"

"She said we weren't *friends*." Kevlar pouts, a terrifying expression on six feet of grown hockey player.

When Lindy moves, the traitor, Kevlar pounces, and wraps Sophie up in a tight hug. He rubs his face in her hair and asks, "Are we friends yet?" over and over and until she's laughing so hard she can't even answer. She's still laughing when he sets her back on her feet. She fixes her ponytail as he snatches a cupcake off the table. He peels the wrapper off and shoves the whole thing into his mouth in two bites.

"Gross," she says.

He grins at her with pink frosting smeared across his cheek.

LATER, WHEN SOPHIE has a plate with two burgers and four different kinds of vegetables on it, she realizes she lost her Gatorade. She detours away from the table, food still in hand, so she can poke through the coolers.

"Looking for this?" Merlin asks. He dangles a half-empty bottle of purple Gatorade in front of her. Did she drink that much? Did someone else drink out of it? How long was it out of her sight for? She glances at her teammates, almost everyone sitting and eating, and grabs a water out of the blue cooler.

She returns to the table she picked out, and Merlin trails after her. "I thought you were showing off your feminine side."

"Are we even allowed to talk about Sofe's feminine side?" Zinger asks as Sophie sits down.

Zinger, Kevlar, and Theo are already at the table. When Merlin sits next to her, it means the table has a lot of returning players at it, but Jordan Clifford and Spitzweg are here too so she counts it as mingling.

Merlin sets Sophie's Gatorade next to her plate. She ignores it as she untwists the cap on her water. Unfortunately, Merlin doesn't lose interest. "You're being weird."

Teddy drops down next to Clifford. "What's Sofe being weird about?"

"Nothing," Sophie answers. The back of her neck prickles and she draws her shoulders up.

"Her Gatorade," Merlin says. "She dropped it when Kevlar chased her around the backyard and even though I rescued it from being thrown out, she won't drink it."

"Let it go." An edge hardens her words, but Merlin misses it, oblivious.

He opens his mouth, but Clifford beats him to it. "She said, let it go."

Merlin isn't the only one too surprised to talk. Sophie looks over at the new kid, a winger from St. Cloud State. He catches her looking and shrugs his narrow shoulders. He's too skinny. Whatever they feed their athletes in college, it isn't enough. He'll have to bulk up if he doesn't want to be knocked around the ice all season.

"You don't drink anything if it's been out of your sight," Clifford says as if it's normal.

See, she thinks at Merlin, *I'm not weird.*

Clifford keeps talking. "It's what all the girls at school do. I think they had a meeting about it freshman year or something."

Shit.

"Isn't it to make sure you don't end up roofied?" Merlin asks. He looks at Sophie, hurt.

"Sofe?" Matty asks from the other table. His tone is gentle, concerned, and Sophie's shoulders draw up even more when she realizes the entire team is now staring at her.

Whatever worst-case scenarios they're thinking, they aren't true. But if she doesn't tell them what actually happened, they're going to spend months looking at her like this and treating her as if she's fragile. She picks at the label of her water bottle. "When I was at Chilton someone put Ex-Lax in my water bottle. I missed an entire practice shitting my intestines out. When I told my coach, he told me I was lucky it wasn't something worse."

He'd been pissed. Sophie learned early on no matter how many coaches or well-meaning parent assistants said, "Come to me if you have problems," none of them actually wanted to listen to her. If she told them something was wrong, they felt like they had to do something. She kept the harmless pranks to herself and didn't breathe a word of the teasing or bullying to anyone.

This had crossed a line. It kept her from practice and, more importantly, it left her scared. She told Coach what happened and he made the whole team bag skate while she watched, too weak to join them. Things were bad after the incident for a while. Travis was the only one who didn't hate her, but she kept her distance from him so the guys would leave him alone.

Eventually, she recovered and began putting up big points again and everything was fine.

"Holy shit," Theo says.

Sophie glances at Merlin. He's gone pale around his mouth. "There are some things I'm weird about," she says gently. Her food, her drinks, people touching her gear. "I have reasons for it."

She can almost see him running through all the strange things she does; how she won't drink from a water bottle she hasn't seen someone else drink from, how she won't sleep on the plane no matter how tired she is, or how she checks the insides of her skates before she puts them on.

Sophie wants to hunch her shoulders against the stares of her teammates. Instead, she takes a bite of her first burger. "Good job with the food," she tells Matty.

"He's King of the Grill," X says, automatic. There's none of the usual chirping in his tone.

Chapter Five

THEY OPEN THEIR season in Cleveland on a Tuesday. *The National Sports Network* flies in to cover the season's first Tuesday Throwdown. As a kid, Sophie loved Tuesday Throwdown. *TNSN* would always pick a couple of Montreal-Quebec games, and she watched them on the couch with her billet family. At Chilton, she and Travis would make bags of popcorn before the Philly-Boston match-ups.

There's a saying in hockey: if you want to see two teams brawl, you go to a Boston-Philadelphia game but if you want to see the *fans* brawl, you go to a Montreal-Quebec game.

Sophie wonders who will throw down at tonight's game. The Concord-Cleveland rivalry began last season when Michael Hayes was traded to the Presidents. Concord picked Sophie to build their team around and packed Hayes off to Ohio. Their uneasy truce was snapped, and they were free to play each other as hard and nasty as they wanted. Their teams followed suit. Then, in the final game of the season, Concord won, officially eliminating Cleveland from the playoffs.

"It's a game," Sophie says when she's asked about it after morning skate. "We play eighty-three of them a season." She doesn't put much effort into her answer, because she knows no one will believe this game is like all the others she plays.

"It's not." Carol Rogers has been in the hockey business far longer than Sophie. She smiles pleasantly, but she narrows her eyes slightly, a warning to quit trying to bullshit her. "This is Cleveland."

"It's the first game of the season, and I'm excited for it, but we've prepared the same way we prepare for all our games. I don't know if you've heard, but routine is important to hockey players."

No one laughs at her joke. If anything, Rogers grows more serious. "Your personal rivalry with Michael Hayes is entering into its sixth year. What impact will it have on tonight's game?"

"Teams are made up of more than one person. This game is the Condors against the Presidents."

"You're starting the season with McArthur and Aronowitz on your wings," Ed Rickers says. "Are you hoping to pick up where you left off last season?"

"Yes. We're looking to start where we ended last season and improve from there."

SHE CAN TELL the media this game is like any other but, even as stubborn as she is, she can't convince herself of the same thing. She has an A on the front of her jersey and a target on her back.

Cleveland didn't like her last season, but it was the same mild distaste every team had. They didn't truly begin to hate her until Hayes joined their ranks. He and Sophie were high school rivals turned teammates after Concord drafted him second and her two hundred and twenty-fourth. When Concord traded him, choosing Sophie to lead their franchise, he took all his hate for her and found a fertile breeding ground in Cleveland.

The fans boo loudly enough for Sophie to feel it vibrate against her skin as she takes the ice for warm-ups. She skates her two half-laps and ignores the people banging against the glass, wanting her attention. There are fans here in Condors shirts, but she knows from experience it isn't her condor on their shirt, proud and majestic, its wings spread wide. The Cleveland Condor hunches over a body with long brown hair, its beak stained red. And on the back it will say *LAST* with the number 224 instead of 93.

This isn't the first hostile rink she's played in, and she allows herself a brief glance at a pair of fans who wave their middle fingers at her. Her lips peel back in a slow smile. No, this isn't the first crowd to hate her, and it's cute they think they'll break her. If she crumpled under pressure, she never would've made it to the NAHL.

She grabs a puck so she can do her stickhandling. A glance up shows Spitzweg hovering next to her. His eyes are wide as he looks around the stadium. "They said Cleveland would be rough but..." He shakes his head as if he didn't understand how bad it would be.

"They'll try and get you off your game. Don't let them." The A presses against her chest, letting her know it's there. "They'll talk shit about your mom and your sister and me and your play. They'll run through everything they have until something sticks. Don't let it stick."

"I don't have a sister." Spitzweg flashes her a small smile before he squares his shoulders. "I won't let you down."

"Play your game. Be responsible in our zone and make good passes on the breakout the way you've done all preseason." She claps him on the shoulder. "The louder they boo, the better you're playing."

It's the same thing her dad told her growing up. There wasn't a single rink she played in where she wasn't booed. She's learned to hear it as a sign she's playing well. And, as the "Sophie sucks" chants begin, she can't help a tiny spark of satisfaction. They'd rather heckle her than cheer for their own team.

She looks across the ice at where Hayes is warming up. As if he can feel her gaze, he looks up. She smiles, nothing nice about it. *They'd rather use their energy on me than you. Always falling short, even in your home stadium.*

He adjusts his grip on his stick as if he wants to skate over and cross-check her with it.

She turns and joins her teammates in a three-on-two drill.

MATTY'S LINE STARTS the game, and she can't help her jealousy as he lines up against Farage. Her captain has earned every minute of playing time he receives, but the harsh truth is she won't be the 1C or have the privilege of taking the opening faceoff as long as she and Matty are on the same team.

She presses her fist against the logo on the front of her jersey. Team is what matters. She cheers with the rest of the bench as Matty wins the first faceoff of the season. A small part of her still wishes she was the one out there.

The puck clunks against Garfield's stick before Garfield's rammed into the boards, a sharp crack which brings the crowd to life. Sophie leans forward to get a good look at the action. Garfield shakes himself and jumps into the battle for the puck.

Hockey is back.

Garfield wins the puck to Matty who passes to X before dropping down toward Strindberg. It forces the defense to shift their coverage. X passes to Kuzy who sends the puck to Matty. He wrists a shot on Strindberg, but the Cleveland goalie knocks the puck away.

Farage gathers the rebound and flicks the puck out of his zone.

Garfield races Caldwell for the puck. He reaches it first and takes the puck behind Lindy's net so the rest of his line can change. Sophie switches for Matty. Garfield passes to her so he and Merlin can trade places.

She carries the puck up the ice as Cleveland makes changes of their own. The defensemen skate backward, and she tracks where they are and what lanes they leave open as a new line of forwards take the ice. Hayes skates out to challenge her.

You want him on the ice with me? She spares a moment to scoff at Cleveland's coach. She drives toward the net and stops, sharply enough for Hayes to lose an edge and fall on his ass. She passes to Merlin and skates around the back of the net. With Hayes out of the play, there's more room, and Merlin drops down by the hash marks, forcing the defense to come up and meet him.

Sophie taps her stick once on the ice. Merlin passes back to her and she shoots. Strindberg snaps his glove up, but he's too slow, and she has the first goal of the season.

She throws her hands up in the air. First shift of her sophomore season and she *scored*. The crowd boos, but her teammates drown them out as they converge on her.

WHEN SHE AND Hayes were Condors last year, they had to pretend to like each other. Sophie sucked it up and did it, playing Ping-Pong against him and allowing her hair to be curled before she went on camera to compliment his grit on the penalty kill. But now what's best for the team is getting under Hayes's skin.

It comes more naturally to her, a skill she acquired freshman year and honed over the next four. Hayes is *easy*. He's part of the class of hockey player who can't stand a girl being better than them so all she has to do to get in his head is play good hockey.

She breaks through the neutral zone, and dances around his coverage before she passes to Witzer. His stick is a second too slow to intercept her pass. "Maybe next time," she tells him sweetly.

On the next play, she meets him in open ice and hip checks him, sending him to the ground. "A real hockey player would stay on their skates," she says. Then, as if she planned it, Olsson tries to bury her in return. Two hundred pounds of Swedish defenseman knocks into her, but she weathers the hit. She flashes Hayes a smile. "See?"

IT TAKES TWO periods, but Sophie goads Hayes into a penalty. She waves at him as he's escorted to the box. He spits his mouth guard into his glove so she can clearly hear him when he calls her "a fucking bitch!"

She grins as she skates to her bench. "So, who's scoring on the power play?"

Clifford and Spitzweg stare at Sophie as if they've never seen her before. The guys who were on the team last year are used to the way she gets against Cleveland. Kevlar knocks his shoulder into Garfield's. "I bet it's a d-man."

"Ha! Right winger for sure."

"I bet on Sophie," Merlin says.

Sophie doesn't try to hide her smile.

IT'S MATTY WHO scores, a gorgeous goal, but Sophie sets him up for it so she takes half-credit.

"Half?" Matty asks, amused as they skate to the bench.

"It was practically an empty net. It's okay, you get 45 percent of the credit. Kevlar gets 5 percent."

"Hey! My pass was worth more than 5 percent."

Sophie shrugs. "Seven then?"

She laughs as he rubs his smelly glove in her face.

SOPHIE ENDS THE game with two points, and it's a struggle to sit in her stall for the media. She's buzzing from the win and a whole season of hockey ahead of her and beating Hayes. She taps her foot and fidgets with her ball cap.

When the media pours in, she forces herself still. Rickers is wearing a tie patterned with the Condors logo. Marty Owen's rumpled suit of choice for the night is navy blue. It's too big in the shoulders and too tight across the waist. She wants to ask him if he's heard of a tailor. Or a dry cleaner.

"First goal in your first game," Rickers says. "It's a better start than last year."

Last year, she didn't score her first goal until her fifteenth game of the season. It became a *thing*, taking over all the coverage. There were actually people suggesting her lack of goals was proof women shouldn't have been allowed in the League. Never mind she was leading all rookies in points with only assists. Never mind she broke Kyle Sorkin's twenty-nine-year-old record by tallying at least one point in her first thirteen games. Her entire life, coaches and her dad have preached selflessness. Play for the team on the front of the jersey rather than the name on the back. Pass first. She's molded herself into the ideal hockey player and she's still criticized.

It's why she's learned to tune out all but the important voices. Is her coach happy with her play? Is her team? Analysts and broadcasters and the media can say whatever they want. She knows better than to take any of it to heart.

"It's nice to get the first one out of the way early," she says neutrally.

Marty Owen puffs up to claim her attention. "You had thirty-three goals in your rookie season. Do you think you'll score more this one?"

"I expect I'll score around the same number. I'm more of a playmaker than a goal scorer. If I have a good opportunity, I'll shoot, but it's not where my strength lies."

"You made a beautiful play to get Mathers the puck on the power play," Danielle Rossetti from *The Burlington Times* says.

Sophie allows them to see a small smile. "Thank you."

She finishes up her media and, like usual, she's the last person on the bus. Unlike Chilton where her teammates would complain when she held up the bus or even last year when her teammates would stare, not saying anything, no one seems to notice. The few guys who look over at her are more relieved than anything else. As long as she wears a Condors jersey, she'll take the bulk of the media, and it means the rest of them are safe.

She sinks into her usual seat next to Teddy. He came over in the Hayes trade last season, and she likes to think he's happier in Concord than he was in Cleveland. They've never talked much about the trade since it's widely accepted it's her fault he's here. It's why he spent the last half of the season apart from his girlfriend and why he's had to uproot his life and move *again.*

She tries not to think about how soon he'll have to leave. He's good enough to be a starting goaltender but Lindy is only twenty-nine; there's a lot of hockey left in him. Teddy will have to find a new team to play for if he wants to be the starter. It's different for Sophie. She'll be the 2C as long as Matty is on their team, but she's still able to play. Her name might not be announced at the start of the game, and she isn't the one taking the opening faceoff, but she doesn't have to sit on the bench with a ball cap pulled low over her eyes and watch the team play without her.

She leans into Teddy's side.

"You do know we won, right?" Despite the teasing, Teddy lifts his arm so he can tuck her against him. "We showed Cleveland who's boss."

"Fucking right we did!" Theo shouts.

It sparks a robust "Cleveland sucks" chant which lasts all the way to the airport.

BY THE TIME they land in Manchester, the adrenaline from the game has worn off. Sophie rolls down the windows and blasts her music, the wind and the noise helping to keep her awake on the drive home. She trudges up the one flight of stairs to her apartment, and each step feels like a monumental effort. Last year, she told the guys she was buying a first-floor apartment so she wouldn't have to put up with stairs after a grueling practice or a late night.

When she toured apartments, though, she didn't like the thought of people walking by and looking in her windows. She compromised with a second-floor apartment but tonight she regrets it. She fumbles with her keys, at first trying to unlock her door with her car key.

When she finally pushes the door open, her apartment is dark, long shadows on the walls. There's no one waiting for her to come home the way Marissa waits for Merlin or Alyssa waits for Teddy. And it's not like Theo and Kevlar where they head home together.

She flips the lights on and then dims them. It's her and her empty rooms. She drops her bag by the door, something to deal with tomorrow, and goes to her room to change. Once she's in her pajamas, she grabs an ice pack out of the freezer and stretches out across her couch. As much as she wants to fall asleep, there's one thing she has to do first.

She gasps as she lays the ice against the worst of her bruises. Her toes curl as if she can run away from the cold seeping into her skin. She pulls her phone out, both to set a timer and so she can find a distraction. She browses NAHL.com and, after seeing Dima had three points in their 7-5 win over DC, she texts him.

Good start, she says. She ignores how the box score implies the game was a shit show, more penalty minutes than shots on goal.

DIMA: *More points than you*
SOPHIE: *Don't get used to it*

He sends her a picture of him sticking his tongue out at her. She laughs and then hisses out a slow breath as she jostles her bruise. She's not sure who this one is from, probably Olsson—he seemed to have it out for her all night. In the moment, none of his hits felt this bad. She stayed on her skates, she jumped back into the play, but it was the adrenaline more than anything which kept her going. Tomorrow, she'll wake up sore all over.

Her phone pings with a message from Dima. *Late. Why not sleep?*

She moves her ice pack and lifts her shirt up to take a picture of her bruise.

DIMA: *Is this sexting? Captain warned me about this.*

She laughs again, hard enough to hurt. Next time, she'll have to text someone else to keep her awake. Someone less funny. Dima sends her a return picture. It's a close-up of his mouth and his split lip.

High stick (((((.

SOPHIE: *You don't look any uglier. It's fine.*

He sends her a bunch of scowly emojis and she grins as she tangles her feet in her throw blanket. For some reason, icing always makes her toes cold. She's reluctant to say goodnight to Dima when her timer goes off, but her home opener is in two days. She needs to be well-rested for it.

SHE WAKES UP to a text from Elsa.

Pretty goal!!!!

Her chest twists, a painful squeeze when she sees Elsa's name on her phone. She knows it's unfair to feel abandoned. Being drafted to a team isn't a commitment, and she can't begrudge Elsa for wanting to play hockey closer to her family. Besides, Sophie had the opportunity to play in the SHL, and she chose the NAHL. It's as much Sophie's fault as Elsa's they're not playing together.

It's too early to deal with complicated feelings so she doesn't answer right away. She tucks her phone into her pocket and heads to the kitchen for breakfast. As she goes, she pulls a Condors sweatshirt over her head and flips the hood up.

She browses Gothenburg's schedule as she eats. Their regular season hasn't begun. She taps her fork on the table as she chews her eggs. One bite. A second. She groans and pulls her phone out so she can text back.

You'll score in your first game too.

She keeps her phone on the table but it doesn't light up as she finishes her breakfast. She continues to check it as she dresses for practice and reviews the game tape before it's time to drive to the rink.

She's walking into the locker room when Elsa answers with a video of her at practice. It's fifteen shaky seconds of Elsa doing some filthy stick work before she roofs the puck.

Sophie's mouth goes dry. She rallies enough to type out, *it's more impressive when there's a goalie in the net.*

ELSA: *Guess I'll have to try harder.*

"Hey!" Merlin snatches her phone out her hands. "No phones in the locker room."

"Like you don't play Candy Crush every day." She steals her phone back. If her team knows Elsa's sending her videos, they'll ask if Elsa's coming next year. Or, worse, they'll see Elsa sending her hockey videos, and it will reignite the hockey-porn folder discussion. Not wanting to deal with either, she drops her phone into her bag.

"I wouldn't have to entertain myself if you didn't take forever in the shower."

Sophie slowly turns to Merlin. "I take too long in the shower?" she repeats.

Merlin inches away from her and looks to Theo for help. The big d-man shakes his head shakes his head. "Your grave, buddy."

"I'm pretty sure you're waiting for me because I have a shit-ton of media to do every day, but if you want to help, I could probably manage to get out of here faster."

"No way. You have a better face for cameras. I mean—"

"You should've kept your mouth shut," Theo says.

Sophie lets it go, but later, when she's talking to Mary Beth, she makes sure to look over at Merlin. He ducks behind Lindy, and Sophie's smile sharpens.

"Do I want to know?" Mary Beth asks.

"Probably not. How early should I be here tomorrow?"

"Don't mess with your pregame routine but as early as you can. The first home game is always a big one."

Sophie's smile softens into something gentler.

Chapter Six

THEY OPEN AT home against Montreal. Despite facing them five times last season, Sophie still feels a buzz of excitement as the game approaches. It will always be surreal to play against the Mammoths. Her dad's side of the family lives in Montreal so she grew up watching the Mammoths play, live if they were in-season or reruns of their historic Cup season if they weren't.

Her first hockey jersey had Bobby Brindle's name on the back. He's a commentator now instead of a player, but it's still weird to play against his team. Watching him lift the Cup was her inspiration to play in the NAHL. Part of her wishes she could play against him to prove herself against a childhood hero.

She'll have to settle for beating his team. They're still a challenge even with Brindle retired. Gabriel Ducasse, Captain Canada, plays for them, and he works as a measuring stick. They briefly crossed paths at the Stuttgart Winter Games. It was her first invitation to the big stage, and he was a veteran. He congratulated her on being the top scorer on the women's side, a memory she'll carry with her for the rest of her life.

She also remembers the way he dumped her on her ass in her first NAHL game against him. She'll be better this game.

She shows up to the Northeastern Mountain Sports Arena two hours earlier than usual, well-rested from her nap. She heads into the lobby to meet with the fans who are already here. She isn't the only one. Matty, X, and Garfield are here in their game day suits. They wave to the fans who jump and cheer in excitement.

Sophie goes for the far end of the crowd and smiles at a teenager in a Condors jersey and a Red Sox hat.

"If you win tonight, I can sleep in and skip first period tomorrow."

"But no pressure." Sophie smiles at him. "What do you have first period?"

"Chemistry. It sucks."

"I wasn't very good at chemistry." She signs the outstretched sleeve of his jersey. "One of my teammates was so he helped me study on long bus rides."

A girl with a high ponytail pushes her way to the font of the crowd. "I get popcorn for every goal you score."

There's something unfair about parents who offer their kids rewards based on Sophie's play.

"Well, *I* get to go to Disney if you win the Maple Cup," another girl volunteers.

"We'll do our best," Sophie says and moves down the line.

"DISNEY," SOPHIE REPEATS as she straps her pads on.

"Do you remember who said it?" Zinger asks. "Maybe if we win, they'll take you with them."

She facewashes him but without her gloves on it isn't nearly as effective. Last year, she came into the League as the last pick of the draft, and she had to prove she was better than everyone thought she was. Now, returning for her second season as the reigning Maddow Trophy winner, she has to prove she's better than herself. The

Maple Cup is too lofty a goal to be thinking about now. First, they need to actually make the playoffs. They begin with tonight's game. The secret to a winning season is taking it one game at a time.

"Maybe the parents won't even go." Zinger waits for her to pull her jersey over her head so he can tap the A. "You're responsible and shit now."

Merlin raps his knuckles furiously on the wooden stalls and glares at Zinger.

"The A means I'm responsible for wrangling you lot, not some stranger's kids."

Zinger strokes his chin as if he has a beard and not a few scattered hairs. "So you'll take *me* to Disney if we win the Cup this year?"

Merlin groans and looks as if he's considering knocking Zinger's head against the stall so Sophie laughs and smoothly changes the subject.

TONIGHT'S CROWD IS as loud as Cleveland's but this one cheers *for* her. The stands are filled with girls wearing her jersey and there are signs reading "If she can do it, I can do it" with pictures of kids in their hockey gear.

Sophie takes a minute to look around, and she waves at as many fans as she can. She's spent most of her hockey career proving people wrong but tonight, as the stadium swells with noise for her team and as people wave their arms to capture her attention, she has the opportunity to prove them *right*.

When she's playing at the top of her game, it feels as if she's playing chess while everyone else is playing checkers. They skip over pieces as they try to move from one end to the other, but she sees the whole board and all the options laid out before her. If she brings the puck here then the defense will move there, and her team will open up there and—

She dekes around a defender and flicks the puck over to Theo. He rifles it on the net. Merlin's there, his stick on the ice, and the puck hits the shaft of his stick and changes direction enough to get by the goalie.

Merlin throws his hands up in the air. Sophie crashes into him and wraps him up in a hug. "Way to be in the right place."

Theo knocks the two of them into the boards with the force of his hug. "He's a small target. I'm glad I could make it work."

"Fuck you! I'm not small!"

They bicker on the way to the bench, moving on from size to whether it takes more skill to aim the puck at the deflector or to be the deflector. Sophie jumps in to say, "I think I was the real MVP of the play," and laughs as they both puff up and tell her a secondary assist is basically a pity point.

DUCASSE KNOCKS SOPHIE into the glass hard enough to stun her. While she regains her bearings, he steals the puck. She chases him down the length of the ice and catches up to him in time to poke the puck away before he can do anything dangerous with it.

The puck trickles to the corner and Witzer battles Cassady for it. They exchange elbows and hip checks as they each try to gain the advantage. Sophie lurks at the edge of their battle, waiting to see which way the puck will go.

"We're going to wipe the ice with you," Ducasse says.

Witzer works the puck loose, and Merlin scoops it up.

"Not with that work ethic," Sophie tells him.

He cross-checks her as they skate after Merlin.

SOPHIE PLANTS HERSELF in front of LaJoie and holds her ground even as he tries to swat her away with his paddle. She shifts her weight to her left skate so he can't see around her and then shifts to the right when the play moves in the other direction. He whacks at her again and she grins. The more attention he pays to her, the less he pays to what's happening around him.

When McClure skates out to challenge Merlin for the puck, Ducasse drops down to take his defensive coverage. He knocks into Sophie, but she holds her position against him too. He loads up for his next shot, shoving her with both hands on his stick. She shoves him back.

"Yeah?" he demands. He glances at her gloves as if he's willing to drop his if she'll drop hers.

The unspoken rules are very clear about her gloves staying on so she shoves him again. He pushes his glove into her face, not a punch so much as a tap, but the officials swoop in, assigning them matching minors for roughing.

After their stint in the box, Ducasse seems as if he's stuck to her. He checks her into the boards and slashes her ankles when she's on the breakaway. At one point, after LaJoie's covered the puck, Ducasse tips her helmet off her head.

It clatters harmlessly to the ice, and Sophie steps up, ready to cross-check him and take another penalty. Merlin's there in a moment, and pulls Sophie back as Theo slots into her place.

"What?" Theo challenges as Ducasse backs down. "Too afraid to fight someone who's allowed to fight back?"

"I could've taken him," Sophie mutters.

"Uh huh." Merlin ushers her back to the bench as Theo and Ducasse shout at each other until the officials grow bored and separate them.

"Are you saying I can't?" Sophie twists back towards the argument. It isn't too late to stand up for herself. She appreciates Theo's willingness to step in and help her, but she can't come across as timid or unable to defend herself or she'll be run all game by every player on the other team.

"Calm yourself." Merlin opens the bench door for her. "No one's questioning your ability, but you're not the guy, uh, teammate, we tap for a fight."

"It wasn't going to escalate to a fight. This isn't my first hockey game."

"Ugh. Cap, you talk some sense into her."

"*Talk some sense into me?*" Sophie demands.

"Aw, fuck," X says.

Sophie plants herself as far away from Matty as she can and bites down on her mouth guard.

SHE DOESN'T DROP her gloves, but she and Ducasse come together after every whistle to exchange hissed insults in French and unfriendly cross-checks. It isn't Sophie's preferred playing style, but being a woman doesn't mean she shies away from the physical side of the game.

Apparently, it's something she has to prove to her team and all the others.

THEY WIN 4-3, and Sophie meets her family in the guest room after her media responsibilities are done. Teddy and Colby are talking about goaltending which makes it easy for Sophie to sneak up on her brother. She wraps her arms around him from behind and lifts him off the ground in a hug.

"Why are you like this?" he asks, but as soon she puts him down, he turns to give her a proper hug.

As a goalie, he was never bulky, but he's even smaller now, because he doesn't play competitively anymore. His hair is still stupid, too much gel and not enough styling. She runs her hand through it to mess it up and wipes her palm on Colby's pants.

"Thanks," he says.

"You played well, sweetie." Sophie's mom kisses her cheek, and Teddy slips away to give her some time alone with her family.

They head out too, Sophie leading them down the hallway to the parking lot. "Are you staying at my place tonight? We're going out, but I'll be quiet when I come home, and I can make you breakfast before you hit the road again."

She isn't about to tell her parents her apartment is lonely with only her in it. It will only lead to her mom worrying and her dad giving her more lectures on how she can't rely on anyone but herself.

"We have a hotel," her dad says.

Of course. Her mom must pick up on some of Sophie's disappointment, because she asks, with forced cheerfulness, "Pierre, didn't your mother call?"

"Your *mémé* asks you not to provoke Ducasse into a fight, because he's her favorite player. You're family so she'll take your side, but she'd rather not have to."

If Sophie didn't know how Montreal lives and dies by their team, she'd be hurt. As it is, she wouldn't expect her *mémé* to say anything different. "I wasn't going to fight Ducasse. We had a few disagreements but it was hockey."

"Anything I should know about?"

"For Heaven's sake, Ellen, she's a hockey player not a kid anymore."

Sophie's glad the parking lot is empty so there isn't anyone to hear her dad's outburst. Of course, her mom hears it, and she wraps an arm around Sophie's shoulders as if to say Sophie will always be her kid, no matter how old she is or how many hockey games she's played.

It's a familiar argument, and as much as she wants to linger in her mom's hug, she forces herself to step away. "Which hotel are you staying at? We can still meet up for breakfast in the morning. You can see my apartment."

HER APARTMENT SEEMS especially empty when she gets home from the game. She flips on all the lights and pulls up some song Zinger was trying to make her listen to the other day. The music fills the room as she heads down the hall to change out of her suit and pick what she's wearing to the bar.

She hangs her suit up and pulls on her comfy jeans and a plain black T-shirt. Her hair is still damp from her shower so she braids it. All it takes is ten minutes and she's ready to go.

The team is already there when she shows up. The table has eight bowls of popcorn, which seems like a lot until she looks around and sees all the empty tables near them. Apparently, her team is full of popcorn thieves. She'll make sure they leave a big tip.

"Sofe!" Merlin raises his beer in greeting and almost spills it on Zinger.

The rest of the guys turn to wave or shout hellos of their own.

"I see you dressed up for us," Merlin says.

"Only the best for you."

Theo pushes Spitz and Clifford out of the booth so Sophie can slide in. Deep in the booth, with teammates on either side of her, there's no pressure for her to dance. She slides Teddy's bowl of popcorn closer to her and takes a handful. "There's a sad girl somewhere in Concord tonight, because I didn't score a goal."

Teddy rolls his eyes. "You're not a sad girl, because we won tonight." He pulls the bowl closer to him, as stingy with popcorn as he is with bread rolls.

"She's not a girl, she's a *woman*," Merlin says. He looks to Sophie as if he wants her to tell him she's proud of him.

She offers him a smile and Teddy's popcorn.

She's glad they won tonight, but she can't help but wish her parents were staying at the apartment. Or her parents could stay at the hotel and Colby could crash with her. She spent the summer making a big deal about being independent and having an apartment, but she never intended to be *alone*.

She leans into Theo, who's big and solid and lifts his arm so he can tuck her more comfortably against his side. He offers her a shot and when she shakes her head, he hands it to Spitz instead.

"You good?" he asks, quiet, so no one else overhears.

"Yeah. Thanks for stepping in with Ducasse."

"I didn't do it because I thought you couldn't handle things yourself. I know you can. But as long as I'm on the ice, you don't need to."

"Thanks," Sophie says again and the word seems insufficient for everything she wants to say.

Then Kevlar comes over with two pitchers of beer, and the table erupts into cheers. He also has a bottle of water, and he passes it down to her. The cap is screwed on tight, the seal unbroken, and tears sting the corners of her eyes. She raises the bottle in thanks, because she doesn't trust her voice.

This is a good team, she thinks as she opens her water.

THEY FLY TO Toronto and record their first loss against the Griffons. Toronto was in the Maple Cup Finals last year, and most of their players returned, making them one of the favorites to win it all, but it doesn't make Sophie feel better about losing.

She feels even worse when she checks her phone on the plane and sees Gothenburg won their home opener with a hat trick for Elsa. She watches the highlights before opening her chat with Elsa. She considers a few responses: *We could've used those goals tonight* and *I wish you were on my wing* before she goes with *You could've had four if Thaulow was a better center.*

It's petty but Sophie feels better after sending it. Well, she feels better until guilt hits her, sharp and twisting. It makes her add more. *The three you did have were pretty.* Then, *Well, the first two. The third was a garbage goal, but it gave you a hat trick so it wasn't all bad.* She winces at the last message and adds, *I didn't mean garbage. Inelegant. The other two were breathtaking.*

Sophie groans as she scrolls through her last few responses. She locks her phone and hands it to Teddy. "Don't let me have this back until we land."

HE RAISES HIS eyebrows but when she doesn't elaborate, he takes her phone and tucks it into his bag. Then he points to his headphone splitter. "I'm watching *Hocus Pocus*."

"It's way too early for Halloween movies," she says. She still digs her headphones out of her bag. Her fingers brush her iPad, and she takes it out too. Coach Vorgen has already sent her her shifts from the game. This the perfect time to review where she fell short and how to be better for their next game.

"Maybe next flight," she tells Teddy. She turns her iPad on and plugs her headphones in.

He sighs but doesn't pressure her.

SOPHIE WAKES UP to a single response from Elsa.

Four if you were my center?

"Fuck," Sophie says. She drags a hand down her face. It isn't humble to say yes, but her fingers hover over the keys anyway. She wants to tell Elsa to book the next flight and come to Concord. Sophie will be the best center she's ever played with.

She spends so much of her life pushing down what she thinks. She gives the media bland soundbites, and she moderates what she says to her teammates as well. She walks a thin line between confident and arrogant. But with Elsa, she can say, *Yes*.

Her phone pings as she scrambles some eggs and broccoli.

ELSA: *I'm holding you to it.*

It sounds like a promise. *This* is the danger of talking to Elsa. It gets her hopes up, and Sophie can't do this. Not again.

SOPHIE: *Concord isn't getting any closer to Sweden.*

She puts her phone on silent and eats her breakfast.

ELSA NEVER ANSWERS.

Sophie tells herself it's what she wants.

AFTER THEIR FIRST road trip, she comes home to a package. It's large and flat and...from *Elsa*? She opens it and pulls out Styrofoam and bubble wrap until her fingers wrap around a framed painting. She slides the picture out of the packaging. The canvas is twice as long as it is tall. It looks as if someone took a blank canvas and splattered paint on it. Did Elsa paint this and send it to her? Sophie snaps a picture with her phone and sends it along with a direct, *What is this?*

ELSA: *A promise.*

Sophie drops down onto her couch. She drags a hand down her face and looks over her shoulder at the closed door to Elsa's room.

Chapter Seven

MILWAUKEE COMES TO town, bringing with them Travis Mollett, one of her former Chilton teammates. Sophie hangs around after morning skate to see Sarah Keller, their head trainer. Her shoulder's been bothering her since a hit she took late in their loss against Atlanta. Keller stretches Sophie's shoulder past comfort, poking and prodding it until it loosens up. Then she tells her what Sophie expected to hear. "Ice and take it easy in the weight room."

After she finishes with Keller, Sophie swings by the ice to see if Milwaukee's done with their practice yet. She troops up the tunnel and leans against the wall as she watches the Engineers skate around the rink.

One of Milwaukee's coaches steps in front of her, blocking her view. He's the younger of the two assistant coaches which means he must be Coach Neuberger. He scowls at her as if he thinks she's here to steal hockey secrets. "What're you doing back here?"

"Waiting for Travis."

Neuberger rolls his eyes. "Does the kid have a girl in *every* city?"

Oh, Neuberger wasn't glaring at her because he thought she was here to spy on a morning skate. He thinks she's a *groupie*. She fixes him with a dead stare and points her finger at the Condors logo on her sweatshirt.

Neuberger's face flushes a deep red. "I—uh, very sorry. When you're not in your pads..."

Sophie tucks her hands into the pouch of her sweatshirt and rocks back on her heels. She refuses to give him an out, watching instead as he grows more and more uncomfortable. Outside of Concord, Sophie still isn't recognized much. It's true without her pads and her jersey, she looks like an ordinary person and not the first woman to be drafted into the League. It doesn't mean she's okay with being mistaken for one of Travis's hookups.

Neuberger is still trying to dig himself out of his hole when the Engineers file off the ice. Forbes is the first one to spot her. Sophie hadn't made a good impression on him last year, and his eyes narrow after he wipes his sweaty face on the sleeve of his practice jersey. "You."

The rest of the team crowds around, surrounding her. She feels backed into a corner and maybe it's what makes her smile, a little mean. "Yep, me. It's almost like this is my home rink."

Forbes shakes his head, but Sophie sees a tiny smile tug at his lips. "Mullet, your friend is here."

"Friend?" Travis pushes through his teammates. He has his helmet tucked under his arm, and his hair is sweaty and plastered to his forehead. He has patchy stubble growing on his chin, and he lights up as soon as he sees her. He takes a step forward and opens his arms as if he's going to hug her.

Sophie jumps back. "No way. I just showered. You're not getting your slime all over me."

"Aw, come on." Travis pouts as he wiggles his fingers at her. "Hockey players don't smell *that* bad."

"Uh-uh. Try it on someone who doesn't spend most of her time in locker rooms."

"Isn't hockey what gets you going?" Thelin, a big hulking defenseman, asks with a cruel twist to his mouth. A couple of his teammates laugh.

Sophie meets his gaze evenly. She won't let him intimidate her in her own damn rink.

"Hey," Travis snaps.

"You can't fight the world." It's the same thing she used to tell him when people tried to start shit in high school. "Hurry up and shower, I'm hungry."

"Eat a protein bar," he says before he heads down to the locker room.

She leans against the wall and stares down every Milwaukee player brave enough to meet her gaze. Most of them shuffle by. A couple, like Thelin, scowl at her, a promise of pain to come in the game. But number 9 stops and grins at her.

"Long time no see, rookie," Mikhail Figuli says.

Mikhail Figuli is an NAHL legend. He's played in this League longer than Sophie's franchise has existed. He's played longer than she's been *alive*. She still has a poster of him hanging up in her room back in Thunder Bay. When he played for Edmonton, he and his center, Jonathan Stucki, traded the Maddow Trophy back and forth for ten years. One day, Sophie wants to play with a winger like Figuli.

Of course, their decade of dominance ended when Stucki suffered a career-ending injury, forcing him into early retirement. Figuli requested a trade, because he couldn't keep playing in Edmonton where the ghost of his center would haunt him.

"I'm not a rookie anymore."

Figuli waves a dismissive hand. "Once you're my age, everyone's a rookie."

"You're pulling the old card?"

"Maybe I want you to go easy on me tonight." Figuli winks at her, and Sophie has to duck her head to hide her blush.

"You don't need me going easy. You've had a good start to your season."

With the corridor empty, she walks with him down to the visitors' locker room. "We always have a good start. It's the end we struggle with." Figuli sounds every one of his forty-one years.

It's a reminder he's never lifted the Maple Cup or medaled in the Winter Games. He's one of the best individual players of all time, but he's never had the supporting cast to help him win at the highest levels. It could happen to her too. There are no guarantees in hockey. She could play for twenty years and never lift the Maple Cup.

They pause outside the room. "My team, earlier, they shouldn't have—"

Sophie cuts him off, because she doesn't need Figuli fighting her battles for her. "Tell them to say it to me on the ice and we'll see how tough they are."

Figuli laughs which means he doesn't realize she's being serious. "You're a good kid. But before you go getting any ideas, the Maddow Trophy is mine this year."

A four-point night in the last game of her rookie season gave her the edge to beat Figuli out for the trophy. She flashes him a smile. "If you can keep up with me, sure, but remember, I'm not going easy on you."

"You should respect your elders."

Travis comes out of the locker room, his hair still damp, and he pauses when he sees Sophie and Figuli laughing together.

"You never told me your captain is funny," she tells Travis.

"You only tell her the bad things?" Figuli tsks.

"What?" Travis asks.

Sophie takes pity on him. "Come on, let's feed you. I can give you the tour of my apartment."

Travis smiles at her, a grin she knows better than to trust. "I've seen your apartment already. Your TV is pretty small."

Sophie shoves his shoulder. "I can't believe you watch CondorsTV."

"How else would I keep up with my favorite former captain?" He slings an arm around her shoulders. "Your bedroom is fucking sad. Forget about lunch, we should go shopping for curtains."

"Quit talking about my bedroom. Neuberger thought I was a groupie. Do you seriously have a hookup in every city?"

"What? No!"

His face is way too red to be telling the truth. Sophie chirps him the whole way out to her car.

TEDDY STAYED WITH Sophie for Fan Fest and CondorsTV invaded for their special, but Travis is her first real guest. It's time she stops wallowing because Elsa left her on her own. She should invite Merlin and Marissa to her place, return the favor by cooking for them for a change.

"Congrats on the A by the way." Travis piles his sandwich high with slices of turkey and cheese. "Took them long enough to give it to you."

"Shut up." She elbows him so he squirts mustard all over his plate instead of his sandwich.

"What was that for? I'm telling the truth! Team Canada gave you an A at your first Winter Games. You were the youngest player to play, the youngest to win, and the youngest to do it with a letter on your chest."

Sophie flushes as she finishes making her own sandwich. "Why are you like this?"

"Speaking of international play..." Travis pushes his sandwich aside to plant his forearms on the table. The look on his face means trouble as he leans forward. "Elsa Nyberg."

Sophie groans. "No." She finally stopped thinking about Elsa. She takes her sandwich and sits at the counter. She runs through topics of conversation, hoping for one which will serve as a good distraction.

Travis sits next to her. He runs his hand through his brown hair and it falls back into his eyes. "Don't try and pull this crap on me. I'm not the media. I remember freshman year when you came back from Zimbabwe or whatever—"

"Zurich."

"You came back from *Zurich* with hearts in your eyes."

No she didn't. Elsa was one of the best hockey players she'd ever played against, but it doesn't mean she returned with a crush on her or anything. "Zurich's in Switzerland. Where did you even get Zimbabwe from?"

"Stop trying to distract me, I'm mocking *you* right now. *Elsa Nyberg was so nice. We didn't even speak the same language but we became best friends then I stomped all over her heart and her gold medal aspirations.* Oh, then junior year when you came back from Tanzania—"

"*Turin.* Are you doing this on purpose?"

"Duh." Travis kicks her lightly under the table. "Teasing aside, it sucks she didn't come over this year. I know you were looking forward to it."

"Maybe next year."

Travis looks at her, his gaze too sharp and assessing. She forgets he knows her in ways her current teammates don't. She can't feed him media lines and expect him to buy them. But, because he knows her as well as he does, he says, "I hope she does. I want to see this winger you think is better than me."

"I centered Figuli at the All-Star Game last year. You've definitely been replaced as my best winger."

Travis draws a breath as if to protest before he nods. "Yeah, fair enough. Isn't he amazing to play with?"

Sophie takes a giant bite of her sandwich and settles in to listen as Travis regales her with stories from this season.

THELIN SLAMS SOPHIE into the boards on her second shift, hard enough to jar her shoulder. She'll have to visit Keller again. For now, she ignores the pain and tries to shove him off her. He presses her into the boards and leans in close to whisper. "Is this doing it for you?"

She elbows him. "How about you let me score and I'll get back to you?"

He presses on the back of her helmet, grinding her visor into the glass. She slips his hold in time to chase down the puck and outlet it up to Witzer. Confident he can carry the puck into the zone, she skates to the bench for a change.

She sits at the end of the bench. X hands her a water bottle. "Tonight's going to be one of those nights then?"

"Always."

SPITZ SITS NEXT to her at intermission. Merlin slides over to make space for him, and Sophie's careful not to elbow him as she massages the worst of the ache from her shoulder. "The guys said not to jump to your defense after every hit."

She goes through a version of this talk with every new teammate she has. It isn't Spitz's fault he's new, and it isn't his fault she's been through this so many times. She pushes down her irritation as she answers. "Yep."

Spitz nods. "Watch out for Kaltz. I played with him in Germany. He thinks he's a tough guy."

"Thinks?"

"You play tougher than he ever did." Spitz beams at her, brimming with confidence even though they've only played a handful of games together.

SOPHIE AND KALTZ lock sticks midway through the second period. He tries to use his height to force her to her knees. She's stronger than him, though, and with a twist of her stick, she uses momentum and surprise to send him sprawling to the ice.

She stands over him for a moment before she skates back into the play.

THEY LOSE 2-4 with Figuli scoring the game-winner and the insurance goal. He smiles cheerfully at her as the buzzer sounds and she almost wishes he was an asshole, because then she wouldn't feel guilty for wanting to punch him in the face. She wipes her sweaty face on the damp sleeve of her sweater and troops down to the locker room to face the media.

She has enough time to strip to her Under Armour and shove down the worst of her disappointment. By the time Rickers and the rest of them pour in, she has a neutral expression fixed to her face.

"Mikhail Figuli is unstoppable," Ed Rickers says. He fidgets with his tie. "Sometimes it feels as if he still hasn't hit his peak."

"He's good." Sophie is a firm believer in giving credit where it's due, but, "Lindy had an unreal stop on him on the penalty kill."

"If he had a couple more, you might've won the game," Marty Owen says.

She doesn't know how Owen can twist compliments into criticism so easily. "We played a tight first period but we were sloppy in the third. We need to work on playing a full sixty minutes."

She answers questions for another twenty minutes before Mary Beth clears the locker room of everyone who isn't on the team. She gives Matty a significant look before she follows the reporters out.

Matty stands up, drawing everyone's attention to him. "Tomorrow, Mister Lightbody's fifth grade science class is visiting which means leave all your foul language at home."

"If we're Condors then isn't *all* our language fowl language?" Merlin asks.

Four different guys throw their sweaty socks at Merlin's head. Zinger loudly declares how he should be fined. Sophie laughs and dodges the incoming sock balls by escaping to the shower.

KID EVENTS ALWAYS means Sophie's the focus of the cameras. Of course, any event involving the Condors means Sophie's the focus of the cameras. At least, since there are kids here, she can wear her Under Armour leggings and one of her jerseys instead of a suit. Kids remind her of a promise she made last year, and she finds Mary Beth when she arrives at the rink.

"Can we put together a visit to Jessi's school?"

"Show-and-tell?" Mary Beth nods. "We'll schedule it for late November. Napoli likes me to space out the kid stuff."

She wishes she could ask for them to leave the cameras behind. She's visiting Jessi's class because it'll make Jessi happy, not because it's an opportunity to promote the team with a feel-good story. But Concord's still a fledging franchise which means they have to turn everything to their advantage.

At least Sophie doesn't have to curl her hair for the kids. She tugs on the end of her ponytail and heads into the locker room. Ben Granlund, their equipment manager, has worked some kind of magic, because it doesn't smell like stale sweat and grungy hockey gear. The stalls are clean, and their nameplates have been replaced with the names of the kids. There's a whole slew of fifth graders, standing next to their poster boards, proud of their diagrams and drawings and fact sheets.

On the far end is a boy with dark hair and even darker eyes. He looks around the room, hesitant, as if he's afraid. He tracks the cameras and then Theo as the big defenseman is drawn to a group of boys in the corner.

Sophie offers the boy a friendly smile and crouches so she doesn't loom as tall over him. "Hi, I'm Sophie. What's your name?"

He blinks at her and shrinks closer to his poster.

"This is Tito." A girl with ringed blonde curls comes over. She smiles at Tito and then at Sophie. "His family moved here from Guatemala. He's shy. Mister Lightbody says to talk slowly and enunciate clearly, because when we talk too fast all our words jumble together and it's hard for Tito to understand."

"Did you say Guatemala?" J-Rod drops to one knee in front of Tito so the kid is taller than him. He holds a fist out for the kid to bump as he says something in Spanish.

Tito lights up, and he answers, pointing to himself and J-Rod and then his poster. Given the way he points to different pictures and graphs, Sophie thinks he's giving his presentation in his native language. Mr. Lightbody, a man in his late fifties, takes a step toward the small group as if he wants to break it up, but Mary Beth smoothly intercepts him as the camera crew flocks around Tito and J-Rod.

"Which one is your poster?" Sophie asks.

The girl leads her over to Kevlar's stall, only the nameplate reads *Lee-Ann* today. Her poster board is bright yellow with pictures and maps all over it. "This is my presentation on the California condor. Hey, why are you called the condors when they live in California, Utah, Arizona, and Mexico?" She taps the map in the left corner of her poster. All the states she mentioned have been shaded red, along with the part of Mexico where the condor can be found.

"How come they're California condors if you can find them other places?" Sophie asks.

"It's also called the New World condor. Did you know they can travel up to a hundred and fifty miles in only one day to find food? Sometimes, they eat so much at once they don't need to eat for days after."

"They must not be hockey players then. I have to eat multiple times a day to have the energy I need."

"And you don't eat carcasses. Carcass is one of our vocabulary words. It means dead animal."

"Charming."

Across the room, a boy stands on the bench so he can touch the top of X's head where he's going bald. "Condors are bald too. It's so their faces stay clean while they dig their beaks into all the blood and guts."

Lee-Ann tugs on Sophie's jersey sleeve to claim her attention again. "Do you want to hear about mating rituals?"

Merlin appears at her side as if he's been summoned. He slings an arm around her shoulders before she can even consider escaping. "Mating rituals? Maybe Sophie can pick up a few tips."

Sophie pinches him, hard, and he yelps. Fortunately, Lee-Ann continues as if they aren't even here. "Male condors blush."

"Do not!" The kid next to her—Gregory—puffs up, offended on behalf of all male condors. "Their heads turn red but it isn't a blush."

"It's a blush," Lee-Ann whispers. "I think it's cute. And once two condors have bonded, they stay together forever. They fly together, doing tricks and stuff."

Gregory steps up next to Lee-Ann's poster. "Once they have a baby chick, the mom and dad take turns throwing up in its mouth to feed it."

"Regurgitation," Lee-Ann happily informs them.

Sophie thinks she would've been happier being a condor if she didn't know all this trivia about them. But after Lee-Ann's presentation, Sophie listens to Gregory's and then she moves over to Mark. His poster says *Condors: Nature's Clean-Up Crew* at the top, and Sophie already regrets being here.

He's the same kid who used X's head to demonstrate earlier, and he tells Sophie about why condors are bald before moving onto their other characteristics. "They have tough beaks so they can rip through thick skin. And even though they eat carrion, their immune systems keeps them from getting sick. My mom says I can't eat raw cookie dough, but I bet a condor could. Neat, huh?"

"Neat," Sophie agrees.

"Do you want to know the best part? Condors don't sweat like we do." A big smile stretches across Mark's face, one Sophie knows better than to trust. "To keep cool, they shit all over themselves!"

All of the kids in the room, and some of Sophie's teammates, burst into laughter. Mr. Lightbody's mouth presses into a thin line, but he doesn't interfere.

Lee-Ann skips over to say, "It's called urohidrosis."

"You're learning all sorts of new words with this project," Sophie says.

They send the kids home with autographed shirseys with their name on the back. Lee-Ann pulls hers on over her dress right away. Tito stares at his for a long time and traces his finger over his last name before he throws his arms around Ben Granlund's legs in thanks.

Once the kids clear out, Napoli does a little dance. "It's like Christmas," he says as he holds one of his cameras to review some of the footage.

Kevlar leans over his shoulder. "Please tell me you have Sofe's face when the kid talked about birds shitting themselves."

"How come we weren't allowed to swear if the kids were?" Merlin asks.

"They were talking about a biological function," Matty says.

Merlin grins, the same way Mark did earlier, and Sophie shakes her head even before he says, "Fucking is a biological function."

X throws Matty a look full of judgment. "You have children. You should've known better."

"Hey, Garfield!" Merlin calls across the locker room. "Next time there are kids here we can talk about fucking because it's a biological function."

"I learned all about the mechanics of bird fucking," says Garfield. "I'm all set."

"Condors mate for life," Theo tells them as if he's the only one who listened to Lee-Ann's presentation. "They do beautiful aerials with their one true loves." He slants a glance at Sophie. "Who are you wooing with your hockey?"

She flips him off.

"Touchy, touchy." Theo drapes his arms over Kevlar's shoulders. "Hey, if we're d-partners then are we together for life?"

"Till trades or retirement do us part," Kevlar says.

Chapter Eight

SOPHIE STREAMS ONE of Gothenburg's games so she can watch Elsa play. She's a force on the ice, snatching the puck off her opponents' sticks, and sometimes the sticks of her teammates, so she can make a breathtaking play. She barrels into the offensive zone, cuts through three defenders, and it takes a hook and a trip to slow her up enough for the goalie to make the stop.

Gothenburg goes on the power play, and Elsa argues with her coach, probably because she wants to be on the ice. It's a different style of hockey than Sophie plays, showier, demand written into every stride and every bark of her voice, but there's no denying she loves the game.

Sophie props herself up on her elbows as Elsa gets her way and hits the ice for the power play. Thaulow wins the faceoff and Gothenburg goes to work. Elsa cradles the puck as she skates down low for better position. The defense shifts to cover her so she passes up to the point. The puck moves and so do the players until Elsa has the puck again. She fakes a pass before she fires the puck on net.

She follows her shot in which means when it rebounds off the goalie's pads she's there to bang it home.

Sophie lets herself daydream about what it would be like to have Elsa on her wing. She has no problem passing when she has a teammate with hot hands. She would feed Elsa without complaint until the winger put up fifty goals in a season. Between Sophie's playmaking and Elsa's finish, they could be an unstoppable duo. All Sophie would have to do is pass and watch as Elsa scored.

A couple of shifts later, Elsa streaks toward the net. *Look up*, Sophie thinks at Thaulow. Elsa bangs her stick on the ice to get his attention. It means the defense is paying attention now too and Thaulow's pass, a beat too late, is intercepted. *I would've been able to do it.*

She's a mix of frustrated and impressed by the time she shuts the game off so she can go to bed. She has an important game tomorrow, and she can't lose sleep wishing for something which isn't happening.

EDMONTON BRINGS SHAWN Wedin, another one of her former Chilton teammates, when they come to Concord. Unlike with Travis, there won't be a lunch invite for Wedin. He was one of her enforcers, tasked with keeping her safe on the ice when they played together. Her sophomore year, she learned his protection of her depended on her production level. If she wasn't putting up points, he wouldn't stick his neck out for her.

It shouldn't have been a surprise when, once they were no longer teammates, he felt no loyalty to her. But it caught her off guard when he crushed her into the boards and told her he'd been waiting years to be able to do it.

He visits her during warm-ups as she stretches by her bench. He bulked up over the summer or maybe it's because she's down on the ice as he looms over her, but he's bigger than she remembers.

It's a stupid bit of gamesmanship, but she responds to it, standing up. He's still taller than her, but she steps into his space, refusing to be intimidated. He wants to come at her? He won't have many opportunities to do it. He's a third pairing defenseman who spends as much time out of the lineup as in. She's the one with a record and a trophy to her name. She's the one making an impact on this league. He can't even make an impact on his own team.

She bares her teeth in a smile. "You're on the wrong side of the ice."

"I came to say hi to an old friend." His smile matches hers, too many teeth to be friendly. He taps his fingers against her chin. "Head up, today, I'll be saying my real hello later."

"Are you threatening me?"

Before things can escalate, Witzer skates over. "This looks like a nice reunion."

"You want to jump in and shoot on Lindy? I'm scoring a goal tonight." She lets her gaze linger on Wedin. "Two if they bump up your minutes."

"Bitch," he sneers.

She shrugs, letting the word roll off her shoulders. She hooks her arm through Witzer's, and they skate away.

"I wasn't trying to rescue you," he says. "I wanted to make sure you had an out if you wanted it."

LATE IN THE second period, Sophie slides a puck across the goal mouth for Witzer to tap in. When he pats her helmet and says, "Thank you," she thinks, *no, thank you.*

THEY WIN 4-1 which isn't the statement game she wanted, but she scored the fourth goal of the game while

Wedin was on the ice. He hung his head on the replay as if he knew his blown coverage gave her the open lane to shoot. She would've thanked him for it the next time they were on the ice, but their paths didn't cross again.

"Big win for you," Ed Rickers says.

Sophie wipes her face the best she can with her towel. As soon as she clears a layer of sweat, a new one rises up to take its place. She wipes underneath her eyes and above her top lip before sets her towel in her lap. "It was a good one."

"Was this a comeback game for Lindholm?" Marty Owen asks. Sophie can't raise her eyebrows or give a sarcastic response so she stares, unblinking, at Owen as she waits for him to realize what a monumentally stupid question he asked. He, of course, doubles down. "He gave up four goals last game and only one tonight."

"Lindy played better tonight, but we also played better in front of him. It was a team effort." They controlled play tonight and, shocker, there are fewer shots against the team with higher possession numbers. They drove the game, shelling Edmonton's goalie on shift after shift. When the Hydras had the puck, Concord collapsed their coverage to protect their goal.

"You were chatting with your Chilton teammate, Shawn Wedin, before the game. It didn't look very friendly."

She finds Christina Rossetti through the crowd of reporters to make sure *The Burlington Times* camera catches her dismissive shrug. "We aren't teammates anymore. Tonight, my job was to beat his team and his job was to beat mine. There isn't a lot of room for friendliness there."

"Harsh," Nelson mutters from his stall.

Sophie drags her towel down her face again.

FOR ONCE, SOPHIE isn't the last one out of the locker room. Matty and Lindy are chatting about something in quiet voices. It's odd they're having a private conversation here, but she gives them as much space as she can, leaving without saying goodbye.

She debates how to celebrate tonight's win. She has frozen yogurt in her freezer and one of Elsa's games saved on her computer. Or she could call Dima; she hasn't talked to him in a while. Mary Beth waves to her from the far end of the hallway, and Sophie freezes in place. Her brain kicks into overdrive, turning over every interaction she's had with another person today from the moment she woke up to now. She doubts anyone overheard her conversation with Wedin and even if he said something stupid in his scrum, his team lost tonight so it could be easily wiped aside as sour grapes.

"What happened?" Sophie asks as Mary Beth reaches her.

"Nothing bad," Mary Beth reassures her. Of course, she follows it up by leading Sophie down the hall to her former locker room, a storage closet with enough space for a couple of stalls and a shower.

"Napoli and CondorsTV did another *What's in Your Bag?* segment tonight. They're airing it during tomorrow's game against Seattle."

It's one of their standard bits. The camera crew roams the stadium during games, and they'll pull aside a couple of fans to rifle through their bags. It's where gems like the Matty bobblehead have been uncovered. There's always a few fans who have a copy of one of Sophie's biographies, and Napoli will occasionally grab her and ask her to sign them, because it's good press. This feels different.

Mary Beth hands over her iPad. She has the unedited footage pulled up, and Sophie hits play. Napoli leads the camera through an empty hallway rather than the concourse. There are no brightly colored signs drawing people in to buy hot dogs or fried dough or ice cream. He's...near the team kitchen?

Theo and Kevlar come into view, their bags slung over their shoulders as they walk down the hallway. Napoli calls out to them and waves them over.

"Can I poke around your bag?" Napoli asks. "For the fans, of course."

Sophie, protective of what little privacy she manages to carve out, would've hesitated, but Kevlar hands his bag over with a smile.

"If we find anything embarrassing, we won't show it," Napoli promises.

"He keeps all his embarrassing stuff tucked under his mattress." Theo grins and dodges Kevlar's half-hearted swing.

"Ignore him, it's what I do."

"Is this the secret to a good d-pairing?" Napoli asks.

"Selective hearing and never go to bed angry," Theo says.

They're loose in front of the camera, comfortable with themselves and Napoli's attention in a way Sophie's never been. She spends so much time being filmed and studied and stared at, she should be more natural in front of a camera, due to sheer exposure if anything. But the only time she feels settled when there's attention on her is on the ice.

Kevlar holds his bag at waist level as Napoli unzips it. He pulls two spare ties out. "Doubly prepared?"

"Well, I need one for me and one for this guy."

Theo scoffs. "Like I'd wear your ties. They're all ugly."

"Not as ugly as your face."

Sophie huffs out a quiet laugh as the d-men play-fight. One of Napoli's assistants has to dart in to grab Kevlar's bag as he drops it so he has both his hands free. Napoli ignores the commotion and digs through Kevlar's bag. He uncovers more spare clothes, a paperback book, and a few protein bars. Sophie can't help but wonder why she's watching this. Then Napoli unzips one of the side pockets. He pulls out a travel shaving kit, a box of Band-Aids and...a box of tampons.

"Oh," Sophie says.

Napoli drops the box on the ground before he picks it up with the very tips of his fingers. "What are these for?"

Theo stares at Kevlar as if he wants to know the same thing. Kevlar raises his eyebrows and a smile tugs at his lips. "You don't know what tampons are for?"

Hilariously, Napoli flushes bright red as he drops the box back into Kevlar's bag. He zips the pocket up so he can't see the teal packaging any longer. "I know what they're for. Why do you have them?"

"In case Sophie needs them." He says it matter-of-fact as if he can't understand why Napoli wouldn't know. "Have you ever been in her bag? She has extra stick tape, a whole first aid kit, even extra shaving kits. If anyone's forgotten something on a roadie, all they have to do is knock on Sofe's door, she probably has it. She has our backs, we should have hers."

"It was a variety pack."

"Yeah, well, I wasn't going to ask her what size she uses."

Napoli winces. "Good idea."

He looks the most uncomfortable Sophie's ever seen him. She's never understood why guys are so uptight about pads and tampons, but it is kind of funny to see the guy who teased her for having a small TV slowly edge away from Kevlar's bag as if the tampons will jump out and attack him.

"My bag next?" Theo offers. "I promise I don't have any tampons. I won't make any promises about condoms."

Napoli sighs and the footage cuts out.

Mary Beth takes her iPad back. "We aren't airing the clip, but I thought you'd want to see it."

She has a bruise blooming on her shoulder from Wedin hitting her during the game tonight. She tries to imagine him carrying emergency tampons for her and can't quite hold back her laugh. "We have a good group of guys here." If she's ever traded, and she hopes she isn't, she doesn't think Kevlar would try to run her through the boards.

Mary Beth squeezes Sophie's good shoulder. "We have a good team. Are you going out tonight?"

"Not with Seattle tomorrow. Besides, two more games until our Halloween party. Everyone's saving their livers for the big bash."

"Are you going this year?"

Last year, Sophie went trick-or-treating with the Wilcox kids instead of going to her team's party. It was in the midst of her feud with Hayes, and for a brief time it spilled over into her whole team. She didn't want to be around them more than she had to so she hid out with her GM's kids. It wasn't one of her prouder moments.

This year is different. She glances at Mary Beth's iPad, the screen blank now. Management chose her over

Hayes last season but at the end of the season, her team chose *her*. They rallied around her after their playoffs hopes were dashed, lifting her to her Maddow Trophy win. Coming into this season, she has an A, she has the respect of her teammates, and, if a peek inside Kevlar's bag is any indication, she has their support.

"I'm planning on it. Since we call McArthur Merlin, someone decided we should go as the Knights of the Round Table. Witzer's going as Guinevere, because he claims no one else has the legs for it."

"Please do not send me any pictures," Mary Beth says.

Sophie laughs and follows her PR manager out of the room.

SHE TAKES THE second faceoff of the game and lines up against Eldon Carruthers. His black hair pokes out from underneath his helmet, and his eyes are bright and focused under the stadium lights. He doesn't have the slump to his shoulders or defeat written into the lines of his face.

Not yet.

By the end of the night, he will. He's Sophie's personal measuring stick, and she intends to beat him in every category tonight. Faceoffs, board battles, assists, goals; hell, she'll even out-hit him if it means proving herself the better player.

She's going to show her home crowd she's better than the first overall pick at her draft. Maybe, though she doesn't hold her breath on it, she'll convince the whole League. Concord drafted her last because they could exploit the rules, but there was a large percentage of people who thought even last at the draft was too high.

Fuck them.

She wins the faceoff, sparking an offensive push from her team. On her next shift, an on-the-fly change, she chases Carruthers down and shoves him up against the glass so Witzer can dart in and steal the puck.

Halfway through the game, Carruthers seems to finally catch a clue, or he's tired of her shoving him around. She has the puck on her stick and she's racing up the ice when he shoulders her into Seattle's bench. She tips into enemy territory, but she's quickly pushed out of it. She regains her bearings and tracks him down to reclaim the puck.

Carruthers scores to make it 4-2, a power play goal while Sophie's stuck on the bench. She chews on the end of her mouth guard. Her team still has a lead, but she hasn't scored which means there's at least one category where Carruthers is beating her.

She narrows her eyes as she tugs on Witzer's sleeve. "We're scoring on the next shift."

Seattle's bench is still smiling when she turns the D inside-out and lifts the puck up and over the goalie's pad. The entire stadium leaps to their feet for her goal. As they chant her name, she turns to stare down the Seafarers' bench. There are no more smiles there.

She grins and throws her arms out to welcome her teammates as they crash into her.

ONE GOAL IS good. Two would be better.

There's four minutes left in the game when she hits post on back-to-back shots. She returns to the bench, shoulders tight. If she'd pulled the puck in a little tighter on the last one, she would've hit top corner. And on the first one she had a fucking wide-open net and couldn't put the puck away. Is this what Concord drafted her for? To miss the net?

"Relax," Merlin tells her. "It's Seattle."

Exactly. "Any team can beat us if we give them the opportunity."

"I'll roll my eyes at you. Don't think the A on your sweater protects you."

You wouldn't understand.

THERE'S THREE MINUTES left in the game when Seattle pulls their goalie. *You could only score two goals in forty-seven minutes, what makes you think you can score three now?* With the extra skater on the ice, Seattle manages two solid shots on net before Teddy covers the puck.

"Fournier, you're up," Coach Butler says. "Smith and Faulkner, you're on the backend."

Theo and Kevlar high-five. Merlin hands Sophie a water bottle so she can have a quick drink before they head out for the defensive zone faceoff. She lines her skates up and crouches, ready. She glances up at Carruthers and grins.

"Psycho," he mutters as he adjusts his grip on his stick.

After a night of losing to Sophie, Carruthers is too quick on the draw and they toss him out of the faceoff dot. She narrows her eyes, annoyed she's lost the opportunity to beat him again. She still wins the faceoff, but her joy doesn't last as long. A goal will make her feel better.

As soon as she's won the puck back to her team, she skates for the blue line. Merlin sends a stretch pass up the ice, and she chases it.

"Go! Go!" Matty shouts from the bench.

A glance over her shoulder shows Carruthers racing her for the loose puck. She skates harder. She's the first one to the puck and she turns her back to him to protect it. One easy move and she can flick the puck into the net, giving herself two goals to his one. She spins around him so he's no longer between her and the net.

Kevlar taps his stick on the ice, letting her know where he is in case she needs help.

She doesn't. But then she remembers the *What's in Your Bag?* segment. She hesitates for one moment before she slides the puck across the ice to her d-man. He taps the puck into the empty net, and the crowd cheers for him.

Sophie shoulders past Carruthers, barely even noting the slumped, defeated posture she was hoping he would have by the end of the game. She rubs her glove over Kevlar's helmet.

"You had it," he says.

"I didn't want to take the chance."

Besides, a goal and an assist are still better than Carruthers's single goal.

THEY PLAY DC to end the first month of the season and lose, 1-3, in front of their home crowd. Disappointment settles, an ache in her chest, one she won't be able to dislodge until next game when they have a fresh opportunity to win. This has been the biggest adjustment since entering the NAHL. She loses a lot more.

They weren't undefeated for four years at Chilton, but they won the majority of their games, and they went to the playoffs every year and won it all three times. Here in Concord, they can't even make it to the first round of the playoffs. *This year. We step up, we play better, and the playoffs are within our reach.*

"Your team combined to score ten goals in the previous two games," Marty Owen says. Sophie leans back in her stall and waits for the follow-up which will turn what could be a compliment into a certain criticism. "Tonight, you only had one. Did you burn yourselves out?"

Stupid fucking question. She eyes his suit, loose again, and thinks about giving him her tailor's number. She wouldn't inflict him on her least favorite tailor, though, let alone the one she trusts to make sure she's presentable for games. "The puck didn't go in tonight. We'll review the game tape, learn what we can, and move on."

"You won more games than you lost in October. It's a much better start than last season."

Sophie offers Ed Rickers a fleeting smile. "We're a better team than we were last year. Our GM made some important moves this summer, and we're settling into our new lines. The more we play together, the more we'll improve."

"You scored your thirty-eighth career goal tonight," Owen says. Again, Sophie waits. "Dmitry Ivanov scored his fiftieth."

There it is. Knowing this footage will be played on all the major channels, dissected by analysts with nothing better to do, she makes sure she smiles, supportive of her fellow NAHLer. "Let me guess, it was on the power play?"

"He sniped it right from the hash marks," Rickers answers.

"I'll have to congratulate him once we're done here."

"I thought you were rivals." Rickers smiles, teasing.

"We're competitors and we push each other to be better, but once we're—" she catches herself before she says *out of our jerseys*—"once the game is over we're friends."

"When will you score your fiftieth?" Owen asks.

"Hopefully this season but I'm not focused on it."

SHE STICKS A candle in her brownie and lights it before sending a picture to Dima. She blows the candle out and takes her brownie and an ice pack back to her couch. She stretches out, ice pack on her shoulder and brownie balanced on her stomach.

Dima calls instead of texting her back. "Brownie for me?"

"Depends, how fast can you get to Concord?" She takes a big bite of her dessert. "Clock's ticking."

"Mean."

She laughs, refusing to buy it for a second. "You scored your fiftieth goal tonight, and you're telling me your teammates aren't celebrating?"

"Vodka shots but you make *brownies*."

"A whole pan of them. And since I don't have a roommate, I don't have to share."

"Terrible at share. Even with roommate."

"Nah." Another bite and her brownie's almost gone. "It's only you I don't share with."

He makes an outraged sound before his attention's dragged away by someone shouting on the other end of the line. Sophie finishes her brownie and debates how much she wants another one. Is it worth getting off the couch? She wonders if she should tell her trainer laziness saved her nutrition plan tonight.

"Party time," Dima says. "Because I'm most famous."

"For tonight. I'll have to score my first hat trick next game to take the spotlight back. You know, because I'm so bad at sharing."

Dima's still laughing when he hangs up.

"BORS!" MERLIN GREETS, already drunk by the sound of his voice and the way he sways alarmingly to one side as he greets her. Sophie laughs and rushes over to catch him before he takes out any of their teammates.

Bors the Younger is the knight Sophie was assigned because "you're young and boring" but joke's on all of them because she looked him up and he slayed three dragons with a single swing of his sword, officially making him the coolest knight. She steadies Merlin and can't help but tug on the long, white beard he's wearing to help complete his costume. She lets the elastic snap back against his chin and he steps away from her with a scowl.

"Respect the beard."

She laughs again, unable to help it. "You're wearing a dress, a fake beard, and a sparkly hat. There is no respect for you."

"They're robes! And I look good." He gestures to himself and sloshes beer down the front of his robes. He frowns at the spill before he shrugs and chugs the rest of his drink.

Sophie leaves him to his drinking and wanders deeper into the back room of the club so she can greet her other teammates. Zinger offers her a drink but she holds up her bottle of orange Gatorade and tells him she's all set.

"Let me know when you need a refill," he tells her.

She nods and shifts over to where Witzer, who is actually in a dress, is being wrangled into a picture with Kevlar and Theo, who are Galahad and Percival respectively. They spot her and drag her into the picture. She ends up squashed between the two d-men, both of them leaning heavily on her. She's strong but not *this* strong.

She walks them backward until they can lean against the wall. "How early did you start?"

Theo holds up a plastic goblet covered in gold glitter. "We went in search of the Holy Grail and it was full of beer. Want some?" He holds the cup up to her lips, but she weaves away from him and shows off her Gatorade.

"I brought my own."

"Good plan." Theo pats her cheek, and his hand is warm and damp from the heat of the club. "We can't share drinks. It's how the mumps spread."

"Okay, buddy. Next time you refill your grail maybe some water?"

"You're the smartest of us all," Kevlar says.

"I'm the fairest!" Witzer interjects.

"That's Snow White, you dumbass."

The two of them bicker until Theo shoves off the wall and steps between them. They both fall silent and turn to him. "Where's King Arthur? We need a picture with all of us."

They follow Theo until they find Matty, stretched out in a booth with a lopsided crown on his head and a beer in his hand. As they approach, she realizes the crown isn't only lopsided but it's handmade with pink and purple rhinestones scattered across it.

"Yeah, yeah," Matty says, waving his hand for her to laugh. "My kids made it."

Sophie holds up her shield, a piece of painted cardboard with a condor on it. "This is left over from Kaylee's Halloween costume last year."

"Matty!" Theo shouts, far too loud for how close all of them are. "We need a picture!"

"How many fucking pictures do we need?" Matty grumbles but he hauls himself out of the booth and they flag down a waitress to take their picture.

Afterward, Sophie steals Kevlar's phone so she can send the picture to herself. It's the five of them, Matty's crown almost as tall as Theo. Sophie's squished between Theo and Kevlar again, but Matty's hand rests on her shoulder. Witzer stands in front of all them and he hikes his dress up to show off his hairy legs. She laughs and, deciding no one looks incriminatingly drunk, sends the picture to Dima.

He sends her one back of himself in his Catwoman costume which is entirely too much spandex for her to have to see him in.

Chapter Nine

CONCORD STARTS NOVEMBER the same way they finished October, by losing. They hit the road for three straight losses and return home only to lose against New Orleans in overtime before losing to Detroit in a shootout.

It isn't exactly the kind of play she was hoping for, especially as they fly to Cleveland for their second game against the Presidents. They're on a six-game losing streak, about to play their biggest rivals in a hostile stadium, and in case there wasn't enough pressure, rumors are spreading. Rumblings Coach Butler isn't the right coach to lead Concord out of their playoff drought woes. Whispers maybe Matty isn't the right captain for the team. People are outright saying Sophie used up all her luck as a rookie, and she'll continue to decline until Concord smartens up and cuts her loose.

She's never gotten anywhere because of luck. She's the player she is because of hard work and a refusal to quit when things are tough. She'll bring her best game tonight, and snap this losing skid. With a couple of wins, everyone will remember Coach Butler was brought in because he has the résumé to make Concord a contender, and Matty is the best captain this franchise has ever had.

SOPHIE MISSES TWO easy shots on net during warm-ups. She circles to the back of the line, her stick clutched tightly in her gloves. It's been three games without a point for her. If she scored against New Orleans, they could've won in regulation or even OT. If she scored against Detroit, they wouldn't have gone to the shootout.

She has an A on her sweater now. It means she's supposed to lead her team, and leaders score important goals in big moments.

"We're winning this one," she tells Merlin. It's become automatic to say, something expected of her rather than something she believes.

She clangs her next shot off the post, and she bites back a frustrated growl. She can't even hit an open net.

"You're getting all your misses out in warm-ups," Merlin says. He smiles, but it's the same smile she's worn the past two weeks; it fools the cameras but doesn't make it all the way to the eyes.

SHE HITS THE post on back-to-back shifts to start the game.

The crowd chants "Hayes is better."

She skates back to the bench after a third unfruitful shift and drops hard into an open space. "They do realize he hasn't scored either, right?"

"Relax," Witzer says.

She grabs a water bottle and sprays some water on her face to try to cool down. It's better than snarling at her linemate. He doesn't know what it's been like for her, going up against Hayes for the past five years. Every single game, she has to prove herself better than him or it's like everything she did before was erased.

She scored a Chilton Academy record six goals in a game against the Weston School her junior year. It was a double hat trick, and she added four assists to her point total, giving her a ten-point night and another school record.

The next time she faced Hayes, she was held off the scoresheet. Hayes had an assist on an empty net and people were quick to jump on the decline on her career. So no, she won't *relax*.

Every time they're on the ice together, it's a story. They're *rivals*. Bullshit. He'd be nothing without her. She's the one who has set records since she first hit the ice. She's the one who had to fight against an entire system in order to play. No one would even know his name if he didn't make such a big deal out of losing to her.

She goes out for her next shift, determined to make something happen. If she can't put the puck in the net herself, she'll have to make space for her teammates and then set them up to score. Only, no one's been on a streak recently so when she passes to Merlin, he shuffles it to Witzer who sends it to Theo and no one shoots.

Theo's return pass is picked off by Hayes, who streaks down the ice. Only a quick glove by Lindy keeps the game tied at zero.

Sophie skates to the bench, even more frustrated than before she started her shift.

"You need to shoot more," Coach Vorgen tells her.

She grinds her teeth into her mouth guard so she doesn't say anything.

CLEVELAND SCORES THE first goal of the game when Olsson takes a shot from the point, and the puck deflects off Spitz's skate and into the net. Sophie's on the ice for the goal, boxing Hayes out, but she lets up as soon as the light flashes. Her stomach sinks, disappointed. She hates being on the ice for a goal against, because it means if she'd done more, she could've stopped it. If she'd held Hayes up when he carried the puck in, she could've forced an offside or if she'd been quicker, they could've cleared the puck out of the zone.

All those ifs will help her prevent the next goal, but it doesn't do anything to negate this one. She pushes her irritation down and skates over to Lindy to tap his pads with her stick. It wasn't his fault the puck went in. He was squared up to Olsson, and it would've been an easy save if the puck hadn't changed direction at the last second.

She skates with Spitz to the bench. He looks gutted and avoids Coach Butler as if he's afraid he'll be benched for the rest of the game if he's noticed.

"Chin up," Sophie tells him as they sit down. "We still have a lot more game left to play."

TWO MINUTES LATER, she's on the bench when Garfield and Nelson collide at center ice. They're still untangling themselves when Farage puts the puck past Lindy.

Nil-two.

As much as she hates being on the ice for a goal against, she hates being stuck on the bench watching even more.

"IT'S ONLY TWO goals," Matty tells them during intermission.

Coach Butler has already come in, yelled at them, and stormed out. Matty's doing the *we're in this together* shit which, when it works, works well. But when it falls flat, it falls really flat. Sophie isn't the only one who can't meet her captain's gaze for long.

It's only two goals for them to tie it. It's *three* to win it.

They haven't posted three goals in a game since Seattle.

She hangs her head. It's bad body language, especially for someone with a letter on their jersey, but she can't summon the energy to pick her head back up.

CLEVELAND SCORES OFF the opening faceoff.

It's only three goals, she thinks and almost bursts into laughter. She bites down on her glove, hard, to keep it in.

Lindy makes an easy save on the next play and the crowd mockingly cheers for him. Immediately, her hysteria and her frustration whoosh out of her, leaving her with a cold fury. No one's allowed to jeer her goalie. It isn't his fault his team has fallen apart around him. She can't fight the fans and she isn't supposed to fight any players, but she does put an edge in her game.

She finishes her checks with an extra elbow or jab of her stick. She boxes out in front of the net and doesn't let anyone push her around. She exchanges shoves and heated words after the whistle blows, but she's careful to keep everything on the right side of the line.

At first, anyway.

The second period is dwindling down when Hayes finds her. Lindy bobbled the puck, managing to save a goal and draw a whistle. Hayes skates by Sophie and bumps his shoulder into hers. "I'm glad I got off this garbage heap of a team."

Sophie's stick is up before she knows what she's doing. "They didn't want you." She cross-checks him across the chest. She wants to hit higher and make him bleed. Fuck him and his fucking face and stupid fucking team. She hits him again, higher this time, her stick glancing off his chin.

He grins as she's hauled off him by two of his teammates. He presses his fingers to his chin as if he's trying to make himself bleed. She rips herself away from the two Cleveland players only to be caught by an official who nudges her in the direction of the penalty box.

The crowd cheers as she skates to the open door, and they cheer even louder when it closes, shutting her in.

She takes off her helmet and draws a deep breath. She wants to put her head in her hands or maybe scream. She can't do either. She shouldn't have let Hayes get to her. They're down by three and now she's in the box, giving Cleveland an opportunity to score again.

"Gatorade?" the attendant offers her. The red Gatorade he holds out already has the seal broken.

"I'm good but thanks."

Her team goes to work on the PK. Lindy makes a flurry of saves, kicking the puck out and then fighting off the second chance with the knob of his stick. Her team gathers the puck long enough to send it down the ice. The puck skips to temporary safety and something hits Sophie's head and bounces off. It's light enough she thinks she imagined it until it happens again.

"Enjoying the show?" someone calls down at her.

Someone else slams the glass behind her. She doesn't turn around. She keeps her eyes glued to the ice. Something hits her again and then it's like little paper balls being rained down on her head. No, not paper, she realizes as she glances at the floor of the penalty box. *Popcorn.* Someone is throwing popcorn at her.

She puts her helmet back on and the kernels stuck in her hair crunch.

"Sorry," she tells the penalty box attendant.

"Could be beer."

Farage, Cleveland's captain, scores with ten seconds left on the power play. She's released from the box as Cleveland celebrates. She skates back to her bench and sits down on the far end where Coach Butler can't see her.

Coach Vorgen pats her shoulder. "We'll get it back."

THEY'RE DOWN 0-4 going into second intermission.

Coach Butler yells at them some more while Sophie picks popcorn out of her braid.

THEY'RE THREE MINUTES into the third period, still down by four when X skates to the bench for a change. It's a routine defense change until Donny *fucking* McGuire barrels into him. It's knee-on-knee, and X goes down hard.

Sophie's breath catches in her throat. Like the rest of her teammates on the bench, she stands up as if there's something she can do. But she's stuck here and X isn't getting back up. *He isn't getting up.*

Matty glances at X, still face down on the ice. He shakes off his gloves. He grabs McGuire by the front of his jersey and hauls him away from the growing crowd. He gets in two big blows before McGuire fights back. They whale on each other as two of the officials hover nearby, waiting for their opportunity to jump in and separate them.

It takes Kuzy and two trainers to help X to his skates and off the ice. The Cleveland fans cheer because they're classless pieces of shit. Sophie doesn't know what she wants more, to jump in and help Matty with McGuire or to vault into the stands and fight everyone there.

The trainers take X down the tunnel.

The bench is silent.

Their captain is escorted to the box and their oldest player, their rock, won't be back in this game. From the looks of it, he won't be back for a long time. Sophie glances down the ice at Lindy. She wishes he was here on the bench. They need him here to settle them.

There's an A on Sophie's sweater burning through her skin. She doesn't know what to say. Their captain is in the box, X is down the tunnel, and their goalie is at the far end of the ice. She needs to pull herself together so she can pull her team together.

Coach Butler's lips are pressed so tight it looks as if he doesn't have a mouth. He sends her over the boards for the first shift.

"Hayes is better!" the crowd chants.

She skates up to the faceoff dot, and Hayes smirks at her. She pops her mouth guard into her mouth. "You've never been better than me."

She wins the faceoff and then charges into the offensive zone. Merlin carries the puck in and drops a pass back for her. She shoots, no pause to overthink her shot, and the puck whips past Strindberg.

The crowd hushes, stunned. Then they recover and chant "Scoreboard" as loud as they can.

DESPITE SOPHIE'S BEST efforts, they lose 1-6. Matty lingers by the bench, ushering them down the tunnel, his gaze far away as they troop to the locker room. Sophie falls into step with Lindy.

"Sorry," she tells him. They should've played better in front of him. They played a shit game which devolved into chaos after X went down. They hung their goalie out to dry, and Lindy will take the brunt of the blame for the loss.

He shrugs. There are dark circles under his eyes. His pads, bigger than hers, don't make him look like the towering goalie she's used to seeing. Instead, they weigh him down, his shoulders slumped and his blocker tucked under his arm. "Been here before, kid."

But did you get out? She doesn't need to ask him. She knows Concord's record.

THE LOCKER ROOM is silent as they strip out of their gear. Everyone knows they played a terrible game. It's another loss in a long string of losses, but this one is more than an L on the stat sheet. X is out long-term, and no one knows how to react to it. They all stay quiet, hunched in on themselves.

They can't—how are they *this* bad? When they lost to DC, she was pissed they couldn't pull off the win, but losses happen. In an eighty-three-game season, they're bound to happen quite a few times. But the losing streak gained steam, taking on a life of its own. Maybe they aren't better than this. Will they limp through the next sixty-four games until the season is mercifully over?

Her entire life, all Sophie has wanted was to play hockey and right now, she wishes she didn't have to lace up and practice tomorrow. She tosses her jersey into the laundry bin, unable to stand wearing anything with their team logo on it. She doesn't deserve it. None of them do.

She's down to her Under Armour and her pads when Matty stops in front of her stall. He has the same dark circles under his eyes Lindy does. There's no teasing tug of his lips, no friendly shoulder punch. He looks exhausted, as if this game wrung him out.

She knows why he's come to fetch her so she doesn't make him say anything. "Let me finish changing."

She unbuckles all her padding and leaves it in a pile. She switches her skates out for her sliders. She pats her hair, damp from sweat and with bits of popcorn still in it, but she doesn't grab her ball cap. No team logos for her right now and no brim to hide behind. She'll face the media and take every criticism they lay on her.

She, Matty, and Lindy head outside the locker room. Normally, Mary Beth invites the media in, lets them swarm the stalls, but today they'll answer questions out here so they can shield the rest of their team the best they can.

They're barely through the doors when the reporters surge forward. Marty Owen elbows his way to the front and shoves his phone in front of Lindy's face. "Do you think you could've stopped a few more pucks and given your team a fighting chance?"

"I always want to stop more pucks."

Matty's grilled on whether he's losing control of the room and if a better leader could turn the season around. Sophie's hands start to curl into fists before she remembers all the cameras around her right now. She flexes her hands instead and then links them in front of her to eliminate the temptation.

"November hasn't been a good month for you," Rossetti says and everyone's attention swings to Sophie.

"It's early. We can still turn things around." Sophie's voice sounds dead, even to her own ears. Her go-to media strategy is bland soundbites, but usually she at least has to work for it. She's monotone, distant as if she isn't standing in front of a crowd of reporters. She tries to summon a spark of *something* so she doesn't wake up tomorrow to articles accusing her of being catatonic but she can't. There isn't anything in her to spark.

"Do you think you'll win a game before November is over?" Marty Owen asks.

She can't even drudge up her usual distaste for *The Concord Courier's* resident hockey writer. Her gaze slides over the assembled crowd in front of her. "We will. Obviously, we have a long list of things to work on, but we have an experienced coach and a veteran captain. It's a rough patch, but we'll make it through."

The reporters put them out of their misery quicker than Cleveland did, dispersing once they realize they won't get anything worth reporting.

NO ONE SPEAKS on the plane ride home. It isn't unusual for late flights to be quiet, but often there's at least one card game going on or one cluster of guys watching a movie. Tonight, everyone sits in their seat, headphones in and staring straight ahead. Sophie doesn't even have music on, but she wants to appear unapproachable.

It works.

WHEN SHE ARRIVES home at her apartment, she drops her bags next to her shoe rack, a problem to deal with in the morning. She turns the lock on the door and then shuffles over to her couch. She wants to drop face down on it, but she knows she won't get back up if she does. She isn't quite pathetic enough to spend the night on her own couch.

She shuffles into her bedroom and hangs her suit up in her closet. It's all the effort she can manage and she flops down on her bed wearing a tank top and her underwear. She wiggles until she's under her covers. She stares at the ceiling, exhaustion pressing down on her, but it isn't enough to sleep.

She turns onto her stomach and plants her face in her pillow. It's pitch black now, but it's also hard to breathe. She moves so she's stretched out on her right side. Then she flips to her left. The red numbers on her clock shine at her, judging her for being awake. She needs her sleep. Experience shows Coach Butler will put them through a brutal practice, and she needs her energy for it.

Does it even matter?

What has her energy and effort gotten her lately? A string of losses. Her chest aches as if there's a weight pressing down on it. She pulls her phone off her nightstand and opens up her contacts. She wants to call her mom. She's always made Sophie feel better, but it's the middle of the night, and she can't wake her mom up and make her worry. Dima? No, Boston's doing well right now. He won't understand.

She scrolls through her whole contacts list and then scrolls back up again. Her thumb hovers over *Elsa Nyberg*. Before she can talk herself out of it, she hits call. Two rings in, she remembers time differences exist. It's early morning in Sweden, early enough she hopes Elsa doesn't sleep with her phone. What would she even say if Elsa picks up?

The phone rings and rings and rings.

Tears fill Sophie's eyes. They lost a lot last year, but it's supposed to be better now. They paid their dues. This isn't what her dreams of the NAHL were like. She saw herself lifting the Maple Cup the same way Bobby Brindle did. She saw herself scoring slick goals like Gabriel Ducasse. She was the hero of her dreams, the one who swooped in and transformed her franchise from a League-wide joke into a Cup contender.

But the reality is she's alone in her apartment, crying because her team is on a seven-game losing streak, and she isn't good enough to snap them out of it.

She doesn't realize Elsa's phone went to voicemail until it clicks off. She pinches at the bridge of her nose as she realizes she left an entire voicemail of her crying into the phone. Crying to a teammate who isn't even a teammate because she chose not to come. She's probably glad she stayed in Gothenburg. Their team is much better than Concord.

She sends Elsa a text—*delete voicemail, didn't mean to call*—and sets her phone on the nightstand.

She turns away from her clock so she won't have to see how long it takes her to fall asleep.

IN THE MORNING, everything is marginally better. They have another sixty-four games to play, and they won't suck for all of them. Statistically, it's impossible. But more importantly, Sophie won't let it happen. She played poorly against Cleveland, she will fully admit to it, but she'll be better tomorrow against DC. Her entire team will be.

With X out, she needs to step up, both as a player and as a teammate. When she shows up to practice, early like Matty's group text asked, they're told X has been diagnosed with a Grade Three MCL sprain. He'll be out for at least two months, maybe more, depending on his recovery.

It means Spitz is bumped up to the first d-pairing with Kuzy. It's obvious to anyone with eyes Spitz is nervous about the move from the third pairing to the first, but no one does anything, everyone too focused on their own game. There are no letters on their practice jerseys, but Sophie feels the imprint of her A anyway, and she makes sure to find Spitz after practice.

She took a quick shower so she wouldn't miss him, and she nudges his knee as he pulls a sweatshirt over his head. "Lunch at my place."

He looks up, wary. "Are we ordering takeout?"

"Are you saying you think I can't cook?" They head out together, no one paying them any mind. Normally, a teammate would walk out with them so it didn't look like they were going somewhere alone or Merlin would complain about how he wasn't being fed.

"But Witzer says you only eat healthy shit."

"We'll do sandwiches. You can make yours however you like." She'll save the new recipes for herself.

This morning, she decided today was a new day and she needed to get her life in order if she wanted to get her game in order. She cleaned her entire apartment, opened all the curtains, and went to the grocery store. She wrote out a week's worth of recipes with two new ones making the list.

Having a list always makes her feel better. Maybe it's the years of playing hockey, but instructions settle her. Planning her meals and neatly writing out all the ingredients she needs to buy at the store is somehow more manageable than trying to force herself there because she knows she should.

It's why practice, even when Coach Butler is pissed, is a refuge for her. He tears apart their play during video review, and he doesn't go easy on them in drills, but he always explains how to fix what's wrong after pointing out the ways they screwed up. Be faster, cut off the angle this way instead of that way. The directions seem so simple which is where her frustration bubbles up, when she can't do something *easy*. She has to trust the system. The results will come.

Hopefully before they dig themselves into a hole they can't climb out of.

They drive their separate cars to her apartment, and she's more relieved than she wants to admit when Spitz pulls into the spot next to her. She was afraid he'd lose his nerve and head home, but here he is, climbing out of his front seat and narrowing judgmental eyes at her. "Yellow means speed up not slow down."

She laughs, surprised by the sound, but doesn't stop because it feels good to laugh. She waves to her doorman as she ushers Spitz inside. "I try not to run yellow lights when someone's following me in case it turns red."

"Is this a Canadian thing?" Spitz asks as he follows her up the stairs. "Because in Germany you hold onto the *oh shit* handle and pray for the best."

"*Oh shit* handle? I don't remember those from my time in Germany."

Spitz shrugs. "Maybe because it was the Games? They probably didn't want to break any of the athletes. I was able to see one of Team Canada's practices. We couldn't afford tickets to an actual game, and the Team Germany practices were packed, but me and some buddies slipped in while you were on the ice. I never thought I'd play with you."

Sophie opened her apartment door while Spitz talked and led him into the kitchen, but by the time she's pulling sandwich stuff out of the fridge, he's frozen up as if he's a kid again watching the Winter Games practice. His smile fades, and he draws his shoulders up tight.

"What if I can't do it? Who would look at my game against Cleveland and think I belong on the top pairing?"

She grabs the bread from the basket on the counter and motions for Spitz to make himself a sandwich. Then she leans back against her granite countertop. "They wouldn't look at your game against Cleveland. They'd look at all the ones before it. You've played well this season. You and Kuzy will be a good match."

"I can't replace X. He's—" Spitz waves his hand around as if to encompass everything Delacroix brings to the team.

"You can't," Sophie agrees. "No single player can. It means we all step up to fill in the gaps. You'll take top pairing minutes every game and the forwards will play better defense. We'll push the other team to the outsides and make sure Lindy has a fighting chance."

"You make it sound easy."

"It isn't." She stacks cold cuts on her own sandwich. "We still have a lot of season left and it means we'll lose games and we'll have losing streaks, and we'll make silly mistakes, but we need to put those things behind us. They're flukes, not our identity."

Spitz still doesn't look convinced.

"One shift at a time," she tells him, and his lips quirk up in a smile before he smooths his expression out, guilty, as if she'll think he's mocking her. It's a hockey platitude, but there's a reason it's used so much. "We can't think about the rest of the season. Right now, even thinking about a whole game is overwhelming. We play one good shift. Then another and another until we've played a whole period. Then two periods. Then a game. It's slow and it'll be hard, but this is a team built to succeed."

Sensing he needs a break, Sophie opens the fridge. "What do you want to drink?"

"Gatorade. Water doesn't taste like anything."

She grabs three Gatorades and a water and sets them in front of the bar stools. "There's nothing wrong with water. It's neutral, like beige. Everything goes with it."

Spitz looks around the apartment, the living room walls bare except for the TV and the gray couch with two cream-colored pillows. The teal ones are hidden in the ottoman. "Your decorating scheme suddenly makes a lot more sense."

"You don't even have a place of your own," she says as she finishes making her sandwich. "You aren't allowed to judge."

"I had an apartment in Manchester. I lived with two other guys and our place was nicer than this."

Sophie arches her eyebrows.

"Decorated nicer. It definitely wasn't cleaner."

"HERE'S MY QUESTION," Teddy says as they warm up for their game against DC. "How come Cleveland is the Presidents and DC is the Founders?"

"Beats me," Theo answers.

"You're American. You should know these things."

"Like you know everything about Canada."

They're bickering good-naturedly, something they wouldn't have been doing even two days ago. Sophie's relaxing into their argument, a smile tugging at her lips when Matty skates over. Immediately, the smile drops off. She doesn't want him thinking she isn't taking warm-ups seriously.

"Seven US presidents were born in Ohio," he says. "Virginia had eight, but they don't have a hockey team."

"History boner," Merlin whispers, loud enough for Matty to hear him.

"You're from Massachusetts. You should know your American history."

"I know enough to know DC shouldn't be the Founders. Massachusetts is the only reason we even have a country."

"Oh, here we go," Nelson mutters as Matty puffs up and defends his home state of Pennsylvania.

Teddy leans against the boards, grinning, as the team debates if Ben Franklin would've made a good president and whether it would be more ridiculous for a turkey or a condor to be the national bird of America. This is exactly what their team needs, a bit of light-hearted bickering to keep them loose and remind them this is *fun*.

Once the puck drops, they'll be all business.

TEDDY HAS THE start for them tonight. It isn't Lindy's fault they were lit up against Cleveland—everyone is to blame—but Lindy bears the brunt of the loss. He also bears the brunt of the punishment. She can't help but remember last year when Coach Butler scratched a bunch of players after a bad game.

She wasn't scratched then, but Coach did scratch her later, keeping her out of the lineup to teach her a lesson. She wouldn't put it past him to do it again. But for right now, it's Lindy who is at the far end of the bench, ball cap pulled down low over his eyes.

Sophie taps Teddy's pads as he hops into the net to face a few warm-up shots. "You've got this." She knows it isn't easy for him playing backup. He only plays a handful of games, expected to be sharp on a moment's notice, and every game he's given is one taken away from Lindy. She thought she wanted to be a goalie once. She's glad she isn't.

But Teddy grins at her as if there isn't any pressure on him at all. "Of course I do. Didn't you hear? The Founders are phonies." His eyes crinkle behind his mask as he smiles.

ON SOPHIE'S FIRST shift, she bats the puck out of midair, catches it on her stick, and puts it on goal for a shot attempt which is swallowed up by the goalie. Last game, the puck would've bounced over her stick and been picked up by the other team. She didn't score but she made a good play and got them an offensive zone faceoff.

She takes her seat on the bench and Spitz bumps his knee with hers. "Good shift," he says.

She flashes him a smile. "Now we have another one."

THEY ENTER INTERMISSION tied at zero. For a team who has been bleeding goals recently, it isn't a bad start.

Sophie makes sure to sit next to Spitz in the locker room. She breaks off a piece of granola bar and offers it to him. He holds up his own snack so she nods and leans back against the smooth wood. "You had a bunch of good shifts there in the first."

"You too." There's a confidence in his shoulders she hasn't seen in a while. "It's like you said. I concentrate for a minute or so, get a break, then do it again. It's easier when I break it up."

Focusing on one shift at a time can sometimes make the game seem to stretch forever, but it's a good strategy when they're stuck in a rut like this. All she has to do is play well for forty-five seconds, maybe a little longer. On the bench, she reviews what she did well, what she should focus on next time, and waits for her next opportunity. So far, it's a working strategy.

She talks up the high points of Spitz's period, because he's still looking spooked at the big jump in minutes and pressure. She highlights his exit passing, compliments the way he hangs back so Kuzy can jump in on the rush, and she notes his good gap management when defending off the Founders' rush.

Then Coach Butler enters, and she quiets so he can have the room. He's stingy with his praise, but Sophie chooses to focus on the fact there is something to praise. He emphasizes what they did well, reminds them to continue doing it before he moves on to the improvements they need to make.

At the end of it, there's doubt lurking in Spitz's eyes again. She nudges him, trying to gently knock it out of him, but he only offers her a tight smile before finding Kuzy so he can quiz the older defenseman on how to be better.

Sophie finds Merlin who channels his discouragement into snide comments. "Oh, sure. No problem. Do everything we did then *more.*"

"We can do it," Sophie says. She notes his eye roll and the way he doesn't quite face her as he does it. She bumps his shoulders with hers, forcing him to pay attention. "I mean, unless you're afraid of a little hard work?"

Predictably, Merlin juts his chin out. "I'm not afraid of anything."

She fights her smile. "Give me a hard first shift then. We get behind their D and go to work."

"Can I invite Witzer to the party too?" Already, Merlin is looser, and they sandwich Witzer between them on the bench when they reach ice level. He nods as they detail their plans for their first shift. When Coach takes his place on the far end of the bench, Sophie talks a little louder so they don't look to him. He coaches with a mixture of guilt and fear and yelling and sometimes it's what they need. Right now, it isn't.

Matty's line secures them an offensive zone faceoff. Sophie runs through the plan with her linemates one last time as they take the ice. Then she squares up against her opponent and takes a deep breath. For their plan to work, she needs to win this faceoff.

She does.

Witzer takes the puck behind the net, drawing two players to him. He passes the puck up the boards to Sophie who battles against a Founder in order to keep possession. She absorbs a hit from a second player before she's able to work the puck free and up to Theo. They cycle the puck and generate three shots before the goalie falls on top of the puck for a whistle.

Sophie's line switches out for Peets', and she bumps his glove with hers as they pass each other. "Your turn."

He pauses for a moment before he nods and skates over to the faceoff dot. Sophie sits at the far end of the bench and her linemates sit on either side of her. "I want the same thing from you next shift."

Merlin, breathing heavy, picks up a water bottle. He sprays some on his face and takes a drink. "What's gotten into you?"

"We're winning this game," she tells him.

THERE'S LESS THAN a minute left in the period when Theo winds up for a shot. The puck hits the goalie in the chest, but he can't trap it with his glove so Sophie tries to knock it into the net. He kicks out, but she grabs the puck before it can skitter harmlessly away. She's shoved and cross-checked, and she slides the puck through a maze of legs and sticks to Merlin. He slaps at the puck, and the goalie makes another save, but he still can't cover up.

Merlin whacks at the puck again and then again. Finally, he shoves the blade of his stick at the puck and pushes it over the goal line.

Immediately, a whistle is blown. The official has his arm up in the air, and Sophie backs out of the crease before the scrum really starts. She finds Merlin and throws her arms around his shoulders. "I guess you had more in you after all."

"Are you being smug about *my* goal?"

She laughs and facewashes him before stepping back so Theo and Kevlar can pile on him.

She catches Spitz's eye as she returns to the bench.

One shift at a time.

THEY WIN 3-1, and the team leaps off the bench as if they won Game Seven in the Cup Finals. They rush Teddy's net, fighting over who can pat his helmet first. Their good mood carries into the locker room as the guys laugh and mime their favorite plays from the game and plan where they're celebrating tonight.

Witzer playfully punches Kuzy's shoulder and weaves around him and punches the other. Kuzy wrangles him into a headlock and waves Spitz over to help as Witzer tries to break free. On the other side of the locker room, Garfield and Nelson communicate in their half-telepathy, half-facial expressions code which has made them such dominant linemates. Matty wriggles his way between them and they cheerfully give him shit for his empty netter.

Sophie doesn't think things can improve any more. But X crutches in, and the entire room lights up and chants his name as if *he* scored the empty netter to seal the win. He tries to look grumpy for all of two seconds before he grins and whacks Matty's shins with one of his crutches.

She's still smiling when the media pour in, invited to the locker room today so they can see how high everyone's spirits are.

"It's only one game," Marty Owen says.

Her smile brightens even more. "It's how we're going to do this, one game at a time."

Chapter Ten

THE WIN AGAINST DC snaps their seven-game losing streak, and they board the plane for Denver, determined to put together back-to-back wins. This will be Sophie's first time in Denver since her draft. Landing in Denver International and later, stepping into the Boulders' stadium, brings back memories she's done her best to keep down.

Her draft will always be a mix of emotions for her; the elation of being the first woman drafted, the cold fear on the first day when her name wasn't called, and the hot, burning anger when she was picked last. She spent all of last year telling reporters she didn't care about draft order, she was glad for the opportunity to prove herself, but like a lot of things she tells the media, it isn't strictly true.

She deserved to go higher. Setting records her rookie season and earning herself the Maddow Trophy as the regular season point leader wasn't enough to quiet the doubters. It wasn't even enough for everyone to admit she was the best rookie. She knows Dima worked hard for the honor, but she worked harder. She always works harder and what does she have to show for it?

Right now, the worst record of any team in the League. *Seattle* is higher in the standings than them which is fucking embarrassing.

Her thoughts churn in her head as she laces up her skates. The seven-game losing streak lurks in the back of her mind along with last summer. Maybe she isn't as good as she thinks she is. She knots her laces tightly and looks around the room for X. He's been with Concord since the beginning and it feels as if he'll still be there at the end. He's the one who's seen everything, who reminds her to breathe because if he's battled through tough season after tough season, then she can make it through one game.

But X's stall is empty, and her stomach drops out on her. Merlin goes through his own pregame warm-ups, oblivious to how unsettled she is. She needs someone to help settle her. A hand on her knee or her shoulder, someone to crack a joke.

Instead, she takes the ice for warm-ups, and the crowd chants, "Two-two-four! Two-two-four!" as loudly as they can.

MATTY SECURES AN offensive zone faceoff, and Sophie's line is sent over the ice. It's her first shift of the game, and Denver counters with their top line. Anthony Sinclair, their captain, takes his place across the dot from her. He was a graduate of The Weston School, same as Hayes, and the banners in The Weston School's rink all had his name on them.

In between setting records for most fights and most penalty minutes, he scored a few goals and even managed a championship. Years in the NAHL have made him tougher, and he sneers at her as she adjusts her grip on her stick.

She wins the faceoff, but he slashes her wrists in the process, hard enough to sting. She glares at him, and she almost misses a pass from Witzer. She rims the puck around the boards to Merlin's waiting stick. Sinclair shadows her as she drifts closer to the net. He knocks her into his d-man who scowls and knocks her back.

She skates up to take a pass from Kevlar. Normally, she'd hold the puck for a few seconds to survey her options but Sinclair is right on her, and she has to make a split-second pass. It's almost picked off, but her team manages to hold on to possession. Two passes later, she has the puck behind the net, and Sinclair shoulders her into the glass.

By the fourth time he's rammed her into the boards, Sophie has a pretty good idea of how this night will go. This time, the puck is long gone, but he holds her there because he can and she doesn't have any leverage to shove him off with.

"How long until one of your boys comes to your rescue?" he asks.

Right now, "her boys" are streaking up the ice on a four-on-four. She twists, trying to dislodge the bigger player. "How long until Lenno gives up his first goal?"

Sinclair laughs and gives her one last shove before he takes off down the ice. She scrambles to follow.

THEY START THE second period down 0-2, but it isn't an insurmountable deficit. It felt like it entering intermission, but Matty preached patience and discipline, Coach Butler outlined how they can be better, and Sophie's ready for the next twenty minutes.

Her first shift is a scramble in the defensive zone. Pickard winds up at the point, but Theo drops down to block his shot, and the puck hits his shin pad and skitters away. Sophie sprints for the puck. She's the first to reach it and she takes off down the ice, blowing past Pickard and even Kirkland who dropped back to cover his d-partner.

Kirkland turns and skates after her, coming up on the inside to try to put himself between her and the net. But Merlin streaks up the far wing, a two-on-one, the kind of play they've practiced hundreds of times.

Lenno stays where he is, waiting to see which way his d-man will go. Kirkland shifts to the passing lane so she can't slide the puck to Merlin as if he's the bigger threat. Lenno pushes off his goal line to challenge her.

She dekes around him and taps the puck into the net.

"Ha!" Merlin points to her and shoulders through Kirkland to reach her. "He didn't think you could put it in."

She taps his helmet. "Thanks for being a good distraction."

"Distraction?" He puffs up, mock offended, and she laughs as Witzer and their d-men join the celebration.

THE SCORE IS stubbornly 1-2 after Matty hits the post twice. On the other side, Lindy has three highlight-reel-worthy saves, and Kevlar is living up to his name, having blocked two shots on the same shift.

Sophie's across the dot from Sinclair again, and his face has somehow gotten even uglier as he smirks. "Trying real hard to win."

She rolls her eyes. "It's the point of the game."

He leans in with a nasty grin. "I heard they pass you around after." He waggles his eyebrows, meaning clear, and Sophie jerks back, surprised. It's a mistake, because his smile only grows.

He wins the faceoff.

SHE ISN'T A stranger to people talking shit during games. It's hockey so she's been called a wide range of names and accused of sleeping with everyone from her team's enforcer to the owner of her team to the Commissioner. It happened when she was a kid and got worse when she went to high school. For some reason, she thought it would be better in the NAHL.

But when Matty scores with a minute left in the second to tie the game 2-2, Sinclair points down the benches at her. He doesn't even have to say anything. Her shoulders draw up, and she hates herself for giving him the reaction he wants.

Witzer slings an arm around her shoulders, and she pulls back. He looks at her strangely but drops his arm. "Our turn next, yeah?"

"For sure," Sophie answers. She shakes Sinclair and his mind games off. They have a game to win.

FOR ONCE, COACH Butler spends intermission talking up their game. His pride is evident as he praises Zinger for his tenacity and Nelson for his big hits. Matty's goal is given a shout-out, and so is Merlin's net front presence on hers. The room feels lighter than it has all month, everyone on board and focused for the next period.

Sophie finds another gear as she hits the ice for the third. She feels as if she could go one-on-five and come out on top. She could play another four periods without tiring. Shift after shift she plays hard, and she drags

Witzer and Merlin with her. Coach Butler taps her shoulder more often than usual, sending them out because they're the best line on the ice.

They haven't scored yet, but they're building to something big.

With 3:27 left in the game, she goes coast-to-coast and snipes the puck over Lenno's shoulder. She throws her arms up in the air and laughs as the stadium pours their hatred on her. *Fuck you*, she thinks as her teammates crash into her. *I scored the go-ahead goal.* Her teammates whoop and cheer and it's almost loud enough to drown out the crowd's favorite chant. "Two-two-four! Two-two-four!"

SINCLAIR FINDS HER on her very next shift. She passed up the boards to Witzer for a breakout, and Sinclair pins her behind her own net so she can't join the rush.

"You worked real hard for your goal," he says. He leans on her as if he can push her down to the ice. "You must really like being on your knees."

She sees red. Years of proving to herself she's a hockey player and deserves to be on the ice, years of putting up with shit other players don't have to and not complaining so she isn't seen as a whiner or a liability. Years of bullshit like this. She bucks him off her and then, gripping her stick in two hands, hits him in the face.

His head snaps back as her stick cracks against his nose.

She snarls at him, angry heated French, because she doesn't have the English for what she wants to say. Maxime Proust, the first official to reach them, looks horrified as he pulls her off Sinclair. Another time it would be funny, but he's the one keeping her from beating Sinclair's smug fucking face in and—

Sinclair laughs as blood drips down his nose.

Proust escorts Sophie to the box for a double minor.

Fuck.

She sits down hard on the penalty box bench and tosses her gloves on the floor. If only she could toss her gloves aside on the ice. At least then she could've broken his nose *and* he'd have a matching penalty. Instead, she's stuck in the box for the rest of the game unless Denver scores.

She tugs at the end of her braid, blood still humming for a fight. She only hit him once, and it doesn't feel like nearly enough.

The attendant hesitantly offers her a Gatorade.

"Like you haven't seen worse," she says. She plants her elbows on her knees and watches as her team's penalty kill goes to work.

With 1:27 left on the clock, Denver ties the game.

With 0:03 left, Sinclair wins it.

Sophie's shoulders slump as the door swings open to let her out. Sinclair makes sure to skate over to her. "Sorry for ruining your night." The stupid smirk is back. "But if you need a pity fuck, let me know. We'll be celebrating tonight."

Sophie brings her stick up again, ready to knock out a few teeth this time, when Kevlar grabs her, a hand on her shoulder and his other arm across her chest, holding her back. "Let's avoid a suspension, eh?"

He skates with her back to the bench. Garfield opens the bench door for her but won't look at her as she sits, as far from Coach Butler as she can be. There's 0:03 left on the clock, and the fans give it to her the whole time, jeering her name and telling her she sucks. She grinds her teeth into her mouth guard.

She had the game won, a rare two-goal night for her, and then she lost the game for her team. It's even worse because they'd finally snapped their losing streak. They had the opportunity to build on something and instead she undid all their hard work with a temper tantrum.

When the buzzer sounds, she lets her teammates file down the tunnel first. She lingers, absorbing the cheers for the home team.

"Come on," Matty says, tired as if he aged five years over the course of one game, and she knows it's her fault. "It happens," he says as they head down the tunnel, forgiving even though she doesn't deserve it. "Next game will be better."

If she has a next game. She stumbles on her next step and slaps her hand against the wall to keep her balance. Last season, Coach Butler scratched her after she didn't bring enough grit and compete to their game against Denver. Tonight, she brought too much. Is another scratch in her future?

Past the locker room, Coach Butler has a crowd of reporters around him. Fortunately, their backs are to Sophie so they don't notice her, even though she knows it's only a matter of time before she has to face them and explain what happened tonight.

Coach Butler spots her, though, and he glances at her for a brief, dismissive moment, before he turns back to the media. "Fournier's young and tonight she let her emotions get the better of her."

Fuck. Sophie looks over at Matty who has the same stricken expression on his face. "I'll be in the locker room in a minute," she says, shoving all her panic down until a more appropriate time. "I'm not ducking my responsibilities, I promise. I need to check in with Mary Beth."

"Yeah." Matty's shoulders slump, and he gains another five years.

Sophie heads away from the locker room and away from Coach Butler's impromptu scrum. She meets Mary Beth halfway as if the woman was looking for her as well. It's been a while since Sophie needed to be prepped for some postgame soundbites, but this wasn't exactly a normal game for her.

"Coach told all our reporters I'm emotional."

Mary Beth raises her eyes to the ceiling. Then she squares her shoulders. "Damage control tonight. At least we have your show-and-tell tomorrow. I'm dressing you, you'll let your hair be curled, and you'll smile and be nice to little kids."

Sophie nods. She hates it when they curl her hair. They do it to soften her, but she's a hockey player, not a doll. After making Mary Beth's life more difficult, she accepts her punishment without complaint.

"Can you keep your cool tonight during interviews?"

It's a fair question given her meltdown earlier but it still stings. "Yes."

"You're a hockey player." Mary Beth leads her back to the locker room. "Sometimes, hockey players lose their cool, and you're disappointed it cost your team the game, but you'll be better next game."

Sophie nods, grateful to have a game plan to latch onto. Thankfully, Coach Butler's scrum doesn't notice them as they pause outside the locker room.

"Deep breath," Mary Beth says.

Sophie takes a deep breath and pushes down all her frustration, her anger, her tears, every shred of emotion. She takes another deep breath for good measure and enters the locker room.

Chatter pauses and then picks up again, but it's forced. She ignores the stares and the glares and the indifference as she goes to her stall. She hangs up her helmet and wipes her face with a towel. She doesn't change out of her gear. If her angle is hockey player, she'd better look the part.

When the media's let in, Merlin shifts away from her as they descend. They circle around her, cutting her off from the rest of her team. She sits tall and doesn't shrink back against the wall as they push even their thin boundaries for personal space.

Marty Owen is positively gleeful as he says, "Your coach is on record saying you let your emotions get the better of you tonight. Do you think women are too emotional to play hockey?"

There are a few outraged sounds throughout the locker room, and she wants to join them but it would be *emotional*. Theo is praised when tempers lead to him dropping his gloves and coaches praise the "edge" a lot of their guys play with. Sophie knows she crossed a line tonight, but too emotional to play hockey? Seriously?

"I played some of my best hockey tonight and some of my worst," she answers. "Obviously, I'd rather we talk about my two goals, but I let Sinclair goad me into a penalty, and it cost us the game. I let my teammates down tonight. I'll make it up to them the next time I'm on the ice."

"I've never seen you lose your composure," Ed Rickers says. There's a hint of fear in his expression as if he thinks she'll come after him.

"I'm a hockey player. It happens sometimes."

"You broke his nose," Rossetti says.

Sophie tries to look at least a little apologetic. "Agitators agitate and when they're good at their job there's often blood involved."

"What'd he say to you?" Owen asks. "Does Anthony Sinclair know the secret to cracking Sophie Fournier?"

Sophie's stomach twists as she realizes he'll definitely tell his buddies in the League how he threw her off her game. Which means she's going to put up with guys running their mouths for the next month if not for the rest of the season. *One game at a time*, she counsels, as a wave of nausea unsettles her stomach. If she thinks about the whole season stretching out before her, she'll crumble.

By the time the media's filed out, her whole team has showered. They linger in the locker room and none of them try to hide the way they stare. Some of them look even more freaked out now than they did after she snapped during the game.

"What?" Sophie asks.

"I see where the 'hockey bot' articles come from now," Nelson says. "Why weren't you this chill during the game?"

Sophie's hands shake as she pulls her jersey over her head. She tosses it in the laundry bin and rips the tape off her socks. "Because I'm *not* a hockey bot. But my coach told a cluster of reporters I'm *emotional,* and women aren't allowed to be emotional if they want to play hockey."

She chucks the balled-up tape at the nearest trashcan and misses, but no one dares move and pick it up. Something is building, everything she pushed down for the interviews wants to come back up, and it feels good so she lets it. She looks around the room and almost laughs at the shocked expression on everyone's faces. Did they really believe the bland persona she projects to the media is who she is? Do they think Sophie Fournier is made up of hockey soundbites and drop passes?

"Tomorrow, all the headlines will be how I blew my fucking lid against Sinclair and how I followed it up by being nearly catatonic in my interviews. 'Hockey bot' will be the nicest thing they have to say. Then, they'll ask the same question you did."

She stares down Nelson who does his best to tuck himself against his stall.

Sophie unbuckles her padding and tosses it on the bench. "They'll ask—which is the real Sophie Fournier? Is she the hotheaded, irrational woman we saw in the final minutes of the Denver game or is she the boring soundbite dispenser? Because heaven forbid she be *multi-dimensional*. A couple good games, a couple bland interviews and everyone will be reassured."

She's down to her spandex now, but she doesn't want to take it off. She has her sports bra and underwear underneath, and she has a towel hanging up, but she's too angry to be half-naked. "As long as Denver's an exception, they'll let me keep playing." She wishes she had something else to throw. "As if Scott fucking Pearce didn't break his defensemen's sticks one game because 'it's not like you're even using them.' Or the time Justin Rust thought the official called a penalty when it should've been a dive and he speared the other guy in the dick because 'that's what a penalty looks like.'"

She's breathing heavy, another rant or two from losing her temper again. Showing her teammates a flash of what she's feeling is okay, but she can't completely fall apart again. She closes her eyes and takes a deep breath. Then another. Her skin still buzzes, and her heart still pounds, her body gearing up for a fight it won't get. But she feels calmer and when she opens her eyes, she knows she has everything locked down tight.

"Holy shit," Nelson says.

She grabs her towel and shoves her feet into her sliders. "I'll be quick so I don't hold up the bus."

SHE WISHES THEY were home so she could linger in the shower until she scrubbed the game from her skin. But they're on the road and no amount of soap will wash Sinclair's words out of her head. They troop onto the plane, and Sophie takes her now customary seat next to Teddy.

Her dad calls once they've reached cruising attitude. She stares at her phone as it vibrates, his number displayed across the screen. She doesn't want to answer, but he won't stop until he's said his piece.

She answers with a quiet, "Hello," so she doesn't disturb everyone trying to sleep.

"You have to be better," her dad tells her, anger heavy in his voice.

Teddy picks his head up from his sweatshirt as if he can hear, and she digs her headphones out of her bag. "I know."

"What were you *thinking?*" He's louder through the headphones, as if he's here in person yelling at her. "Clearly, you weren't."

"I know. I—" She wants to defend herself. Her dad's thrown punches for less, surely he'd understand, but it's exactly why she has to stay quiet. Her dad was banned from four different hockey rinks before she learned she couldn't tell him what the guys on the ice said to her. She was *eight*. The last thing she needs is for him to be banned from NAHL rinks.

"I'll be better," she finishes weakly.

"Damn right you will. You don't need to give your coach excuses to drop your ice time."

"I know." She tips her head back against the seat. She knows what she did was wrong, she knows all the consequences she might wake up to tomorrow morning. Does he really think she isn't running through worst-case scenarios right now? "I had two goals tonight."

"Which were overshadowed by your penalty. You could've seriously hurt him."

I wish I had. "Can I talk to Colby?"

Teddy reaches between them to curl his fingers over Sophie's.

"He won't coddle you."

"I know." She tries to pull away from Teddy, but he holds on tighter. "I need to ask him something."

"Maybe you can talk some sense into her," her dad mutters before Colby says, "Holy shit, Sofe."

"I know." She's starting to sound like a broken record. "It won't happen again. Has Ritchie graduated yet?"

"From UNH? No, he's a senior. Why?"

"Can I have his number?"

"Sofe—"

"Colb, please." Her voice cracks embarrassingly.

"Yeah, of course. You're going to be okay, right?"

"I always am."

Colby passes the phone off to her mom and then her dad takes it back for another lecture on anger management and proper discipline. By the time she's hung up, she has a text with Ritchie's phone number. She texts him one-handed, because she doesn't want to give up the small comfort Teddy's offering her even though she's done nothing to deserve it.

SOPHIE: *Hey, this is Sophie Fournier, Colby's little sister. You want to meet up for lunch? Concord isn't far from Durham.*

Colby and Ritchie were teammates back in high school. She still remembers tagging along to a couple of practices and the pride she felt about gearing up with them. Other guys warn their teammates off dating their sisters, but Colby warned his team to keep their heads up or she'd kick their asses on the ice.

She's trusting his friendship with Colby will mean Ritchie will help her. She can't have another slipup like she did with Sinclair. She needs to be better, which means she needs to practice.

Chapter Eleven

LENNY DERNIER, THE former player and former coach who now serves as a loud-mouth personality for *The National Sports Network's* show *Rinkside* calls for a ten-game suspension to give the League and her coach time to decide if she's a worthwhile risk to have on the ice.

She's learned to take Dernier's proclamations with a healthy dose of skepticism. He's the guy who bemoaned the end of hockey last season when the finalists for the Clayton Trophy were "two Russians and a girl." His job is to say outlandish things designed to appeal to the lowest portion of the fanbase while his cohost frantically walks back what he said to appeal to the other side of the fanbase.

She supposes it's a good strategy—his show always has high ratings—but whenever she hears him, she mutes him, and whenever she sees him, she narrows her eyes.

It's worse now, because he has a point. Not about the suspension or her ejection from the League, but she definitely crossed the line even though he's all praise when his favorite players cross the same line. Of course, she doesn't look anything like his favorite players. She's not a good Canadian boy playing for a Canadian team. She has the gall to not fit into his hockey player mold and still be good.

She puts Lenny Dernier out of her head as she prepares for her show-and-tell appearance. She's allowed to wear jeans and one of her jerseys instead of the dress she feared, but she has to sit still as her hair is curled to Mary Beth's exacting standards. She even has to wear makeup. The end result is a softer version of herself rather than the person who broke a guy's nose last night.

Miss Donovan's second grade classroom has the kids' latest projects hanging up around the room. There's a whole wall dedicated to the life cycle of the frog, which explains why Jessi has been campaigning for tadpoles in addition to the family hamster they already have.

Jessi Wilcox is at her desk, a red bow in her hair and a giant smile on her face as Sophie comes in, led and trailed by cameras. She sits up straighter and waves excitedly. In the back of the room, Kaylee's here too, because she convinced her mom to let her skip class as it was only fair.

Sophie waves back.

There's a long flat table at the front of the room, and Sophie lays her hockey stick across it and rests her skates there too. She checks the skate guards again to make sure they're secure. The last thing she needs is to be the reason some poor second grader is missing a finger.

"Good morning," she tells the class.

"Good morning," they chorus back.

"My name is Sophie Fournier and I play hockey for the Concord Condors."

"You're the first girl!" someone in the front row shouts. Her hair is in two pigtails, and she squirms in her seat as if she has too much energy to hold still.

"We raise our hands when we have something to say," Miss Donovan reminds the class.

"You're right, I was the first woman drafted into the NAHL, and I'm the first woman to play in it. But there were two more women drafted last year. Does anyone know who they are?"

Five hands shoot up in the air.

Sophie points to the girl in a pink sequined top who answers, "Gabrielle Gagnon. She's *beautiful*. And her hair is so long. I'm growing mine out like her." She twists in her chair so Sophie can see her braids, the tips of them reaching her shoulder blades. She still has a ways to go before she matches Gabrielle's hair.

"Do you want to be a goalie like her too?"

The girl shakes her head. "Whenever we play broom hockey in gym, people hit my shins and it hurts."

Sophie nods and looks out at the class again. "Does anyone know who the second woman drafted is?" Only Jessi and Kaylee's hands are in the air now. "Jessi?"

"Elsa Nyberg," Jessi says, proud. "She was supposed to come play with us this season but she didn't."

"She plays in a city called Gothenburg in Sweden. It's close to where she grew up. How many of you think it would be tough to have to move really far away to play hockey?"

Everyone's hands shoot up.

"It would be tough for Elsa too. I played against her once at an international tournament. She played for Team Sweden. Who knows what team I played for?"

Five hands go up.

"Canada!" Nick answers after Miss Donovan calls on him. "Who's your favorite hockey player?"

"Mikhail Figuli. Have any of you seen him play?"

She smiles and relaxes as they throw question after question at her. After last night's mess, she forgot she'd been looking forward to this. Kids want to know her favorite color and if anyone's ever pulled her hair in a scrum and how many mouth guards she goes through in a year. It's *fun*.

"One last question," Miss Donovan eventually says. "Lucy, you've waited very patiently."

Lucy pushes her glasses up her nose and folds her hands on her desk. "Miss Donovan always tells us if a bully is being mean, we should tell a teacher and we *always* keep our hands and feet to ourselves. How come you hit the guy with your stick?"

This second grader's judgment hits her harder than Lenny Dernier's and even her dad's. "I lost my temper. Has it ever happened to you?" Everyone in the room nods. "Miss Donovan is right, though. You shouldn't use your hands or your feet or even your hockey stick to hurt someone when you're mad. After I hit him, I had to sit in the penalty box."

"Like the take-a-break chair?" Lucy asks.

"Yes."

"Why didn't you tell a teacher? He was saying mean things to you. Miss Donovan says bullying with your words is as bad as bullying with your fists."

Sophie hesitates. Chirping, even trash talking, isn't bullying. It's part of the game. Three cameras are fixed on her, and there's a whole class of eager seven and eight-year-olds waiting for her answer. "Miss Donovan sounds like a good teacher. Maybe I can learn something from her even though I'm not in school anymore. But there aren't any teachers in hockey, so who can I talk to if I need help?"

"The officials!" Nick calls out.

"Your captain!"

"Your coach!"

"Those are all really good suggestions. Who wants a T-shirt?"

TOMORROW, THEY PLAY the Empires at home but today, Sophie leaves practice and drives to Durham to meet with Ritchie. She brings sandwiches from her favorite place in Concord. She's glad for her foresight when she arrives at Ritchie's off-campus house.

Her shoes stick to the floor as if someone spilled beer and let it dry rather than cleaning it up. The counters look as if they haven't been wiped down in months. She doesn't want to know what the inside of the fridge looks like. Sandwiches from the shop are a much better choice.

"Hungry?" she asks. She sets her brown paper bag on the counter and pulls out four sandwiches, two bottles of water, and two Gatorades.

"Always."

Sophie eyes the bar stools, all of them wobbly, and decides to stand. "I need your help with something."

Ritchie unwraps his first sandwich, and his gaze flicks up to her. "No offense but you're a professional hockey player. Don't you have teammates and shit for this?"

For a guy going on his fourth year in college, he isn't very smart. "If it was something I could ask my teammates for, I wouldn't be here. Look, I'm asking you for help, and I'm hoping you'll keep your mouth shut about it as a favor for Colby."

"Dude, I'd die for Colbs. He's my goalie."

It's exactly what she was counting on. "Let me know what your team's schedule looks like, and I'll get you all tickets to see a game."

Ritchie looks up from his sandwich, lettuce dangling from his mouth. "Seriously?" The lettuce falls to the floor. He leaves it there but sets his sandwich down on the counter near a suspicious stain. "You're not going to ask me to do anything illegal, are you?"

"I want to play some one-on-one with you, and I want you to run your mouth the whole time."

Ritchie holds his hands up as if she's asked him to do something he can't do. "It's against the bro code."

"Remember the time you bet your per diem I couldn't go one-on-two against you and your d-partner and score? And how I did. *Twice.* Or the time your team had to run suicides for every goal I scored on you in practice until your coach took pity on you and called it at ten?"

Ritchie scowls at her. "Fine. I have, in the past, thought some bad things about you."

"I know." Everyone she's played against has. "Now, I want you to say those things to me while we fight for the puck."

"Is this about the game the other night?"

Maybe he's smarter than she originally gave him credit for. "This is about me wanting to be the best player I can be." She flashes him a smile and takes a giant bite out of her sandwich.

SHE WORKS WITH Ritchie for an hour, battling with him along the boards and letting him chase her around the ice while he runs his mouth. She trips him up a few times and throws an elbow or two until he puts some heat into his insults. It isn't the same as being in a game, but she still arranges to meet a couple of times a month to keep working at it.

She's always had an analytical approach to the game, helped by her dad. He would film her practices, first on a shaky camcorder and later on his iPad. He downloaded coaching software so he could slow the video down, draw on it, even compare it to other video he had of her or players he wanted her to play like. She knows how to pick out one, or two or three, things from her game, isolate the problem and fix it.

Too slow on the draw for the faceoff? She has a reaction ball, bright pink and covered in irregular bumps. When she drops it on the ground, it could go anywhere and the goal is to catch it before it can bounce more than once. If her edges aren't good enough, she has drills. Same for her net front presence and her tip-in goals and her board battles. If there's a weakness in her game, she has a fix for it and from there it's a matter of effort and putting in the time.

Keeping her temper is too important for her to brush off an opportunity to shore up her emotional strength. It doesn't keep her from being angry which is why, after her session with Ritchie, she drives back to the practice rink and tapes up her hands for a few rounds with the punching bag.

"I thought you were curbing your violent outbursts."

She spins around, her hair falling out of its ponytail. Coach Butler stands by the doors. His arms are crossed over his chest and his severe face looks even more disapproving today as he presses his lips into a thin line.

She steps away from the bag, but there's no hiding the sweat-soaked spots on her shirt. "I am working on them. No more outbursts during games." But she needs some kind of outlet or she'll have a breakdown.

"You're a good hockey player, but there are a lot of good hockey players in our program. I want the focus to be on our team. If it isn't, changes will be made. Do you understand?"

If you're a problem, I will bury you.

It's unfair. Everyone in the League knows Coach Butler likes his teams to play with an edge. It's one of the reasons why she doesn't understand his hiring here. Boston is the New England team known for its bruising players and big fights. Concord's game has always trended toward speed and skill which is why she's a good fit for the team. She knows the double-minor she took cost them the game, but she bets if it was Theo or Nelson or even Matty who did the same thing, Coach would defend them.

"I understand," she says. She'll be better. She doesn't have any other options.

Coach Butler stays in the doorway, staring her down, until she unwinds the tape from her hands. Once he's satisfied his message has gotten across, he leaves. She's tempted to re-tape her hands and have a go at the heavy weight bag, but she won't risk digging herself into a deeper hole. Besides, while there's something cathartic about punching things, it isn't making her a better player.

She loads up a bar instead so she can squat. Her lower body strength is one of her best assets. She's difficult to knock off the puck, and she has one of the quickest first strides in the League. She uses her second hair elastic to twist her hair into a bun so the ponytail won't catch on the bar when she ducks under it.

She takes a deep breath and releases it as she stands up, lifting the bar from its resting place. Another deep breath as she sinks down. She exhales as she stands. She does it again. And again until her legs give out. She drops to the floor and the bar slams down on the spotter rails.

She sits there on the dirty floor, breathing hard. She's still there when the doors open again. If it's Coach Butler he can yell at her, she's exhausted enough she won't be tempted to snap back at him.

"Hey, I saw your car in the—are you okay?" Teddy rushes over.

"I'm fine." Stupid, because she shouldn't squat to failure the day before a game, and she certainly shouldn't do it without a spotter, but this is apparently her week for being stupid. Maybe she'll get it all out of her system. "What're you still doing here?"

"I came back to look at some tape with Richelieu. I'm starting against the Empires tomorrow."

"Awesome!" She drags herself off the floor and onto a nearby bench.

Teddy shrugs. "Lindy let in six against Cleveland, and Butler was pissed so I played against DC and then Lindy played against Denver and we lost so"—another shrug—"I'm back in net."

"Lindy isn't the reason we lost to Denver. I mean, I'm excited for you, but *I* lost us the game." And now their starting goalie is paying for it.

"I get it. Being a backup is shitty. Every start I'm given is one taken away from Lindy."

"Hey." Sophie pulls herself out of her guilt spiral and gives Teddy a sweaty hug. "You're going to crush it against the Empires. You want to grab dinner and talk about what you and Richelieu saw?"

"Only if you shower." He pushes her off him, but he's grinning as he does it. "You're disgusting."

She exaggeratedly sniffs her sweat-soaked shirt. "Smells like hard work and dedication to me."

Teddy laughs as he helps her take the weight off her squat bar.

THEY KICK OFF their home-and-home against the Empires at home. It only takes two shifts for Roesner to check her into the boards. He leers at her as he has her trapped there. She shoves him off and joins the play, banging her stick on the ice so Merlin notices her and passes her the puck.

The next time she's on the ice, it's Supinski who trips her, sweeping his stick out. She lands hard on the ice and then scrambles to her skates. He smirks around his mouth guard. "Guess my stick's too much for you to handle."

She wants to slash his stick, snap it in two to watch him flinch. Instead, she skates to the bench for a change. *Discipline*, she chants to herself as Coach Richelieu claps her shoulder, a silent acknowledgment for her keeping her temper in check.

On the next shift it's Roesner again and then Supinski. By the time she's in the locker room for intermission, she wants to break something. She tosses a roll of tape from hand to hand, wishing she could wrap up and spend even five minutes with the punching bag. She's stuck here, on the wooden bench as Coach Butler drones on about the period, picking apart their weaknesses and glossing over their strengths.

Merlin hands her a granola bar. It makes a satisfying *crack* when she breaks off the first piece.

It'll have to do.

A FEW MINUTES into the second period, Supinski loads up for a shot. Sophie drops into the shooting lane and braces herself for the sting of the puck. But Supinski fans on his shot, completely missing it.

It's Witzer who darts in to steal the puck, because Sophie's laughing too hard to do it herself. She slants a look at Supinski and laughs even harder. He skates up to her and cross-checks her across the chest, hard enough to push her back a few inches. She flicks her mouth guard out and dares him to do it again.

He does.

The second one is enough for an official to skate in, arm raised.

Concord scores on the power play; Matty off Sophie and Kevlar.

SHE TALLIES ANOTHER two assists before the game is over, and Concord wins, 5-1.

She gives Teddy extra helmet rubs when she finds him in his crease. "You're a rock star."

He taps her calves with his paddle, a thank-you, before she moves aside so Witzer can slap his back and yell.

TEDDY'S GIVEN THEIR next start, this time against the Empires in New York City. The opposing team tries a new strategy; instead of running their mouths, they take runs at her. She comes out of the game with a split lip and three new bruises. She doesn't take a single penalty.

More importantly, Concord wins 3-2.

THEY FLY TO Phoenix, and Sophie dumps her bags on the extra bed in her hotel room. It's too much effort to unpack so she digs out her pajamas and her toiletry bag. She'll figure the rest out in the morning.

Her phone buzzes while she brushes her teeth. She hurriedly spits and half-heartedly rinses before she answers.

"I'll fucking kill him," Travis says.

"No, you won't." She drops her toothbrush in its holder, wipes her mouth, and sits down on her bed. "It wasn't your job to fight for me when we were teammates and it's still not your job."

"I thought this shit would be done by now."

Me too. "At least I've had a lot of practice." She laughs weakly and Travis doesn't laugh with her. "Look, I slipped up and now every guy in the League thinks they have an edge on me. They don't. I know how to lock shit down. I've been better since the Denver game."

"Figs says anyone on our team who says shit to you gets a beatdown from him."

"Tell him he doesn't need to fight for me either. He should focus on scoring more beautiful goals from your assists. You hit fifty last game."

"Yeah." He sounds pleased, a little embarrassed, and quickly follows it up with, "But you had your fiftieth assist in your first season."

"Then tell your center to start putting some goals away too. You'll catch up in no time."

Travis laughs. "Yeah, let me tell *Richard DePalo* he needs to play better."

"Eh, I'll do it for you. When do we play you next?"

"You don't have our match-ups memorized?" Travis sniffles. "It's like all the love has gone out of our relationship."

"Because there was so much to begin with," she says, dryly. She does look up their schedule and cheerfully picks apart DePalo's game until Travis is laughing too hard to tell her to stop.

THEY PLAY A few more games before they fly to LA, and Sophie spends the night before the game hanging out with Teddy. They're stretched across his bed, a poker tournament on, because he has the worst taste in TV. She almost wishes Big Red, his roommate this season, had stayed. If she had an ally, they wouldn't be watching a bunch of dudes sitting around a table.

But Clifford is hanging out with Spitz, claiming it's rookie time. At least poker is easy to talk over.

"They call him the Goalie Killer," Teddy says, seemingly out of nowhere.

He's played every start since the Empires, and Sophie isn't about to let *Carl Alstead* force him out of the lineup. The Orca has a reputation for taking out goalies. He drives the net hard and sometimes...doesn't stop. He's mastered the art of "accidentally on purpose," and she's seen more than one goalie lose weeks of their season thanks to him. Teddy won't be one of his casualties.

"He won't touch you," she promises.

"You'll break his nose if he gets too close?"

Teddy grins and nudges her shoulder. She nudges him back. "You bet your skinny chicken legs I will."

"I'm more like a gazelle; quick and graceful."

"Quick, I'll give you. Not so sure about graceful."

"Like you're one to talk. You fell over the boards yesterday!"

"Merlin pushed me."

Teddy laughs. "So you fell with help."

"Chicken legs."

He laughs harder and slings an arm around her shoulders when she tries to roll away from him.

MARY BETH FINDS Sophie after morning skate. She crooks her finger, and Sophie breaks away from the guys, ignoring their dramatic "oohs". Theo hums the *Jaws* theme as Sophie thinks of what this could be about. She's been on her best behavior since Denver.

Did Big Red say something about Sophie and Teddy hanging out last night? All they did was talk hockey and watch poker. She knows she isn't supposed to go anywhere alone with a teammate, the optics aren't good, which means being alone in a hotel room is definitely off limits but...

"No fights tonight," Mary Beth says.

Sophie draws up, preparing for a fight right now. "If Alstead goes anywhere near Teddy—"

"None," Mary Beth says, firm. "You have a whole bench full of teammates to defend Teddy's honor. You're still on probation."

Probation with PR, probation with Coach Butler; hell, her dad's still pissed at her for the double-minor and even he has nothing on her mom's quiet disappointment. She knew it would take her a long time to dig herself out of this particular hole, but she's taken each insult and cross-check as penance. Standing by, doing nothing as guys go after Teddy is unacceptable.

Rule one of hockey is *always protect your goalie*, and she's supposed to sit back and watch Alstead take runs at hers? No.

"Focus on what you're good at," Mary Beth tells her.

She's been on a tear since the Denver game, netting as many assists as possible and propelling her team to wins. She's sitting at ninety-seven career assists, and if she plays as well as she did against San Francisco, she'll hit one hundred tonight, the first in her draft class to do it. It's an impressive accomplishment, and maybe it's the thing she needs to make everyone shut up about Sinclair, but she'd rather defend her goalie.

One hundred assists can come next game. She promised Teddy she has his back. She won't break her promise to him.

Sophie offers Mary Beth a smile, but no guarantees, and slips away from her PR manager. She almost makes it to the locker room before Coach Butler lays a heavy hand on her shoulder.

"Nothing extra tonight," he tells her. "You play hockey, it's what you're on this roster for. Anything else, and you sit."

Well, she can't shake his direct order as easily as Mary Beth's. She turns so she can go into the locker room and change, but Coach Butler's hand squeezes her shoulder, holding her still. "Do you understand?"

"I understand," she dutifully repeats.

As soon as he lets her go, she storms into the locker room. Fuck him and fuck Mary Beth and fuck the entire fucking League. Matty's never been told to sit back and let his teammates get taken out by a dirty player. And she bets Theo's never been kept out of a scuffle because he fought in a recent game.

But she's *Sophie Fournier* and the rules are different for her.

Fuck the rules too.

"Whoa," Merlin says as she slams things around in her stall. "Save some of the aggression for the game, yeah?"

Too bad she *can't*. She does, however, take a deep breath. A temper tantrum in the locker room is marginally better than one on the ice, but Coach Butler's threat still echoes in her head. She won't risk being benched tonight or finding a yellow jersey in her stall.

The team splits into groups for lunch, and her crew lingers after they eat, talking about the upcoming road trip. They fly home to play Indianapolis before they head out for their west coast trip.

"It's stupid is what it is," Theo says. "We're in LA right now. Why do we have to fly across the country only to haul our asses back again?"

"The League hates us," Kevlar says, far too solemn.

"Damn right it does." Theo slips into a familiar rant, and Kevlar's lips twitch as he tries not to smile.

Sophie makes sure to find him as they walk back to the hotel. She slaps his arm. "Two for instigating."

He laughs and drags her up to his room with him and Theo.

"I have to take a nap," she says.

He checks his phone. "You have plenty of time."

Theo drops down onto his bed and sticks his headphones in. This feels like the setup for something, and Sophie draws her shoulders up toward her ears.

"You got the Butler special?" Kevlar asks. "Part threat-part condescension but full asshole?"

"Coach Butler knows how to get the best out of his players."

Kevlar opens his mouth like he's going to argue but shakes it off. "Your leash is short tonight, and you're already angling for a fight. Let's do something about it before you get your ass nailed to the bench. We need you on the ice."

He pulls off his sweater, revealing a white V-neck shirt underneath. He shucks his pants next and pulls on a pair of mesh shorts. "Do you want to change before we wrestle?"

She looks down at her blouse and jeans and walks down the hall to her room. She changes into a T-shirt and shorts and hesitates, wondering if this is a good idea. She and Travis used to mock-fight, when they were both too keyed up to sleep or pissed off after a game and needed an outlet. This is the same thing, except Kevlar might understand where she's coming from more than Travis did.

He knows what it's like to play by a different set of rules, half of them unspoken. And if they don't live up to expectations, they might not be given a second chance. By the time she knocks on Kevlar's door, she's even more pissed off.

Kevlar lets her in and backs up until he's standing in the cleared area of the floor. He beckons to her with a crook of his fingers. "Think you can take me down?"

She narrows her eyes.

Challenge accepted.

She runs at him. She crouches to knock him off balance, but he uses her momentum to shove her down onto the floor. She twists and hooks her legs around his waist to bring him down with her. He plants a hand on the rug so he doesn't crush her. It's a moment of weakness she uses to flip them, pinning him against the floor.

He flashes a smile at her, draws his knees up, and pushes her off him. She lands flat on her back, the wind temporarily knocked out of her. He pins her with an arm against her shoulders and his knees against her thighs.

She drops her head back against the carpet and he eases up on her. "Again?" he asks.

They go again.

And again.

She's breathing hard by the end of it, her shirt sticking to the sweat on her back, but the worst of her restlessness gone. There's still a little bit there; she never beat him once, and part of her doesn't want to give up until she's won, but they have a game later tonight. Kevlar gives her a hand up, pulling her to her feet. He reels her the rest of the way in until they're hugging.

With her face tucked into his shoulder, it's easier to mumble, "They won't let me protect Teddy." She would take back the cross-check to Sinclair if it meant she could knock Alstead around the ice. She should've known she was only allowed one violent outburst per season. She'll have to ration it better next year.

"Trust the rest of us to do it then."

It's similar to what Mary Beth told her, but she doesn't snap at Kevlar or storm out of his room. He understands the position she's in. He knows how much it sucks to be held back, and he knows the frustration of battling back against a narrative. It doesn't stop her from balling her hands into fists against his back.

"Every single guy on this team will defend Teddy if Alstead tries anything. We need you doing the things no one else can do." He leans back and tilts her chin up, forcing her to look at him.

"Yeah." Her voice comes out too quiet so she clears her throat. "Set up some goals, maybe score one of my own. Keep your head up on the power play. I'll look for you."

By the time she's tucked into her bed for her pregame nap, she feels settled enough to actually sleep.

IN ALL HER worry about Teddy, she forgot Alstead has more than one target in his sights for the game. He jaws at her from the moment they step onto the ice together. He's one of the more creative opponents she's had, but she doesn't let him goad her into a penalty.

Midway through the second period, he's on a breakaway when Garfield swings out with his stick and taps Alstead's skates. The Orca goes down easy and doesn't even try to avoid contract with Teddy. He slams into Sophie's goaltender and they knock the net off its moorings.

She starts to stand up, but Kevlar puts a hand on her shoulder. She settles for grumbling and outraged swearing when *Garfield's* sent to the box. They blame the tripping on Alstead's contact which is fucking bullshit.

Garfield must think so too because as soon as he's out of the box, he grabs Alstead by the front of his jersey, and they exchange blows until they're both sent to the penalty box with matching five-minute majors.

There's a freeness to the next five minutes. She isn't looking over her shoulder, wondering where the next hit or insult is coming from, and she doesn't keep half her attention on Alstead, tracking his movements to make sure he stays away from her goalie.

They don't manage to score, but they have a few good looks. Besides, she's on the ice when Alstead's released from the box and as much fun as it would be to score while he's stuck watching in there, she'd rather do it while he's stuck watching here.

She takes a pass from Witzer and streaks into the offensive zone, dodging checks and sticks. Two players drop down with her, and they realize their mistake at the same time. One scrambles back to his defensive position, but she snakes a pass to a wide-open Merlin who puts the puck home.

She spares a glance at Alstead before she joins her team to celebrate.

THERE'S A HAIR less than five minutes left in the game when Alstead is sprung for a breakaway. He takes off down the ice, and Kuzy, who pinched too deep, won't be able to catch him. Spitz skates after the streaking winger, but he isn't fast enough.

Sophie bites down on her mouth guard as Teddy pushes himself out of his crease to challenge. He's square to the shot, his glove up and ready. Alstead's running out of space, and he isn't good enough to pull the kind of move he'd need to score. He also isn't slowing down. He knows better than to barrel into a goalie with the entire stadium watching, but...Teddy flinches and it's enough to freeze him. Alstead taps the puck into the net and screeches to a halt, showering Teddy in ice flakes.

The home crowd erupts into cheers as the goal light flashes. Teddy tips his mask up and skates away from his goal.

No, she thinks as she watches the Orcas celebrate. *They aren't winning this game. They won't even make it to overtime.* Teddy deserves this win.

TWO SHIFTS LATER, Rowan only gets half his glove on a shot from the puck so Peets whacks at it a couple times. Rumfield, one of LA's d-men, hauls Peets out of the crease which is hilarious given how Alstead's tried to make his home in Teddy's net all game.

"Fournier, you're up," Coach Butler says.

She checks the clock. They're down to 0:52.

"Don't tell me you're nervous," Alstead says, catching her look.

"Nervous?" she allows herself a smile. "I have plenty of time." *You won't even make it back into the offensive zone this game.*

She wins the faceoff and cycles around to the far faceoff dot. Theo passes across the blue line to Kevlar who passes down to Witzer. Sophie creeps closer to Rowan's net as everyone's attention is taken up by watching the puck. Witzer fakes a pass to Kevlar and slides the puck to Sophie.

Rumfield drops to block her shot, Rowan pushes post-to-post, and it opens a sliver of a lane for her to shoot the puck. She fires, and the puck skims over Rumfield's shoulder and hits top corner.

Two-one.

She checks the clock again—0:14. She taps her helmet and points to Alstead before her team swarms her.

THEY'RE HOME FOR their next game, and the crowd is raucous, even though it's warm-ups. Sophie stretches as the fans shout and chant and bang on the glass, hoping for a puck tossed their way or even a quick selfie.

She knows the seats are packed because they're finally winning again, but she likes to think it's because they all want to see her hit one hundred assists tonight. She's sitting on ninety-eight, and two tonight is within her reach. She could reach a milestone at home in front of her fans. And if she doesn't...well, Edmonton is the first game of their road trip, and she wouldn't mind hitting one hundred with Shawn Wedin on the ice.

She's stretching her hip flexors when Riley Dennison drops down next to her. He's one of Indy's forwards, and she exchanged a handful of words with him at last year's All-Star Game, but she doesn't know him, and he doesn't know her. There's only one reason opposing players find her before games. She narrows her eyes, a warning he doesn't heed.

"We're not Denver," Dennison says. "None of my guys will hassle you."

Her gaze dips to the A on his sweater, but she doesn't let herself believe him. Sinclair has a C, and he's a first rate asshole.

"Sure," she says.

Dennison opens his mouth as if he has more to say before he shrugs. "Won't stop us from shutting you out."

She laughs, sharp and surprised. He's gone before she can say anything else.

SEROV, ONE OF Indy's d-men, battles with her in front of Hyde's net as Sophie tries to screen the goalie, and Serov tries to clear her from the crease. They were two of the finalists for the Clayton Trophy last season, and tonight they lock into a struggle neither of them wins before Dennison clears the puck.

THE RENEGADES STRIKE first, flipping the puck past Teddy once he's braced for a hard slapshot.

Sophie misses a wide-open net on the next shift, but Turner doesn't ask if Sophie needs some help getting it in as they battle for the loose puck. He shoulders her to make some space and she pins the puck against the boards and holds it there until Witzer drops down for support.

IT TAKES ANOTHER four shifts, but she assists on Witzer's goal. *We have a tie game*, she thinks, laughing as she pats his helmet and is patted in return. All across the stands, fans wave signs with the number 99 on them.

"Focus," Coach Butler says when her line reaches the bench.

Oh, she's focused.

SPITZ SCORES TO give them the lead, and Sophie braces herself as she hits the ice for her next shift. It's one thing for Dennison to make promises before a game. It's another to expect him to keep them when his team is down by one and desperately needs a win. Indy's situation isn't nearly as dire as Seattle's or even Concord's, but they've had their struggles.

Serov hits her harder, slamming her into the boards so Turner can scoop up the puck.

Two shifts later, when she draws a tripping penalty, Turner spits his mouth guard out to accuse her of diving.

Normal hockey stuff.

She grins and skates to the bench to hear Coach's plan for the power play.

IT'S IMPOSSIBLE TO keep from thinking this power play could be what gets her a hundred. She's on the first unit with Matty, and they've connected enough times for her to know where he likes the puck and where he's most effective with it.

Kevlar carries the puck into the zone, dodging a half-hearted stick lift. He passes to Sophie, and she takes the puck around the back of the net. It forces the penalty kill to split their attention between her and their assignments. It isn't a big advantage, but it's enough for her to have a clear pass up to Merlin. He fires the puck on goal, but Hyde fights it off with his blocker.

She collects the rebound, defends it, and passes up to Merlin. He cradles the puck as he looks for the pass he wants, but a defender drifts up to cut off his pass to the point, and there's too much traffic for him to make a cross-ice pass. He sends the puck back to Sophie. She sees an opening he didn't, and she threads the puck through sticks and legs until it lands right on Matty's tape.

Hyde pushes off his post, but he isn't quick enough, and Matty slams the puck home.

She skates right for her captain, laughing and knocking him gently into the boards. "I knew I could trust you! Knew you'd put it in."

"Was that an important goal or something?" he asks. He laughs and then laughs harder as she punches his shoulder.

One hundred assists in 111 NAHL games. The crowd chants her name and hold up their "100" signs. Matty rubs her helmet, smiling even though she's taking some of the spotlight away from him.

When they reach the bench, Kevlar tosses the puck to Ben Granlund, their equipment manager. He'll give it to her after the game with today's date written on it so she can put it with her first NAHL goal puck and her fiftieth assist puck and her one hundredth point puck. Before the end of the season, her fiftieth goal puck will join the collection.

SOPHIE TAKES HER puck home with her and places it in the display case alongside her others. She changes out of her suit and pulls on one of her tighter pair of jeans. She debates between a T-shirt and a V-neck. She goes with the V-neck, and Zinger gives her an over-the-top double-take when she joins them at their favorite bar.

"Is that *skin* you're showing?" he asks.

"Fuck off," she tells him, smiling too much to mean it.

"Do you want a water?" Theo asks before she can slip into the booth and hide from all the offers to dance. "There's a guy at the bar who is definitely checking out your ass. I can chaperone."

"Chaperone?" Sophie echoes.

"You know, I'll make sure he checks out before you go home with him."

"What?" Nelson asks. "Sophie doesn't go home with people."

"One hundred career assists, she can do whatever the hell she wants tonight." Theo looks over at Sophie as if to ask *I did the right thing, yeah?*

But Matty's gripping his beer, obviously uncomfortable, and Nelson looks one wrong word away from springing out of the booth. "Yes on the water, no on the guy."

If she wanted to pick up, she would, even if it forced her teammates to confront how she's a healthy young woman with a sex drive. But after listening to the Sinclairs and Supinskis of the League spew shit at her for the past two weeks, she doesn't want to let anyone with a dick near her. She hasn't even wanted to touch herself recently, but tonight's different.

There's adrenaline still humming under her skin— *one hundred assists*—and she's definitely celebrating tonight.

SHE STAYS UNTIL the first wave of teammates head back, and splits a cab with Spitz and Big Red. As soon as she's home, she flips the lock on her apartment door and pulls her shirt over her head. She tosses it on her floor and pops the button on her jeans. She has one leg freed and one leg still stuck when her phone rings.

She ignores it as she strips all the way down. It finally stops ringing, and she breathes a sigh of relief as she takes her vibrator out of her drawer. Then her phone rings again. She groans and snatches it off her bedside table.

It's Dima calling which means she can't silence her phone or she'll end up with ten missed calls, six voicemails, and upwards of twenty texts.

"Hey," she says.

"Not excited?" Dima asks. "Big point for you tonight."

Normally, she loves talking hockey achievements with Dima, especially when it's a milestone she's hit before him, but she's never been naked before when he called. She covers her vibrator with her blanket. "Of course I'm excited, but I'm home from the bar and, uh, celebrating."

"Oh. Be safe!"

He hangs up on her, and she turns her phone on silent. Tomorrow, she'll call him back or maybe send him a picture of her puck. But for now she stretches out across her bed and thinks about how good her pass to Matty felt. She knew from the moment she slung the puck across the ice, he would put it in. One-fucking-hundred-assists. And hundreds more in her future.

She smiles as she skims her fingers down her stomach and sets aside thoughts of hockey.

Chapter Twelve

THEY HAVE AN off-day after Indianapolis, and Sophie takes full advantage, knowing they're about to spend the next few days in western Canada. She goes to optional skate, puts in some time in the weight room, and drives out to Durham to work with Ritchie again.

She only has a seven-game sample size, but she hasn't broken anyone's nose or even taken a retaliatory penalty in those seven games which means this must be working. They play for two hours, one hour on the ice, one hour in sneakers on a hard-top rink because ice time is hard to find.

Afterward, they pick up pizzas and bring them back to his house. He lives with some other guys on the UNH team, and they clearly don't know what to make of her. But once she puts away her fourth slice of pizza, they stop tiptoeing around her and start viciously chirping her every time she loses at Mario Kart.

It feels like Chilton and even a little bit like Concord, and it's definitely a good way to spend her day. She leaves feeling on top of her shit which means it's time to sort out her team. Hockey coaches were often once hockey players, and there's an unspoken rule you don't mess with what works. Some players take this to the extreme; they wear the same jock year in and year out until the straps wear through and some players don't wear socks because one time they forgot their socks and scored a hat trick which means going sock-less is lucky.

She isn't on the extreme side of the "change is bad" spectrum, and she doesn't think Coach Butler is either, but he hasn't given Lindy a start since the Empires. They lost seven in a row backed by their starter and they've won six out of the most recent seven with Teddy in net. The losses weren't all on Lindy and the wins weren't all on Teddy, but he doesn't want to mess with what's working.

Hot goalies are given starts.

She's proud of Teddy—he deserves every start he earns—but it's been tough on Lindy. For the past week or so, he's left every practice with his shoulders drawn up tight. More often than not, Matty leaves with him, and Teddy tracks both of them, his own shoulders drawing up.

She hasn't had the emotional energy to deal with it until now, but today after practice, she snags Teddy and drags him back to her apartment.

"It's not your fault," she tells him.

"I know. It's Coach Butler's decision to put me in. But goalie is such a shit position sometimes. You can work with Peets on faceoffs and know if the third line plays better the team will be better. And if for some reason he took the 2C spot, you'd still have the 3C. You wouldn't be stuck on the bench watching."

Teddy drops onto one of the bar stools at her island and runs his hands through his hair. "Lindy's the starter, he deserves it, but it means the moment I have a bad game, Butler's going to yank me. I'm playing because he doesn't want to mess with a good thing but once I'm not a good thing, I'm back to baseball caps and bubblegum during games. And it might not even come down to how I play. If the team sucks and I let in three quick goals, I'm out whether I had a chance at stopping them or not."

He takes the glass of water she offers him and downs it in three large gulps. "Every start I have is one Lindy doesn't. I don't want to feel guilty for playing well."

"Then don't. You told me starts were up to Coach Butler. He'll start whoever he wants. All the guilt and blame and responsibility is his. All you have to do is play the best game you can whenever you're tapped to start. Lindy won't hold it against you."

"I know." Teddy tugs on his hair. "But this is his team. I'm the one intruding."

"This is *our* team. Lindy knows it, and he might be frustrated because he isn't playing, but he doesn't resent you for it. I bet you anything he'd rather share starts with you than any other goalie in the League."

Teddy rolls his eyes. "You're reaching, Sofe."

"He's your mentor which means you're his favorite."

"I thought I was *your* favorite."

She grins. "See? Look at all these people who love you." Teddy shakes his head, but his lips twitch as if he's fighting a smile. She leans on her counter. "So, what can I make for dinner to tempt Alyssa over here too?"

SHE TEXTS MATTY to meet her early for their flight to Edmonton and makes sure she has coffee for him when he shows up. She's listened to Matty and X complain enough about not seeing their wives and kids as often as they'd like to feel guilty about dragging him away from them even earlier. But this is a conversation they need to have, and she wants it to be private. At least she can count on no one else showing up early.

Everyone shows up to practice, because there's hell to pay if they're late, but the plane is different. No one's stupid enough to miss it, but some of them cut it pretty close.

She hands him the coffee and leans back against her bag. He sits down next to her and tugs off his toque. *Beanie*, his voice says in her head. *No respectable American wears a toque.* He stuffs it in his coat pocket and sips his coffee. He hums, pleased. "You know how I take my coffee."

"I also know it's about time you get a new jock strap."

"Yeah, I'm not talking about my jock strap with you." He laughs and takes another sip of his coffee. "So, what's up?"

"Lindy's frustrated."

If he was anyone else, if he wasn't her captain or her mentor, he'd probably give her a *no shit* look. Instead, he wraps his hands around his coffee cup and says, "Yeah. One of the hardest things in hockey is learning how to deal with your team winning without you."

She appreciates the wisdom, but she didn't come here for advice. She came with a problem. Though maybe...it isn't her place to say anything? She doesn't want to disrupt the locker room or be labeled difficult. Matty and Lindy, they're at the same level as X, experienced vets. She's still new.

But Teddy being a back-up goalie doesn't make him less of a teammate, and she might only be in her second season, but they gave her an A. "Some of the other guys are picking up on his frustration."

Sophie's always been able to read a room well. It came from the painful awareness of how she disrupted it and her never-ending attempts to fit in. The first time she realized something was sour with one of her teams, she brought it up to Colby, because she was afraid to talk to her coach. She didn't want him to laugh at her for being caught up in *feelings*. Colby set her straight. Team dynamics make or break a season.

There's nuance to it, of course. Some things need to be worked out by the players involved, there are things captains need to be brought into, and sometimes there are things Coach needs to know. Their goalie situation is a mess in part because of their coach so she's hoping Matty can fix it. Teddy's uncertain, and Lindy's frustration is leaking, and if they don't get on top of it, it'll spread until the team is uneasy even if they don't know the reason why.

"Ah." Matty doesn't ask her to elaborate. "I'll talk to Lindy. He's been struggling, but he doesn't mean to take it out on Teddy. Another one of the hardest things in hockey is when they ask you to train your replacement."

Matty glances up from his coffee. His eyes are pinched, sad almost. Out of respect, she doesn't roll her eyes, but it's a near thing. "Teddy isn't his replacement. Lindy's young, and he still has three years left on his contract. He's our guy. Both of you are our guys. You signed the biggest contract in Concord's history. You and Lindy and X; Condors for life."

It's her dream too, to stay with Concord until she retires.

"Why do you know that?" Matty asks.

"Why do you know so much history shit? I like hockey facts."

"You like hockey facts." He's outright laughing at her. "Our little hockey nerd."

"Whatever." Important conversation over, she stands up and stretches her legs. "I'm going to track down a juice or something. Do you want anything?"

He lifts his coffee. "I'm good."

When she comes back, they sit in companionable silence until the rest of the team shows up, en masse as if they met up in the parking lot so they could come in all together. Nelson pauses when he sees the two of them. "How come we weren't invited to the party?"

"We should've invited you, I'm sorry. You might've actually made it on time for once."

"Hey! I'm here fifteen minutes early today."

It's a miracle, Garfield mouths over his shoulder.

"Remember the time we had to hold the plane for Odie?" Theo asks loudly.

"Fuck you." There's no bite in Nelson's words as if he knows the story's going to be told whether he protests or not.

Kevlar grins as he picks up the story, clearly enjoying the way Nelson squirms. "I can never remember, did your alarm go off while you were making her brunch or going for round three? Careful, one answer makes you a gentleman, the other makes you an asshole with poor time management skills."

"You almost missed hockey for a *girl*?" Spitz winces as if he didn't mean to talk.

"Was she hot?" Peets asks.

Theo grins and tucks Peets under one arm and Spitz under the other. "Let me tell you about the glorious afternoon."

"*Afternoon*?" Spitz asks as if he can't help himself.

"You should've seen his neck," Theo says. "I'm pretty sure she was a vampire."

"His neck? Did you see his *chest*?" Witzer chimes in with a giant grin. "He took his shirt off in the locker room, and we all understood why it took him so long to get his ass to the plane."

"I bet Butler's still pissed about it," Garfield says.

Merlin slings an arm around Nelson. His expression spells nothing but trouble. "Would you say Butler...put you in the doghouse?"

Half the team groans, and Theo loudly calls on him to be fined. In the resulting chaos, Matty tugs on Lindy's sleeve and pulls him into a quiet conversation.

THEY'VE MOSTLY SETTLED by the time they board the plane. Sophie hangs back with Spitz who's still baffled Nelson would miss hockey for a girl. Sophie, who wouldn't miss hockey for anything or anyone, doesn't get it either. She nudges him down the aisle to where the rest of the Manchester crew is.

She stops at her row and pauses when she doesn't see Teddy in his usual seat. He's a few rows past hers, sitting with Lindy. She smiles as she sits down and pulls out her headphones.

THE TWO GOALIES stick close to each other on the plane, the next day at morning skate, and again during warm-ups for their game against Edmonton. Sophie tracks them as she skates her first lap. They're both on the ice stretching, but Lindy points out Edmonton players, and Sophie can see his mouth move and Teddy nod along, even if she isn't close enough to hear what they're saying.

"Oh good." Merlin falls into stride with her for her second lap. "Was it just me or were things awkward?"

"Just you. They look fine to me."

"Huh." Merlin glance back at their goalies and then shrugs, letting it go. "Are we kicking Hydra ass tonight, or what?"

"As long as we don't chop off any heads. I heard if you cut off one, three more take its place."

"Really?" Witzer asks, joining them. "Does it work the same way with their dicks?"

Sophie isn't the only one to give him an incredulous look. Merlin stops skating, accidentally snow-showering Zinger. His eyebrows climb up to his forward. "What?"

Witzer shrugs. "They're mythological beasts with multiple heads. Why would it be weird if they had multi-pronged dicks?"

"I'm not having this conversation." Sophie claps Merlin's back. "All you, buddy." She skates over to Theo who's looking their way.

"You don't want to know." She inspects the water bottles on the bench. Theo takes a drink from his and hands it to her. She catches him still staring at where her wingers are. "You really don't want to know."

"I trust you."

Sophie takes a drink of water as Merlin and Witzer bring their conversation to the bench. Witzer waves his free hand around. "All I'm saying is this; three heads, three prongs. With some coordination, it's totally possible."

Sophie spits her water out on the ice. "I hate you." She wipes her mouth and then points down the bench at Matty. "Cap, we're switching lines tonight. And possibly forever."

"What?" Merlin gasps.

"But we're *lineys*." Witzer sniffles.

"Wait, so what has three prongs?" Zinger asks.

"Hydra dick," Witzer cheerfully answers.

"What?" Theo demands, voice flat.

Sophie pats him on the back. "I told you you didn't want to know."

THEY WIN 7-5 over Edmonton in what's far from a defensively sound game. They troop down to the locker room with a victory under their belts, but Sophie can't muster the energy to match the rookies' excitement. Big Red bounces between Witzer and Zinger, keyed up from his first three-point night. Spitz beams as Kuzy clasps the back of his neck and praises the shot block which saved a goal and set up the breakout pass for the empty netter.

"It's a start," Coach Butler says and the team reins their excitement in. "Wins are good, but you have to step it up for Vancouver. Lindholm's back in net."

Which means they better tighten up their defense or they'll hang their starter out to dry. Again.

Teddy's back in his seat beside her on their flight to Vancouver. The lights in the cabin are dimmed so guys can sleep, but Sophie's too restless. She tips her head back and runs through everything she remembers on Vancouver; their goalie's weaknesses, their forwards' favorite shots, and if there are any players she has to keep an eye out for.

At the hotel, she struggles to fall asleep. Once she finally does, she doesn't stay asleep. She wakes up every time she rolls over or stretches too far, pain blossoming from the bruises she accumulated thanks to Shawn Wedin. When she wakes up, the bruise on her hip throbs, a hot insistent pain. Her whole body protests as she stretches, her muscles tight from a hard-hitting game. She wants to turn her alarm off and sink back against her pillows but she can't.

No more sleep until her game day nap.

Only, when she takes her nap she rolls onto her bruise and hisses out a sharp breath. Then she turns on her side and her calf cramps up. She rolls onto her bruise *again* and by the time her alarm goes off she's crankier than she was before her nap.

Merlin's mouth actually falls open when she boards the bus. "Woah. You look—"

"If the next word out of your mouth is tired, I swear I will call Marissa and we'll see how you look after a week of sleeping on the couch."

The bus is silent save for Nelson's muttered, "Oh, shit."

Sophie drags a hand down her face. "Sorry."

Merlin doesn't say anything as she passes him to reach her seat. Teddy doesn't spare her more than a glance. His headphones are in, and he's halfway into his goalie zone already. She sinks into her seat with a sigh and winces as she isn't as careful of her bruises as she should be.

Fuck Shawn Wedin.

They file off the bus in their game day suits, and she summons a smile for Napoli and the CondorsTV crew, but it feels more like a grimace. It must look like one too, because Napoli nudges Bowman toward Theo and Kevlar as they try to pull each other's toques over their eyes.

When they reach the rink, Sophie takes some time to put her head on straight. She's played in back-to-backs before. She's played fatigued before. She's played banged up before. No matter how she feels today, she's played like this before.

She stops in the bathroom on her way to find a pregame snack and figures out why she's so run down. She's on her period. She raises her gaze to the ceiling. *Well, this will be fun.* She sorts herself out and heads into the tiny visitors' kitchen to find a snack.

"Crackers?" Theo asks, offering her the sleeve of Triscuits in his hand. Kevlar offers her a slice of cheese.

"No thank you."

"Cookie?" Zinger holds up a Fig Newton.

"I stopped believing those were cookies when I was five."

She sorts through the bags of dried fruit and mixed nuts, but nothing jumps out at her. She hasn't hit the "voraciously hungry" or "mildly nauseous" stage yet. She's stuck in the "everything is bleh" stage. At least her cramps are mild compared to some of the stories she heard at the Winter Games. She had teammates who can't get out of bed some days because they're so bad.

She absently knocks on the wooden cabinet even though she isn't superstitious and a stray thought won't change her biology.

"Jerky?" Merlin asks, hesitant as if he's afraid she'll snap at him again.

It isn't what she'd usually pick for a pregame snack, but nothing else looks good and it's an easy way to apologize for earlier. She takes two pieces with a, "Thank you," and sifts through the snacks again. She ends up with a Tupperware of melon and sits next to him to eat.

They don't talk, but it isn't a strained silence. She's too tired to think of anything to say, and he—well, she doesn't know his excuse. She fussily eats her melon, picking out all the best looking pieces and leaving the rest for someone else.

Everything improves once they're on the ice. Their passes connect, long stretch passes and cross-ice ones as they lay siege to Vancouver's net. They don't have anything to show for it by the end of the period, but it isn't for lack of trying.

BY THE THIRD period, Concord's feeling the effects of the back-to-back. Coach shortens their shifts and uses all four lines equally, but they're all breathing hard when they get back to the bench. Sophie's muscles scream at her as she drops hard onto her seat. She braces her arms on the boards and watches Peets' line skate out. She's running on empty, wrung out the way she usually only feels after a grueling shift.

Merlin nudges her. "We've got this. We haven't battled this hard to let the game go."

She nods, agreeing with him. If she had the breath, she'd say something.

Every shift turns into a battle against her own body. Her legs don't want to move fast enough, her reflexes are a touch too slow, and her passes stop connecting. Instead of threading the puck to her teammates, she passes it into the other team's skates or worse, onto their sticks.

As the period winds down, they stop spending as much time in the offensive zone. It's all they can do to keep the puck out of their own net, and they switch lines before they can begin any kind of push. Sophie knows she needs to give more, but she doesn't have anything left to give.

When the clock hits zero, the whole bench breathes a sigh of relief. Surviving to OT means they've earned at least a point tonight. It also means a short five-minute break at the bench until they have to play more.

"We're not done," Coach Butler tells them. "If you settle for the pity point, you're setting Lindholm up to fail."

Well, shit.

Sophie picks up a water bottle and sprays some water on her face to wake herself up.

She's rocked into the boards on her first shift out. She manages to stay on her skates, but she loses the puck and has to immediately chase.

Four shifts into overtime, she's panting on the bench and tries to summon the energy for her next time out. Her mouth guard rests on the boards so she can suck in as much air as possible. If it's an offensive zone faceoff, she knows the set play she wants to run. If it's defensive zone faceoff, the best they can do is to get the puck out and hope the next line has better luck.

But then Spitz breaks out with a burst of speed. It's dangerous for a d-man to commit, especially this late in the game, but he passes to Peets and stays up on the rush. Sophie leans forward as Peets challenges the goalie and slips the puck under his arm and in.

"Fucking hell," Merlin says.

Sophie nods her agreement and slaps his back.

MEDIA IS EXTRA-long because of the win, but most of them want to crowd around Lindy and ask how he feels posting a shutout after "an extended vacation." It means Sophie isn't the last one doing media and she celebrates with a long shower, the water as hot as she can stand it.

When she emerges, clean and her skin pink, the cameras have all cleared out. She takes her time changing, another luxury, and one she needs right now because she feels as if she's moving through molasses. She definitely won't have any trouble sleeping tonight.

"Yikes," Merlin says as he spots the bruise curling around her side. "You should ice."

She's still pleasantly flushed from her shower, and there's even some sweat pooling in the small of her back. The last thing she wants to do is ruin her pocket of warmth. "Ice is cold."

Merlin stares at her, unholy glee in his expression. Witzer stops pulling his shirt over his head. A few other guys turn to look as well.

"Ice is cold?" Merlin repeats, delighted. "What a stunning observation."

She tries to glare at him, but the effect is ruined when she has to cover a yawn with her hand. She settles for flipping him off and buttoning her dress shirt to hide her bruise.

When she makes it to her row on the plane she pauses because Teddy's in the aisle seat. She isn't militant about traditions, and Teddy isn't married to his routines, but this is new. He pulls his legs up so she can get by him. "Take the window. You're two seconds from falling asleep."

"It's a short flight." She takes the window seat so she doesn't hold up the line, but she won't sleep. It's safer to stay awake on planes and buses.

"You deserve a nap. Besides, I didn't play tonight, I can stay awake and watch over you."

"I don't—" She doesn't have the energy to lie. And, even if she did, Teddy doesn't look like he'd believe her. "Okay."

He rewards her with a smile and hands over his sweatshirt. "It's the best plane pillow I've ever had."

"Thank you." She tucks the sweatshirt against the window and closes her eyes.

When she wakes up, she's resting against Teddy's shoulder. She starts to pull away, but he shushes her and guides her head back down. "We're not there yet."

"M'kay," she says and goes back to sleep.

Chapter Thirteen

SOPHIE PULLS INTO the driveway with her backseat full of food. Fortunately, the Delacroix kids come out to see who's here, and she ropes them into helping her carry everything in. She hands one of the lasagnas to Benoit Junior who holds it carefully in both arms. Catherine accepts the salad bowl, and Sabrina darts in to snatch the bag of cookies.

"I bet I could eat them all before we get in the house." She opens the bag and peers inside. "Chocolate chip is the best kind of cookie."

"You would make yourself sick." Sophie takes the second lasagna and follows the kids up the brick walkway.

Sabrina huffs with all the judgment a nine-year-old can muster. "Maybe, but I could still do it."

Aline, X's wife, is in the kitchen with an open cooler on the counter. She looks over the procession of food and smiles fondly. "You didn't have to do this." Her accent is thick, and Sophie knows she's speaking English for Sophie's benefit.

"I had some downtime."

"Clearly." She takes the lasagna from Benoit and slides it into the fridge. Sophie puts hers on top of it. "But thank you for bringing this and for visiting."

"How is he today?"

"Grumpy." Aline closes the fridge door and taps the detailed schedule showing ice-times and painkiller doses. "He needs to ice soon."

"We're going to the ice castles," Sabrina tells Sophie. She takes four cookies out of the bag and puts them in a second bag. When no one says anything, she adds another four.

"Eight cookies are enough," Aline says.

"It's going to be really cool," Catherine says.

"Ice cold." Benoit waggles his eyebrows and laughs as Catherine chases him around the counter, threatening to slap a better sense of humor into him.

Once their lunch is packed, Aline ushers her children out of the house. Sophie leans against the island for another moment, adjusting to the sudden quiet, before she searches for X. He's in the living room, stretched out on the sectional. His bad leg is propped up and carefully supported. His chin is stubbled with brown and gray hairs, but it doesn't look as if he's cultivating a mid-season beard; rather, she has the impression he can't be bothered to shave.

His sweatpants are old and his shirt is older, the Condor on it from before Concord rebranded a few years back. He's slumped against the cushions and the lines around his face make him look like he's pushing fifty.

"Hey," Sophie says.

He pauses his show and looks over at her. "What're you doing here?"

She sits down, careful not to jostle him. "I thought I'd drop off some dinner and do some babysitting."

"Aline took the kids out for the day—oh." He rolls his eyes. "Very funny."

She grins. "What're we watching?"

"*NCIS*. There's a shit-ton of seasons and a bunch of spinoffs so it's kept me entertained. I might even get off this damn couch before I'm done with the show."

"Is it any good?"

She wouldn't mind watching a couple of episodes even if it isn't. She's used to seeing X in the locker room where he's a stable, comforting presence. He can give a speech to fire them up or poke Lindy into a smile. He's one of the few who can pull Matty out of his own head. She used to him having all the answers, but right now, he's tired. And, not in the "in the third period of a back-to-back" kind of way but a "he may not get off the couch today" way.

Sure, she has a letter, and she's his teammate, but she doesn't know what to say to make this better. She's never had an injury like this, something long term. Hopefully she never will.

"It's decent." He unpauses the show but lowers the volume so they can still talk. "Did Matty put you up to this? He and Lindy keep showing up and distracting my kids with theirs."

"I don't have any kids to bring over."

"Don't even joke about that. I'm too weak to worry about you having kids."

"It's not something you need to worry about."

X looks as though he wants to pursue the subject but then he says, "Matty tells me you've taken Spitz under your wing."

She huffs. "He's two years older than me, he isn't my kid, but yeah, I've been helping him. He was spooked by playing on the first pairing, but he's relaxed some. He was thinking too much."

"Sounds like someone else I know."

Sophie thinks exactly the right amount, thank you very much. "The first pairing experience is good for him. When he was on the third, Coach would bench him for tiny mistakes. Now, he has the opportunity to play through them and learn."

"Look at you, being all wise. Spitz isn't the only one getting good experience out of this season."

Something explodes on the TV screen, but Sophie only notices it out of the corner of her eye. X's smile dims too fast, and she's reminded of what Matty told her in the airport. *One of the hardest things in hockey is learning how to deal with the team winning without you.*

"Spitz is only holding your spot until you come back. We aren't moving on without you." *You're the cornerstone of this franchise. We wouldn't be who we are without you.*

"The team looks good," he says. He doesn't sound upset. He sounds as if he wants the team to move on without him. At Sophie's frown, he sighs. "Kid, I know you're feeling old, because you're a half year out from no longer being a teenager but this"—he gestures to himself—"is old. I was having knee trouble before the sprain, and it'll be worse now."

"The trainers said you'll make a full recovery." He's talking as if...*no.* He'll follow the plan, recover, and he'll be back on the ice where he belongs.

"I can't play forever. Look, I'm not rushing into anything. I'm coming back from this injury, and I'll see how I play. If I'm dragging the team down then..." He shrugs as if he's not quite able to say the word "retire."

And he shouldn't be able to. It isn't time for him to retire. They have to make the playoffs. They have to win the Cup, and they can't do it without him. "Did you run this by Matty?"

"He told me he was going to get me so drunk I forgot I ever had the thought."

"Clearly it didn't work."

"I popped one of my painkillers and told him they didn't mix well with alcohol."

"He had the right idea." *Retiring?* No. X is synonymous with Concord. He was the first player on the team's roster, and they're going to win it all for him before he's allowed to retire. "Aren't you sick of being stuck on the couch? Don't you wish you were back on the ice?"

X glares at her, the first spark of emotion she's seen from him. "Of course I do."

"So why are you trying to find ways to stay off it? We're stringing together some wins. We're making the playoffs this year, and we need you to do it. You've been with us since the beginning. Don't you want to see what we can be?"

X takes a deep breath and looks ten years older after. "Kid, you're the future, and it looks bright, but I don't have enough years left in me to see it through."

Tears prickle at the corners of her eyes. If she'd been better last year, then maybe he'd have more hope. She knows no one except herself thought she'd come and turn the team around in one season, but she thought she'd be enough. Instead, they missed the playoffs again. She has to be better this year. The team has to be better. They need to show X they're a contender. They make the playoffs this year, show him it's possible, then they win next year.

He's lifting the fucking Cup before he's allowed to retire.

Her phone dings with a reminder for him to ice. "I'm grabbing you an icepack and we're talking about happier things."

"Like our upcoming game against Boston? You'll be able to see your secret boyfriend. I heard his stick's been hot lately."

Sophie rolls her eyes as she heads into the kitchen. She raises her voice so X can still hear her. "Dima's not my boyfriend. And we're snapping his point streak."

"Not going to let him score? You're going to give him the ol' shutout?"

She grabs two icepacks and a roll of kitchen towel. "Did you sneak a painkiller while I wasn't looking?" She returns to the couch and arranges the ice around his knee.

X pats her head. "Remember, fight for your children to play for Canada."

"Oh yeah, you took something." She finishes with the ice and tucks a blanket around him.

By the time she takes the ice off, twenty minutes later, X is asleep. He looks more pained than he did while he was awake, as if he doesn't have to pretend to feel better than he does. She smooths the worst of the wrinkles out of his forehead and returns the ice packs to the fridge.

She sits down next to him and lowers the volume on his show.

AS SOON AS she's home, she drops onto her couch and calls Dima. "X is thinking about retiring," she blurts out.

"X?"

"Delacroix. He's been with Concord since the beginning, but he hasn't been to the playoffs or lifted the Cup. He can't retire yet. I won't let him."

"Most stubborn."

She stretches out until her toes reach the far end of her couch. She missed her nap by visiting X, and she tugs the blanket off the back of the couch as if she's ready to make up for it. "Will we ever be old like X? I can't imagine retirement."

"Still our second year. Lots of time."

"Yeah. We'll play forever."

"Even longer than Figuli."

She doesn't want to think about her favorite players retiring. "Let's talk about something happier, like how we're going to kick your ass when you come to town."

"What?" Dima squawks, outraged.

Sophie laughs and sits up, fully awake as they trash talk each other.

THEY LOSE TO Boston but snap Dima's point streak. After the game, she meets Dima for dinner, and he pokes her about the loss, and she reminds him he doesn't have a point streak anymore. They stop bickering long enough to share a piece of chocolate cake.

She doesn't know if it was all the talk about retirement or her visit with X, but she finds herself wanting to spend more time with her team. Maybe it's because, retirement or not, this won't be the same team they have next year. It won't even be the same team they have headed into the playoffs.

Mid-season trades, deadline deals, even injury, the lineup is constantly changing. For this moment, these people in the locker room are her team, and maybe realizing it could change at any time prompts her to clear her throat and say, "Surprise pizza today. The rookies haven't had it yet."

"Surprise pizza!" Theo exclaims. He pulls Spitz into a friendly headlock. "You're going to love it."

"I know better than to trust you." He wriggles free and looks to Sophie as if she'll give him an honest answer. "What's surprise pizza?"

She grins. "A surprise."

Spitz groans. Big Red throws a piece of balled-up tape at her. She catches it and flings it back at him.

Surprise pizza is a Concord tradition. The whole team piles into a pizza joint and one teammate is tasked with writing out every ingredient available and assigning them numbers. Then, a different teammate picks two, three, sometimes five random numbers to determine the toppings on their pizza.

Everyone has to have one bite before they're allowed to eat whatever they actually ordered for lunch. Sauces used to be part of the ingredient list until the time they ordered a pineapple, shrimp, and olive pizza with Alfredo sauce and Wilchinski threw up. At least he made it to the bathroom first.

Whatever expression is on Sophie's face is enough to make Spitz back up as if he can escape without anyone noticing. He bumps into Kevlar who grins at him, and slings an arm around his shoulders to hold him in place. "Our alternate said surprise pizza which means we're all in. No ducking out."

"I second surprise pizza," Nelson says. He's been wearing the other A since X went down. The two of them look to Matty.

"Mandatory pizza," he says and the locker room erupts into cheers.

THEY TAKE OVER the whole back of the place. Garfield's the unlucky sucker who has to write out all the ingredients while everyone else jostles for position in line.

"Eggplant parm?" Spitz could be asking what it is or if it's good here.

Either way, "Pizza," Sophie reminds him. It's the entire reason they're here.

His gaze flicks over to where Garfield's diligently working. "I think you're about to ruin pizza for me."

Merlin joins them by draping his arms over Sophie's shoulders and dropping all his weight on her. Her knees buckle but hold steady. She elbows him, lightly, in the gut.

"Where the fuck is our captain?" he asks.

Sophie looks around. Zinger is trying to con Big Red into something not on their diet plans if his giant grin is anything to go by, J-Rod is wrestling Kevlar for a place in line, and Kuzy and Peets are talking quietly in Russian, probably despairing of their North American teammates. She doesn't see Matty anywhere.

"Penalty for ditching is a whole slice," Witzer decrees. "We'll bring it to him when we're done."

Kuzy winces as he looks up from his conversation. "Cold surprise pizza?"

He looks even more pained after they reveal their pizza for the day: bacon, ricotta cheese, jalapeños, and green peppers. The girl behind the counter is horrified as she punches the order in, her polite customer service smile slipping after the third ingredient.

Kevlar leans on the counter and offers her a smile. "Don't worry, we won't make you try it."

"Good," she says. "I mean, no offense."

Spitz puts in his eggplant parm order as the head cook comes out from the back. His shirt is splattered with pizza sauce and there's a bit of mozzarella cheese sticking to his shoulder. He has a slip of paper in his hand, but his confusion melts away when he spots them. "You guys."

"Gary!" Theo exclaims. "You know you miss us when we're away too long."

"You and your gross-ass pizzas." He laughs and claps the counter girl on the back. "Mia, this is our city's illustrious hockey team. If any of them try to give you their number, rip it up. They're all scoundrels, excepting Miss Fournier, of course."

"Sophie's fine," she tells Gary, the same as she does every time they come here.

"And she's no angel," Theo adds. "Didn't you see her break Sinclair's nose?"

"I'm sure he deserved it." Gary follows it up with a wink, and Sophie ducks her head to hide her smile. Then he taps Mia's arm. "Send Miss Fournier's order back first."

"It's Sophie!" she reminds him but he waves and heads back to the kitchen.

Merlin groans and pokes Sophie's side. "How do I get special treatment? I'm *starving*."

"Wah wah," Sophie says.

THEY'VE DIVVIED UP their surprise pizza and made the rookies take the biggest pieces when Matty shows up with X. Theo stands up and waves as if it's possible to miss the cluster of rowdy hockey players taking up four tables.

"Look who finally showed up," Merlin says but his giant grin takes any possible sting out of the words. "Don't worry, you didn't miss surprise pizza."

"Whatever it is, it doesn't mix with my medication," X says. Theo and Kevlar shove deeper into their booth to make room for X next to them. Lindy scoffs and hands him a bite of surprise pizza. There's a little bit of everything on it, and X makes a face but he dutifully eats it.

All four tables erupt into cheers.

"Now it's your turn," Merlin says, nudging Spitz. "Big Red already ate his."

"You want seconds?" Spitz asks.

Clifford shakes his head.

"It's not so bad," Sophie tells their baby defenseman. She's already eaten her piece and it was gross but, "There are worse bonding activities. We could be breaking into the trainers' Icy Hot stash right now."

"Are you ever going to let this go?" Teddy asks.

Sophie grins and takes a bite of her real pizza.

X picks up his phone and checks something before he says, "The countdown is on. In twenty minutes, we find out which unlucky sucker's been roped into the dog and pony show this year."

"Dogs?" Peets asks. A frown wrinkles his forehead. Kuzy says something in Russian and Peets nod.

Every year, the NAHL selects players from every team in the League to participate in the All-Star Weekend, three days of skills competitions and good press ending in a game pitting best against best. In theory, at least. No one takes the weekend too seriously, refusing to risk an injury in a game with no meaning.

Most guys treat the weekend like a death sentence. They'd rather spend time with their family or go someplace warm with their buddies. Sophie went last year and loved it. It felt like validation, being chosen as one of the top players in the league. Plenty of people called it a PR stunt, recycling an old accusation as if *this* time it would get under her skin. And maybe the League did choose her to drive up ratings, but she showed up and she put her skillset on display, winning two individual competitions. She was also part of the winning team, and she was able to center Mikhail Figuli and Dima, something only possible there.

Around her, the guys laugh about what injury they'll fake to get out of it and the plans they have, but she quietly hopes she's selected again. She'll take every stage and every opportunity to prove she's an elite player.

"All-Star Weekend was my first introduction to hockey," J-Rod tells Zinger, quietly so they don't draw any attention away from the debate over whether beaches or skiing is a better use of the All-Star break. Sophie's pretty sure the skiing camp is only doing it to fuck with Matty, and she's positive once Merlin loudly speculates about snowboarding.

"I was visiting my cousins in Detroit. They didn't have tickets or anything, and I didn't even know what the sport was, but there was all the stuff going on outside the rink, you know? There were goalie simulations and the slapshot competitions and there were like five mini-rinks set up. We went the first day and waited forever in line, and I thought it was such bullshit until someone put a crappy hockey stick in my hands and told me to see how hard I could hit the puck."

"Then you were a stud?" Zinger asks.

J-Rod laughs. "Completely whiffed. Swung as hard as I could and landed on my ass. A couple of the kids behind me in line laughed but the guy running it showed me how to hold the stick and then how to make sure I hit the puck. I didn't hit it very hard even after the lesson. But it turned out Remi Corcoran taught me how to shoot a puck."

"No fucking way." Zinger looks impressed.

"And I didn't even have a clue." J-Rod laughs again. "But he took a picture with me and signed my shirt, and I went back to the desert convinced I was going to be a hockey player when I grew up. My mom called to yell at my aunt, but she signed me up for lessons. I keep hoping they'll let Phoenix or Santa Fe host the All-Star Game so more kids like me can see how awesome hockey is."

"Maybe next year."

"I think Edmonton and Winnipeg are making bids to host it."

"Then the year after. It'll give you some time to shore up your game so you get invited."

"You're so full of shit." J-Rod throws an ice cube at him. Zinger catches it and drops it in his nest of used napkins.

"Maybe we'll play a preseason game in Taiwan or something, and I can invite my family to come watch."

J-Rod holds his glass of water in a mockery of a toast. Zinger clinks their glasses together and Sophie goes back to her pizza before they catch her eavesdropping.

X INSISTS EVERYONE turn their phones face-down on the table and give him a drumroll before he opens the 2013 NAHL All-Star selections. "Mikhail Figuli from Milwaukee, no surprise there. Justin Rust from Minneapolis, yawn. Farage from Cleveland but not Hayes, no hometown pity pick this year. Ooh, Ivanov's going, your Boston beau." He winks at Sophie. "Dubs too. Good guy, good d-man."

Matty snatches X's phone away from him. "Last time we played Boston, you cursed him and every ancestor he has."

"Give me back my phone!"

Matty bats X's hands away. "You're taking too long, and I want to know if I have to reschedule my vacation plans." He scrolls through the list. "Sofe, I hope you didn't book any flights."

"My weekend's open."

Matty flashes her a smile and turns to Garfield. "I hope yours is too."

All the color drains from Garfield's face. "Are you joking? I'm taking Josie to the Bahamas. I'm *proposing*. If the NAHL fucks this up I swear—"

Matty bursts into laughter and Garfield growls before he throws his greasy napkins at him.

"You're proposing?" Kuzy asks. "Congratulations."

"About damn time," Nelson mutters.

"Shut up." Garfield's cheeks are flushed pink. "And don't say anything. I want her to be surprised."

"Of course." Nelson claps Garfield on the back and then looks around the table, his glare a promise there will be hell to pay for anyone who leaks Garfield's plans.

The moment's broken when *All Star* by Smash Mouth blares loudly over the speakers. Gary emerges from the kitchen to wave his dishrag like a victory towel, and Sophie can't help but laugh and give him a thumbs-up.

Chapter Fourteen

THERE'S STILL SOME hockey to be played before it's time for the All-Star Weekend so Sophie puts her excitement aside and focuses. They fly to Atlanta where Sophie scores a beauty of a goal which ends up as the game winner. The Atlanta crowd boos her off the ice.

"They're not going to forget or forgive you," Merlin says as they troop down to the locker room.

Sophie grins, flushed with the win. "Maybe I'll pull the same move in the shootout competition."

"I fucking dare you."

"Like hell am I doing the shootout competition." It's one of the more popular events at the All-Star Weekend, because it's showy. There will be plenty of people wanting to do it, and Sophie would rather do something more in line with her skills. Speed work, stick work, showing off her edges; she'll excel in those competitions.

"For me?" Merlin bats his eyelashes and she laughs and shoves him into the locker room.

"Put your face away. No one wants to see it."

"Ooooh," Kevlar choruses.

"Roasted," Theo adds.

Sophie rolls her eyes, but she smiles as she strips out of her gear.

AFTER ATLANTA THEY fly home and lose to Montreal before beating Orlando. Their last game before the Christmas break is up in Quebec. They fly out tonight and play tomorrow, an afternoon game so everyone can start their celebrations early.

When she comes home from practice, she has another package slip. Her parents are bringing their presents when they fly down so she doesn't know who sent her something, but she goes downstairs to find out.

It's another flat, cardboard box.

And, when she opens it, it's a landscape with melting clocks everywhere, and she recognizes the painting even if she doesn't remember what it's called. She carries it into Elsa's room and then calls the woman herself.

"You got my present?" Elsa asks when she picks up.

"What is this?"

"It's a Dali. I like the melting clocks, they help me fall asleep."

There's an empty space on the wall across from Elsa's bed, the perfect place to hang the painting. Her parents are coming down for Christmas so she could ask her dad to help her hang it up but—*no*. She won't get carried away again.

The last time Elsa sent Sophie a painting, she told Sophie it was a promise. She can't go through this again. She's worked hard to put her team back on track after a disastrous start to November and a key injury to their lineup. She's fought to keep her emotions calmer after her blowup against Sinclair, and this won't help.

She leans the painting against the wall and shuts the door to Elsa's room on her way out. "You need to stop."

"Stop?" Elsa's voice wavers, unsure.

"Sweden's far away and it isn't getting closer. I understand why you stayed in Gothenburg. And I can't—I *won't*—ask you to give up your family and your team. Don't ask me to get my hopes up again."

Elsa's silent for so long Sophie checks to make sure the call hasn't dropped. Guilt curdles in her stomach. She didn't mean to upset her, but Sophie needs to set boundaries. She was so excited when Elsa was drafted. Elsa choosing to stay in Sweden didn't occur to Sophie while she was picking out furniture and bedspreads and planning what it would be like to have a roommate and dreaming of the goals they'd score together.

"Next year," Elsa finally says. "No matter what Mamma says. I want to play with you."

"Sure," Sophie says but she doesn't let herself believe.

ELSA ISN'T IN the NAHL right now, she isn't even in North America, but she wasn't the only woman drafted last year. Gabrielle Gagnon was drafted too and while she isn't in the NAHL either, she is playing for the Trois-Rivières Bobcats. Sophie looks up their schedule, and they play an evening game, the same day Concord plays their afternoon game in Quebec.

She glances at Elsa's closed door and makes her plans. She cleans her apartment, makes a trip to the grocery store to stock up in case her family makes it here before she does, and heads to the airport to meet up with her teammates.

"Do you think Coach Butler will let me arrange my own flight home?" Sophie asks Teddy.

"A bunch of us already have. I thought your parents were flying to you, though?"

"Gabrielle's starting tomorrow for Trois-Rivières. If I left after our game, I could make it to hers in time for puck drop."

"Road trip? I'm in."

"Aren't you going to see your family?"

"Yeah but I'm driving and it isn't far. Besides, I've heard you speak French. You won't make it out of the rental agency without help, and I've volunteered myself. Besides, I need to scout my competition for your favorite goaltender."

"She'll probably be my goalie at the next Winter Games, but you're mine forever."

In two years, the top athletes in the world will compete in Helsinki. Sophie played in her first Games in Stuttgart, and she expects to be invited back for Finland. She expects Gabrielle to be there too. She put up an unreal performance at the U-Tourneys last year, and even if Quebec's front office can't see it, Sophie knows she's the future of Canadian goaltending. She tracks the puck better than any goalie Sophie's seen before.

At the draft, management told Sophie if Gabrielle was still available, they'd draft her. Quebec snapped her up instead which means Sophie will only have a chance to play with her when they're representing their country.

When they board the plane, Teddy taps Matty's shoulder. "Sophie's not coming back on the team plane." They move on before Matty's even looked up from his crossword.

"Don't I have to tell Coach Butler?"

"Matty's not as grumpy as Butler. Did you hear him barking at practice yesterday? *Someone's* not in the holiday spirit."

Teddy slides into the window seat in their row and Sophie drops down next to him. "Maybe he's in the spirit of the Grinch."

"I would fucking believe it after those sprints he made us skate the other day. His heart is definitely three sizes too small." Teddy pulls his iPad and his headphones out of his bag before tucking the bag under the seat in front of him.

"The upcoming breaks mess with the schedule." The end of December and start of January is all start-stop with the time off for various holidays and the All-Star weekend. They struggled to find consistency through this stretch last season, and Coach Butler's only trying to keep the same thing from happening this year.

Teddy holds his headphone splitter out to Sophie. "We're watching *The Grinch*."

"Jim Carrey freaks me out," she says even as she digs her own headphones out.

Teddy pats her shoulder but still cues up the movie.

IT TAKES OVERTIME for them to beat Quebec, and Coach Butler stands in front of them in the locker room, seething. Sophie tucks herself deeper into her stall. Whenever he's too angry to yell right away it means he's really pissed.

"Get your shit together over the break," he finally says. "Be ready to play on the 27th. If this is the effort you bring, it'll be the last game you play until the new year."

She's never had a coach make use of scratches the way Coach Butler does. She should ask Dima if Boston does it the same way. Sophie was briefly scratched last season, and the fear she'd blown her chance to play in the NAHL was enough to make her clean up her game.

But they weren't bad tonight. It certainly wasn't their best game, but there weren't any egregious turnovers. Lindy didn't let in any soft goals, and there wasn't a lack of effort. Coach Butler has yelled at them plenty tonight, but he hasn't told them what they did wrong. How are they supposed to solve a problem if they don't know what the problem is?

Coach Butler stares Matty down, placing the responsibility of the team on their captain's shoulders, before he walks out.

Fuck.

Sophie pulls her jersey over her head and drops it in her stall. The bubbling excitement over the win and everyone's plans for the holiday has evaporated with Coach's scolding. She's not sure she's seen a locker room so sullen after a win.

Media is short, because they have holiday plans too, and after Sophie's done, she tucks her wet hair under her toque and meets up with Teddy.

"Told you it was safer to go through Matty," he mutters.

Yeah, she's glad she doesn't have to talk to Coach again until after their break.

"You ready for our road trip?" she asks.

"I'm driving and picking the music."

"No country."

"Duh. We're listening to Christmas carols."

THEIR ONLY OPTIONS for clothes were their game day suits and Condors gear, which means Sophie shows up to Quebec's minor league game in a T-shirt with her name and number on the back. Teddy at least had a general long-sleeve. Sophie has a ball cap on and hopes it'll be enough for her to pass as a fan.

"Fucking punks!" a drunk fan shouts as they look for their seats. "Go back to fucking America!"

"You should've brought your Bobby Brindle jersey," Teddy whispers.

"Then they'd be throwing punches. Besides, it's from when I was a kid. It wouldn't fit me."

They take their seats, only a handful of rows back from the glass. On their left is a young girl and her father. Sophie elbows Teddy as they sit down. "Make sure you watch your language."

Teddy glances over at the girl and nods. "Okay, *Mom*."

She elbows him hard enough for him to grunt. She smiles angelically when he glares at her.

"It's okay," the girl says as Sophie sits next to her. She's in a Bobcats T-shirt, and she has a dozen clips holding her hair back. They're all bedazzled and catch the light every time her turns her head. "I know all the bad words. In English *and* French."

"You must go to a lot of hockey games then," Teddy says.

The girl's smile falters. "We go to Trois-Rivières games sometimes. I asked Santa if I could go to a Quebec game this year, but there are a lot of kids in the world, and sometimes Santa runs out of money before he reaches our house."

The girl's dad shoves his hands into his pockets and carefully doesn't look over at them. Sophie's family didn't grow up with a lot of money. Her dad's parents were the ones who took them to hockey games and bought her her Brindle jersey. Her parents wouldn't have been able to afford Sophie and Colby both playing hockey if her *mémé* and *pépé* didn't help. Sophie took care of her equipment to make it last as long as possible, because Christmas was the only time she'd get new gear.

The girl plays with her hair, twisting it up in the style Gabrielle prefers before letting it drop back down. Sophie does a mental check of their schedule. "Would you like to go to a Quebec game in March? The Concord Condors come to town on the 3rd."

Now the dad looks over. "Lady, if this is a joke—"

"It's not," Sophie promises. She pulls out her phone and opens ticket sales for the Quebec-Concord game. She turns the phone so the girl and her father can see as Sophie navigates the site. "Okay, so you and your dad. Is there anyone else in your family? Mom? Brother or sister?"

"I have a mom and a little brother, but they don't care about hockey." The girl glances at her dad as if she wants to know if she gave the right answer.

Sophie buys four tickets. "Where should I send these?"

"You—" The guy shakes his head but types his email in.

"Will you be there?" the girl asks. She tugs on the sleeve of Sophie's shirt. "Are they your favorite team or something?"

"I will be there. Maybe I'll even see you." Sophie bought them tickets near the glass so she can find them during warm-ups. The girl probably won't remember her by then, and she certainly won't be there cheering for Concord but it's okay.

"I'm Estelle. You're really nice for a stranger." Introductions half-done, the girl throws herself into Sophie's lap so she can hug her.

"Oh, um, nice to meet you." Sophie awkwardly pats her back until Estelle slips back into her own seat again."

The dad clears his throat. "Yes, thank you, Miss…"

Aware of the FOURNIER stamped across her back, she says, "It's Sophie."

Teddy laughs himself silly next to her, and he only laughs harder when Sophie elbows him to try to shut him up.

"How come you're here in Concord stuff?" Estelle asks. "We're playing Sherbrooke tonight, not Manchester."

Teddy continues to laugh and Sophie decides to ignore him. "We're big Concord fans. I grew up a Montreal fan, though."

Estelle scrunches up her nose. "You're not cheering for Sherbrooke, are you?"

"Definitely not. We're here to see Gabrielle play."

It's the right answer, because Estelle lights up. "She's the best. She's my favorite player in the whole world." The players pour onto the ice for their warm-ups and Estelle taps Sophie's arm. "Do you want to come bang on the glass with me? Sometimes, if you're loud enough, the players notice you."

It's a terrible idea. There's a chance they won't be noticed if they stick to their seats and Sophie keeps the brim of her cap tipped down. Standing at the glass will definitely get her noticed and will probably end in at least a dozen pictures of her up on Twitter. But Estelle's wiggling in her seat, anxious to go, and Sophie's not very good at saying no.

"As long as your dad's okay with it."

"He is!" Estelle leaps out of her seat and grabs Sophie's hand. "Come on, we don't want to miss Gabrielle!"

Sophie's tugged down to ice level. Estelle presses her face against the glass, but she doesn't bang on it until Gabrielle skates toward them. The goalie's in her pads, but she isn't wearing her helmet yet, and Estelle pounds both her fists and calls out Gabrielle's name.

Gabrielle spots Estelle first and then Sophie. She comes to a dead stop, snow-showering one of her own teammates. The guy grumbles and wipes the water off his face. Then he looks up and his mouth falls open.

Sophie gives an awkward two-fingered wave.

Estelle jumps up and down, delighted Gabrielle's stopped, and Gabrielle skates over until she can tap her paddle against the glass, right where Estelle's face is. Estelle squeals and launches into French too fast for Sophie to keep up with.

Eventually, Gabrielle has to finish her warm-up, and Sophie and Estelle return to their seats. Estelle throws herself into her dad's lap as soon as they're there. "Gabrielle noticed me! This is the best game ever! Thank you!"

SOPHIE CAN'T REMEMBER the last time she watched a hockey game to enjoy it. This isn't a tape to review for a scouting report, this isn't her own game to pick apart. She splits a bag of popcorn with Teddy, but she forgets about it when a play in the defensive end takes all her attention.

The Bobcats have numbers back, but they lose track of their coverage and the Mammoths set up in their zone without a problem. Gabrielle squares up to the shooter and bats the puck away when it comes at her. Her teammates fail to clear the puck and she has to fight off another shot.

Another failed clearing attempt leads to one of the Mammoths' defensemen taking a monster of a shot from the point. There's a Mammoth planted in the crease, and he whacks Gabrielle with his stick as she tries to make the save. Instead of catching the puck in her glove, she bobbles it. It lands on the ice, and as she tries to cover it up her own teammate, while trying to clear the Mammoth out of the crease, knocks her out of position. A second Mammoth player finds the loose puck and tries to stuff it home. Gabrielle kicks out her pad to block the initial shot and throws herself down on top of the puck.

"Holy shit," Teddy breathes, reverent. "You were right."

"Future of Canadian goaltending," Sophie says.

THE GAME ENDS in a shutout for Gabrielle despite her team's defensive failings. Once it's over, she tips her mask off her face as her teammates swarm her to give her head pats. Then she looks over at where Sophie had stood during warm-ups. She doesn't look for where Sophie is now, but the message is clear.

"We've been summoned," Teddy whispers.

Sophie says goodbye to Estelle and her dad. She and Teddy head into the bowels of the stadium to find the locker room. It doesn't take long before they're stopped by a haggard employee with a "STAFF" lanyard. Sophie would guess he's a college intern, and he puffs himself up to block their way.

"Don't make me call security," he says.

There had been four brawls in the stands during the game, proving the Montreal-Quebec rivalry begins early. Sophie isn't trying to make this guy's night any harder so she smiles as she takes off her ball cap and says, "I'm looking for Gabrielle."

As far as big reveals go, it's anti-climactic, because the guy doesn't recognize her. "You and everyone else in this building. Look, whatever you're offering, she isn't interested."

"People have been harassing her?"

The guy rolls his eyes. "She's hot as fuck, of course people are bothering her." At Sophie's glare, he holds up his hands. "Not *me*. I, of course, respect her greatly and would never look at her too long and—do I need to call security?"

Their standoff is interrupted when a man in a full suit rounds the corner. He gestures at the kid with his clipboard. "Jeremy, there you are! Where the fuck have you been?" He notices Sophie and coughs. "Uh, pardon my language, ma'am."

Sophie ignores Teddy's laughter. "Ma'am isn't necessary. I prefer Sophie Fournier."

The kid—Jeremy—shakes his head. "You have got to be fucking kidding me."

"I was hoping to see Gabrielle before I have to fly back to Concord," Sophie tells the man in the suit.

"Of course. I'm Brett Meyers, assistant coach for the Bobcats."

"Nice to meet you. This is Teddy Augereau, one of my teammates."

Meyers leads them down the hall and stops outside the locker room. "Wait here, I'll make sure everyone's decent."

"Because we've never been in a locker room before," Teddy mutters.

Sophie elbows him—even though it hasn't shut him up the past four times she's done it tonight. The next time he volunteers to road trip with her, she'll remember he's doing it so he has a front row seat to making fun of her.

"The Fournier VIP experience is fun," he adds. "We should do this more often."

"Never again."

Gabrielle emerges from the locker room, somehow regal in her Under Armour. Her face is flushed from the game, but it doesn't make her look like an angry tomato the way Sophie always does. Her hair is still in the elaborate crown she does for games, not a single strand out of place. Honestly, Sophie finds her a little intimidating.

"What are you doing here?" Gabrielle asks.

"We were in the area, and I wanted to see you play. Do you want to grab dinner before we have to head home?" Maybe this was a mistake. They don't know each other so Sophie wasn't expecting Gabrielle to be friendly but this is borderline hostile.

"I need to shower. Can you wait?"

"Of course," Sophie answers.

Gabrielle looks between them as if they're a puzzle to be solved before she goes back into the locker room. Sophie doesn't breathe again until the doors close behind her.

"She's, uh, kind of intense," Sophie says.

Teddy barks out a laugh. "No fucking shit."

GABRIELLE WARMS UP during dinner which Sophie attributes both to good food and the steady stream of goalie talk. She and Teddy discuss positioning and share horror stories, and she relaxes the more the meal goes on as if she realizes this wasn't some kind of trick or trap.

They're nearly done when she glances at Teddy's empty glass of water. "You should use the bathroom so you don't have to make five stops on your way to the airport."

Teddy lifts his eyebrows as if he's going to protest. Then he shrugs. "I could take a piss."

Once he's out of earshot, Gabrielle fixes Sophie with an inscrutable goalie stare. "Why are you here?"

"Our schedules lined up and I wanted to see you play."

"You wanted to see me play?"

Sophie feels judged or maybe accused, and she squirms in her seat even though she hasn't done anything wrong. "It's you and me in the League. I want to support you as much as I can." Maybe next year Elsa will come over and maybe at this upcoming draft more women will be drafted but it isn't a guarantee.

She braces herself for another dismissal, but Gabrielle breaks their eye contract as she says, "It's lonely sometimes."

"My teammates are great, but they don't always get it."

"I spend all this time training them only for them to be called up or traded. Do you know how many times I've had to tell them not to touch my hair?"

"The first time I ordered chocolate cake at a restaurant they shied away, because they thought I was on my period."

"Idiots."

Speaking of her idiots, Teddy should be back by now. She glances around the room, and a smile tugs at her lips when she sees him chatting with the bartender.

"Did he get lost?" Gabrielle asks.

"I think he's giving us space. They do try. But sometimes...this was nice."

Teddy spots her looking and takes it as his cue to wander back over.

"I have a phone," Gabrielle says. "You can call me."

Sophie's smile grows as they exchange phone numbers.

IT'S LATE ENOUGH when Sophie lands in Manchester for her to consider napping on one of the airport couches, but she knows her mom would be able to tell. Instead, she drives home and sleeps long enough to be functional but not personable.

She wears her ball cap tipped low, because she doesn't want to talk to any fans while she's half-asleep and grumpy. Her mom, of course, takes her hat off after hugging Sophie. She tsks at the dark circles under her eyes. "You're not driving home. You look exhausted. Give your father your keys."

Her dad waits until he has her keys to ask, "Late night?" with enough derision in his tone for her to know pictures have been posted of her at the Trois-Rivières game last night.

She itches to take her keys back. It's not like she has a game today or even a practice. She's on her Christmas break, and if she wanted to spend the first few hours of it watching a hockey game it's her choice. She doesn't need to defend herself. She still jams her hands into her pockets and says, in her bland media voice, "It's important to support the other women in the League."

"If she makes it, she'll be your competition. You should be focused on your game."

"Elsa's going to be my teammate. Does that mean I can support her?"

"If she ever comes over."

He's always been able to cut at her without even trying.

COLBY'S QUIET THE whole way home. He doesn't even sing along when her mom finds the radio station with Christmas carols. It takes Sophie most of the drive to realize he isn't being quiet because he's tired like her but because something's wrong. She waits until they're home and her parents are unpacking in the guest room to corner him in the kitchen.

"Is everything okay?" she asks.

"Shayna and I broke up."

Sophie isn't prepared to be comforting, and she scrambles for something appropriate to say. All she comes up with is, "Sucks."

He shrugs. "We both knew it wasn't working, but I thought if we tried a little harder then maybe...I still gave her her Christmas present. I wasn't sure what else to do with it. I shouldn't be bringing you down."

"You can talk to me." They've always been close, but it's been harder to keep in touch since she made the jump to the NAHL. There's a million different demands on her time, and she feels guilty for not making more of an effort. "Hey, why don't you come down for a week at the end of January or February? We can hang out, and I'll introduce you to the guys. I'm sure they'd take you to a bar and get drunk with you or whatever it is people do when they break up."

"Hopefully I'll be past that stage by then but sure. I have some vacation time I can use."

"Vacation?" their mom asks, coming into the kitchen. "Are you going somewhere?"

"I'm visiting Sofe for a week."

"No!" their dad calls from the guest room.

Sophie narrows her eyes, a bit of fight still left over from the airport this morning. "You're coming. It should be the week we play Philly. Ritchie and the UNH guys are driving down for the game. You can sit with them and heckle all the Falcons."

"Ritchie's coming to a game?"

Colby looks like he has a dozen questions so Sophie opens the fridge. "Who's hungry? I have a ton of food."

THERE'S A FAMILY and Friends skate on the 26th, and Sophie laces up and hits the ice, because even if it isn't a formal practice, it's nice to be able to skate. The team kitchen is full of hot chocolate and pastries, things not on their diet plans but the kids will be happy. She's pretty sure she saw Nelson's nephew with two munchkins covered in snowflake sprinkles when she stopped in to grab a Gatorade.

The ice is full of her teammates and their families, and she only feels a small pang as she skates her first lap. Yesterday morning, her mom made blueberry pancakes and they ate around her island counter before opening presents. She drove them to the airport yesterday afternoon and now her apartment feels too empty with only her in it.

"Where's your brother?" Teddy asks as he falls into stride with her.

"Back home. They left last night." Her attention is caught by X, sitting in a sled as his kids try to pull him around the ice. She laughs as Benoit Jr. grunts and pulls harder.

"You spent Christmas alone?"

Sophie rolls her eyes. "Hardly. I spent Christmas Eve and morning with them. And you're one to talk. I thought you stayed in Canada."

"I spent half of Christmas with my family, now I'm spending the second half with Alyssa's. Her parents flew in to visit, and I was told I wasn't allowed to hide in Canada the whole time. But I'm still with family."

Sophie looks around. X tells Benoit Jr. to put his back into it and laughs as Sabrina plops herself down on his lap, tired of trying to pull the sled. Witzer and Zinger are play-fighting as Kevlar's niece blows her whistle and tries to give them each five-minute majors. On the other side of the ice, Lindy's in goal in all his pads so the older kids can practice their shots.

"So am I," she says.

Teddy waves his girlfriend over. Alyssa brings Marissa and Merlin with her. As soon as she's in reach, Teddy winds an arm around Alyssa's waist and pulls her closer. "Did you know Sophie's family is already back in Thunder Bay?"

Sophie glares at her goalie and then glares harder when Alyssa says, "You'll have to have dinner with us tonight."

"And your parents?" Teddy asks.

"We can host dinner tonight," Marissa volunteers. "Jeff's parents left last night, and his dad bought the biggest roast you've seen. But if you don't want leftovers—"

"It sounds perfect," Alyssa says. "We'll bring a bottle of wine."

It almost makes her dizzy as they plan but by the end of it, it's decided Sophie's coming over for dinner and she doesn't have to bring anything. She'll bring the gingerbread cookies her mom baked yesterday, because she certainly isn't showing up empty-handed, and she can't eat all those cookies on her own.

Chapter Fifteen

THEY LOSE FOUR of their six games between Christmas break and the All-Star break, including back-to-back losses to close out the stretch. Sophie's glad to escape Concord and fly down to Atlanta.

Last year, the Commissioner made a big deal about Sophie during the All-Star Weekend, because she was the first woman drafted into the League. This year, he schedules as many photo-ops and press availabilities, because she's the only woman in the League. When she first sees her schedule, crammed as full as possible, she snaps a picture and sends it to Gabrielle.

SOPHIE: *Looking forward to some help with this.*

Gabrielle sends back a picture of her in goal, her mask covering her face. Sophie laughs and tucks her phone away so she can change for her first event.

By the time she makes it to the draft, in her third outfit of the day, her feet ache because her stylist forced her into heels. She's in sneakers now at least, but she sits next to Dima and pouts as she leans against his side.

"You're already tired?" Dubya asks.

"The Mayor of Atlanta staged a street hockey game with the local Girl Scouts. I'm exhausted."

Dima laughs and pats her head. "Hard to be so famous."

She jabs him viciously in the side and he yelps and jabs her back.

"Children," Dubya sighs.

Riley Dennison joins their table, and he lifts his opaque water bottle in a toast. "To the players on shitty teams who still get stuck in this farce."

Dubya laughs. "Speak for yourself. We're good enough to have two of us." He glances at Sophie. "Concord sucks, though."

Sophie rolls her eyes. To Dennison she says, "Sorry about your season," because right now Indy makes Concord look like Cup contenders.

"Someone has to snap Seattle's first overall pick streak." He takes a long drink from his bottle and makes a face as he swallows.

A couple of tables over, Eldon Carruthers sits with some of the Western Conference guys. Sophie hopes they're drafted to separate teams so she has an extra opportunity to compete against him this year. So far she's winning her battle with him, but this is the biggest stage they've been at together. Neither Seattle nor Concord are talented enough to attract anything beyond local attention. The All-Star Game will have a wider reaching audience, and she'll make another argument for why she should've been picked first at their draft instead of him.

As if he can feel her gaze, Carruthers looks over. He frowns when he catches her staring, and she lifts her water bottle in what could be considered a friendly gesture.

"Besides, this is a good year to suck." Dennison's still talking, and Sophie forces her attention back to her table. "Chad Kensington is something else."

Sophie huffs. All the talking heads are playing up the small American forward who has a decent shot at being the first pick this year, but Sophie doesn't care about him. She'd much rather talk about the power forward who has the potential to force herself into the conversation and, in Sophie's hopes, to the number one slot. "Alexis Engelking is better."

To her surprise, Dennison shrugs instead of immediately disputing it. "Maybe, but your girl staying in Sweden dampened the excitement over drafting women. They're flaky, can't be relied on."

Sophie narrows her eyes. "Elsa isn't 'my girl' and she didn't ruin anything."

Dennison holds his hands up. "Hot button issue, sorry. Maybe we'll get Kensington *and* Engelking. We have New Orleans' first round pick and they suck almost as badly as we do. You think she'll go first round?"

"She's hard on the puck, she doesn't quit on plays, and she has the kind of fight your team's lacking." Sophie could give a much more in-depth scouting report, but this isn't the time or place for it.

"I already apologized for the dig against Nyberg. No need to drag my team."

Sophie shrugs. It's a deserved criticism, but she lets it go as the Commissioner approaches the microphone on stage and is booed by everyone packed into the venue. The players are in a separate room, watching the opening address from the TV screens scattered across the room or, in the case of two tables over, making a drinking game out of the Commissioner's speech.

After the Commissioner, the two All-Star captains for the year walk through separate doors. Corey Freedman, Atlanta's captain, is greeted by rousing cheers. Anthony Sinclair's entrance is barely noticed. They step up to the microphone as the draft begins.

"Fucking Sinclair," Dennison mutters. He takes a long drink from his bottle.

"You better save the rest," Dubya advises. "You'll need it if he picks you."

At least Sophie won't go last this year. Sinclair would rather play down a forward than select her for his team. It's not like second-to-last is much better, but it'll still be an improvement over last year.

"Sophie's here to protect me." Dennison grins, pleased with his joke, but he cuts her a glance as if he's worried she'll be mad.

"Haven't you heard? I'm reformed. No more breaking noses for me."

"It was a long time coming." Dubya taps his fingers on the table as Freedman selects his Atlanta teammate, James Levesque, as his first pick.

"Maybe I'll fight him this weekend," Dima says.

"You definitely will not."

Sinclair selects Rawlings, his Denver teammate, as his first pick and Dubya covers a yawn when the cameras pan the room for a reaction. Figuli is chosen next and then Dima. Sophie kicks him under the table when it looks like he might not walk out. Eventually, he goes and accepts the Team Sinclair jersey his temporary captain hands him.

Sophie's selected next. She's disappointed she won't have a chance to center Dima again, but she pulls her Team Freedman jersey over her head and sits down next to Figuli.

"Hey, rookie," Figuli says. "How many points do you think we'll score this time?"

"I'm not focused on numbers. I want to play the best hockey I can. If we focus and work hard, the points will come." She manages a straight face until she spots Levesque, staring as if he thinks she's being serious. She cracks then, smiling and holding back her laughter as the draft continues.

In the second-to-last pick, Freedman selects Dubya. He has to pass the Team Sinclair section, and Dima grabs Dubya's hand and tries to steal him for his side. Freedman playfully breaks it up and the crowd laughs and cheers as Dima wipes away fake tears.

He has a talent for charming the cameras, and the crowds. Sophie was fiercely jealous of it last season. Cameras are her enemy, hovering as they search for any sign of weakness they can turn back on her. Dima's ease with them made her angry until she realized he hammed it up in order to hide how his English wasn't perfect. He always laughed first because it meant everyone would be laughing with him instead of at him.

When the cameras land on her, looking for a reaction, she shakes her head, only a hint of a smile on her face as if to say *Oh Ivanov. Never focused, never serious.*

They all have their parts to play.

THE POST-DRAFT Team Freedman party is held in Figuli's room. Sophie navigates it with her Gatorade bottle clutched in her hands like a lifeline. Despite the knowing look Ducasse gives her, she only has Gatorade in it. There's no Dima to hang out with this year, no cluster of rookies to seek refuge with. She's debating whether or not she's been here long enough to justify ducking out when Eldon Carruthers finds her.

He's drunk and bumps into her shoulder as if he misjudged the distance between them. He squints, dark eyes even darker in their corner of the room. "You don't like me."

Sophie opens her mouth and closes it again. Of all the things she expected him to lead with, this wasn't one of them. She doesn't know what to say, no hockey clichés to fall back on. Because he's right, she doesn't like him. He went first in their draft when it should've been her, and she knows it isn't his fault, but he's a convenient person to blame.

Carruthers, apparently, doesn't need a response from her. "I mean, it's whatever. Everyone knows why you broke Sinclair's nose, but I never did anything to you. I don't think I did, at least."

Tucked away in their corner of the room, no one's paying attention to them. Maybe it's what makes her brave enough to tell the truth. "You went first in our draft. You're my measuring stick." It won't change how she was picked last, but maybe it will pave the way for another woman to be chosen first.

"Not really." Carruthers' shoulders slump as if all those expectations are finally hitting him. "I was first overall and what did I do? Sucked enough for us to get another first overall. It's kind of nice, though. When I came in last year, Hippo looked so fucking happy, and I didn't get it. I thought he'd be jealous, y'know? He was supposed to be the savior of the franchise and here I was replacing him. But we lost and lost and lost and when we drafted Tippy, I finally understood. Let *him* be the savior. All I want is to play hockey."

This is the most she's ever heard him say in his life, but she still doesn't know how to respond. *Sorry Seattle sucks?*

"It's fucking depressing," Carruthers continues. "It rains all the fucking time and a good season is one where we don't get a top-five pick. I don't want to be stuck here for the rest of my career." He sways into her, and she can smell the booze on his breath. When she steadies him, she notices the tears gathering in his eyes. "Sometimes, I forget how much I love hockey."

"O-kay," Sophie says. "You need a Gatorade hat trick and to go to sleep. Who're you staying with?"

"So you don't need to hate me." He keeps on going as if she didn't say anything at all. "I'm suffering enough."

He drapes his arms over her, half-hug, half-bid for support. She holds him up and looks around, hoping for someone to help her.

Freedman and Figuli head over, her captain for the weekend taking Carruthers from her. He wraps an arm around the Seafarer's waist and talks quietly as he leads him out of the room.

"Everything okay?" Figuli asks.

Sophie's chest is heavy as if she's about to cry. "Seattle sounds rough."

"It's hard not to win."

Figuli's never won the Cup in all his years in the League. If Carruthers is broken after only a season and a half in Seattle, how much worse is it for Figuli who has been here for so much longer? Is it easier for him since he's made it to the playoffs, even made it to the Finals? Or is it worse having come so close and never winning?

They're winning the game this weekend. She knows it isn't the same as lifting the Cup, it isn't even close, but she'll set her rivalry with Carruthers aside and remind him hockey is fun. There's a reason they've dedicated their lives to the sport, sacrificed time with their family, and collected a myriad of bruises.

They love this sport, even if it doesn't always love them back.

SOPHIE'S THE FIRST one at breakfast the next morning by virtue of being the only hockey player in the hotel who isn't sleeping off a hangover. She's done with her eggs when Dima and Dubya stumble in. Dennison and Ducasse trail them. The older players find a table together, but Dima brings his coffee to where she is.

He clutches his mug like a lifeline and breathes in the steam.

"I heard it works better if you drink it."

Dima flips her off, and she laughs and keeps eating. A few minutes later, Carruthers wanders in. Sophie waves him over to their table. The Seafarer squints at her as if he's not sure what he's seeing.

Dima fetches him and grabs some breakfast while he's up.

"It's way too early," Carruthers says as he sits down. "Berry hid his phone, turned the alarm up to full volume, and crashed in someone else's room. Asshole."

"Kids up even earlier," Dima says. "Outside rink already."

Sophie checks her phone. It's quarter past nine. "They've set everything up?" Her hotel room faces the wrong way so she can't see the stadium from her window.

"Oh yeah. Camp is there. Everyone is in bright pink T-shirts."

She thinks about what J-Rod told Zinger at surprise pizza. He was introduced to hockey at the All-Star Weekend when a player took the time to talk to him. He wishes one of the southwest cities would host so hockey could pick up traction in places where it isn't already popular. Atlanta isn't one of the big hockey markets. How many kids are here because they're bored and it's something to do? How many might fall in love with hockey if someone would only nudge them toward it?

She eats faster. It doesn't go unnoticed by her companions.

"Where's the fire?" Carruthers asks.

"I want to go outside."

Dima wrinkles his nose. "Photos?"

"This isn't part of my schedule. I want to try some of the games. You can play goalie against me."

"Not stupid." Dima laughs, though, and drinks the rest of his coffee in two big swallows. "Change first?"

Dima's currently wearing sweatpants and a T-shirt covered in sheep gleefully bounding over a fence. She's almost afraid of what he'll choose to wear outside. His fashion decisions are...creative. Sophie stands up, done with her breakfast. Dima stands too and, when Carruthers doesn't stand with him, he clears his throat. "You come too."

"What?"

Dima wraps Carruthers' bagel in a napkin and says, "Eat and walk."

Carruthers looks to Sophie for help but she grins instead of saying anything, so he shrugs and follows them. They stop off at their rooms long enough to change. Sophie puts on one of her pairs of Under Armour, the warm ones because it's chilly out this morning. She layers a long-sleeve shirt and her All-Star sweatshirt. It has her name and number on the sleeve and, more importantly, it has a hood.

She flips the hood up and meets Dima and Carruthers outside her door. They're dressed the same except their hoods are down. Dima laughs at her but as soon as they're outside, he flips his hood up too, because even though it's Georgia, it's still winter and it's cold.

They hear the kids before they see them, but when they turn the corner of the hotel, Sophie pauses because the front of the stadium is packed. There are mini-rinks set up and shooting challenges and tables of official NAHL merchants hawking their wares. Dima nudges her and points to the rack of Fournier jerseys, both Concord and All-Star styled ones, as if she hadn't noticed them.

"I already have a few of those but thanks." She laughs as he shoves her. She leads them across the street to pick what they're doing first.

There's a cutout of a goalie guarding a net with a few open spaces to try to shoot the puck. Kid after kid takes the stick the attendant offers them and tries to score five-hole or high corner.

A couple of kids have brought their own sticks, and they fare much better. There's one, a girl who doesn't look more than ten, who's wearing a pink Fournier jersey who steps in to try, holding a neon pink hockey stick.

"Wait!" Dima shouts. He vaults into the setup, and the attendant opens his mouth to scold him before he realizes who it is. Then he freezes as if he wasn't trained on how to react to a NAHL player hijacking his station. Dima pushes the fake goalie out of the way and then crouches in front of the net. "Now you go."

The girl looks from Dima to her mom as if to ask *is this okay?*

"Sir," the mother says, and Sophie has to bite back her laugh. "Could you please let my daughter shoot?"

Sophie steps in next, offering the mother and daughter a reassuring smile. "It's okay. You can shoot at him. Do you want me to demonstrate for you?"

The girl looks at Sophie, then Dima, and hesitantly hands her stick over. It's much shorter than Sophie's preferred stick and the blade has the wrong curve, but she can work with this. She shows the girl where to put her hands. "A lot of people think it's about the wind-up, but you don't need a big swing to be effective. Where do you want me to put the puck?"

"Hey!" Dima protests. "I didn't sign up for *you*. I'm not wearing a cup!"

Sophie's smile grows. "Poor choice on your part."

Dima shields himself with his hands, leading to laughter from the growing crowd. Sophie snipes the puck top corner. "Now, you try," she tells the girl. "I'll be here to help you."

Dima tosses Sophie the puck and she sets it down on the ground. Once the girl is holding her stick again, Sophie stands behind her and adjusts her grip. She guides her through the motion twice before stepping back. Dima moves too, and the girl knocks the puck into an unguarded net.

"Now you have to practice a thousand more times."

The girl's eyes grow wide. "A thousand?"

"A thousand a day," Dima adds, joining them. He opens the door so they can step out and the next kid can take his turn. "Two thousand if you want to be great like me. Only one to be like Sophie."

Sophie rolls her eyes but lets it go. She glances at Carruthers, hanging back and looking as overwhelmed as the girl. "Do you have any advice for an aspiring hockey player?"

"Oh, she doesn't play hockey," the girl's mom says even as Carruthers crouches down to say, "Have fun. You'll never get better if you don't want to be at the rink every day."

"I'm a gymnast but hockey seems kinda cool. Do you wanna see my cartwheel?"

They have to find somewhere less crowded, but she's able to show off her cartwheel, and all three hockey players clap approvingly.

"We're going to check out the accuracy shooting, but can we sign your hockey stick before we go?" Sophie asks.

The mom eyes them with suspicion again. "Who *are* you?"

Sophie smiles. "This is Dmitri Ivanov, Eldon Carruthers, and I'm Sophie Fournier. We—"

The mom's mouth drops open. "You're hockey players. Tom's going to be so jealous."

"Daddy slept in today," the girl pipes up. "He didn't want to come with us."

"Do you want a picture?" Sophie offers.

After they part ways with the mom and daughter, they stop by the accuracy booth. Dima jumps into line and sets the fastest record. He cellies as if he scored the game-winner in the Maple Cup final. The kids in line eat it up, and they take another round of pictures.

SOPHIE DEFENDS BOTH her titles from last year, winning the stickhandling competition and the obstacle course. The next day is the All-Star game itself, but it isn't until the afternoon. In part, it's to give the players time to recover from their hangovers, but there's also a Family Skate held in the morning. Sophie has to go even though she doesn't have any family here.

Dima's parents didn't fly in from Russia, but he scoops up one of Dubya's kids and skates around the ice, dodging other players and their families. Sophie finds a quiet corner where she juggles a puck because if she's boring enough, the cameras won't linger on her.

She holds her stick behind her back, tosses the puck up into the air, finds it, and catches it in front of her.

"Wow."

Sophie drops the puck, startled. The speaker is a woman in thick leggings and an even thicker sweater. Her hair is pulled back into a high ponytail, and she looks unsteady on her skates, holding onto Dennison's arm for balance.

"She's one of the best in the League," Dennison says. Then, to Sophie. "This is my wife, Laura. Laura, this is Sophie Fournier."

"It's a pleasure to meet you," Laura says.

"Same." Sophie glances at Dennison, wondering what the hell he's playing at. They barely even know each other. Why is he introducing her to his wife?

"No boyfriend to skate with?" Laura's smile is friendly, but Sophie still draws her shoulders up.

She can't help but check to see if there are any cameras lurking. She doesn't see any, but it doesn't mean Dennison or Laura aren't mic'd up. "I'm focusing on hockey right now."

Her answer catches Laura off guard. Her smile slips and she glances at Dennison who offers no help. "Hockey does take up a lot of time. I feel like I never see Riley once he's in season."

"I live alone."

Laura nods and the conversation sputters out. Dennison doesn't seem bothered by it. Before things can grow too awkward, a little girl skates over with unsteady strides. She alternates between staring at her skates and staring at Sophie, awed and overwhelmed. She's wearing a black All-Star jersey which means her father is on Team Freedman. Sophie takes a knee as the girl reaches them. "Hi."

"You're Sophie Fournier." The girl's English is heavy with a French accent. "You were my favorite in the Winter Games."

"I was proud to represent Team Canada."

The girl nods, solemn. "My papa too. He was captain. Will you be captain next Games?"

This is a little Ducasse, then. "I don't think I'll be captain. Do you remember Adrienne Stewart?" The girl nods. "She'll be my captain in Helsinki, but I'll be proud to be one of her alternates."

"Were the Mammoths really your favorite team growing up?"

Sophie shares a secret smile with her. "Bobby Brindle was my first hockey jersey."

"The Mammoths are my favorite team too. My papa's my favorite boy player in the whole NAHL. You're my favorite girl player." She shyly holds out a silver Sharpie. "Will you sign my jersey?"

"Of course. What's your name?"

"Ada," she says as she turns so Sophie can write on the back. *To Ada and a forever love of Team Canada, Sophie Fournier 93.* Ada giggles as the marker loops across her back. "You're writing a lot."

"I want it to be special for you."

Ada's cheeks are pink as she turns back around. "*Merci.*"

Sophie hands her the marker. "*De rien.*" It's a mistake, because suddenly Ada's chatting in French, and Sophie's command of the language isn't strong enough to keep up with an overexcited kid.

Fortunately, Ducasse skates over, visible relief on his face when he sees his daughter. It shifts into something more guarded when he sees Sophie, still kneeling on the ice.

"Papa!" Ada somehow starts talking even *faster* as she skates over, arms held up. Her dad lifts her into his arms as Sophie gets back to her skates.

"I hope she wasn't any trouble," Ducasse says.

"She's a sweet girl even if she's cheering for the wrong team."

Ada twists in her dad's arms. "Am not!"

"It's okay," Sophie tells her, full-out grinning. "I was a Mammoths fan when I was little too, but I grew out of it. There's still hope for you."

Ada draws a breath to defend her dad's team and then pauses. "Maybe I can have two favorite teams. The Mammoths can be my favorite Canadian team and the Condors can be my favorite American team."

"You'll be just like my *mémé*. Do you know who her favorite player on the Mammoths is?"

Ada's gaze darts to her dad. When Sophie nods, Ada tugs on her dad's jersey sleeve. "You have to sign something for Sophie's *mémé*. She signed my jersey for me. Wanna see?" She twists again and Ducasse narrowly avoids dropping her as she shows off the back of her jersey.

"It was very nice of her." Ducasse looks over at Sophie. "I can give you one of my All-Star jerseys if you want."

Sophie doesn't answer right away, because *Captain Canada* is offering her one of his jerseys. "Um, thank you. You don't have to."

"We're countrymen, eh? I'll have it for you before the game this afternoon."

"Thank you," Sophie says again.

Ducasse nods and then skates away with his daughter, lightly scolding her for disappearing without any warning.

"Wow," Dennison says, and Sophie startles because she forgot he and Laura were still here. "I'm not sure who was more starstruck there, you or Ada."

"Fuck off," Sophie says and Dennison laughs, delighted.

SOPHIE CENTERS FIGULI again and even without Dima on the wing, their line puts up half their team's goals and leads Team Freedman to the win. Afterward, they take a bunch of pictures, of the team and the oversized check they're donating to the Freedman Foundation which provides hockey equipment to underprivileged kids in the Atlanta area. The home crowd cheers the announcement and there are more pictures before another round of media and they're finally allowed to leave.

It was a good weekend, but as soon as she lands, fun time is over. There's still a lot of work to be done so Concord can make the playoffs this year.

Chapter Sixteen

CONCORD DREW THE short scheduling straw this year. They have a road game the Monday after the All-Star break which means an early flight to Pittsburgh and a brief pregame skate before they play. To make matters worse, it's the first game of a back-to-back which means a late night flight to Memphis for another game.

They won't have a real practice until three days after their break, and Sophie's nervous. They haven't played together as a team since their loss to DC and most of her teammates haven't touched a hockey stick since then. She reminds herself they're all professional athletes and have been playing hockey for at least a decade if not more. A couple of days off won't make them all forget how to play.

They skate a few easy laps on Pittsburgh's ice and swap stories from their breaks. They partner up to pass back and forth.

"Beaches." Merlin sighs happily as he passes to Sophie. She has to reach to catch it on her tape. "Plural, as in many beaches. Sand and sun all day long."

"I had hockey. I win."

Down the line, Garfield's pass takes a weird bounce and skitters over Nelson's stick. They cheerfully heckle each other, blaming each other for the missed pass as the puck bumps gently against the boards.

"Is this social hour or hockey practice?" Coach Butler demands.

The rink falls silent. Spitz turns to Coach and misses Kuzy's pass. Their puck clunks against the boards near Garfield and Nelson's.

Coach Butler's face turns an unflattering shade of red. "You were shit going into the break and none of you practiced over the break so you haven't gotten any better. The only one of you who had a stick in their hands recently was Fournier but with all the circus shit at the All-Star Weekend, it'll be a miracle if she remembers how to play hockey. So cut the chatter and up the effort."

Spitz ventures across the ice to pick up the errant puck. While he's there, he grabs Nelson's as well.

Coach blows his whistle, sharp, the noise cutting through the quiet rink, and Sophie winces. "What did I just fucking say? Effort! Nelson can get his own puck. Maybe next time he'll catch it on his stick instead of letting it by him."

Spitz glances at Kuzy and then Matty, panic in the wide set of his eyes. At Matty's nod, he drops the puck back to the ice. He skates by Nelson on his way back to his position, and Sophie sees his lips move in an apology.

Well, she thinks as she turns back to Merlin. *This is a great start to the final push of our season.*

THEY LOSE TO Pittsburgh and Memphis. It drops them down to sixth in their division, two places out of a playoff spot. When they come to practice on January 16, Coach Butler does nothing but skate them for the first half of their practice. They skate red line to red line until Sophie's quads burn, and she doesn't have enough time to catch her breath between whistles.

Finally, Coach takes his whistle out of his mouth. Sophie doesn't dare bend over, but she takes advantage of the pause to drag in a few desperate lungfuls of air.

"Do you want to give up?" Coach Butler demands. He looks down the line, and Sophie forces herself to meet his gaze. "Maybe you think if you suck enough, we'll draft Chad Kensington this summer. You want the flashy new kid on our team?"

No one has the breath to answer, but he doesn't need one.

"You want Kensington? Fine. First, look around and decide who we're giving up to get him. If this team tanks, we're selling at the trade deadline. Who will go? Nelson? Garfield? Lindholm? Hell, if you're not going to try, why not trade Mathers? What does a bottom of the League team need with a captain anyway?"

Sophie's chest squeezes tight. *No.* Before she can formulate a more coherent thought, Coach blows his whistle, and they skate again.

"FUCKING *FUCK!*" MERLIN shouts once they're in the locker room. He throws his helmet at his stall and it makes a loud sound before it drops to the floor. He rips off his chest protector and throws it too.

Theo and Kevlar sit side by side, turned to each other, whispering quietly. Nelson drops into his stall, head in his hands. Garfield sits next to him, their shoulders touching in a silent show of support.

Sophie takes an extra-long shower. This is their team, the one she wants to keep this year *and* next year. They need to play well enough to keep everyone at the trade deadline and to keep them through summer signings too.

After her shower, she rearranges her stall until Matty's the only one left in the locker room. Most of the guys cleared out right away, ready to be out of the rink after a practice like today, which is a problem for another day. The rink is somewhere they should want to be. They should have to be thrown out by the coaches they stay so long.

Today, she approaches her captain, her bag slung over her shoulder. "I'll walk out with you."

He looks over at her, surprised he isn't the only one here. His shoulders slump before he can catch it, but he musters up a smile for her. "We're going to be okay."

"I don't need a pep talk. Coach Butler told me exactly what I needed to hear. We aren't losing you. You're our captain. We'll play better so we buy at the deadline. You're going to lead Concord to their first playoff appearance in franchise history."

She's giving a pep talk, but somehow Matty looks even more defeated. He shakes his head but she keeps going. "You're ours and we're making the playoffs this year. Come on, we're getting takeout and bringing it to X's."

She refuses to lose anyone this season. They're keeping Lindy, the longest tenured goalie in Concord's history, and Matty, their captain, and X, who has been with Concord since the beginning. Garfield and Nelson will stay a unit and Theo and Kevlar are staying a pairing. She's keeping Merlin and Witzer on her wings. *This* is the team which will make the playoffs for the first time in franchise history.

All they have to do is win hockey games.

THEY DROP THEIR game against Detroit. Minei, the center Sophie's been matched up against all game, scores the OT-winner, but she doesn't hang her head in the locker room. She won't let anyone else either.

"We pushed this one to OT." She stands up, speaking louder until she has the attention of the whole team. "We got a point out of this one. Next game, we get two."

"One shift at a time," Spitz says.

"Exactly."

Coach Butler comes in to yell at them, but Sophie tunes it out. She knows what she needs to do, and she knows what's at stake if she doesn't.

ATLANTA TIES THE game with seconds left on the clock, and the home crowd falls silent. They've seen this show before, and some of them even stand up and leave, not wanting to see their team lose again. More troubling, Sophie's teammates hang their heads, because this is playing out like Detroit.

Not tonight. Sophie tightens her grip on her stick. *We're winning this one.*

Coach Butler doesn't speak to them during the brief intermission, leaving them to Coach Vorgen and Coach Richelieu. Sophie ducks out of their speech about playing with energy and focus and approaches her head coach.

His clipboard is cracked from how hard he's gripped it tonight, and he spares her a glance before looking at his numbers again.

"Put me on Matty's wing to start overtime. Double shift me when you need to. I can handle it."

"You've had sixty minutes to do something and you haven't."

This is different. Why won't you trust me? "I will."

"You better. If you're on the ice for Atlanta's game-winning goal, you're on the third line against Boston."

"Deal."

She rejoins the huddle, intending to stand between her wingers, but Teddy snags her first. He pulls her close and drops his voice to a whisper. "He shouldn't put the game on you."

"You think my shoulders aren't broad enough?" She flexes but doesn't even score a smile. "I play my best when I'm challenged, and Coach Butler knows it. We're winning tonight and going out. The team needs the morale boost."

"Sofe—"

The horn sounds, ending intermission, before Teddy can finish his thought.

"Mathers, Fournier, and Garfield out for the first faceoff," Coach Butler says.

Nelson sits back down on the bench and Wilchinski pats his knee.

I'm not replacing you. It's only for overtime, I'm doing this so we can keep you. You and Matty and Lindy and everyone.

Matty wins the faceoff, and they go to work in Atlanta's zone. Sophie fires a puck at Vanderbilt, but he stops it with his shoulder. The puck drops to the ice, and Freedman sweeps it away, out of danger. Theo cuts off the clearing pass, knocking it down and sliding the puck to Kevlar who takes a shot of his own.

Freedman goes down on one knee to the block the shot, and the puck ricochets off him and out of play. The first line is given a break as Peets takes the third line over the boards. Sophie has enough time to catch her breath before she takes her usual line out for a shift.

She plays and plays, sometimes with a shift between hers and sometimes with only the length of a stoppage to catch her breath. Nelson goes out with his line, and Sophie sits at the end of the bench and sucks in some much-needed air. Teddy reaches over to tap her shin with his paddle. She nods at him, unable to speak.

"Vanderbilt has a weak glove," Teddy tells her. "A hard, fast shot and it'll go past him or he'll bobble it, and you'll have a good second chance."

She nods again.

The next time she takes the ice it's with Matty's line. Her captain looks tired, and she pulls him aside on their way to Atlanta's zone. "Let me take this faceoff. We can both win them, but you're the one who can score off them." She tugs him away from where the Lancers are having a pre-faceoff huddle of their own. "Teddy says Vanderbilt is weak glove side. A quick shot, and he won't stop it. Me-you-score."

"Bang-bang play." Matty nods and pats her helmet.

She skates up to the faceoff dot even as Coach Butler shouts something from the bench. She doesn't hear what it is. She's locked in now, nothing but her and Freedman and the official holding the puck. She takes one last deep breath and springs into action as soon as the puck is dropped.

She knocks the puck over to where Matty's waiting, and he snaps it on net. Vanderbilt shoots his glove up, catching a piece of the puck but not enough, and Matty scores.

Sophie raises her gaze to the ceiling.

Kuzy crashes into her, shouting and hugging her. He opens the celebration to Spitz and then Matty and Garfield. She can't do more than smile and nod and try to breathe as the rest of them celebrate.

She looks past her teammates to the bench where Coach Butler is standing, arms crossed, his permanent half-frown on his face. *See? We need Matty. He plays big in big moments. Don't trade our captain.*

"YOU TOOK THE final faceoff of the game. You don't usually take the faceoff when you and Matty are on the ice together."

Ed Rickers brings up the point Sophie's been waiting for all scrum. She tamps down her smile so she doesn't look too eager to answer the question. "Shooting isn't one of my strengths, something you've all written at length about for the past two years, but Matty scores clutch goals when we need him to, and we needed one tonight. I took the faceoff, freeing him to be the shooter. It was a good play from our captain."

She pours praise on her captain in each of the follow-up questions, knowing at least some of what she says will make it into the articles printed tonight and tomorrow morning. She wants everyone in her organization and her city to know how important Matty is to them.

"We don't win this one without him," she tells Marty Owen.

Across the room, Matty frowns faintly at her.

THEY GAINED AN important two points, showcased the skill of their captain, and, as a bonus, won a game with Sophie's brother in the stadium. Now, they're both in Sophie's apartment, Colby sitting on her bed as she shifts through her closet for something to wear out with the team.

"We're in fifth now," she tells him as she holds up a black V-neck T-shirt. "This?"

"This is how you celebrate a big win?"

"Too dark? I have a gray one."

Colby laughs but trails off when she doesn't laugh along with him. He shakes his head. "Wear whatever you want. Hey, do you think Ivanov will sign my trading card after the Boston game?"

"Of course. He wants to get drinks too. Well, I say drinks but neither of us are legal in the US. He wants to meet you for some reason."

"I'm a treasure. And *I'm* US legal."

"I don't drink in public." She pulls her black V-neck on and tugs the fabric up so it doesn't show her sports bra. She exchanges her sweatpants for a worn pair of jeans and declares herself ready.

THE NEXT DAY, she leaves her brother with Teddy, Theo, and Kevlar so she can drive out to Durham one last time. Ritchie is waiting for her, and he takes his usual place outside the locker room, standing guard as she changes into her practice gear.

"Are you still on for the Philly game?" she asks as she troops out, pads and skates in place, mouth guard hooked through her sports bra. "O'Reilly's an instigator so you'll have a chance to see all our lessons pay off."

"Drew O'Reilly?" Ritchie opens the bench door for her and ushers her onto the ice. "He's on my fantasy team. You're not going to fight him, are you?"

"I don't fight people."

"You break their noses."

Ritchie grins, proud of his joke, and Sophie rolls her eyes. She skates backward, waiting for Ritchie to hop on the ice and join her. "I'm working with you so I won't break anyone's nose. Colby will be in town for the game too. I figured you'd want to catch up."

"Hell fucking yeah! How's Colbs doing?"

"You can catch up at the game. We have work to do."

"Bossy," Ritchie says but there's no heat in his words. Unlike a few minutes later when he shoves her up against the boards.

It's their hardest session yet, but at the end of it, she feels ready.

BEFORE THEY CAN play Philly they face Boston, and they rout their rivals in a 6-2 win. There were five power plays for her team during the game, and she played with Matty on every single one of them. All three of her assists came on power play goals by her captain, and she beams during her postgame scrum.

"He's a leader in the room," Sophie says with a glance to the other side of the locker room. "There's a confidence when you step onto the ice with him. It's hard to explain, but you saw it tonight."

"It's easy to be confident when you have an extra player on the ice," Marty Owen says.

She doesn't let him get her down tonight. Matty had the OT winner last game, a hat trick this game. One game at a time they're proving they need their captain. They're doing exactly what Coach Butler told them to do; they're winning.

Once the media's cleared out, Merlin drapes his arms over Sophie's shoulders. "Where are we celebrating tonight?"

"Matty's the man of the hour. Hat trick, remember?"

"Yeah but you did all the work."

Sophie elbows him, making him yelp and back off.

"You did," Matty agrees from his stall. He's smiling, relaxed for the first time in far too long. "The net was wide fucking open on my second goal."

Sophie smiles again, so wide it hurts her cheeks. "Well, you're still picking the bar. I'm going out with Colby and Dima."

She expects a hard time about not celebrating with the team and, if they push hard enough, she'll meet up with Dima another time, but Merlin nods and says, "It's about time. Make sure to remind him we scored six goals on his team tonight."

It's about time?

"Tell us what Colby thinks of him," Theo adds.

This conversation has officially gotten weird. She looks to Matty for help, but he's failing at hiding a smile. "I can already tell you. He's in awe of Dima's shot and a little part of him wants to gear up against him and the rest of him is glad his goaltending days are over."

"Not exactly what I meant." Now Theo's smiling too, but he doesn't push it.

Sophie shrugs and rushes through her shower so she can grab Colby and change. He sits on her bed again as she picks through her closet, but she doesn't take long to decide. She goes with the gray V-neck tonight.

"Good choice," Colby tells her. "It brings out your eyes. And your pit stains."

She flips him off. "Dima's always more of a fashion disaster than I am." She pulls her hair up into a simple ponytail. "The guys want to know what you think of him."

Colby grins. "Do they?"

"They were being weird about it but they're weird about a lot of things."

"Sofe..." Colby shakes his head, thinking better of what he was going to say. "Are you ready to go?"

THEY MEET DIMA at one of the quieter bars in Concord, because Sophie doesn't want to run into her team. He's wearing jeans with holes in the knees and a black T-shirt covered in zippers. He meets him outside the bar and gives Sophie a hug when he sees her. He also hugs Colby, lifting Sophie's brother right off his feet.

"He has a trading card he wants you sign," Sophie says.

"Sofe," Colby groans.

"What? You do."

Dima laughs and ushers them inside. Sophie leaves them to figure out drinks while she hunts down a table. The place is mostly full, men and women in business casual as if they came here right after work. Or, also possible, as if they dress up before going out. The bar counter is crowded, but there's a section of empty tables, away from the dance floor and the pool tables.

Sophie slides into the booth, claiming the table. Colby and Dima join her a few minutes later. Colby sets the pitcher of beer down and drops his coat on the empty side of the table. "I'll be back."

"How come he gets a whole side to himself?" she asks even as she lets Dima push her deeper into the booth. She puts up a fight as soon as she realizes he's trying to squish her against the wall. "You don't need this much space."

"We're *friends*," Dima coos. He snakes an arm around her shoulders and pulls her tight against his side. "Friends are close."

"This might be too close."

Dima laughs and, when she doesn't elbow him away, he drops his arm to her waist and stays pressed up against her. She lets herself lean into his side. With Colby here, she's been hugged more than she has the whole rest of her season combined. It's made her spoiled, and this isn't something she can get from her team.

They treat her as a teammate when she's in her pads, slapping her helmet, her shoulders, her ass, giving her fist bumps, but as soon as the hockey gear is gone it's as if a switch is flicked in their heads; she goes from hockey player to *girl* and they're afraid to touch her. It's better than the alternative but it means she's barely ever hugged.

Dima's sipping his beer when Colby returns to the table with a platter of nachos, piled high with shredded chicken, cheese, black olives, and salsa. Sophie shakes her head even as Colby sets them down in the middle of the table. "These aren't on my diet plan."

"Not all for you," Dima says. "We share." He slants a look at Colby, nothing but trouble in his expression. "Always so bad at share?"

"I'm not bad at sharing!" Sophie knocks her shoulder into Dima's, but he doesn't even budge. "Did you see how many assists I had tonight?" She winces as soon as she says it. "Sorry. No game talk."

Dima rolls his eyes and tugs on her ponytail. "Is one loss. Not end of the world."

Colby looks between them, amused. "You did have a lot of assists tonight. You played possessed." He pauses, thinking, which is never a good thing. "You played hard against Atlanta too."

"It's the push to the playoffs, everyone's stepping their game up." She shrugs as if it isn't a big deal. She finds a chip with the least amount of cheese and dips it in the salsa. "Besides, Coach lit into us after the break. If we don't pick it up, we're losing Matty at the trade deadline."

Colby stops piling olives on his chip. "What?"

"Serious?" Dima asks.

"He doesn't have full power over trades, but he can make recommendations to Mister Wilcox, and I won't risk it. Matty's our captain. We aren't losing him."

"Sofe," Colby begins and he sounds like Teddy, angry but completely on her side.

She doesn't need either of them handling her with kid gloves. "It motivated us, didn't it? Coach Butler knows what he's doing."

Colby and Dima exchange a look before her brother says, "Guess he does."

WHEN SOPHIE HITS the ice for warm-ups, there's a loud cheer from the far side of the ice. She looks down to see the UNH men's hockey team lined up against the glass. They wave and, once they're satisfied she's noticed them, they turn their full attention to heckling every Philly player who skates by them.

"Wow," Merlin says. "Usually we're on the receiving end."

"Friends of Colby. Now concentrate, we have a game to win."

O'REILLY SHOVES SOPHIE into the boards on her first shift of the night. In theory, they're battling for the puck, but he elbows her and tips her helmet forward and slashes at her ankles, trying to rile her up. "Get used to this. I'm going to be on you all night."

The puck's knocked free and Sophie checks to make sure the officials are focused on the breakout before she sweeps her foot out and dumps him on his ass. She smiles sweetly down at him. "I don't think you can handle me."

She skates to the bench for a change and sits between Merlin and Garfield.

"What was that?" Garfield asks.

"Nothing you need to worry about. I have it under control."

Garfield glances at her, no doubt full of questions, but he shrugs and lets it go.

Two shifts later, after the play's blown dead, O'Reilly snow-showers her. He smirks as she wipes shaved ice from her visor. "If you ask me nicely, I'll give you a real facial later."

She doesn't give him the satisfaction of looking at him. "Not interested." She skates to the bench, herding Merlin so he doesn't do something stupid like start a fight.

Teddy opens the bench door for her and Matty tosses her a towel. "If you want backup let me know."

"He's annoying but he won't draw a penalty."

It's part promise, part threat, and even though she doesn't stare her bench down, she trusts they've received the message.

SHE CHANNELS HER irritation with O'Reilly into good, hard hockey. She checks players when she needs to and then she takes the puck and skates down the ice, dancing away from stick checks and clumsy attempts to cut off her path to the net. She peppers the goal with shots, and she's rewarded when Witzer scoops up one of her rebounds and slams it home.

The next time she's on the ice, it's Theo who scores, a bomb from the point no one reacts to until it's in the net. Sophie knocks shoulders with O'Reilly as she skates to her d-man, arms raised in celebration.

O'Reilly comes at her even harder after Theo's goal. He checks her and shoves her as much as he can get away with when the officials are looking and even more once they aren't. He cross-checks her and it sends her helmet skittering across the ice. She spins to him, fury in her gaze, a heartbeat away from slamming her stick into his smug fucking face. He smirks, showing off two missing teeth, because he has the kind of face which invites people to hit it.

Focus, we have a game to win. They're on a two-game winning streak, and she won't jeopardize their momentum with a selfish penalty. She takes a deep breath, ready to skate away. Theo flies in to shove O'Reilly away from her. "What the fuck is your problem?"

O'Reilly pretends to be confused. "I'm doing her a favor. I heard she likes it rough." He spins his mouth guard around, and Sophie steps between him and her d-man before Theo throws the kind of punch which'll get him ejected.

Theo's tall enough to glare at O'Reilly over her so she plants her hands on Theo's shoulders and skates him to the bench. "Play smart."

"Did you hear what he said?"

"I was standing right there, and if I'm not allowed to hit him, you aren't either."

They're at the bench now, but Theo's still looking past her, still locked in his fight with O'Reilly. Irritation prickles under her skin. She grabs a fistful of his jersey and yanks until he looks down at her, surprised. "Do you respect me?"

Behind them, the bench falls completely silent.

"What the fuck?" Theo demands. "*Yes.*"

"Then listen to me. He isn't worth your time. Don't fight him, don't leave your position to lay a hit on him. We are winning this game." She looks down the bench at everyone who's pretending they aren't paying attention. "Same goes for all of you. The only reason he's on his team is to instigate. It sure as hell isn't for his hockey skill." There are a few laughs. "Don't play his game. Play ours."

She looks at Theo one last time. He doesn't look happy about it, but he nods. Sophie takes her place on the bench and takes another deep breath. Now she really has to keep her cool for the rest of the game.

THEY WIN 4-2, and Sophie has two points on the night, but it isn't enough. She wanted to thrash them, pile on goals until it was 8-2 or 10-2. She's restless during her postgame responsibilities, and she doesn't shower. She sends her brother out with his friends and goes to the weight room, tapes up her hands, and takes on the heavy weight bag.

She adds another layer of sweat to her game-sweat, and her knuckles sting, but she doesn't stop hitting. There's still something twisted and ugly nestled deep inside her and she wants it out. She lands a hit hard enough to move the bag.

"I was wondering where you'd gone."

She looks over her shoulder to see Matty standing inside the doors, back in his game day suit. The punching bag knocks gently into her stomach, a reminder she was here for a reason. "I have some energy."

"So I can see." His smile shifts into something more serious. "You'll need it for our next game. Don't wear yourself out in here."

"I need to hit something."

He looks pointedly at the sweat stains on her stomach and under her arms. "Looks like you did. It's time to shower and change. Everyone's coming to my place for video games. Shooting shit always makes me feel better."

Sophie unwraps her hands and winces when she notices her knuckles are red and even purple in some places.

"You're smarter than this." Matty crosses the room until he can examine her hands, gently touching her new bruises. "Ice when you get home and we'll ice again at my place. No more sneaking in here. We need you on the ice, not on IR."

"I'll be fine tomorrow." She pulls her hands out of his grasp and closes them into fists. Her skin is tender, but she isn't *hurt*. "And this is better than being stuck in the box for a double minor."

"If someone gives you trouble, tell me."

"We need you on the ice too." She hasn't put in all this effort to highlight how important he is only to be the reason he's put in time out for two minutes.

"I know how to keep from getting caught." He tugs on her ponytail. "Shower, I'm not leaving until I see you get in your car."

"Bossy," she grumbles, no real heat behind it.

"It's why they gave me the C."

Chapter Seventeen

X RETURNS TO the lineup, and he slots into the third d-pairing the way he predicted. Spitz is jumpy for a few games, making boneheaded passes and forgetting his coverage until Sophie finally pulls him aside. She tells him one of two things will happen; X will play his top pairing position again or the coaching staff will protect his knee by giving him fewer minutes on the third.

Spitz calms down after their talk. He still makes mistakes, same as any of them, and he still glances at the bench each time as if he's wondering if *this* is the play Coach will yank him for. There isn't anything else Sophie can do to assure him. Coach is still talking about big moves at the deadline and no one feels safe.

At this point, Sophie almost wishes the deadline was here so they'd know.

And then it's the final game before the deadline and they're not ready. They're sixth in the standings again, Atlanta and DC ahead of them. The team hasn't made any moves yet, and Sophie clings to the small hope, with a win tonight, they can prove they shouldn't.

They're in Philadelphia, and they allow a goal on the very first shift of the game. She doesn't raise her eyes to the ceiling even though she wants to, because there's no telling how many cameras are on her right now.

Instead, she takes a deep breath then says, "No," as calmly and measured as she can.

"Not even you can will a goal into being called back," Merlin says.

"I can say no more. We're winning this game."

"Sofe…" Merlin trails off as Banks grinds Matty into the boards. Ralden scoops up the loose puck and takes off. "We—"

"No," she repeats. "We're winning this game for Lindy and Matty and X. We're winning it for *us*. A win tonight puts us back in fifth place in the standings. There's plenty of time for us to secure fourth. We're going to the playoffs, and this is the team we're doing it with."

"Hell, yeah," Witzer agrees.

Coach Vorgen puts his hands on Sophie's shoulders. "Herman is weak glove side. Bring two forwards down the wing—"

"Get him to bite on one, drop pass, score." Sophie nods and then nudges Merlin's knee. "You ready for this?"

"We're going to score and you're going to *told you so* me."

"Should've believed in me from the beginning."

SOPHIE CARRIES THE puck down the wing, Merlin and O'Reilly hot on her skates. She knows Herman will bite on her the same way she knows O'Reilly would rather lay a hit than cover Merlin. She slows down enough to let O'Reilly catch up and then three things happen at once; Herman goes down for her shot, Sophie drops a pass back for Merlin, and O'Reilly slams into her from the side.

It's like being hit by a sack of bricks, and she goes down hard to the ice. But she sees the goal light flash, and she ignores the ache in her side as she scrambles back to her skates. Witzer reaches Merlin first, but she joins their celebration with a giant grin. "Fucking told you so."

Merlin tries to shake his head at her, but he's beaming, too excited about the goal.

One-one.

Only one more to give them the lead and then they hold it.

This game is theirs.

X NOTCHES AN assist on Peet's goal to put them ahead 2-1.

They get a handful of power plays, but they don't manage to convert on any of them. Sophie's so close, the puck partially crosses the goal line before Herman slaps his glove down over it. She skates away from the goal, frustrated and even more determined to score on her next opportunity.

She's sitting on forty-nine career goals. Her next one is a big one.

Dima reached this milestone earlier in the season, and she's sure it'll be a talking point how she hit hers so late in the same season, but she's never been a goal scorer the way Dima is.

In the dwindling seconds of the game, she has the chance for her fiftieth. There's an open net and no one standing in her way. But skating up the far side of the ice is Matty, and she slides the puck over to him.

He passes it back to her. "Shoot."

"You shoot." She sends the puck back across the ice to him.

Two Falcons are gaining on them; they can't play not-it with the puck forever. She can see Matty preparing to pass to her again so she adds a spark of speed to her stride and skates behind the net.

With no other option, Matty taps the puck into the empty net. He doesn't smile, doesn't even celebrate as he bumps her gently into the boards. "Why didn't you shoot? It would've been fifty for you."

"So I score my fiftieth against Toronto." She will get it which is what matters to her. The when doesn't matter as much.

THE GAME ENDS with a win for Lindy, an assist for X, and a goal for Matty. If Coach Butler needed a sign their veteran core is important, he doesn't need to look beyond this game. In case he missed it, she talks up her teammates in her postgame scrum.

"We had a big game from the leaders in the room tonight. Lindy gave us timely saves to keep us in the game, X and Matty gave us the goals for the win. We're fifth in the standings now and ready for the final push of the season."

Marty Owen smiles condescendingly as if he thinks her optimism is cute.

"You and Matty played a nice game of hot potato there at the end," Rickers says. "You could've scored your fiftieth goal." He breaks the news to her gently as if she didn't willingly pass on the milestone.

"There's always next game. Did you see X's shot block that led to the breakout? I told him we just got him back and he smiled and said it's why he's on the ice, to keep the puck out of our net."

IT'S A LATE flight from Philly, but no one sleeps on the plane. They all know come tomorrow, this won't be their team anymore. Maybe when they wake up it'll look the same, but by the end of the day they will have lost a couple of players and gained some others.

Sophie doesn't expect her team to stay exactly the same, but she trusts they'll be buyers at this deadline. They aren't after the big names—they aren't competitive enough in the playoff race—but they've played well enough to deserve a show of support from the front office.

She and Teddy forgo their usual seats to play cards in the back. The veterans play dominoes, and Merlin cheerfully gives them shit for being old.

SHE WAKES UP half an hour early, nauseous as if something's wrong. She dismisses it as deadline jitters. She checks her phone as she eats breakfast, relieved to see none of the early morning headlines are for her team.

She heads to practice once she's ready, because it's better than sitting in her apartment worrying. When she reaches the rink, she has a missed call from Mr. Wilcox. Her stomach twists itself into knots, her earlier nausea returning. There's never a good reason for a call from the GM on deadline day.

She never considered *she* might be on the trading block. She spent her rookie season being told Concord was the only team desperate enough to want her. She figured it was still the same.

It takes two tries to call Mr. Wilcox back. The phone rings and rings as she heads down the hall. Dread sinks in her stomach with each step she takes.

She's a step outside the locker room when he picks up the phone. "It isn't you."

She appreciates the reassurance but still, a personal phone call from her GM? She opens the locker room doors. Matty's sitting in his empty stall, still in his street clothes. There isn't a practice jersey hanging behind him. "No."

Matty looks up, dark rings under his eyes as if he hasn't slept. Mr. Wilcox says something she doesn't hear.

"No," she repeats. She shoves her phone into her bag. She thinks she turned it off. It doesn't matter. "You—*Matty.*"

"You're here early."

"Trouble sleeping. You—" She still can't get the words out as if saying them will make them true.

"Me."

She waits for him to deny what she's thinking, but he returns to staring at the floor. Her mind flits from one thought to the next too quickly for her to say anything so they stand there in silence until X and Lindy burst into the room.

X looks from Matty to Sophie and says, "*Fuck,*" low and defeated.

"The news broke?" Matty asks. "I was hoping to tell the team."

"Ronnie called." Lindy drops his bag where he's standing. "I came over as soon as I was off the phone. Toronto?"

"It's a good fit. They're hoping to make it back to the Finals and win this year. Do you know how long it's been since I was in the playoffs?"

But you're ours, Sophie wants to say. *We're making the playoffs this season.* Or…maybe they aren't. If the front office traded their captain, they clearly don't have high hopes for this season.

Lindy sits down next to Matty, a sight she's seen dozens of time; her captain and his goalie. But now—she turns away from them, tears stingingly hotly in her eyes. Didn't they play well enough to keep their captain? Coach Butler promised and—

She pulls her fist back, prepared to punch through her practice jersey, because the Condor on it is mocking her. X grabs her elbow and then her wrist, holding her back. "Don't be stupid. You need your hands."

She looks over at Matty. *For what? Didn't you hear? Our season is already over.* She drops her arms to her sides and turns to X. "How are we supposed to do it without him?"

"We'll find a way."

She wants to press for more, have him reassure her until she believes in her team again, but she sees the way he looks at Matty, as lost as she feels. She's being selfish, demanding he comfort her when this must be harder for him than it is for her. He's known Matty longer and, as the original member of this team, he's seen everyone come and go.

She takes a deep breath and pushes down the tangle of her emotions. "We will. I promised you the playoffs."

Like I promised to keep Matty? No, Coach Butler promised we'd keep our captain.

Anger simmers under her skin. She tries to tamp it down, but every time someone comes into the locker room and sees Matty, it flares up again. Garfield and Nelson freeze as soon as they step through the door, because it's obvious something's wrong. The kids come in laughing but their laughter's swallowed up by the stillness of the room.

By the time their coach enters the room, Sophie can't look at him, too afraid of what will show on her face. She stares at her skates as Coach gives his pre-practice speech as if everything's normal. When he finishes, no one moves, waiting for Matty to lead them out.

Finally, X stands up. "Time to hit the ice."

One by one they follow their defenseman out. A few people say goodbye to Matty or give him a fist bump. It's hockey so it's not a forever goodbye. They'll see him tomorrow when they face Toronto, but she can't think about it right now; facing off against her captain, seeing him in the wrong jersey.

She's—

She's the last one in the locker room.

"It'll suck for a bit," Matty tells her. His voice sounds steadier now than it did when he told the locker room about the trade. "The first big trade is always the hardest, but it'll get better. And they're all looking to you now."

She shakes her head.

"This is your team."

She's in her skates, and Matty's in his trainers so it means they're eye to eye. She wants to look away from him, but she can't. Instead, she curls her fingers into fists. Matty's been traded so Concord has lost their captain, and he's trying pass the torch to her?

No.

"You're going to do great things, kid."

"I'm not a kid," she snaps and storms out of the locker room, as quickly as she can manage in her skates.

SHE'S THE LAST one on the ice and Coach Butler barely spares her a glance. "You're late. Three laps, and you can join your teammates."

"Coach," Merlin begins.

"You don't have a captain right now. It means you have to show personal responsibility. Do you have a problem being held accountable, Fournier?"

"No, Coach." The urge to punch him returns. He promised they would keep Matty if they pulled themselves together and they did. They kept their side of the promise, and he didn't keep his.

She takes a deep breath and starts the first of her punishment laps.

AFTER PRACTICE, SOPHIE'S thrust in front of the media where reporter after reporter asks her how she *feels* about her captain being traded. Next to her, X patiently answers the same questions. On her other side is Nelson. He's been given the third A since they don't have a captain. Marty Owen flits between them, unsure which one to poke.

Once she's free, Napoli snags her for a last-minute tribute video so they'll have something to show during tomorrow's game. He hands her a makeup kit and fusses over her hair until she glares at him. "Are we doing this or what?"

He holds his hands up and backs up to his camera. "Give me a smile."

She sits on her hands so she doesn't flip him off.

By the time she's done, she's frayed at the edges. She knows she should go home, curl up with a mug of hot chocolate, and call her mom. Instead, she heads upstairs to Coach Butler's office. She enters without knocking and closes the door behind her so the entire hall won't hear what she has to say.

Coach Butler glances up at her as if to say *what are you doing here* before he returns to attention to his phone.

All her anger flares up. She steps up to his desk and curls her hands into fists when he won't look at her again. "You *promised*. You said if we improved, we would keep everyone, and you traded Matty anyway."

"I'm your coach not your GM. Trade decisions aren't mine to make."

"You're a liar."

Coach Butler plants his hands on his desk and stands up, leaning in, until she wants to back away. She holds her ground even though it was a stupid thing to say and an even stupider one to double down on.

"The front office thinks you're going to save this franchise," he says. "Of course, it's why they brought Mathers in. Are you going to end up like him or are you going to win?"

What about why the front office brought you in? You were hired to turn the franchise around and look where we are. How long until they cut you loose?

She's angry and frustrated and scared, and he's the first available target and probably the worst one. One wrong word and he could scratch her like he did last season or assign her to Manchester. He was right earlier, he doesn't have power over trades, but he does have power over whether or not she plays.

"You're dismissed. Come back tomorrow with a better attitude."

She holds her ground long enough for doubt to flicker across his gaze. When she leaves, it takes all her self-control not to slam the door.

WHEN SHE ARRIVES home, there's evidence her cleaning service has been through. There are lines in the carpet from the vacuum and the room smells faintly of lemon. The counters gleam, and she can walk barefoot through the kitchen without stepping on spilled granola or dried peas.

It's *too* orderly. She wants to rip open a bag of quinoa and toss it around the kitchen. She wants to tip all the books off her bookcase or shove all the cushions off her couch. She wasn't able to unleash her temper at the rink, and it flares up again now, demanding a response to what happened today.

It makes her wish she put in some time with the heavy weight bag. After her meeting with Butler, it would've been cathartic to punch something. It also would've been too easy to accidentally hurt herself, and X had a point earlier this morning. Their season isn't over because Matty was traded, but if she busts up her hands doing something stupid then her season will be.

The truth she isn't ready to accept yet is they can play without Matty. It will be hard, and there will be a huge hole in their lineup, but they'll adjust and recover and, if she trusts the front office, they'll be better for it. She's in the NAHL now, trades are part of the business. If she can't handle it, she won't last much longer in this league.

She won't last if she holds a grudge against her coach, either. Yeah, he promised they could keep Matty and then broke his promise, but if she was thinking clearly, she would've remembered he isn't in charge of trades. His job is to motivate his players to be their best, and he did. He squeezed the best out of Sophie and now it's up to her to keep playing well, even though he can't dangle Matty in front of her as a reward.

Her phone rings, and she glances at it, prepared to ignore the call until she sees it's Colby. He's the only person she'd pick the phone up for right now, and she answers with a sullen, "Hey."

"Do you want to talk about it?"

"No."

"Okay."

And this is why she picked up his call. He won't force her to talk about it. Her mom would sit in silence until Sophie cracked and her dad would talk until Sophie said something to give herself a break from his lecture.

Her dad.

"Do you think it's too late to tell Dad not to come down for the Dads' Trip?" They play Toronto and Quebec before they kick off the Dads' Trip against Denver. Having her dad in town is stressful in the best of situations and having him here in the middle of this mess...

"Probably," Colby answers.

She sighs and sinks down onto her couch. "We play Denver for our first game in front of the dads. At least I can't play worse than I did last time." There's no reason to work herself up over this. She and her dad have their routine down pat by now. She'll play, he'll tell her how she can be better, she'll play again. And he won't let her wallow in the trade the way her mom would.

"You've been on a hot streak recently."

"Because I wanted to keep Matty." And somehow she's talking about the thing she didn't want to talk about. "I know I shouldn't need extra motivation, but what am I supposed to play for now?"

"Play for the team. You told me you're making the playoffs this season."

Concord first.

She takes a deep breath and feels more settled after it. "Tomorrow's going to be a fucking disaster."

"It's hockey. Focus on being your best. It doesn't matter who you face when you're on top of your game."

"Thanks, Colb."

THE NEWS OF the trade spreads quickly. On its heels is speculation over who the next captain of the Concord Condors will be. The general consensus is it will be X. He's their longest tenured player, his name is synonymous with Concord, and if anyone can drag this team to the playoffs it's him.

When he's asked about it after morning skate, he laughs and shakes his head. "I'm flattered you think so, but I've never been interested in being captain. There are plenty of my teammates who are more deserving."

"Like who?" Rossetti presses.

X keeps smiling but doesn't give her the answer she wants.

Sophie hangs back after her shower, waits until X emerges from the trainers' room so she can ambush him. He sighs when he sees her but follows her down the hall to the exit.

"You took yourself out of the running for the captaincy." She doesn't want to see anyone else with the C this season. She knows the team has to move on—they can't linger on the trade forever—but seeing anyone else with Matty's C while the trade is still raw would be wrong. Maybe it would be okay if it was X, but he's made it clear he doesn't want it.

"The next captain should be someone who's going to be here for a long time." He pauses and looks at her, until she gets it.

"We agreed, no retirement talk. You're our guy. You're *the* guy. Who are we without you?" She can't lose Matty and X. The three of them and Lindy were supposed to be the foundation supporting this team. They can't lose half of their veteran squad in one go.

"Sofe..." X drags a hand down his face and keeps walking down the hallway. "I've been here since Concord's beginning. It sounds cool, but it means I'm old. I don't have enough years left in me to lead this team the way a captain should. I'll wear an A, and I'll make my voice heard, but it would be unfair to the team if I accepted the captaincy. There are better options."

"You're the only captain I'd accept this season."

"We both know it isn't true. You're too much of a hockey player. If Butler named Peets captain tomorrow, you'd stand in front of the media and tell them what a good choice he was."

She wants to argue, but he has a point. They fall quiet until they're out of the building. "Tonight's going to be hard."

"It is." X doesn't lie, and she's not sure if she's annoyed with him or not. She's an adult and a professional hockey player, she doesn't need to be coddled, but it would've been nice, even for a few minutes, to believe tonight won't suck as much as she knows it will.

THEY LOSE 2-3 against Toronto.

It isn't an embarrassing showing; they went up against a team who made it all the way to the Maple Cup Finals last season and held their own.

But what the final score doesn't show is how Concord played like they'd never seen a hockey puck before. In the first period they were outshot 17-2.

What the final score doesn't show is the dozens of times Sophie turned to ask Matty how to make the lines click better or how to get their team to stop making stupid mistakes.

What the final score doesn't show is the team in the locker room when the game is over, and they've lost and doubt creeps in. If Matty was traded it means their management doesn't believe in this season. And if management doesn't believe in this season, then why should the team?

The A on Sophie's chest feels as if it's burning into her skin, but she doesn't know what to say. How does she motivate a team of players who have given up? Every person in this room should want to be a part of a history-making team and instead, they quietly undress, shoulders heavy, because tomorrow they have to get out there and do the same thing again.

Chapter Eighteen

THIS IS YOUR team now.

Matty's words stick with her. If he's right, if this is her team, then she damn well better act like it. They have a lot of ground to make up if they want to qualify for the playoffs.

With the back-to-back, her first chance to test her attitude is during warm-ups. She starts with the kids, because they don't have seasons of disappointment weighing them down like X or the pressure of being one of the guys expected to defy the odds like Nelson or Merlin. Big Red and Spitz are still new and Peets looks spooked by being the second line center now, but she can work with this.

"Ready for a big game?" She claps Spitz on the shoulder. "You on the first d-pairing, Peets here as the 2C, you're giving Manchester a good rep."

"I still don't know what Rocky's going to do," Big Red says. He glances over at Peter Rockburn, the guy they picked up in the trade. Everything else was draft picks and prospects, but Toronto wanted to dump his salary, and Concord needed a NAHL-ready center.

"It's hockey," Sophie says. "You both know how to play. Read and react. You can do it."

She skates over to Zinger next. He's working his stickhandling near the bench. He isn't wearing his helmet and his black hair is sticking up in all directions, held together by sweat and too much gel. He looks up as she approaches. "It's weird not playing with Peets."

"You'll settle into playing with Rocky. Do you know what would help?"

"Practice?" he asks drily.

She laughs. "How about a goal?"

She can't imagine what it's like to be Rocky, one moment on a team pushing to win it all and then suddenly on a team far down in the standings. She hasn't talked to him besides a brief welcome, because he's sticking close to the veteran guys, ones who have been traded around like he was.

"Not all of us are you," Zinger says. "We can't decide we want a goal and score on the next shift."

"Then do it the old-fashioned way, hard work and patience."

She laughs again as he swats her. She skates over to Garfield and Nelson next, and her smile is replaced with something more guarded. While some of her teammates have seen a promotion since the trade, Garfield and Nelson were moved to the second line. Sophie's the first line center, and Coach Butler kept her with her usual linemates, because they've spent nearly two seasons building their chemistry. It means a bump up for Merlin and Witzer and a bump down for Garfield and Nelson.

In reality, it isn't a difference in anything but name, but it doesn't mean they'll take it well. She and Nelson have always had a strained relationship. He wasn't comfortable with having a woman on the team, and he puts up with her because he's supposed to, not because he's accepted her. He took Hayes's side last year when she and her fellow rookie feuded. The A he was given after Thurman was traded was given to Sophie to start this season. She doesn't think he'd hold a grudge against her for it, but she's had teammates hate her for less.

The two wingers stop passing the puck back and forth when they spot her. Nelson, now wearing an A again, flips her the puck. She catches it on her stick, tosses it into the air, and catches it with her glove.

"I heard you're rallying the troops," Garfield says. "Silverman tweaked his groin last game. He's slow going post to post."

"Let's make him work then." She hands Nelson his puck back. "Make sure you tell Peets. I need to finish my rounds."

She skates over to her linemates as Nelson gathers his own linemates to him.

"Here comes trouble," Witzer says.

"Traffic and screens in front of Silverman all night. Cut off his lines of sight, force him to move, and we'll score."

She leaves them to continue their warm-ups and seeks out Teddy. He's deep in a split, rocking side-to-side to reach an even deeper stretch. "No groin trouble for you?"

"That's the hope." He shifts into his butterfly. "How tired is everyone after last night's game?"

"We'll be strong in front of you. This is an important game to win." Quebec is in striking distance of Concord in the standings which makes these two critical points. It won't do any good for them to overtake DC only for Quebec to leapfrog them at the last minute. They need to win and to do it in regulation.

"They're all important if we want to make the playoffs."

Sophie grins. "Now you're getting it."

"I didn't…" Teddy shakes his head. "Go practice scoring. I can't do it on my own."

"You won't have to." Promise delivered, she leaves him to his stretches and grabs J-Rod and the other d-men to tell them about Silverman's weakness.

LAST NIGHT, SOPHIE lost the opening faceoff to Matty. Tonight, she beats Coderre to start the game on the right note.

Merlin carries the puck into the offensive zone, and passes to Sophie. She skates around the back of the net and fights off Coderre as he wraps his stick and then his arm around her to slow her progress. She collides with Rotrand and loses the puck. She steals it back, regaining possession long enough to trap it against the boards.

She battles with Coderre on one side and Rotrand on the other until Witzer drops down to help her. They emerge with the puck, and Witzer passes up to Kevlar. He walks the blue line, evaluating, until Witzer pushes his way to the front of the net to act as a screen. Only then does Kevlar unload his shot.

It's blocked by Galloway, and the Bobcats start the puck the other way.

Sophie's first four shifts fall into a similar pattern; strong offensive work followed by scrambling on defense until Teddy bails them out.

Her fifth shift is the same, a good push on Silverman's net before a blocked shot sends Quebec the other way. But then it's Concord's turn to block a shot, and Sophie's the one on the breakaway. She takes off down the ice, big powerful strides, until she's too far ahead for any of the Quebec players to catch her.

She approaches Silverman from the side, waits until he seals his post, and she crosses over, forcing him to push to the opposite post. Like Garfield told her during warm-ups, he's slow, and she pokes the puck between his skate and the post before he can close the gap.

One-nil.

And the big five-oh.

She spits her mouth guard into her glove, raises her arms above her head, and roars as the goal light flashes. Fifty fucking goals. She slaps the glass, laughing as the Quebec fans slap back, booing as if they can bring her down.

She turns around in time for Merlin to knock into her. "Fuck yeah!" he shouts as he slaps her helmet.

Witzer flies in, yelling more of the same, and chest bumps her into the boards.

Kevlar and Theo are the last to reach her, but they each pat her helmet before Theo gives her a push toward the bench. She skates through the fist bump line and sits down next to Garfield. "Thanks for the tip. Silverman definitely isn't as quick as he usually is."

"The goal was all you."

She raps her knuckles against his helmet. "Little bit you. Now, it's your turn to make Silverman work, eh?"

GARFIELD SCORES WITH two minutes left in the period. He and Sophie exchange a grin as he skates through the line at the bench. "Can't let you have all the fun," he says.

With thirty seconds left in the game, Quebec cuts Concord's lead in half. The stadium cheers as if they've won the game. There's still another forty minutes left to play, but Sophie knows a goal can change the momentum of the game.

She gathers her teammates to her on the bench. "We can't get sloppy." She has to shout to be heard above the crowd. "We play hard for the last thirty seconds and we carry our focus into the next period."

When they get to the locker room, Coach Butler throws his clipboard and says the same thing Sophie did but with more expletives.

AFTER INTERMISSION, SOPHIE leads her team to ice level, but she doesn't jump on the ice right away. In the buildup to the game, she almost forgot something important. She slips behind her bench to the glass seats and ignores the jeers and the middle fingers, the fans who light up and show her the worst sides of themselves because they think she's paying attention to them.

She ignores them all as she searches the rows for the fan she wants to see. There, in a Trois-Rivières jersey, is Estelle. Sophie waves. When Estelle frowns, confused, she takes her helmet off and waves again. Estelle's mouth drops open. She tugs her dad's sleeve and points.

Sophie waves again before she turns around and right into—Coach Butler.

"The team needs you focused," he says.

She's the most focused one on the team right now. She's the only one who believes there's still hope left for her season, and he's wasting his time on her? "I am."

His gaze flicks behind her. "Are you?"

She pops her mouth guard in and steps by him so she can get on the ice.

SHE SCORES ON the opening shift of the period. When she stares down her coach, he nods, pleased as if he's the reason she put the puck in the back of the net. Her eyes narrow and frustration prickles under her skin until Kevlar crashes into her, knocking her irritation away.

THEY WIN 3-1, and Sophie's delayed with Teddy, because they're both named as stars of the game. Teddy's announced as the third star, Coderre is the second. As soon as Sophie's announced as the first star, the few remaining fans boo as heartily as they can. She waves to them as she skates out to accept the accolades. Then she returns to the bench where none of her teammates are waiting for her.

She doesn't blame them. She's cautious as she enters the locker room, prepared for a whipped cream pie to the face or a bucket of water dropped on her head, something light-hearted to welcome her to the fifty-goal club.

Instead, Theo hands her a pizza box. The bottom of the box is still warm which means he ordered her a pizza to Quebec's stadium. Why? And when?

"Um." She looks up from the box at Theo who grins as men with cameras crowd closer to catch her reaction. She opens the lid, half-expecting something to jump out at her. Instead, it's a normal pizza. Well, not quite normal. There's pineapple and ham on it, and she doesn't understand why people insist on putting fruit on pizza. She glances up at him, still confused. "Thank you?"

"Pineapple and ham." Theo looks proud of himself. "It's a Hawaiian pizza."

Sophie nods, hoping to stall until someone explains the joke to her.

"Like *Hawaii Five-o*?" Theo asks.

She ups her smile and holds the box out. "Anyone want a slice?"

"Hopeless," Theo says but he snags two pieces.

SOPHIE'S PHONE BUZZES nonstop from the locker room to the bus. She has congratulatory texts from Colby and Matty and some of the guys she played with at Chilton. Travis sent her a series of exclamation points and passed on Figuli's congratulations. Her response to him is interrupted four times by texts from Dima. It takes her an embarrassingly long time to realize Dima is sending her fifty puck emojis one at a time.

SOPHIE: *I hate you. Why are you like this?*

Her phone buzzes with another three pucks.

SOPHIE: *Seriously. Why?*

Another seven come in while she's texting Colby.

"Someone's popular," Teddy says.

"Dima." Sophie glares at her phone as if it will make him stop. "Next time we play Boston, I'm going to check him so hard he forgets his name."

Teddy leans over to look at her phone. He laughs as more pucks pop up. "He's being supportive."

"He's being a pain in the ass," she grumbles but she can't quite keep the smile off her face.

Buried in her texts from Dima is a message from Elsa congratulating her on the milestone. Sophie opens it a few times, intending to answer, but she doesn't know what to say. Elsa knows how she feels. Sophie wants her on her wing more than anything, but she promised herself she wouldn't pressure Elsa to come over. She opens the message again to stare at the words.

Congrats on 50 goals. You would've had it sooner with a better left winger.

It's an echo of what Sophie told her after her four-goal opener this season. Is this another promise? Sophie's musing is interrupted by another three pucks from Dima. She laughs and tucks her phone into her pocket.

She pokes Teddy's side. "When are you scoring your first goal? I'm running away with the competition here."

THE FINAL PRACTICE before their Denver game is brutal. Coach Butler pushes them hard and Sophie pushes herself even harder. She was the weak link last time they played, and she can't afford a slipup tomorrow. Sure, they're only on a one-game winning streak, but tonight could make it two. *Has* to make it two if they want a shot at the playoffs.

She stumbles up the stairs to her apartment, wrung out in the best of ways. Her legs tremble and her hands shake, nothing a solid meal and a long nap won't fix. She unlocks her door, turns the handle and...runs into her closed door.

She rubs her shoulder and frowns at her door before she tries the handle again. It's locked. She must be more tired than she thought. She unlocks her door for real this time and opens it.

Her dad is sitting on her couch. He has broad shoulders and a thick waist, two things she inherited from him. His hair is a light brown, almost blond in the summer. From the shoulders down she looks like her dad. From the neck up, the dark brown hair, blue eyes, pointed nose, she looks like her mom.

Her dad insisted on renting a car at the airport, because he didn't want to be stuck at the apartment while she's at practice or games, which is fair, but she figured he would at least tell her when he arrived. Apparently not.

"You should've told me you were here, I would've picked up something for lunch." Her plan for herself was leftovers, but she feels weird offering them to her dad. He was her first coach, her first trainer, the first person to see potential in her and push her to reach it. She's spent a lifetime trying to live up to his expectations of her, and two-day-old quinoa won't cut it.

"I ate at the airport."

He has a newspaper arranged on her coffee table, the sports section folded and waiting until he's read everything else. She leaves him to his reading and pulls a couple of Tupperware boxes out of the fridge to heat up.

Already, this is different than last year when her mom visited. She isn't sure why she expected anything else. If Sophie's team was blown out 2-9, her mom could find something positive to say about Sophie's game. On the flipside, if her team won 9-2, her dad could find a dozen things for her to improve on.

"Denver tomorrow," her dad says. "Will you keep your cool this time?"

She sighs and hopes the sound is covered by the microwave.

"Don't get huffy with me. You're the one who lost your composure and broke a man's nose."

Yeah, months ago. And he deserved it. She pulls her lunch out of the microwave. "It won't happen again." She eats standing up at the island counter as her dad reads his newspaper in the other room.

"This Marty Owen fellow is critical. It's important having reporters willing to challenge you."

"For sure. I have to nap. Do you want me to set you up with the TV?"

"I'm going to call your mother. I'll tell her you said hello."

Sophie lingers in the kitchen for another moment, but she doesn't have anything else to say. She nods, mostly to herself, and heads down the hall to her room.

SHE WAKES UP refreshed but not prepared for her dad to insist he drive to dinner. She should've been, she's known him her entire life and he hasn't changed, but it still takes her a few seconds to gather her thoughts enough to say, "I've lived here for two years now, I know where we're going."

"GPS," her dad dismisses. He holds up the keys to his rental.

She imagines what her teammates will say if her dad drives her to team dinner as if she's still in midget. "I'm driving." She grabs her own keys from where they hang near the door.

Her dad's caught off guard by her assertion, and after a five-count with nothing from him, she's afraid he'll insist on taking two cars to dinner. Finally, he tucks his keys into his pockets. "I suppose I could have a beer or two with dinner. Your mother can't stand the smell."

Sophie nods and, glad she's won, hurries them out the door before he can change his mind. Her dad talks about beer the whole drive there, his favorites and how he should try something local even though he's certain it will be disappointing. Sophie doesn't even drink, but anger still prickles under her skin at the slight against her city. She answers in "huhs" and "hmms", not speaking an actual word for the whole ride.

By the time they arrive at the steakhouse, her patience is frayed, and she's perhaps too enthusiastic when she spots Teddy and his dad getting out of Teddy's Escalade. Sophie waves and Teddy pauses long enough for them to catch up to him.

"Good evening, Mister Augereau," she greets. "You grew up in Montreal, didn't you?"

Mr. Augereau answers in French, a twinkle in his eye, which tells her Teddy inherited his sense of humor from his dad. Sophie answers in halting French before, thankfully, her dad takes over, and Sophie and Teddy are ignored in favor of comparing favorite places in the city.

Teddy, cementing his standing as her favorite teammate, urges their dads to sit together at dinner and guides Sophie to the far end of the table.

"Thank you," she murmurs. "If I make it through this week it will be a miracle."

She glances down the table. Her dad shakes his cloth napkin out and lays it carefully across his lap. He plucks the drink menu from its place, nestled between the salt and pepper shaker. He gave up nights out with his buddies from work to stay home and train her or to drive her to practice. He and her mom both sacrificed so she and her brother could play hockey.

She wouldn't be here, with Teddy on one side and Zinger on the other, if it weren't for her dad. She shakes her own napkin out and lays it across her lap. "I wouldn't in the NAHL if he hadn't pushed me. But...sometimes I wish he could start a game breakdown with 'you did well.'"

It's a silly hope; he didn't do it when she was a kid, so why should he start now?

COACH BUTLER DOESN'T avoid the Sophie-Sinclair matchup which either means he has faith in her or, more likely, it's a test. He wants to see if she can keep her cool better than the last time they played the Boulders. He wants to see if she's *less emotional.*

Thinking about the previous game makes anger prickle along her spine. But if Coach Butler wants to see her growth, she'll put it on display.

She has her first opportunity on her third shift. They're pinned in their own zone, and she battles with Kirkland against the boards for possession of the puck. She wins the puck to Witzer, but it's intercepted by Pickard and thrown on net. Lindy slaps his glove down, but Pickard takes a few extra jabs. Kevlar puts himself between the Boulders' defenseman and his goalie and glowers. When the officials go to make sure it doesn't escalate, Sinclair shoves Sophie.

He glances up at the box where all the dads are sitting. "Daddy gonna get mad if I rough up his little girl?"

She doesn't have the time for his bullshit. She shoulders past him and he puts his stick out, stopping her. The crowd, restless from the almost-goal and disappointed with the lack of Pickard-Kevlar fight, perk up at the prospect of a Sophie-Sinclair fight.

It's Merlin who knocks Sinclair's stick out of his hands. It clatters loudly on the ice. "Fuck off."

Sinclair smirks, his attention never leaving Sophie. "Well-trained."

She grabs a handful of Merlin's jersey before he launches himself at Sinclair. She tugs him toward the bench and, once he realizes it's skate on his own or be towed, he shakes off her grip. "I'm going to deck him. Fucking asshole."

"You're going to play hard and stay out of the box."

Merlin knocks the bench door open and clambers through. He sits heavily next to Zinger and glares at the Boulders bench.

Sophie takes a deep breath and sits next to him.

KELLMAN, DENVER'S RESIDENT brute, has an extra elbow for Sophie every time they fight for the puck. He can't keep up with her skill-wise so he wraps his stick around her waist in a hold the officials don't call, he slashes her ankles when she beats him to the puck and, once one of his teammates stops her along the boards, he throws a shoulder into her to knock her off the puck.

She ends up on the ice with Rawlings, Sinclair 2.0, and he crushes her into the boards. She wobbles but stays on her skates. He shoves her again as Kirkland sweeps his stick out, in theory going for the puck, but he hits her ankles instead and between the two of them, she goes down, landing hard on her knees.

"This is a good place for you," Rawlings says.

She grits her teeth and, seizing on their distraction, pokes the puck free to Merlin. As soon as he scoops it up, she pushes to her skates and plants herself in front of the net. Merlin passes up to Kevlar then drifts to the far dot. He takes the return pass and drops to one knee as he shoots. Pickard's in the right place; the puck deflects off his skate but it lands on Sophie's stick. She slips the puck under Lenno's pads and pushes it across the goal line.

She seeks out Rawlings as she lifts her arms in celebration. *Fuck you and your piece of shit team.*

SINCLAIR IS SMARTER than she gives him credit for. It only takes him a period and a half before he realizes he won't throw her off her game like he did last time. She's practiced with Ritchie, and she's been given the responsibility of the Condors; she won't lose her composure this time.

So he turns to easier targets.

She doesn't know what he says to Theo but one moment, Sophie's skating to the bench for a change, the next there are gloves on the ground and both men are snarling as they try to punch the teeth out of each other's mouths.

"Aw, hell," Sophie says.

"About damn time," Merlin says. "He's been running his fucking mouth all night."

"And now you're letting him fire up his team and take one of our best d-men out of the game for five minutes. He's all talk and no action until you give him some action."

Merlin turns away from the fight to stare at her. "You have no idea how you sounded, do you?"

She glares at him.

The fight ends with Theo pinned to the ice, and the Denver bench roars for their captain. Theo and Sinclair continue to shout at each other as they're escorted to the penalty boxes, and they keep going after they're shut in.

Merlin, energized by the fight, sits near the glass separating the two benches so he can shout over the poor broadcaster caught between the two teams. Kellman, looking gleeful, stands on his bench so he can shout back. Spitz and Big Red are pulled into the yelling, and Sophie looks to Coach Butler to do something, because the team is losing their damn minds.

He crosses his arms over his chest and looks as happy as she's ever seen him in a game.

She's tempted to throw her hands up in the air. Instead, she sits down next to Kevlar. "Tell me you still have your head screwed on straight."

"I wouldn't say straight, but I'm not about to fight anyone."

"Good. Talk to the kids, would you?"

J-Rod's drawn into the fray before Coach Butler sends J-Rod and X over the boards with Peets' line. She chews on her mouth guard and hopes J-Rod doesn't do something stupid and get his head pounded by Rawlings.

Ten seconds into the shift it's *Garfield* who drops his gloves. *You're supposed to know better*, she thinks as he throws punches in a fight he's outmatched in.

There's a whole three minutes before Kuzy and Kellman drop the gloves. She's so angry she sees red as more people are added to the penalty boxes.

"Fournier, you're up," Coach Butler says.

She takes Merlin and Witzer over the boards with them, but they have J-Rod and X on the back end thanks to two of their d-men being in the box. She lines up for the faceoff against Denver's third line center.

It seems as if it takes an eternity for the horn to sound, ending the second period. As they pass their coach on their way to the locker room, she can't help but notice he still looks cheery. *So it's only too emotional when I fight in a game? If it's the guys then you're* proud?

She's practically vibrating with anger when she enters the locker room. She's been on her best behavior all game, putting up with Denver and their fucking bullshit, because they have a game to win. And her teammates are...comparing bloodied knuckles.

Theo shows off his hands and mimes a few on the punches he threw as if Sinclair didn't hand his ass to him.

"You seem awfully proud of yourselves," Sophie says, her voice low and dangerous. The entire locker room falls silent as they look to her. Coach Butler won't do anything to curb this? Fine. Sophie will. Matty told her this was her team now and they're going to play Condors hockey, not some Boulders knockoff.

She stops in front of Theo, towering over in him in her skates as he sits in his stall. "Why'd you fight?"

"Sinclair said something he shouldn't have about you." He puffs up, as if he wants her to pat him on the head and thank him.

She turns to Garfield. "You?"

He, at least, has the sense to look wary. "Same."

Kuzy is the last she faces, and he doesn't even wait for her to ask the question. "Kellman was talking shit."

"Did you know Sinclair spent the first damn period spewing shit to try and get me off my game? Rawlings did the same. Kellman plays fucking dirty but he kept his damn mouth shut at least. I didn't let them get under my skin, because we have a game to win, but as soon as Sinclair turned his attention to you, you folded like a fucking chair."

She looks at Garfield again. "So, seeing his captain's success, Rawlings thought he'd try the same thing. How'd he do, Garfield? Did he get to you?"

Garfield narrows his eyes but he doesn't say anything.

"Then they send out a guy who scores ten goals a season if it's a good one for him, because why risk putting one of their best players in the box when Concord's *easy* to bait?"

Kuzy flinches.

Sophie turns away, because she can't stand the sight of them right now. When she was weak against Denver, she was deservedly called out by everyone from her mom to Lenny Dernier. But she took the lesson to heart and adjusted her game. And now her teammates are being dumbasses.

"Sofe, you didn't hear what they were saying."

She spins to Merlin who sinks into his stall as if he regrets opening his mouth. "Of course I heard what they were saying. They tried all their lines on me first. And do you know what I did? I played fucking hockey. Do you think you're being chivalrous by punching every guy who says something about me? You're not. You're inviting every single guy on every damn team to think of his worst lines, because if he can't get to me then he'll at least get to you. I don't want you fighting for me. I want you playing hockey."

Nelson's gaze darts to Coach Butler, and it takes every ounce of her self-control not to scream. "This next period will be hard," she says, reclaiming the attention of the room. "Denver thinks they can get to you now. When you don't respond, they'll escalate. Do not engage."

"Play fucking hockey?" X asks. There's a smile tugging at his lips, but it isn't teasing. "I think we can handle it."

"We have a game to win." Sophie finally returns to her own stall. She sits down and looks to Coach Butler for his input.

It's Coach Vorgen who steps forward. "I think Sophie summed it up well. Play hockey. Make your dads proud."

Coach Butler takes over, but Coach Vorgen pulls Sophie aside on their way back up to the ice to congratulate her on her control of the room.

"Anyone can talk," she says. "What matters is if they listen."

Coach Vorgen claps her on the shoulder and ushers her ahead of him.

TWO MINUTES INTO the third period, Theo scores with a slapper from the point.

Ten minutes into the period, Kellman tries to start something with Merlin. Sophie's winger looks at him as if he's an irritating fly and hooks his arm through Sophie's as they skate away. "Let's score a goal."

It takes a power play opportunity, but they do; Sophie to Merlin to Garfield. She's the first to reach Garfield after the goal, and she can't help but ask, "Better than sitting in the box, eh?"

He tries to look disgruntled, but his smile ruins it. "Better for my hands, certainly."

She laughs and pats his helmet before opening their celebration up to the rest of the guys on the ice.

Realizing something's changed, Denver sends Sinclair's line out against Rocky and the kids. Wimberly knocks into Zinger, shoving the smaller player to the ground. He stands over him and looks at Big Red, challenging. Despite his name, Big Red isn't big and fortunately he doesn't take the bait. Sinclair says something to Rocky, who laughs and skates after the puck.

The clock's winding down on the game, the score is 3-0, and Sophie feels confident even as Denver pulls their goalie. She's on the bench as Denver begins their full-on assault against the net, throwing shot after shot at Lindy. Somehow, they knock down every clearing attempt, and they keep the puck trapped in Concord's zone.

It's Kellman of all people who scores, and Sophie feels a flicker of irritation as Lindy's shutout is ruined. More troubling, the Denver bench is all on their feet, revitalized as if they think they can score another two before time runs out.

"We shut it down now," Sophie says.

"Aye, aye," Kevlar says as he throws one leg then the other over the boards. Theo follows him out, and they successfully defend against another Denver wave. Sophie's on the edge of the bench, her stick planted on the ground, ready to spring into action as soon as Coach Butler calls on her.

Instead, he sends Peets' line out.

Witzer pats her knee consolingly. She chews on her mouth guard as Peets takes a defensive zone faceoff against Sinclair. It's a good learning opportunity for him, and it's important for Coach Butler to show faith in him, but she still wishes she was the one out there.

Peets locks sticks with Sinclair and holds his ground as Sinclair bears down. Garfield darts in, scoops up the loose puck, and outlets a pass to Nelson. Rawlings knocks Nelson off the puck. Pickard ends up with the puck on his stick, and settles it long enough to pass to his d-partner. Denver moves the puck and finally takes a shot. Kevlar drops down to block it and it skitters to open ice.

Even though Denver has six guys to Concord's five, it's Garfield who reaches the puck first. One long stride then another and he's broken out of their zone. A few more strides and he'll hit the red line, and it'll be safe for him to dump the puck in.

Kirkland scrambles, skating backward to keep himself between Garfield and the open net. A feint one way, a lunge the other, and Garfield has a clear lane. He sends the puck skipping down the ice and into the net.

Four-one.

Garfield looks right at her before he's swallowed by the guys on the ice. When they return to the bench, he grins as he sits down next to her. "Am I forgiven?"

She matches his smile. "Getting there."

Rocky and the kids finish out the game and they win 4-1, a decisive victory to kick off the Dads' Trip.

THEY DON'T SEE much of their dads after the game, because the team goes out to celebrate the win and have a belated celebration for Sophie's fiftieth goal. She shows up to the bar early enough to snag a seat deep in the booth.

Theo, spotting her, disappears to the bar and when he comes back, he offers her a yellow drink with an umbrella resting on the rim. "It's non-alcoholic, promise."

She takes a cautious sniff and wrinkles her nose. "What's your obsession with pineapple?"

"It's a great fruit." He grins, showing off his usual missing teeth. He didn't sacrifice any more in tonight's game. Her job is to make sure he doesn't lose any on her behalf. She clinks her glass against his beer, a thank-you, both for the drink and for pulling himself together.

"Are you dancing tonight?" Witzer asks. "I'm sure we can get the DJ to play 'All I Do is Win'."

Merlin rolls his eyes. "Sofe never dances." He looks around the table. "But someone has to celebrate this win in style."

"I will," Spitz volunteers.

"You? You're almost as much of a hermit as Sofe."

"I'm not a hermit," Sophie protests.

Spitz puffs up, offended. "I know how to have fun." He pokes Big Red. "You're coming with me."

"He's the worst wingman," Wilchinski complains. "He always steals your girls."

Big Red grins, accepting the accusation. He's cute in a puppyish sort of way, full of enthusiasm and almost always sporting a wide smile.

"Take Peets with you," Garfield suggests. "He has a girlfriend."

There's some shuffling as the younger guys are shooed from the booth to dance. As they settle back into the booth, Sophie ends up next to Teddy. The guys fight over who has to buy the next round and what kind of beer they want, occasionally taking a pause to laugh at the kids as they dance.

"You have the start against Minneapolis," Sophie tells Teddy.

His smile is fond even if it's also a touch exasperated. "We're out celebrating two wins, and you're already looking forward to our next game?"

"We need to close out the season strong."

Teddy shrugs and loses his smile. He looks older and worried, his shoulders weighted down with the pressure of the start. "Rust is one of the best American players of all time."

"You'll stop him." Sophie nudges her pineapple drink toward him. "Do you want this?"

"Fuck no."

She laughs and braces herself before she takes a long swallow. She grimaces but when Theo looks over she gives him a thumbs-up.

"Liar," Teddy whispers.

She elbows him and lets him steer them away from hockey so he can talk about Alyssa's class. They're gearing up for Colonial Day, which is apparently some kind of American tradition where the kids all wear bonnets and dresses or boots and trousers to school and make candles. It's not the strangest thing she's seen since coming to America, but it's up there.

She finishes her drink as Teddy explains to her how to make a powdered wig out of cotton balls and pieces of yarn. She smiles politely during a breakdown of colonial diets. Finally, though, she checks her phone and decides it's time for her to turn in.

"You're leaving?" Merlin asks as Kevlar hands her her jacket. "Don't tell me you have a curfew because your dad's in town."

"I don't have a curfew."

No one looks as if they believe her, but none of them stop her either so she counts it as a win. She makes it outside in time to see Spitz helping a woman into a cab. He spent most of the night dancing with her; she knows because the guys took bets on whether they'd leave together, and cheered raucously when they finally did. At least the bar was noisy enough Spitz and the woman didn't hear.

The cab drives away with the woman inside and Spitz on the curb. He spots Sophie and shoves his hands deep into his pockets. "She was really drunk. I didn't—I—"

Sophie cuts off his stammering with a hand on his shoulder. He doesn't need to give her an explanation for why he isn't going home with someone. "You're a good guy. Do you want a ride home?" She holds up her car keys.

He hesitates as if he thinks her offer is a trap.

"No girl talk," she promises. "We have the Minneapolis game to look forward to. We're winning it for Teddy."

"One shift at a time?" Spitz guesses.

They share a smile.

Chapter Nineteen

THE NEXT MORNING in the locker room, Sophie's changing from her workout gear into her practice gear when Garfield and Nelson ambush Spitz. Garfield tugs at the collar of his shirt, examining his neck, and he sounds disappointed as he asks, "Not a biter? She looked like a biter."

Spitz flushes and bats Garfield's hands away.

"Maybe the neck's too obvious. Did she bite your thighs?" Nelson eyes Spitz's legs, his thick thighs barely contained by his flimsy spandex. Spitz shuffles backward as if he's afraid Nelson's going to yank down his shorts to check.

"Spitz likes the gentle ones," Peets volunteers. He grins brightly as Spitz glares at him. "You know, hand-holding, whispered confessions while sharing the same pillow..." He touches his hand to his heart and sighs.

Spitz, his face bright red now, flips off his friend which leads to another raucous round of laughter.

"Seriously, though." Nelson's determined not to let this go. "How was your night?"

A few new guys trickle into the locker room, zeroing in on the conversation. It makes it even more obvious when Spitz glances at Sophie. Is he looking for her to rescue him? She could easily shut down this whole conversation by saying he didn't take anyone home, but Spitz could've done it from the beginning. Does he want them thinking he took a girl home?

"Sofe doesn't care if you give us the dirty details," Merlin says. "But if you're concerned about her delicate ears..." He claps his hands over Sophie's ears and then shouts loud enough for her to hear anyway. "You can tell us now!"

Sophie knocks Merlin's hands away. "Hurry up and change." When no one moves, except Nelson so he can lift up Spitz's shirt, she adds, "Last one on the ice has to help Merlin clean up the pucks."

"What?" Merlin squawks.

"If he's last, does he have to do it on his own?" Big Red asks.

Sophie grins and there's suddenly a mad rush to get changed, everyone forgetting about Spitz and his night.

MERLIN IS TRYING, and failing, to use his seniority on the team to make Big Red help him after practice when Coach Butler says, "Fournier, you're with me."

"Oooh," the team choruses.

Coach looks as unimpressed with them as Sophie feels. She looks down at her skates, but before she can even ask her question, he answers. "As you are is fine."

"Someone's in trouble," Wilchinski sing-songs.

X claps Wilchinski on the back. "Thanks for volunteering to help Merlin."

Nelson, because he's an asshole, knocks a bucket of pucks to the ice, scattering them. "Oops."

Sophie's glad to leave X to corral their teammates. She puts her skate guards on and awkwardly waddles after Coach Butler. When they reach his office, she pauses, because Coach Vorgen, Mr. Pauling, and Mr. Wilcox are all there.

Is she in trouble? Why is she having a post-practice meeting with two of her coaches, her GM, and her team's owner? She takes her helmet down and pats her hair once before giving up on it.

"You have exceeded our expectations recently," Mr. Pauling tells her. He offers her a warm smile as she sits cautiously in one of the chairs. "You've had an offensive breakout in the latter half of the season and, more importantly, your game against Denver demonstrated your personal growth."

Mr. Wilcox and Coach Vorgen both nod. She feels like she needs to say something so she offers a tentative, "Thank you."

"The team looks to you now," Coach Vorgen tells her.

She can't help her quick glance at her head coach. His lips are pursed in a straight line, clearly unhappy they look to her first and him second. It's something she'll have to be wary of, because she doesn't want to be seen as stepping on his toes. The coach is the first authority on the team, then the captain, then the As. It's the hierarchy she's had drilled into her since her first organized team.

"For these reasons, and others, we're offering you the captaincy of the Concord Condors," Mr. Pauling says.

Sophie's brain screeches to a halt. Matty's been gone for three games, and they want to pin the C to her sweater? She doesn't command the locker room the way he does. Maybe the team does look to her now, but she doesn't have the answers they need. She—

Another one of the hardest things in hockey is when they ask you to train your replacement.

This is your team now.

They traded Matty with the intention of slotting Sophie into his place.

She sags back against her seat, feeling small inside her pads. She would be the first woman to wear the C, another accomplishment to add to her growing list. But...she isn't ready for it. What has she done to earn it besides not get traded? Yeah, she scored her fiftieth career goal a couple games ago, and she didn't completely lose her shit this time against Denver, but those aren't reasons for a captaincy. Those are basic expectations.

She looks around the room, at the three men smiling as they wait for her acceptance and the one whose expression is neutral as if they're down by two in a big game. She takes a steadying breath. "Thank you for the offer, but I have to decline."

Mr. Wilcox's smile slips from his face.

Mr. Pauling chuckles. "Not ready for it yet?"

"No, sir," she answers, glad he understands. As the first woman in the League, she can't accept the captaincy because she's a convenient body. She has to prove she deserves it before she can wear it. There will always be people willing to tell her how she doesn't deserve her place in hockey which makes it even more important for her to believe she deserves it.

If, when she's ready, they make the offer again she'll accept the responsibility and do her best to live up to it.

"You have sixteen games left this season." Mr. Pauling has grown serious again. "When I ask you again this off-season, I expect you to be ready."

No pressure, though. "Thank you. Is there anything else you need?"

"You're good. Go home, spend some time with your dad. I hope he's enjoying his first Dads' Trip."

"He is." Sophie offers them a strained smile and books it out of there as fast as she can still in her full gear.

She makes it downstairs before she feels safe enough to lean against the wall. They offered her Matty's captaincy after she spent months doing her best to make sure they would keep him. And now she has sixteen games to make sure she's ready to accept it when Mr. Pauling offers it again.

If he offers it again, a small part of her brain whispers.

"Sophie!"

Sophie pushes off the wall, media smile already fixed to her face before she realizes it's only Mary Beth. Her PR manager falters when she sees Sophie's expression. "Congratulations not in order, then?"

How many people know? Will this leak and poison the rest of their season? Is Lenny Dernier going to dedicate an entire segment to how she never should've been offered the letter in the first place?

"Breathe," Mary Beth tells her.

Sophie drags in a shuddering breath. "Sorry. I—I said no." Hearing it out loud makes her wonder, again, if she made the wrong choice. She's spent years and years battling to prove she belongs in the same league as men and now, when she was offered tangible proof her front office at least sees her as belonging, she turned it down?

Mary Beth's expression doesn't change. "Then I guess we don't need an emergency PR meeting."

"Yeah. Um, thank you." Sophie slips into the locker room, hoping for a few moments to collect her thoughts.

Instead, her team is still mostly here and a lot of them are naked. Big Red yelps and grabs a towel as if they haven't been sharing a locker room all season. It's enough to make her laugh as she sits in her stall and unlaces her skates.

She strips out of her gear, down to her spandex when Merlin nudges her. "What did Coach want?" He whispers but the locker room is quiet enough for his words to carry as if everyone was waiting to see who would ask her.

"I saw Pauling and Wilcox in the building," Nelson adds and the scrutiny grows.

Lindy looks at her with his goalie stare as if he can somehow beam the answer out of her head. Next to him, X looks as if he's waiting for confirmation of something he already knows. She's careful not to look at either of them as she answers. "They liked my game against Denver."

"Seriously?" Merlin asks, let down.

He isn't the only one.

Lindy and X are both staring so hard it's as if they're trying to read her mind so Sophie pulls her ace card. She tugs her shirt off and everyone immediately finds somewhere else to look, as if there's something scandalous about a woman in a sports bra.

X LINGERS WHILE she showers so he can walk out with her. Not only does it mean she can't ditch him, there's no one she can pull into their conversation to save her from something she absolutely doesn't want to talk about.

"They liked your game against Denver?" X asks.

She shrugs. It wasn't her best deflection, but it wasn't a lie. They did like her game against Denver, because it apparently showed the kind of growth they wanted in order to name her captain. She isn't sure showing enough restraint to keep from breaking Sinclair's nose again deserves a captaincy, though. A sainthood? Maybe. Not a captaincy.

"And Quebec. They congratulated me on the big five-oh. No pineapple involved which was a relief."

"It's an American thing. They—" X catches himself and frowns at her. "You're trying to distract me. There's only one reason our owner and GM arranged a meeting with you and Butler."

"A couple of reasons," Sophie says, one last desperate attempt to deflect. "I mean, I am the first woman in the League, and women require special handling. They're very *emotional*." X's sharp look makes her sigh. "I'm done. Ask your question."

"Outright or you won't answer it?"

She refuses to give him answers he doesn't request. It's too ingrained in her not to give any more information than necessary. X isn't a reporter or a stranger trying to squeeze out details of her life, but she's still guarded.

"They offered you the C," X says.

It's a relief to hear him say it, even as she flinches away from the words.

"You turned it down?" He sounds incredulous as if he didn't immediately cut off anyone's thoughts of offering him the C once Matty was traded.

They've reached the parking lot now, and Sophie does an instinctive sweep to make sure no one's around to overhear them. "I told you. You're the only person I would accept this season with a C on their sweater."

"You're the next captain of the Concord Condors."

"Maybe. But it isn't happening this season." She holds up a hand as he opens his mouth to protest. "I know Matty's gone, and we aren't getting him back. It doesn't mean I'm ready to lead the way they want me to."

"As soon as they iron the C onto your jersey, everyone will follow you."

She rolls her eyes. "If the only reason my teammates listen to me is because of a letter on my chest, I don't deserve it. They need to listen to me first."

"You're a good kid."

"Not a kid," she mutters and he laughs before he tugs on the end of her ponytail.

SHE'S WRUNG OUT by the time she makes it home, looking forward to eating something and taking a long nap. Only, when she opens her apartment door, the first thing she sees is her dad, sitting on the couch, with a game tape of Minneapolis playing on her TV.

She pauses and only belatedly remembers to close the door behind her. "How do you have this?"

Her dad pauses the game as if he doesn't want to miss a single shift. He studies her, critical, then says, "You don't seem happy."

"Did Coach Vorgen give you this?"

"I was hoping to go over their style with you before Philip and I go out."

Who the hell is Philip?

"But you were late," her dad continues.

Her chest aches, a sharp familiar pain. *Ah, Dad's disappointment.* She drops her bag by the door and wanders into the kitchen to put together something to eat.

"Did something happen at practice?"

She taps her fingers against her fridge as she peers inside. The more people she tells, the more likely something will leak out. But she can trust her dad, and she has to talk about it with someone or she'll end up blurting it to Marty Owen in the middle of her presser tomorrow. Talking to X had been good, but she couldn't tell him how she actually felt. She might be his captain next year. She can't share her doubts or her fears or her blinding rage with him.

She glances at her dad, unsure if she can really share it with him either. "I was offered the captaincy."

"Of course you were. Will you wear the C against Minneapolis?"

She closes the fridge to turn and stare. "What do you mean *of course*?"

"It's obvious they dropped Mathers to make room for you to grow."

Anger bubbles up. She wasn't allowed to be angry in front of her GM or her owner. And forget about showing emotion in front of her coach. But now she curls her fingers around her granite countertop and takes a vicious pleasure in saying, "I'm not the captain."

Her dad stands up so he can see her over the back of the couch. "What?"

She doesn't repeat herself. He knows what she said.

Her dad shakes his head. "You turned it down? What have we been working toward your entire life if it wasn't this?"

"The goal was always the NAHL, and I made it." She might have been drafted last, but she's carving a place for herself in this League. And, apparently, squeezing other people out in the process. When did Matty realize they were grooming her to take his place? How doesn't he hate her for it?

"Making it doesn't mean your place is secure. The C will help."

Sophie can't help but laugh. "It'll protect me the way it protected Matty? I said no. I'm wearing the A for the rest of the season."

"And if they don't offer it to you again?"

"Then I didn't deserve it in the first place."

There's a long, terse silence, before he says, "I see." He goes back to the guest room and Sophie follows him as far as the hallway, but she pauses outside his room, unwilling to intrude in his space even if, technically, every room in this apartment is hers.

"What do you mean *I see*?"

She and her dad have had epic blowups over the years, all stemming from hockey. Sometimes, they shout until they don't have words while her mom wrings her hands and tries to play peacemaker. Sometimes, they yell until Sophie's eyes prickle with tears because *he won't listen* and she has to walk away because *there's no crying in hockey*. Sometimes, rarely, her dad is the one who walks away, because he won't admit to being wrong but he will put a fight on hold if he doesn't think he'll win.

She watches her dad pack his bags. Fury swells inside her with each neatly folded polo he places on top of another. "What are you doing?"

"I'm meeting Philip for dinner."

Who the fuck *is Philip?*

"Why do you need all your shit with you?"

Her dad zips his bags and walks past her. He pauses long enough to point at the TV, still frozen on the third period of the Minneapolis-Chicago game. "I took some notes. Watch the video, read up on my report, and prepare for tomorrow's game."

He walks out and she doesn't stop him, because she doesn't know how.

SHE WATCHES THE game tape on Minneapolis while she eats dinner. She keeps looking to the door, expecting her dad to come through as if summoned by video review. Instead, the door stays stubbornly closed, and her quinoa keeps falling off her spoon so she has to re-scoop it.

Eventually, she accepts he isn't coming back and focuses instead on Justin Rust. Minneapolis's captain is as good as he was last year, maybe even better. Will Coach Butler put her out against his line to neutralize it? Or will he trust Peets to shut them down and task Sophie's line with scoring?

She picks up her dad's notes to study up and prepare herself for either one. His breakdown of Minneapolis's system is insightful. She reads what he has to say and watches it happen on her TV. She sees the gaps to exploit on offense and players she has to be careful of on defense. She taps her phone against her leg. If she were a better person, she'd text her dad and thank him for the analysis.

Instead, she turns off the TV and prepares for bed.

The next morning, the guest room is empty.

She eats breakfast and heads to the rink for morning skate, because there isn't anything else to do. She could text her mom and see if she's heard from him but then she'll have to explain how she lost him in the first place, and she needs her focus to be on tonight's game.

She takes an extra five minutes on the bike to clear her head and drops a yoga mat next to Teddy so she can stretch.

"I think our dads are making friendship bracelets," Teddy says.

"Your dad's name is Philip?"

"Yeah. They went to dinner last night and when my dad came home he had a whole scouting report on Minneapolis's best shooters."

Sounds like her dad. She wants to ask if her dad stayed over at Teddy's place last night, but Teddy would've mentioned if he had. At least she knows he's still in the city. If he was back in Thunder Bay, her mother would've called.

Teddy drops into a stretch which makes Sophie's muscles twinge in sympathy. "Do you think they gave me this game because the season's over?"

"The season isn't over. And they gave you this game because they know you can back us to two points tonight."

Teddy rolls his eyes.

This is why I can't have the C. Maybe I'm ready for it, but they're not ready for me. She punches his shoulder and ignores his grunt. "I need you in my corner."

"Sofe—"

"We're making the playoffs. We do it one game at a time. Are you with me tonight?"

Teddy sighs. "Yeah, I'm with you. How come you never ask me for easy shit?"

Sophie grins and pats his shoulder.

HER APARTMENT'S STILL empty when she returns from morning skate. It takes her a long time to fall asleep for her pregame nap, and she's tense when she shows up to the rink for the game. She spots Mary Beth in the hallway. She glances at the assistant and intern who seem to always shadow her and asks, "Can I talk to you for a second?"

Mary Beth leaves the other two women where they are and leads Sophie far enough away to give them some privacy. "What's up?"

"Will you let me know if my dad makes it to the box?"

"If?" Mary Beth's concern shifts into something more personal. "Is everything okay?"

Sophie shrugs. She shouldn't have brought it up. Now Mary Beth will have questions, and she can't brush off her PR manager the way she does other people. Mary Beth taught her some of her tricks and is wise to all the others.

Mary Beth lays a hand on Sophie's arm. "I'll keep an eye out. Warm up, get your head in the game, and I'll let you know when your dad arrives."

Sophie nods and heads to the locker room to change. Either her dad will show up or he won't; either way, she can't do anything until after the game. For now, she takes a deep breath and pushes him out of her head.

She nudges Merlin. "I need a big game out of you tonight."

"You always do."

"It's crunch time."

If they win tonight and DC loses, they're in a playoff spot. If they win and DC loses in OT, they're tied for fourth place and DC has the tie breaker. Taking sole possession of fourth place will bring new energy to the locker room. Once they're in the playoffs, they'll fight to keep their place. She knows they will.

"Coach is matching us against Rust. Are you ready to shut down your favorite player?"

"Easy peasy."

Sophie laughs and pokes his side. "Dork."

COACH BUTLER'S GIVING them his pregame speech when Mary Beth slips into the locker room. She gives Sophie a discreet nod.

Her dad's here then.

Good.

Now, she needs to win.

MINNEAPOLIS OPENS THE game with their best line. Coach Butler counters with Sophie, Merlin, and Witzer. They exchange fist bumps as they skate to center ice for the faceoff. Sophie comes to a stop across from Rust and grins around her mouth guard.

Pierre Delmonte holds the puck between them and lets it drop. Sophie and Rust both lunge forward. They tie up, their sticks locked together, and the puck forgotten as they lean on each other, vying for leverage.

Merlin swoops in to grab the puck. Sophie ducks away from Rust and follows her winger into the offensive zone. Merlin drops a pass back to her, and she shoots. The puck goes wide, and Johnson reaches it first and passes to Rust who's on a breakaway before Sophie realizes possession has changed.

She takes off after him, but he had a head start, and she won't catch up to him in time. She took a bad shot and now her team's going to pay for it, not even a minute into the period. Still, she pushes her legs to move faster, even as Rust goes forehand-backhand, his signature move. The stadium seems to draw a collective breath, silent as Rust shoots.

Teddy's there, big in his net, and the puck hits the condor on his chest and drops to the ice. He covers it before Rust has a second chance.

"Lucky," Rust tells Teddy as Sophie reaches them.

Teddy scoffs. "Like I need luck to stop you."

Sophie waits until Rust skates away to tap Teddy's skates. "Thanks."

His eyes crinkle as he smiles. "I told you I was with you tonight."

She pats his helmet before she skates to the bench. She pulls Peets, Spitz, and Big Red to her as she sits down. "Teddy bailed us out big time. Now, we give back to him. We play solid defense, we put a goal or two up on the board, and we win this for him."

"How did Rust miss?" Big Red asks. "Shootouts, breakaways, they're his wheelhouse."

"He didn't miss. Teddy stopped him."

Big Red stops staring at Rust and turns to stare at Teddy instead. He laughs and punches Spitz's shoulder. "Fuck yeah, he did."

SOPHIE BREAKS UP a two-on-one before it can develop, lifting Johnson's stick so Witzer can grab the puck.

Two shifts later, Spitz throws himself in the way of Rust's shot and takes the puck off his thigh. He limps back to the bench, but he grins as he accepts back slaps and cheers from the team.

Peets wins important faceoffs and Big Red plays the best defensive hockey he has all year. He fights for pucks along the boards, battles without taking penalties, and, instead of cheating for a breakaway, he commits to assignments.

He returns to the bench, breathing heavy, but with fire in his eyes. Sophie grins and tosses him a bottle of Gatorade. "That's exactly what I want from you."

THE SCORE IS 0-0 headed into first intermission.

It's still 0-0 headed into the second intermission.

There's ten minutes left in the third period when Nolan's shot goes off Teddy's facemask. Teddy throws himself on the puck, stomach first as if he's forgotten he has a glove and a paddle he can use. Rust gets in a few extra jabs before the official blows the play dead.

Sophie skates over to Teddy as Theo hauls his fellow American away from his goalie. "You good?"

Teddy nods. His facemask is dented so he has to get a new one. Their head trainer asks him a few questions while Granlund does the equipment repair, but as soon as the switch is made, Teddy's back on the ice.

There's five minutes left in the period when Johnson tries to go five-hole. Teddy squeezes his knees together and looks over his shoulder as if he isn't sure he has the puck. The puck isn't behind him and, after the play is blown dead and he stands up, there the puck is, safely out of the net.

A few shifts later, he windmills, knocking the puck away from his net. He pushes off his post to challenge the rebound shot. Then he slams his paddle down to stop the next shot, and Sophie loses track of the saves he makes before he manages to cover the puck.

Garfield whistles, low and impressed. "What the fuck did he eat today?"

Nelson slings a leg over the boards. "Whatever it is, I want some."

Peets wins the faceoff, and they have enough time to clear the puck before the horn sounds to end the game. It'll take overtime to decide this one.

Teddy skates over for Coach's intermission pep talk. He tips his helmet back and accepts the Gatorade she offers him. "You never ask me for easy shit."

"And yet, you still deliver. You got us a point, now it's time for us to get you the second."

SOPHIE WINS THE faceoff against Rust to kick off overtime. She spent all last night studying his tendencies at the dot and reviewing her dad's notes on his tells. When someone surprises him, he freezes for half a second instead of going straight for the puck. It's all the advantage she needs.

Her win springs a rush into the offensive zone. Merlin enters first and slings a cross-ice pass to Witzer. He bobbles the pass and Nolan steals the puck, but Sophie knocks down his clearing attempt. She settles the puck and slides it back to Witzer.

They aren't leaving this zone until they win.

She streaks to the net, banging her stick for the puck. Nolan shoves her, but it isn't enough to knock her off balance. She catches Witzer's return pass right on her tape and she cradles the puck as she spins around Nolan and flicks a backhander top corner.

Goal.

They squeezed two points out of tonight, and they have a playoff spot. Now all they have to do is keep it.

She accepts her back pats and butt slaps from her linemates, but it's Teddy she rushes as soon as she's able. Her stick is somewhere on the ice so she clasps his helmet between both of her hands and leans up to bump her visor against his mask. "You were so fucking huge for us. If I could, I would buy you so many drinks tonight."

He laughs and Theo nudges Sophie out of the way so he can shower love on their goalie. She skates over to her stick and plucks it off the ice.

"Two points," she tells X. "Now we need another two."

"Now, we celebrate the game. You can draw up the next battle plan tomorrow."

THEY FLY TO Kansas City and win big, 6-3, for the last game of the Dads' Trip. Sophie had a goal and two assists on the night, but when she sits next to her dad for the flight home, he says, "DC won tonight. You're only one point up on them. You need to be consistent for the rest of the season."

"We can do it."

They're winning which they obviously need to do, but as they win they're building good habits and their confidence. Big Red sneaks looks at the League's standings when he thinks no one's watching, and Spitz has started whistling in the showers. Even the older guys, the ones who have been here and fallen short for season after season, they're beginning to hope as well.

Her dad holds up his iPad. "I have all your shifts from the past three games."

She doesn't ask where he's been since he left her apartment or tell him flights home are prime napping times. Instead, she digs through her bag until she pulls out a notebook and a pen. "Hit me with it."

Chapter Twenty

THE TEAM SEEMS to lose their enthusiasm after the Dads' Trip. They lose to DC, drag a few games to OT where they scrape out one point, but they slip out of their place in the playoffs. There's only a handful of games left, and if they don't turn it around this will be yet another season where Concord misses the postseason.

They string a few wins together, but they're still one point out of a playoff spot going into their final game of the season. A win tonight puts them in fourth place in their division and means their season isn't over. A loss, even an OT loss, and DC makes the playoffs instead.

They need a win tonight.

A win over *Toronto*.

No big deal. All we need is a win over a team we've lost to twice this season. A team our former captain now plays for.

They're better than they were in the third game of the season when they first lost to Toronto, and they're better than they were in Game 65. They've learned to fill some of the gaps Matty left behind, but this won't be an easy game.

Sophie pulls her jersey on. The A presses heavy against her chest. *Not as heavy as a C would.*

When they take the ice for warm-ups, it's in front of a full house. Every seat sold tonight, and the stands are packed with fans hoping to see history made. Sophie looks around as she skates her two laps. Fans are pressed against the glass, trying to be as close to the players as possible. Some have kids hoisted up on their shoulders for a better view. Some have their cameras out, taking pictures as the players skate by them.

Two teenage girls hoist a sign which says "It's been 84 years" and has a picture of an old lady.

"Their sign is wrong," she tells Big Red as he skates up to her. He looks over at the sign and laughs.

"You don't spend a lot of time on the internet, do you?"

"Did they use a picture of their grandmother?"

Big Red laughs again and pats her helmet before he chases after Zinger, a part of their pregame ritual she doesn't entirely understand.

She takes a deep breath and blocks out everything going on around her as she returns to her warm-up.

THE CROWD GROWS louder and louder until the stadium is deafening. They boo each Toronto player as the starting roster is announced and chant for each Concord player when it's their turn. They only quiet down long enough for the anthems to be sung. Coach Butler has to bring the team in for a tight huddle and even when he shouts, they can barely hear him.

Sophie, Merlin, and Witzer skate out as the first line on the ice.

"Did you hear a word he was saying?" Merlin asks.

Witzer shrugs. "I never really pay attention."

Sophie rolls her eyes. "Play hockey. It's all we have to do."

Merlin taps his stick on the ice for her. "Bravo. Inspiring speech."

She gives him a friendly facewash and sets up at center ice. She glances up and her smile slips from her face when she sees Matty across from her.

"You're on the brink of something," he tells her.

She ignores him, looking to Pierre Delmonte instead. As soon as he drops the puck, she springs into action. She lunges forward to sweep the puck away, but her stick clacks loudly against Matty's. She leans in and he leans back. Catching her off balance, he knocks the puck to Poletti, and Sophie breaks free to chase the forward down the ice.

She catches up to him before the blue line, and she pokes the puck off his stick with enough force to send it skittering to Lindy. Her goalie cradles the puck as he surveys his options. He flings a pass down ice to Witzer.

It's Toronto's turn to scramble on defense, and the crowd stays on their feet, cheering the Condors on.

WHEN SOPHIE JUMPS over the boards for her third shift of the game, the fans somehow grow louder. She strips Marcus of the puck and reverses direction for a quick reentry into the offensive zone. Witzer's on the far side of the ice, and she's prepared to pass when Marcus shifts into the passing lane.

Well, then.

She shoots the puck instead, and Lauer kicks the puck out wide. Witzer jumps on the rebound and passes up to Spitz. Sophie drops down to screen, and she holds her ground as Spitz loads up his shot. Unlike Lauer, she has a clear view of the puck as it comes at them. She tilts her stick and the puck hits the shaft and bounces over Lauer's waiting glove.

She throws her hands up in the air as the goal light flashes. She skates right for Spitz who opens his arms and laughs as they collide. "Perfect fucking shot," she tells him.

"Nice deflection."

Witzer and Merlin crash into them at the same time.

"Holy shit!" Merlin shouts, grabbing their necks and shaking them. "We might make the playoffs!"

Sophie smacks his helmet. "We *will*."

THE SCORE IS 1-0 headed into the first intermission. Sometime during the first period, she stops feeling the sharp stab of *not right* whenever she sees Matty. He's a guy on the other team, and she has to beat him if she wants her two points. No one, not even her former captain, is keeping her from the playoffs.

IT'S 1-2 HEADED into the second intermission.

The crowd is silent as the Condors troop down the tunnel, all their excitement replaced with an all too familiar *why do we bother*. It's a one goal deficit in the biggest game of the franchise's history. They can come back from this. They *will*. Given the team's past, she grudgingly understands why the fans are so quick to lose faith, but her teammates hang their heads as they sit in their stalls as if they're wondering why *they* bother.

X's helmet hangs behind him, and he runs his hands through sweaty, gray-speckled hair. He doesn't joke with J-Rod like he did during last intermission or glance over at Sophie with a glimmer of hope in his eyes. Big Red and

Zinger, who were both animated twenty minutes ago, are subdued by the vets beside them. Garfield and Nelson look tired. Merlin hangs his helmet in his stall as if this is the end of their season.

Anger bubbles up inside her. Every single one of them talk about *compete* and *grit* and *toughness* in their interviews as if those are the foundation of a hockey player, but where are those qualities now? They're coming up on the most important twenty minutes of their whole season; hell, of their whole *careers*, and they're giving up?

Her fingers brush the seams holding the A to her sweater. Nelson talks quietly with Garfield. X isn't speaking to anyone. Rocky, the player they brought in from the Toronto trade, stares at his hands as if wondering how he went from a playoff contender to this team.

Spitz meets Sophie's gaze from across the room. He nudges J-Rod who looks up and catches her gaze. Next it's Teddy. And once Teddy's watching her, Lindy looks over. One by one, her teammates turn to her.

"We got sloppy." Before her censure can break them completely, she continues. "We were up by one, and we thought it would be enough when there was still forty minutes left to play. We'll have to work hard in the third period, but we know we can score on them, and we know we can win."

"Two goals in twenty minutes?" Kevlar scoffs. "If Toronto can do it, so can we."

"Lauer's weak glove side," Merlin adds.

"He's good down low," Rocky tells them, "so elevate your shots."

Coach Butler clears his throat. Sophie hadn't even noticed him by the doors. "Maybe I should let you handle the game plan for the third period."

Sophie's not sure he's serious, but Witzer takes him at his word and says, "Convert on our breakaways. We have to take advantage of the opportunities we create. We're hesitating or waiting for support and it gives Toronto enough time to make it back and play defense."

"We need to hustle harder on defense," Spitz says. He stares at the floor as he says it.

Kuzy nudges him and offers him a small smile. "We should shot block more. Help Lindy out."

Lindy throws a lazy salute in their direction.

It's Merlin who says, "So...play hockey. Easy enough."

Laughter ripples through the room until they're all relaxed and ready for the third period.

SOPHIE WINS THE opening faceoff clean. She knocks the puck back to Merlin who carries it into the zone. When no one challenges him, he hazards a shot on net, and it clangs off the goalpost. Jefferson, a Toronto defenseman, tries to clear the puck, but Sophie intercepts the pass and slings the puck to Witzer. They manage four good shots on goal before Lauer finally manages to cover up.

Sophie switches out for Rocky's line. She chews on the edge of her mouth guard as Big Red shoots, gathers his own rebound, and shoots again. He doesn't elevate the puck enough, and Lauer easily kicks the shot away. Needham gathers the loose puck and breaks his team out of the zone.

Zinger hounds him the whole length of the ice until he forces a turnover, and he passes up to Rocky who chips the puck deep and chases, giving the rest of his line a chance to change out.

A couple of shifts later, Nelson goes down on one knee to block a shot. The puck bounces off his shin pad and skitters to Jefferson who rifles a shot off Nelson's helmet and out of play. Garfield grabs Jefferson by the jersey as the trainers run out to help Nelson off the ice.

They take him straight down the tunnel, and Spitz glances back as they go.

"He'll be okay," Sophie promises. "They're following protocol."

"Jefferson aimed for his head."

"Don't start anything," Kuzy tells him.

Spitz mutters something in German, and Kuzy fires back in Russian. They knock shoulders and grin. Trusting Kuzy to keep their young defenseman levelheaded, Sophie turns to her linemates.

"We're scoring a fucking goal for him," Merlin says.

Sophie grins. "Do you have a plan or do you want to hear mine?"

Witzer hands her two water bottles to use as players, and she grabs another couple until she has enough pieces to diagram a play. By the time Coach Butler calls their line, they know what they want to do.

THERE'S THREE MINUTES left in the game when Sophie plasters Matty to the boards so Merlin can grab the puck. She holds her former captain there until Merlin's free. She breaks away to plant herself in front of the net and battles Jefferson for position. He cross-checks her so she elbows him back. She has three minutes to keep their playoff hopes alive. She braces herself for Jefferson's next shove and holds her ground so she's blocking Lauer's view when Kevlar unloads his shot.

Lauer manages to stop it anyway, but Sophie gathers the puck on her stick. She leans on Jefferson, forcing him to hold her weight as she lifts the puck, elevating it despite the tight space. Jefferson steps back so she falls without his support, but it doesn't matter, because the goal light is on and the crowd is screaming.

She's tied the game.

Merlin hauls her to her skates and squeezes her as tightly as he can. "You fucking beauty!"

"We're not done yet. We need two points out of this game."

"We'll get them. We're fucking doing this!"

BOTH TEAMS FIND another gear and the last few minutes of the game are a flurry of chances on either side. When the buzzer finally sounds, the game is tied 2-2. The crowd, on their feet since Sophie's goal, stays standing through the shortened intermission.

They stay standing through overtime, cheering whenever they're in the offensive zone and groaning every time a shot goes wide or Lauer makes a save.

Overtime ends without a goal.

They're going to a shootout.

Nelson rejoins them on the bench, and she sees the moment Garfield reaches out to pat his helmet and pats his shoulder instead. She pops her mouth guard out and pops it back in. If there weren't a dozen cameras on her right now, she'd chew on it. Their entire season comes down to this moment. Three shooters from each team and sudden death if they need it.

Anticipation and excitement prickle under her skin. She wishes she could take all the shootout attempts. She promised X they were making the playoffs this season, and now is when it happens.

Lindy's already in his net, hunched on the goal line, yet somehow still looking big, as if he fills the entire space. Poletti is first up for Toronto and as he skates at Lindy, their goalie pushes off his line to challenge. He looks even bigger now, a fucking wall, and Poletti tries to deke around him but the puck trickles off his stick and goes wide.

The crowd cheers and chants Lindy's name as Coach Butler taps Merlin as their first shooter. Sophie pats his ass as he slings one leg then the other over the boards. This is his bread and butter, and he takes the puck from center ice and skates at Lauer, no fancy moves. He forces Lauer deeper into his crease and, once Lauer doesn't have enough time to react, he snaps the puck past him.

Now the fans chant Merlin's name, and he skates back to the bench, a little stunned.

"Fuck yeah!" Kevlar shouts, slapping his helmet.

Theo whistles and Witzer smacks a kiss to his helmet. He goes all the way down the bench until he takes the empty seat at the end.

Needham takes his attempt for Toronto and misses.

The fans are raucous. If Garfield scores, they win the game and they're going to the playoffs.

Sophie holds her breath as Garfield begins his approach from the left. He winds, taking his time, trying to make Lauer commit. But Lauer holds his ground and when Garfield runs out of space and shoots, he catches the puck in his glove.

The crowd groans, momentarily disappointed, before they begin chanting Lindy's name again.

There's a slight pause when Matty takes his place at center ice for Toronto's third attempt, before they grow even louder.

"Fuck," Theo mutters.

Sophie's seen Matty practice shootout attempts hundreds of times. Lindy's seen it even more. He knows Matty's favorite moves and how to shut them down. All Lindy has to do is stop this puck and they've won.

Matty comes in hard, moves the puck side-to-side until Lindy freezes. He scores.

Fuck.

"Fournier," Coach Butler says.

Sophie climbs over the boards. Merlin hands her stick to her. "You've got this."

She glances down the bench at X. His expression is neutral, but she sees the way he sits on the very edge of the bench and how tightly he grips his stick. She turns back to Merlin and smiles. "Thanks."

The crowd chants her name as she stops in front of the puck. If she scores here, the game is over, and they're playoff bound. This is the moment her entire season has come down to, her with the puck at center ice, determined to score, and Lauer in his net, determined to stop her.

When she was younger, she would spend hours in the driveway going one-on-one against Colby or, if the weather was right, they'd be on the backyard rink. Her dad would come outside at random intervals, and if he crossed his arms over his chest, she knew she had one chance to score. If she did, he would nod, maybe give her some pointers, then go back inside.

But if she didn't, she had to go inside with him, and there was no more hockey for the rest of the day. She could practice her stickhandling or do drills in the basement, but it wasn't the same. *If you're not the best, then you don't get to play,* her dad told her.

Once, her dad came out early. She and Colby didn't want to chance missing out on an entire day of hockey so Colby gave her the five-hole. Her dad noticed. Colby never went easy on her again.

Lauer won't go easy on her either, but she doesn't need him to. He comes out to challenge her, glove raised, as if he can intimidate her. She's already scored twice on him tonight, when he had an entire defense helping him.

She pushes the puck out in front of her to tempt him. As soon as he jabs his paddle forward to poke check, she pulls the puck back. He's extended now, out of position, and she flicks the puck over his shoulder.

The goal light flashes.

The crowd erupts.

She throws her stick and her gloves in the air and turns as her entire team rushes her. They hit her at once, slamming her back into the glass where the fans chant *"Playoffs! Playoffs! Playoffs!"*

She laughs as she's hugged and facewashed, and she finds Lindy to hug him and she finds Merlin so she can slap his helmet. Then, through all the chaos and all the noise, she finds X.

"I promised you."

His eyes shine with tears as he pulls her in for a hug. "I should know better than to doubt you."

Chapter Twenty-One

THE MAPLE CUP Playoffs.

Sophie has dreamed of this moment for years. She watched other teams compete for the Cup as a little girl in the basement of her grandparents' house. She knew one day she would be there. After every season, she and Colby would recreate their favorite moments in the driveway, practicing for the moment they could do it for real.

And now here she is.

Only, when she and Colby played make believe in the driveway, they ran through the highlight reel. She didn't dream of practices more grueling than the toughest games they played all season or of struggling to stay awake in video review. And now, when she collapses in her bed at night, she doesn't dream.

She scours hours of game tape on Montreal for the secret to beating the Mammoths. She doesn't find any. She finds small weaknesses in each game, things they can exploit, but when they take the ice in Montreal, all those weaknesses are gone.

The d-men are smart in their pinches so they don't give up odd man rushes, the forwards cut down on their offsides, and LaJoie is a fucking wall.

Sophie's matched up against Ducasse, and she's constantly scrambling to keep up. During the regular season, she felt as if she could hold her own against him, but tonight it's obvious he's Captain Canada and she's in her first playoff game.

He dodges her check, makes a pass, and crashes Lindy's net, leaving her to play catch-up.

Two shifts later, he wins a faceoff before she even reacts. He takes the time to say, "Welcome to the big leagues, kid," before he's gone.

By the end of the period, she feels as if it's overtime in the second game of a back-to-back. Her eyes sting with sweat, her legs are jelly, and she can't remember the last time she caught her breath. It's taken their full effort to keep the puck out of their net. They've haven't had anything left in the tank to try to score on Montreal.

And they have another two periods of this.

In Game *One*.

One game at a time. She won't make it through if she thinks too far ahead.

"This is the effort you're giving?" Coach Butler demands. "You don't get a trophy for making the playoffs. You have to earn it. You're slow and playing scared. They won't slip up and give you an opening. You have to make your openings. You need to be harder on the puck. All of you."

This is when they miss Matty the most, in the silence after Coach's speech. Everyone looks to X, but he's sitting in his stall, head bowed to hide his grimace. He knee is bothering him, and he won't give them the rousing motivational speech they need.

What would he even say if he did speak up? He hasn't been here before. Almost none of them have. She finds herself turning to Rocky once Coach Butler's gone. He made it all the way to the Finals last year. Surely he has some advice he can pass on to them.

Rocky pushes his hair out of his face and freezes when he catches her staring. He turns, eyes widening when he realizes she isn't the only one.

"I was the fourth line center," he says.

"You were still in the playoffs," Merlin points out.

Rocky looks around as if still hoping for backup. When he realizes no one else will speak up, he says, "Everything is magnified. Every goal for is huge, every goal against is devastating. Every hit feels as if you're carrying an extra ten pounds. The teams who win are the ones who manage their emotions and who dig deep when they don't think they have anything left to give."

It isn't exactly a rallying cry, but she can find something useful in there. The winning team is the one who works the hardest. Concord might be new to the playoffs, but they know how to work.

THEY'RE ENERGIZED TO start the second period. Sophie wins the opening faceoff and then they pin Ducasse's line in their own zone. It's their longest shift in the offensive zone all game, and they force LaJoie to cover the puck to end it.

She taps Garfield's helmet as they pass each other. "Your turn."

Concord pushes, line after line, until Montreal is scrambling on every shift. Rocky's line forces an icing and Coach Butler taps Sophie to go up against the Mammoth's tired fourth line.

It's the best opportunity they've had all game. It might be the best one they have all night, which means they have to take advantage. She pulls Merlin and Witzer in close. "The team who works the hardest, Rocky said. That's us."

They nod, both of them locked in. She takes her place at the faceoff dot. The Montreal crowd, loud from the start, grows even louder as if they can lend their strength to their team.

Sophie wins the faceoff. Two Mammoths swarm J-Rod who holds the puck until Witzer is free. He passes and takes a hit for his trouble. They move the puck, keeping it in the zone as they wear down Montreal's players even more. Merlin plants himself in front of LaJoie's net and weathers the cross-checks and abuse as Sophie skates the puck behind the net.

She waits for a defender to chase her and turns sharply. She passes up to X who unloads on his shot. The puck hits Merlin in front and bounces to Sophie's stick. She shoots, and the puck hits off LaJoie's shoulder and rolls in.

She stands there, stunned, even as the goal light flashes. J-Rod skates in, yelling, and it jolts her into a belated celly. They're up 1-0 in their first playoff game. Merlin and Witzer jump on her and then X hands her the puck. "First playoff goal in Concord history."

She can't say anything as she accepts it from him. Granlund, their equipment manager, will write on it, marking its significance, a piece of Concord history she's undeniably a part of. She looks up at X, their first player, and who notched an assist in the history-making goal, and she tries to give the puck back to him. "This is yours more than it's mine."

X holds his hands up as if he won't take it back. It's Witzer who snatches it away. "We can fight about it later. We have a game to win."

They skate through the fist bump line, and Sophie's smile grows with each teammate who congratulates her.

"It's one goal," Coach Butler says. "We'll need more if we want to win."

With Sophie on the bench, Montreal matches their top line against Concord's second. Ducasse wins the faceoff with ease, and Concord collapses down to play defense.

It only takes two shifts for the high from her goal to wear off. Whenever she looks up at the scoreboard and sees 1-0, she feels a flutter of hope followed by the heavy certainly it won't be enough. Coach Butler is right; they can't beat Montreal with only one goal.

They cling to their lead during the second period, and Sophie allows herself to wonder if maybe Coach Butler's wrong.

She's on the bench when Ducasse scores to tie the game. Her stomach plummets and disappointment hits her hard as the entire stadium celebrates. She takes a deep breath. Teams have scored against them before. All Montreal did was tie the game. There's still plenty of time left on the clock.

Coach Butler taps his clipboard on his thigh. "Fournier, you're up."

She knows he wants the top line playing big minutes, and she sets even higher expectations for herself. She scored the first playoff goal in Concord's history. Time to score the second.

She loses the faceoff, and they spend her whole shift trapped in their own zone. They keep the puck out thanks to the crossbar, but they can't clear the zone. Eventually, a deflection out of play gives her line a desperately needed break.

Rocky's line can't clear the puck either. Sophie's breath sticks in her throat as Big Red flips the puck down the ice. It's a temporary relief, and Zinger leans on his stick as the official fetches the puck. J-Rod taps Lindy's pads and, between the distance and the mask, Sophie can't tell how Lindy feels.

Montreal switches out for fresh bodies. Ducasse easily wins the faceoff. The Mammoths move the puck like a cat playing with its food. Ducasse drops down into the slot, and J-Rod is a step too slow. Ducasse has a clear shot and—

Misses.

Relief crashes through her, sharp and sudden. She raises her gaze to the ceiling. They finally have a change and—the Jumbotron shows the replay. Ducasse missed the puck, because Big Red's stick was hooked around his wrists.

Oh.

The stadium is thunderous as the official makes the call. The fans behind the penalty box laugh and jeer as Big Red's shut in. The ones behind the bench slap the glass as if Sophie's stupid enough to acknowledge them. They grow louder as Ducasse takes the faceoff.

He wins the puck back to Korhonen who snaps it on net and scores. The noise almost drowns out her disappointment. The fans sing along to their goal song then, when Big Red's released from the box, they chant "Thank you" until he looks completely broken. Sophie reaches out to him but he says, "Not now," and sits at the far end of the bench.

It's only 1-2, the game isn't over, but looking at her teammates, it feels as if it is.

At the end of the second period, it's 1-3, and they troop down to the locker room with the Mammoth goal song ringing in their ears.

"You hung with them in the first period so I know you can do it," Coach Butler says. "You slipped in the second, now you need to step it up in the third."

He doesn't look at Sophie, but she feels as if he's speaking directly to her. She didn't accept the captaincy, because she didn't feel as if she was ready for it. There's no better proving grounds than right here.

As soon as Coach leaves them to their own devices, she turns to Merlin. Her winger groans. "What fucking impossible thing are you going to ask of me now?"

"It's not impossible."

"Here we go," he says, but he settles in to listen. Witzer crowds closer, a council of three.

IT TAKES TWO minutes and forty-seven seconds for Concord to score their second ever playoff goal.

Witzer stares at his stick, disbelieving, until the goal light knocks him out of his stupor. He kicks his leg in the air and barrels into Merlin as he shouts his excitement. Sophie claps them both on the back. "*This* is what we need."

They skate back to the bench, energizing their teammates as they go through the line. By the end of it, Nelson and Garfield are refocused, Spitz and J-Rod are talking breakout passes, and Big Red doesn't seem as haunted by his penalty.

She looks down the bench and sees her team *believe*. She grins, sweat-soaked pads feeling as if they weigh nothing. She nudges Kevlar. "Time for the D to contribute?"

Sweat glistens on his skin, and his visor fogs up before he towels it off. She can still see his ruffled indignation. "After the game I'll show you my fucking bruises. *Time to contribute.* Forwards!"

She laughs and slaps him on the back as Coach Richelieu sends him and Theo over the boards. Kevlar blocks two shots and delivers a big hit on Cassady. When he returns to the bench, breathing hard, he arches his eyebrows as if to ask *good enough?*

She hands him a Gatorade bottle. "Yes. Keep it up."

"Your turn." He pats her helmet and drops gratefully onto the bench.

She takes her line out, Spitz and Kuzy on their backend, and they hold their own against Ducasse and the rest of Montreal's top line.

THEY'RE DOWN BY one when Coach Butler signals to Lindy. "As soon as he's here, Fournier, you're up."

She slings one leg over the boards and taps her stick, impatient. Once Lindy's close enough, she hits the ice and skates right for the offensive zone. She crosses the blue line in time to keep the puck in. By the time she's settled it, the crowds is booing her. Booed by the home team in the Maple Cup playoffs. She grins. *Guess I've made it.*

She passes to Nelson and drops into a pocket of open space. He passes and then finds his own open space. They move the puck, using their numbers to their advantage. Only, Montreal has the game clock on their side and time winds down without anyone shooting.

Theo loads up but hesitates long enough to lose his lane. It's a scramble to keep the puck in the zone. The next time, they aren't so lucky. Nelson doesn't take his shot and Ducasse steals the puck and lifts it out of the zone.

Kevlar tracks it down before it can do any damage, but they have to all clear the zone and re-enter. It drains precious seconds off the clock. Someone has to shoot the fucking puck.

Garfield leads them into the zone and then drops a pass back to Sophie. She drifts down, evaluating. She doesn't have a perfect shot, but if they wait for perfect then they'll run out of time. She passes to Theo then, trusting he'll show the same reluctance as before, cuts to the net, banging her stick. He whips her a pass, and she shoves the puck over LaJoie's shoulder.

Three-three.

Relief washes through her, even as her teammates crash into her. The game is tied with…0:05 left. She skates to the bench on shaky legs, and she's grateful to sit as Rocky heads out for the faceoff.

"Cutting it a little close," Merlin teases.

"Fuck you."

He laughs and slaps her helmet.

Five seconds later, the horn sounds on regulation. Unlike the regular season when tie games result in a ten-minute OT and a shootout if needed, the playoffs is twenty-minute periods until someone scores. She's glad they have a full intermission to recover before they play again.

Of course, Montreal also has time to recover, and they come out hard to start the period. McClure slams Sophie into the boards with enough force to rattle the glass as if he wants to make sure she doesn't score the game-winner.

With each passing shift, the pressure grows. OT is sudden death, which means one mistake could cost them the game. Concord tightens up. They stop taking risks, too afraid of the consequences. But it means they're trapped in their own zone, scrambling and making increasingly desperate plays to keep the puck out.

With each shift they're worn down more and more until Lindy's consistently bailing them out. They haven't been scored on yet, but they haven't recorded a shot on goal either.

Sophie switches out for Rocky, but Big Red and Zinger aren't able to switch out for Merlin and Witzer. It's a mishmash of a line, but Sophie sticks to her defensive coverage and keeps her eyes peeled for an opportunity to break out.

Big Red flings his stick out to break up a pass, and Zinger darts in to knock the puck out of the zone. He skates hard to the bench, but he's forced back out after the official declares an icing. He and Big Red both look beat, and Sophie doesn't feel much fresher.

One goal, one opportunity, it's all I need. She takes a deep breath and skates to her place at the faceoff dot. A moment later, Ducasse appears across from her. He smiles but doesn't say anything. He doesn't need to. She knows she's only 40 percent from the dot tonight, and it drops to 35 percent against him. Her team is tired, and his isn't fresh, but they have more energy and momentum on their side.

But this is a new faceoff, a new opportunity.

She loses the faceoff.

Ducasse knocks the puck forward to Cassady who passes up to McClure at the point. Big Red lunges forward to poke the puck away, but he overcommits and McClure easily skates around him. Sophie has to shift her coverage, and it opens a passing lane to Ducasse who accepts McClure's pass, shoots, and—scores.

Sophie looks away from the goal light, and Lindy's hunched defeat. She still hears the goal song and Montreal's celebration. And, of course, she can't avoid the hats as they rain down for Ducasse. X leads the Condors off the ice. Sophie's the last of her teammates, and she pauses to look at the Jumbotron. Final score 3-4, OT.

They'll be better next game.

They have to be.

THE TEAM ALWAYS sticks close on road trips, but they're even closer now, no room for any kind of distraction.

"It's nice," Teddy says at lunch after practice. They're all in the hotel ballroom, eating a catered, team-approved meal. Sophie's with Teddy, her linemates, Spitz, and J-Rod. The older guys are at the table next to them, talking about some fishing show they watched this morning. "Normally, I have to go out with my parents when we're in Montreal. Which is fine, but right now..." He shrugs. "Hey Sofe, you have family in the area too."

"Yeah." As soon as they made the playoffs, *Mémé* called to scold her. *Why didn't you try harder for the third seed? Now you are playing Captain Canada. My heart is too fragile for this.* "But they wouldn't come anyway."

"Gotta limit those distractions," Merlin jokes.

Not quite. Her phone is full of texts and voicemails from her dad, well-meaning advice she can't deal with right now. "More like extra motivation. They only come to the big games. They watched most of the Winter Games from the hotel. The only one they saw in person was the gold medal match."

"What the hell?" Merlin's earlier humor is gone. "Marissa's parents think hockey's a barbaric fucking sport, but they'll be there when we play at home."

Sophie shrugs, uncomfortable with the attention they've drawn from the nearby tables. Rocky's openly staring as if she's an exhibit at the zoo. Garfield and

Nelson are subtler, but she still accidentally catches Garfield's gaze, and they both quickly look away.

"So will mine, if we make it to the Finals." Which means they need to win four games against Montreal, another four, *and* another four in order to make it to hockey's biggest stage. It's exhausting even thinking about it. She spears a broccoli floret with her fork. "My brother wanted to come down but he was overruled."

"Sucks," Teddy says.

"It's how it is. Winning tomorrow's game will bring us a step closer."

Not even Teddy smiles at her attempt at positivity. It took everything they had last night to tie the game and they lost in overtime. Where are they going to find *more*?

BOTH TEAMS PICK up where they left off the night before, Montreal riding the high of a hat trick from their captain, and Concord run down and scrambling to keep up.

Montreal scores two quick goals to open the period. They score a third midway through, and Coach Butler looks down the bench. Teddy pulls out of his slouch, but Coach turns back to the ice to bark at their players.

It's a 0-6 bloodbath, leaving Sophie with the heavy knowledge they weren't ready for the playoffs. They clawed their way into the fourth seed but Montreal is a playoff contender. Toronto, who is easily dismantling their own opponent, is a contender.

Sophie tells herself this is good experience. They'll be better for tasting the playoffs but as she sits in her stall, she can't help but wish experience didn't come through losing all the time.

"Well," Merlin begins but doesn't finish. He pulls his jersey over his head and sits next to Sophie.

No one else tries to speak, and the locker room is silent until the media files in. Sophie's blander than usual, talking about *compete* and *grit* and *battling for pucks*. She misses Matty so much her chest aches with it. He would know the right things to motivate the team. He'd fire them up for their first ever home playoff game. He would know which players need a hand on their shoulder and a quiet word of encouragement and which ones need to be challenged.

But Matty's in Toronto, and Sophie's supposed to fill the space he left behind.

THERE ARE MORE Montreal fans than Concord ones at the first home playoff game in their franchise's history. Sophie's not sure if it makes it better or worse when they lose in front of them.

She stays an extra forty-five minutes to answer reporters' questions, the same questions she's asked herself since Game One. *How will you beat them? Who in the room will breathe life into this team? Do you think you made it to the playoffs a year too early? Is there a leadership vacuum?*

She doesn't have any more answers for them than she does for herself.

IN GAME FOUR, Ducasse hits her hard enough to send her skittering across the ice. It takes her an extra two seconds to get back on her skates, because she wonders if it's worth getting back up.

It's the moment she knows they aren't winning the game.

It takes three goals from Montreal and another forty-seven minutes, but Concord's first playoff experience ends with them being swept in the first round.

She's glad her parents weren't here for it.

SHE DOES HER media on autopilot.

"Yes, it's a disappointing way to end our season."

"It was a good next step. Last year, we didn't make the playoffs, this year we did. Next year, we'll push deeper."

"I don't think the sweep is on any one player. We all could've done better."

"The summer's a good time to work on improving our game."

"I don't know if Matty would've made the difference. Yes, I saw Toronto's up in their series."

"I don't know what changes management is going to make over the summer, but once they make them, the team will adjust."

When it's all over, she's wrung out and wants nothing more than to go home, curl up on her couch, and call her mom. Instead, she avoids her couch, changes into her comfiest clothes, and drives to X's. Aline and the kids are at the Lindholms' tonight so the team can crash here and have a pity party.

X greets her at the door, his playoff stubble speckled with gray. He holds his hand out to her. "Keys."

"I'm not drinking."

"Don't care. Keys."

She hands over her keys but lingers in the door. "Next year—"

"Not now."

Yes now. She steps into his space like she would on the ice. Coach Butler threatened to trade her the way Matty was traded if she doesn't produce. She had a phenomenal run to end the regular season, but the team crashed and burned in the playoffs. Next summer, her contract is up, which means she has one season left to prove why she should stay a Concord Condor. She has one season to prove she deserves her place in the NAHL.

There's no better way than winning the Cup.

She wraps her arms around X's waist, surprising him with the hug. He's smaller when he isn't in his pads, and it's too easy for her to fit her arms around him as if he lost weight when he was injured and never managed to put all of it back on. They both have work to do this summer to be ready for next season.

He hugs her back, careful, as if one of them is on the verge of breaking. "Go mingle." His voice is scratchy as he pats her hair. "Eat junk and drink too much. We'll deal with the rest in the morning."

She lingers in his embrace for another moment before she forces herself to step back. She moves into the kitchen where she looks at the wide array of food on the counter. Queso dip with three bags of chips next to it, a tray of mozzarella sticks, another with buffalo wings. There's a whole bounty of desserts and she grabs two cupcakes, chocolate with a thick smear of fudge frosting.

Her personal belief is any problem can be solved by hockey or chocolate. and hockey is over. She brings her cupcakes into the living room. The couches and other furniture are nowhere to be seen. It's a big open room, and her teammates are sprawled on the floor with various drinks and snacks surrounding them.

She drops down next to Teddy. He glances up, away from the line of shots he was contemplating. His shoulders are heavy with the loss and his chin is dotted with hair, because they weren't in the postseason long enough for him to grow even a bad beard.

She holds out a cupcake. "Want one?"

He stares as if considering it and then lifts the clear shot. "I'll get drunk quicker if I don't eat."

She wants to tell him it's a terrible fucking idea. Instead, she raises her cupcake in a toast.

SHE USES THE bathroom. As she's washing her hands, she looks at her reflection. The end of her ponytail is still Condors red. She turns the water off and tugs on her hair as if she can pull the color off.

While her teammates grew facial hair in honor of the playoffs, she did what she did at Chilton; she dip-dyed her ponytail. For each round they made, she dyed more of it.

Here, of course, it's only the tips. It's still too much, a reminder the season is over before it should be. She opens the top drawer and finds a beard trimmer and nail clippers. The second drawer has Q-tips, a nail file, and a dozen plastic hair clips. The third drawer has a box of tampons.

She takes a detour through the kitchen and rummages through X's drawers until she finds a pair of scissors. She brings them into the living room and surveys her teammates. Garfield face-plants into a plate of cheese puffs. Merlin's half-asleep on Theo, who traces Kevlar's sleeve tattoos with his finger. Beside them, Spitz looks alert and then alarmed when he spots Sophie and the scissors.

She offers them to him, handle first. "I need you to cut my hair."

"No way."

"I'll do it." Merlin pushes off Theo's shoulder but pushes too far and tips alarmingly before Theo reels him back in.

Sophie looks pointedly at Spitz who sighs and, acknowledging her point, takes the scissors. "Next time we do this, I'm drinking too much to be responsible."

There won't be a next time. They're winning it all next season. They were caught off guard by the playoffs but now they know. They'll push themselves harder during the regular season so they're ready for the jump. But for now, she pulls the elastic out of her ponytail and shakes her hair out.

"It doesn't have to be even, I'll get a real cut back home, but I want the red gone."

"Someone get me a trash can. I don't want to make a mess."

J-Rod wrestles a trash can away from Big Red who groans and curls up on the floor.

"Will he need this?"

"I won't take long." Spitz moves behind her, and their teammates crowd around as if they've never seen anything so interesting. Witzer even holds her hair for Spitz to cut. It takes a few false tries before the first chunks fall into the trash can. Once Spitz learns how much hair the scissors can cut at once, the process goes by quickly. When it's done, she pulls her hair into a bun to hide the uneven ends and Spitz gives Big Red his trash can back.

"Is this what girl sleepovers are like?" Merlin asks. "Whose hair are we doing next?"

"No more hair." X takes the scissors away from Spitz. "Nail polish?"

X gives Sophie a look as if this is her fault or, more likely, as if he wants her to put a stop to it. She rolls onto her stomach and props herself up on her elbows. "I've never been to a girl sleepover. Unless you count the Winter Games. There was no nail polish, but we had team cuddles. It was good."

Witzer tucks himself next to her. He smells like locker room soap and, underneath it, the faint staleness of the locker room. They still have cleanout day, but it's only one day and then it's a long summer before she's back in Concord. She turns her face into his shoulder and inhales.

Merlin, never one to be left out, joins them, squishing her between her two wingers. "Can't have you liking a bunch of Canadians more than us."

"Speak for yourself." Kevlar lies across from Sophie and grins when she lifts her head up enough to see him. "Canadians are the best."

"Damn straight." Now Sophie's lying down, the series, the whole season really, feels as if it's finally hitting her. She drops her head back to her arms. "I'm going to take a little nap. Then we can play truth or dare or something."

Someone drapes a blanket over her. It's the last thing she remembers before falling asleep.

LOCKER ROOM CLEANOUT is brutal, and she flies home, still weighed down with disappointment. Next year will be different. It has to be. She taps her fingers on her thighs as she stares out the airplane window. There's talk of re-signing Merlin this summer. His contract is up next year, same as hers, but management might not want to get him under contract again. Or, more likely, they'll trade him next year.

No free agent chooses Concord, and the players who do play here never re-sign. Management knows it and trades the players coming up on the end of their contracts so they can get something for them instead of letting them walk for nothing.

If Merlin doesn't get a shiny new contract this summer, it's a sign he won't be with them at the end of next season. Montreal, Toronto, Boston, those are all teams players gravitate towards, teams with rich history and a tradition of winning even if Boston's been on a downswing.

Everyone said their goodbyes at locker room cleanout, but she didn't think about how many of them were permanent goodbyes. By the start of the upcoming season, her team will look different than it does now. Who should she have hugged longer? Merlin? Teddy? Garfield and Nelson?

She lands in Thunder Bay and lingers by baggage claim long enough to haul her two suitcases off the belt. Her car is in storage back in Concord, and most of her things are locked up in her apartment. She has the important stuff in her bags and what she forgot she can buy here. It seems wasteful to have enough clothes and gear to fill two places, but it's easier than lugging it from one country to another.

She takes a cab to her parents' house. The driver recognizes her and says, "Sucks, we were rooting for you," before he turns the radio up.

She offers him a smile before she fiddles with her phone, pretending it has her full attention.

HOME IS…HOME. It's the street she grew up on, the same nets set up in driveways but different kids playing impromptu games of street hockey. There's the same grocery store and same Tim Hortons and everywhere she goes there are people who know her. They smile and congratulate her on making the postseason before they wince and smile sadly and change the subject.

It's suffocating, but it's nothing compared to her dad.

A few days after she arrives home, she eats dinner with her parents, and everything seems rushed. She doesn't get it until her dad herds her to the TV and sits her down.

"No," she says even as her dad turns the Montreal-Boston game on. She doesn't want to watch this, the pain of her elimination still sharp in her chest.

Her dad hands her a notebook. "Find three things each team does well and three things they need to improve on."

She wants to toss the notebook, wants to argue she isn't a kid anymore. Instead, she grits her teeth and takes the pen he holds out to her.

"You need to learn," he continues. "If you were better, you'd still be playing."

She watches Dima warm up and is hit with a wave of jealousy. The camera pans to Ducasse and she narrows her eyes.

SHE CALLS DIMA to congratulate him on his series-winning goal in Game Seven against Montreal. She calls again, five games later, after Boston loses to Toronto.

Her dad makes her watch the Conference Finals and take notes on Matty's style of play and how she can be more like him. Then, they watch the Maple Cup Finals.

It takes six games but Toronto wins. She watches the Griffons toss their gloves and their sticks, their helmets skittering across the ice as they crash into each other. Some of them are shouting. Others are crying. They grab everyone in reach to hug them.

When it all settles down, the Maple Cup is brought out. Sophie's breath catches at the sight of it. One day, she'll hold it, lift it above her head, and listen to the crowd around her cheer.

But today, she's stuck on her couch in Thunder Bay as Matty takes his turn with the Cup. One of his teammates passes it to him and he stares up at it, stunned, as if he can't believe it's real. He kisses the shiny metal and hoists it high above his head and takes a lap of the rink.

Next year, that will be me.

About the Author

K.R. Collins went to college in Pennsylvania where she learned to write and fell in love with hockey. When she isn't working or writing, she watches hockey games and claims it's for research.

Twitter: @kcollins1394

Other books by this author

Breaking the Ice

Also Available from NineStar Press

Connect with NineStar Press

www.ninestarpress.com

www.facebook.com/ninestarpress

www.facebook.com/groups/NineStarNiche

www.twitter.com/ninestarpress

www.tumblr.com/blog/ninestarpress